Tiger's Tale

Books by Colleen Houck

THE TIGER'S CURSE SERIES

Tiger's Curse

Tiger's Quest

Tiger's Voyage

Tiger's Destiny

Tiger's Promise

Tiger's Dream

Tiger's Tale

REAWAKENED SERIES

Reawakened

Recreated

Reunited

STANDALONE NOVELS

The Lantern's Embers

Terraformer

COLLEEN HOUCK

TIGER'S TALE

BLACK STONE PUBLISHING

Published in 2024 by Blackstone Publishing
Cover design by James Egan of Bookfly Design

Printed in the United States of America

First edition: 2024
ISBN 979-8-212-22169-6
Young Adult Fiction / Fantasy / General

Version 1

Blackstone Publishing
31 Mistletoe Rd.
Ashland, OR 97520

www.BlackstonePublishing.com

For the Kryszek Clan.
We already shared a love of tigers, dogs, and cupcakes.
Now there's even more.

To ***

by Aleksandr Pushkin

I still recall the wondrous moment:
When you appeared before my sight
As though a brief and fleeting omen,
Pure phantom in enchanting light.
In sorrow, when I felt unwell,
Caught in the bustle, in a daze,
I fell under your voice's spell
And dreamt the features of your face.
Years passed and gales had dispelled
My former hopes, and in those days,
I lost your voice's sacred spell, The holy
features of your face.

Detained in darkness, isolation,
My days began to drag in strife.
Without faith and inspiration,
Without tears, and love and life.
My soul attained its waking moment:
You re-appeared before my sight,
As though a brief and fleeting omen,
Pure phantom in enchanting light.
And now, my heart, with fascination,
Beats rapidly and finds revived
Devout faith and inspiration,
And tender tears, and love, and life.

—Translated by Andrey Kneller

CONTENTS

Prologue

As the Call, So the Echo

The sounds of the forest should have comforted him, but he'd spent too many nights listening to the hum of insects, the croaking of frogs, and the death cries of small creatures being silenced by the larger creatures that pursued them. Occasionally, he was the thing that stalked them, that stuffed the gnawing hollowness in his belly with their pulsing life.

Hunting sated his hunger, but it couldn't fill the emptiness that consumed his days. Without Ana, he couldn't find purpose or meaning. She had been his anchor, and now he was adrift on an ocean alone. So many times he wished he could have followed her into death.

Outside he heard a rustle in the trees and the screech of a bird. Kishan covered his golden eyes with his arm, wishing he couldn't see in the dark so well. His stomach rumbled. He'd have to hunt tomorrow.

Then again, he thought. *Maybe not.* "Can I even starve to death? Didn't Ren try that once?" he asked out loud, though no one was there to hear his question. He couldn't remember if it was true. Even if it was, it obviously hadn't worked. Still, hunger pangs would give him something else to focus on. If he could just forget for a while, perhaps he could find a modicum of peace. For the first time in his incredibly long life, he felt . . . *old*.

There was a sudden rustle and a thump on the hut door. Kishan's instincts caused him to spring to his feet immediately, but the moment the scent of the man on the other side of the door tickled his nostrils, his muscles relaxed, and his body slumped back on the too-small cot.

"Come in," he said brusquely. Then, remembering his manners and his training of long, long ago, added a soft, "*Please.*"

"Hello, son," Kadam said, as he entered the hut. His piercing gaze took in the scene. "How are you?" he asked politely, hearing only a tetchy rumble in response coming from beneath the worn blanket, as he drew the wooden chair up to the bed. Stooping to stoke the fire, the visitor then tugged a neglected bundle of tied herbs down from the rafter and began sorting them for a pot of tea. "I see you've been disregarding the care of my hut."

"Your hut?" Kishan grumbled. "I believe I've lived here longer than you have."

Kadam's eyes twinkled in the dark as he ladled water into his favorite mug and replied cryptically, "Perhaps. Perhaps not."

He carried the mug to Kishan, blowing steam away from the brim. "I suppose it depends on your perspective. Now, why don't you sit up for a while, son, and drink this. I promise you'll feel better."

"I really don't think that's possible," he replied, but sat up obediently. Kadam fluffed the meager pillow while Kishan sniffed the contents of the mug, grimacing. Reluctantly, he sipped. Sweat beaded on his upper lip and chest. "Why am I so hot?"

"The medicine is burning the sickness out of you."

"I didn't realize I was ill."

"Yes. You'll get over it, of course. Even without my special concoction. The amulet strengthens you and grants you long life."

Kishan set down the mug and said soberly, "I wish it wouldn't."

"I know, son. You miss her. But it's not your time. Not yet. You still have work to do."

"Do I?"

"Yes."

Kishan picked up his drink and swirled the contents slowly, staring deeply into the cup.

"You want to ask me something," Kadam said astutely. "Go ahead."

The corner of Kishan's mouth lifted briefly, but his sadness tugged it down almost immediately. "You've always been able to read me," he said, then admitted softly, "I . . . I'm afraid of the answer."

Kadam shrugged. "I've never known you to be cowardly. Ask anyway."

Letting out an almost painful sigh, Kishan asked, "Will I see Ana again?" Before Kadam could reply, Kishan held up a hand. "I already know what you're going to say. You can't tell me, right? Or, you don't know. You aren't back from the dead. You haven't technically died yet."

Smiling, Kadam clapped Kishan on the shoulder and squeezed. "While that last part is true, what I can tell you is this . . ." Leaning closer, he peered directly into Kishan's golden eyes. "You absolutely *will* be seeing Anamika again in your future. I guarantee it."

Kishan blinked once, twice, three times, and then seeing that his mentor was perfectly sincere, released a breath he didn't realize he'd been holding. He grunted, lifted the cup to his lips, and quickly downed the rest of the bitter brew before settling back down on the pillow and closing his eyes. "Thank you," he said gratefully.

"You're welcome." Standing, Kadam took the mug, rinsed it out, dried it, and replaced it on the little wooden shelf. "Just keep in mind that seeing your wife again may or may not be the reunion you have in mind at present. Not everything comes easily when you walk through time as we do."

"I know. But I don't care. Just knowing there's a future where she exists is all that matters to me. It's enough."

"Good. Now, is there anything else I can do for you?"

Kishan cracked open an eye. "Can you stay with me for a while? I'm finding being alone difficult."

Taking a seat again in the wooden chair, Kadam removed the Divine Scarf from around his neck and draped it across the cot, asking it to transform into a comfortable blanket for Kishan. "I suppose I can stay for a time," he replied.

"Thank you, again. Why don't you tell me one of your stories, then? That should help me drift off."

Raising an eyebrow, Kadam chuckled. “I didn’t realize my stories bored you so much. They never appeared to tire Miss Kelsey. Very well. Let’s see if I can find one to distract you.” He stared into the flames for a long moment, his mouth slightly lifted as if he were remembering a song or words meant only for him. When he looked at Kishan again, it appeared as if the firelight was dancing in his eyes. Steepling his fingers, Kadam touched them to his bottom lip, considering. “Perhaps the time has come to tell you one of the lost tales.”

“Lost tales? What do you mean?”

“You recall when I was drifting in space and time and that it took me many of your months to return to our world?”

“Yes.”

“As you know, I was searching for a way to remain with you and still have a successful outcome in defeating Lokesh.”

“Right. You told us that you had to die. That there was no other way to defeat him.”

“That is correct. To be exact, there was no other successful way, where all of you would have survived and would have ended up happy. But there are and were many other possibilities. Many other outcomes. In some timelines, we lost the battle. In others, we won, but you or Miss Kelsey perished. Those timelines were . . . not ideal. One or more of you did not become your best selves, or ended up alone; I could not accept that.”

Kadam left off, and Kishan could read between the lines.

The idea of what he might have missed out on had his life not turned out the way it did brought Kishan renewed sadness.

“So I selected the best outcome for all of us,” Kadam finished.

“Then you chose well. I do not regret my life. Though I am grieving over my loss, I’m still grateful for the wealth of memories and experiences I treasure, as well as your sacrifice on our behalf. Without your discerning choice, I would not have those.”

Kadam dipped his head briefly in acknowledgment. “You’ve gained much wisdom over the years, my boy.”

“As you know, there were many others influencing me. It definitely wasn't all my doing. But you're saying there were other possible outcomes? You spoke of lost tales?"

"Yes. Many others. Countless others. In fact, there are many timelines where we don't even exist. These were very dangerous for me, as I nearly came undone in those places. To begin finding myself, I needed to latch on to timelines that closely paralleled our own and seek the aid of those souls that were essentially my mirror image."

"What?" Kishan asked incredulously. "Why have you never told us of this before?"

Kadam smiled wryly. "It was never the right . . . time. Perhaps now you will allow me to tell you the story of one such dimension—the first one, in fact, I ever encountered. Sadly, it also nearly undid me. Though, in truth, I never would have learned what I did had I not struggled to the point of death."

"So, you're saying there's a world somewhere out there with no Tiger's Curse?"

"Ah," Kadam replied, lifting a finger. "I never said that. It would seem the world—or at least the versions of it I encountered—always needed the tigers in one way, shape, or form. There was indeed a Tiger's Curse in this place. But neither you nor Ren nor I were ever born in that place."

"Remarkable!"

"Yes. In that timeline, you see, there was a major shift in history, one mostly due to the actions of one man, Sviatoslav I Igorevich, the Grand Prince of Kiev. Our timelines, as far as I can tell, synced up until his reign. Then, instead of going to war with the Khazars and the Bulgars, he made a treaty with them, allied with the Slavic tribes, and recruited the Varangians to be his Royal Guard.

"Together they created a mighty Kievian Empire, defeating Poland and Hungary. They made inroads with the indigenous tribes to the east, providing enough land and stability in the region for future royal generations to prosper. They took over trade routes and with them incorporated many Chinese and Mongolian cities into their empire. Because of this, Genghis Khan never rose to power."

"That's why we were never born. Our mother was a descendant of Genghis Khan."

"That is correct."

"But . . . then where does the Tiger's Curse come in?"

"Ah . . . that's where it gets interesting. It would seem, in this world, the Damon Amulet was broken not into five pieces, as it was here, but into seven."

"Seven?"

"Yes. And the inscription was different. Not only did it have new words but they were written in Samoyedic or perhaps another Uralic tongue. It's hard for me to remember exactly, as I was looking at it through the eyes of another." Kadam paused for a moment and then added, "Of course, it's entirely possible the language I recall is completely their own, but I suppose for the purposes of our story, it's close enough to the Samoyedic of our own world, as near as I can detect from my memory anyway."

"I'm sure it is," Kishan said. "You'll have to explain what you mean about the eyes of another," he added, both puzzlement and curiosity clear on his face.

Kadam nodded. "I'll get to that. For my survival, I relied greatly upon an ally I discovered in that world. This other gentleman, fortunately for me, was a man of great aptitude, kindness, and empathy. He also happened to be a shaman of renowned skill and intellect. He found me, you see; sheltered the unraveling bits of who I was; and showed me the path back to myself. Without him, I never would have come home. I owe him a great deal. He was the one who mentored the tigers."

"Then he *was* your counterpart."

"He was, in a way, though we never lived in the same century. I have searched for his mirror image through time on our own world and have never found him. As far as I can tell, he was never born here."

"And the tigers?"

Kadam smiled widely, crossed his legs, and laced his fingers, cupping his kneecap. "Ah, we've come to it," he said, "the most interesting thing about this, for lack of a better word, echo, of our own world, is that the tigers . . ."

"Yes?" Kishan prompted, unable to resist leaning forward. "The tigers were . . . what?"

"Kishan, the tigers of that world were not only Siberian cats," Kadam explained, a gleam of excitement in his eyes. "They were . . . *women.* Tsarevnas—*tsarinas,* actually—destined to rule the Kievian Empire."

There wasn't a sound in the little hut except for the deep inhales and exhales of the man on the bed.

"Did you hear me, Kishan?" Kadam asked.

The answer came slowly as the man gripped the worn blanket to his sweaty chest and laid back on the bed. His eyes, burning with fever, stared intently through half-lowered lids, and the room darkened, either with dusk, or the portent of the unshared history.

"I heard," Kishan replied. "Tell me . . . *everything.*"

CHAPTER 1

Each Person Is the Blacksmith of Their Own Destiny

The clash of steel rang out across the training field as the twins' sharp blades connected. The taller of the two warriors slid the weapon down quickly, creating sparks and nicking a barely visible band of flesh at the wrist. A spot of red appeared, rapidly soaking the green fabric, and there was an audible hiss uttered as the shorter twin backed off.

"You'll pay for that, Stacia," the injured sister grumbled from beneath her heavy helmet.

"Not today, my sweet sestra, Verusha," the taller one replied. "Your pretty looks might charm soldiers into dropping their guard, but not me. True, you are better with knives, and you were Papa's favorite despite his best efforts to hide it, but *today* I've got the drop on you. You're slow, Veru. What's the problem? Too much kasha this morning?

"Shut up, Stacia."

"Why don't you make me? Oh, that's right. You can't. I've been telling you to cut down on the pelmeni—unless, of course, your goal is to have some foreign prince pet you and call you his dumpling as you get fat and produce his pink-cheeked detkas."

"That's your life, Stacia, not mine. You were born first. It's your destiny to inherit the throne. You know I've always wanted to leave the capital, lead the Guard, and see the far reaches of the empire," Verusha said, spinning and kicking Stacia's feet out from under her so she fell heavily into the soft dirt of the practice field. Before Verusha could strike a winning blow, Stacia rolled quickly, got to her knees, and lifted her shield.

"You know we don't know who the oldest is," Stacia said, blocking the blow.

Usually, in the case of twins, especially royal births, not one but several midwives are called in. The birth order is carefully monitored, and the babies are kept separate, with the firstborn identified by any notable physical features as well as a red ribbon tied around the wrist.

Somehow that red ribbon slipped off when the nursemaids moved the girls to the nursery. And as there were no discernible birthmarks cataloged at the time, it was anyone's guess as to which twin was technically the eldest. The tsar and tsarina took it well, saying that sometimes providence steps in where people might go about making a mess of things. They believed it was their job to make certain their little girls didn't covet the empire's throne. Perhaps they'd done their work a bit too well, as neither of their daughters wanted to rule.

Though she often mocked her sister, Stacia knew it was all bluster. Veru was small indeed, but she packed a punch when it came to a fight. It was wrong to underestimate her. And many often did. This was what made her particularly effective and often deadly in conflicts. Her short stature made her especially lethal with a blade. She was exactly the right height to slip a sharp knife between gaps in armor, pressing it deep into soft bellies, muscled thighs, or even tender groins.

When their father had been alive, the empire had been at peace. He'd made sure they were well trained, and they often accompanied him on diplomatic missions. Then, after he died, the twins began taking more risks. They always made sure at least one of them was home, but every so often they'd sneak out with select groups of soldiers, never telling their grieving mother. It was how they coped.

One of Veru's favorite knives suddenly made an appearance. Stacia gritted her teeth and twisted, thrusting her shield into Veru's arm, ramming it into the ground so hard she dropped the knife. Sweat pooled between her armored shoulder blades, and she squinted as the salty drops stung her eyes beneath her helmet. Her sister was angry. *Good.* So was she.

As they circled, Veru spat, "You know I hate wearing dresses and putting on a show."

"So do I."

"Well, someone needs to take over. We're turning eighteen soon."

"That's right," Stacia said, swishing her sword slowly back and forth in invitation.

"You're older."

"Even if I was, you're prettier. It'll be easier for you to find an *appropriate* husband."

That did it. Verusha's bloodcurdling scream could be heard throughout the barracks, and curious soldiers rose from their beds to investigate. A vicious sword fight between the royal tsarevnas was a common enough affair that some returned to their warm beds, taking advantage of the early morning hour and the bit of warmth left from the fire made the night before, but others decided to stay and watch the spectacle.

The dawn was lovely. The air brisk with the promise of snow. Hot mugs of sbiten or spiced tea were passed from one pair of hands to another as the soldiers watched and traded coins and quiet bets on which sister would emerge the victor. They shifted back and forth to keep warm, stomping their boots and blowing out their breath in soft clouds, but they never clapped in appreciation, though they might have wanted to, over particularly exciting parries. It wouldn't have been appropriate.

They also didn't debate so much on the skills of the sisters, for each one had defeated the other often enough, but they did discuss other factors that might decide the outcome of the duel, such as which sister fought better in certain weather conditions, with the light in her eyes, or with a certain weapon. And they shared opinions on who had a lingering injury, what might be a distraction to either sister, or perhaps which one was doing a better job riling the other.

Above all else, one thing was certain: not one of them, not a single soldier among all the Royal Guard, was disloyal to the tsarevnas. It was a shame the twins had lost their father in battle. The men blamed themselves for the tsar's death. When Andrey Mikhail Stepanov II insisted on leading the Guard into war, they'd tried to stop him. But just like the twins, there was no persuading the tsar on a different course once he'd set his mind to something.

Another half hour passed, and neither sister was ready to concede, though both were bloody and tiring. It was a time when mistakes were made. The men began to shift uncomfortably. The women sensed it. Almost as one, they stepped apart, each nodding to a man on the sidelines who rushed forward to take their swords. Veru raised tired arms to remove her helmet but felt it lifted from her head before she touched it.

A soldier stepped to her side and began loosening the clasp tightening her chest plate. He glanced up with warm brown eyes and offered a shy smile before nodding. "Tsarevna," he said deferentially. "You fought well."

"Thank you, Nikolai. Did you sleep last night?"

"A bit better with the tonic I made."

"Good."

He lifted away the breastplate, and Verusha let out a long sigh, pulling at the sticky tunic clinging to her chest. When Nikolai glanced up to see what he could help with next, his entire face and neck colored a bright red before he quickly looked down at his feet.

Verusha laughed softly. "Can you bring those back to the palace, Nikolai?" she asked.

"Of course, Tsarevna," he immediately answered.

"There's no need to call me that around the men," Verusha said softly, wrinkling her nose. "I want them to think of me like one of their own." Then a bit more loudly, "Veru is fine with me. We're all soldiers here. At least until I rise to the rank of captain," she added.

"Ha!" Stacia said from beneath her helmet as she struggled to get out of her own armor. Two soldiers stood by waiting to help, but she insisted on doing it alone. She didn't want a man touching her. The very idea of it made her extremely . . . uncomfortable. It wasn't that she didn't like men or appreciate them, but she refused to fawn over them or use them like Verusha did. She hated the way men's eyes fogged over when they saw her sister or how they couldn't seem to focus on her words, only on the way her body moved.

No man had ever looked at her that way, and she never wanted them to. She didn't even know what she'd do about it if one ever did. Veru would laugh endlessly if Stacia ever told her how she truly felt. Though Stacia could appreciate Veru's "talents" when it came to distracting men, it being useful in negotiating contracts and diplomatic sessions, she honestly couldn't see much use for beauty otherwise.

Finally wrenching her helmet from her head, she grimaced as she combed her fingers through the sweaty, frizzy mass of curls that had escaped from her braid and pulled the thick bulk of it away from her neck, letting the nearly frigid air cool her quickly. She shivered and gathered the pieces of her heavy armor, trudging up the path behind her sister and her sister's minion. Her stomach growled, but she pressed her hand against it, willing it to stop. She'd grown thin since her father's death, and her mother kept harping on her about it, but she just didn't have an appetite. Stacia ate when it was necessary, but otherwise considered it a nuisance.

She could hear the men shuffling back to the barracks, preparing for their assigned duties, and envied them. How easy would it be to live among them? Yes, there were battles and skirmishes to fight, but not as often as before. Most of the Guard led simple lives. They trained; fulfilled their duties; advanced as far as their ambition, skill, and intelligence allowed; saw much of the empire; and were free of the mundane toils that limited most.

There were no children to care for. No wives to support. There were no farms or animals to tend to. Essentially, being a member of the Guard meant freedom. And freedom was what she craved beyond anything else. If she took on the role of tsarevna, not only would her entire life be a series of meetings, which was bad enough, but she'd seen firsthand what the pressure had done to her parents. They were the two most intelligent people she had ever known, and there were still days she'd seen her mother cry when she couldn't figure out a problem.

As often as her father had praised Stacia's cleverness with strategy, Stacia had never once beaten him at any game, not unless he let her win. She just knew, deep in her gut, that she wasn't smart enough to do their job. There were too many people to take care of, too many neighboring countries, too many languages to know, too many laws. When she even thought about taking charge, she'd bend over just to catch her breath.

Knowing she'd fail and disappoint her parents and the entire empire and end up destroying everything her parents had worked so hard to build was the one reason Stacia knew she could never be the tsarina. It had to be Veru.

It wasn't that she didn't love her country. She did. She'd lay down her life for it. She just needed to serve the best way she could. And that was with her sword. Her sword, shield, and sweat. Stacia caught the scent of her own perspiration as she finally pulled away her chest plate. All she needed to do was win her freedom by convincing Veru she was the best choice. That was what she wanted. Well, that and a hot bath.

At least there were still some things about the palace she enjoyed. The luxury of a hot bath drawn by someone other than herself was something any exhausted and aching-muscled soldier would relish. But since the death of her father, Stacia found she felt little pleasure in anything. Sometimes she even feigned illness to avoid the evening activities planned by her mother or the social fetes she was expected to attend. She knew her mother had more of a right to grieve than she did, and Stacia was also aware that it wasn't fair to leave everything for Veru and her mother to handle, but it was difficult to make herself care.

Occasionally, she allowed the guilt over such things to stifle the little enjoyment she did find, but not today. On this morning, she would take her time and enjoy the water until it cooled. After all, she was going to win her freedom from rule and beat her sestra. And winning meant she should allow herself a little reward.

—

As Stacia contemplated her impending ablutions, Verusha and Nikolai were deep in conversation about the recent fight.

"Your ribs might be bruised on the right side," Nikolai said. "Your stance was slightly off, and you guarded that side during the fight."

Veru nodded. "You're probably right. They're tender. I'll need them wrapped."

Nik's neck colored, but his expression was rigid and determined. "I can do it. You know I've been apprenticing in medical training. You'll have to remove your tunic though. Perhaps it would be better to do it out of sight of the others. Maybe in the stables?"

Taking the training had been Verusha's idea. His heart had stirred with excitement to learn that she'd wanted him proficient in a specialty that would make him an even more valuable commodity on the battlefield, and as a bonus, it also gave him an excuse to attend to her constantly.

Though they were separate during his lessons, he consoled himself thinking of how much a future Guard leader would rely on a battlefield surgeon. He might even be called upon to save her life someday.

Considering it briefly, Verusha shook her head. "Thank you, Nik, but no. I'll have my nurse do the wrap. It won't likely be as tight as yours, and she'll probably tell Mother, but it would be better if I wasn't found in a compromising position, no matter the excuse."

"You're right, of course, Tsarevna," Nikolai immediately replied. "You know I would never wish to harm either you or your reputation."

"Relax, Nik," Veru said with a sincere smile, a special one she used only with those she truly cared for. "I know you've always had my best interests in mind. Now, quickly, before we get to the palace, tell me what else you saw. And don't pull any punches. This is important. I need to beat my sister. I know you notice everything."

"I do," Nikolai replied quietly. It wasn't true, of course. Nik didn't notice everything, but he liked her thinking he did. He only seemed to know everything because he watched the tsarevna Verusha with near obsessive fixation. He'd been in love with her since the moment he'd met her.

It had been his first day on the practice field when he'd been pitted against her. He'd had no idea he was sparring with one of the famed tsarevnas. An orphan, Nik had joined the Guard as soon as he was eligible at age fourteen. Back then, she'd been only twelve, but she was already strong despite her diminutive size. He'd thought it an insult to be pitted against the smallest trainee in the Guard, but Veru had taken no time at all to knock his skinny self to the ground not once but ten times.

The final time, she offered a gloved hand and removed her helmet. The shock at realizing he'd been bested by a girl—and a tiny one at that—wore off quickly when she smiled and introduced herself. "Sorry about that, Nikolai," she said. "I'm Tsarevna Veru. I hope there aren't any hard feelings. The other recruits all knew to look out for me and would have gone easy on me. You didn't. I appreciate that."

Nik stuttered a lame response. "Right . . . no problem. You beat me soundly. I can promise I didn't hold back at all."

She'd then helped him to his feet and dusted off his armor for him. "And he's humble too. I like you, Nik. Stick around. We'll meet again."

As she headed back to the barracks so the next pair of soldiers could enter the practice field, Nik thought, *I certainly hope so.*

It had been a good thing that he was so obsessive in watching her because Nikolai quickly realized the young tsarevna Verusha Irena Vasilia Stepanov wasn't kidding when she said the other soldiers held back. At first he assumed it was due to her royal status or to her diminutive size. He knew it wasn't because of her gender. There were many other female soldiers in the ranks, and she did fight against some of them with success.

But the more he watched the rapidly blossoming tsarevna, the more he realized the true issue at hand. Verusha wasn't becoming merely pretty; she was truly breathtaking. Even when her hair was damp with sweat, and the dust from the sparring field coated her skin, there was no denying her beauty. Male or female, in love with her or not, which Nik suspected most of them were, not a soldier in the Guard had a wish to damage a royal commodity so precious and valuable.

The one who scarred that beautiful face or disfigured her lush form would be remembered throughout the empire as the most dastardly, most careless, most reckless, most unpatriotic creature who ever walked the earth, and surely he or she would find no resting place or kind soul to console them for such a mistake. Over time, the only one who truly fought Verusha in the way she craved was her sister.

Not even Nik could bring himself to accidentally mar her lovely skin despite his willingness to do absolutely anything to please her. But when he began holding back in sparring, he saw how his actions made her special smile disappear, and he decided then he'd simply throw the match in every competition from that point onward.

That way she wouldn't feel as if he was treating her any differently. When she realized just how truly terrible a fighter he was, she took pity on him, began giving him pointers, and her special smile came back.

It became a careful dance for him. He had to slowly improve in the areas she tutored while secretly training on his own so that he could become so skilled with weapons that he would never ever risk an accidental nick or scratch when she taught him. He felt the most fear when she fought her sister, and his fellow soldiers felt as he did, at least on some level.

When the time came for the culling, a year after his training had begun, he despaired at the idea of being cast aside. He knew the others thought him barely competent enough to keep around. With Verusha's support, he was allowed to remain a Guard member after those deemed unqualified were cut loose and sent home.

Though many teased him, calling him the tsarevna's pet or prize pig, he smiled each time he heard such comments and simply raised his glass with a wink or replied, "I'll take it!" with such enthusiasm it always garnered a laugh. He knew it implied something more to their relationship, but he found he didn't mind it so much and liked to imagine she wouldn't mind it either if she knew he was being mocked for their friendship.

Over the next few years, Nik had become someone Verusha relied upon heavily. She'd grown to rely on him as a sparring companion, then as a friend and confidant. Secretly, Nik hoped for more. He knew it was highly likely she'd be married off to a royal good-for-nothing someday. That she would inherit the throne. It was best for diplomacy and the empire, he knew. And Nikolai considered himself as loyal to the empire as the next. It was the reason he'd joined the Guard.

Well, *that* and guaranteed meals.

But even so, maybe someday, somehow, the tsarevna might come to love him back. Such a thing was possible. Love wasn't exclusive to royals. Marriage might be, but not love. Perhaps they might find it together. At least for a while. He'd try to tell himself it would be enough. But if she ascended to the throne, her marriage date would be pushed forward all the quicker. Even if Veru arranged for him to stay at the palace, the likelihood of his continued presence in her life was slim to none.

It was more probable he'd be shipped off with the Guard on their next venture. Veru would soon forget all about him, begin popping out royal progeny, and he'd be an old friend who stopped by for a visit every once in a while, or, even worse, a headstone in the military cemetery who might—and that was if he was very lucky—get a yearly visit and flower from the royal gardens.

His best option would be to get Stacia to take over as tsarina. Then Veru could be head of the Guard, and he could insert himself as her right hand.

When they parted at the secret door to the palace, she squeezed his upper arm and gave him a tired smile. He encouraged her to rest, and her small shoulders relaxed. It was some consolation to know it was him she listened to and that he was her closest advisor and confidant.

As the door closed behind her, he frowned, his jaw set. Had her stance changed just as she entered the house? It looked like she might have a slight limp or perhaps a broken toe. She wouldn't hide such a thing from him, would she? If so, why?

As he turned, heading for the royal armory, he made a mental note to watch her walk more carefully the next day. Perhaps he'd even insist on looking at her feet himself. He didn't like the idea that she'd hide something from him. *The tsarevna should know by now that I can be trusted with anything. Yes. I'll simply have to insist. It won't do to have her feet compromised.*

Nik rehashed the fight, wondering if there was something he'd missed that might have damaged his precious tsarevna. His hands clenched into fists. It was that awkward Stacia's fault. If she would just be more careful with her sister. It wasn't that Nik particularly disliked Stacia; it was simply that Stacia didn't treat her sister with the respect, care, and admiration she deserved.

In a perfect world, Stacia would rule, and Verusha would become captain of the Guard, taking Nik as her right-hand officer. They'd end up sharing more than just a hot mug of sbiten on cold, dark evenings and, eventually, she'd realize she couldn't live without him in her life.

If Tsarevna Stacia would just accept her calling in life, he'd be happy to bend a knee and place a hand on his chest, pledging his loyalty and support. True, her height and abrupt manner with men made her the more difficult sister to match. But Stacia wasn't unsightly—besides, when did that ever stop a man wanting power? Stacia was . . . *regal.* That was the word.

Stacia took after her father. She was too tall. Too proud. Too imposing. Too . . . unbending. And what man wanted an unbending, unsmiling, cold woman for a wife? Regardless, Nik was certain a match could be made somehow. There were many interested in furthering status and linking their lands and countries to the empire. Someone would come forward. Though that someone would have to be a special man indeed if he could learn to tolerate Tsarevna Stacia.

Nik shifted the armor as he walked, thinking about what kind of a man it would have to be to marry such a woman. She'd hold him beneath her thumb for sure. Verusha often complained that none of the soldiers wanted to fight her fairly, and she wasn't wrong. But it was also true that there weren't too many willing to take on Tsarevna Stacia. Not because they didn't want to mar her skin either. No. They didn't want to take her on because she was just that good.

Often, she ended up fighting the female soldiers. Stacia relaxed a bit more around them, but she seemed to have something to prove when she fought the men. She became almost bitter and cruel. It was as if she was determined to end them as quickly as possible to get her opponents out of her sight. It was almost humiliating to be beaten by her. It wasn't so much training as it was an experience in dodging targeted lightning strikes. When it was over, the struck man wasn't certain he ever wanted to go outside again.

Nik dropped off the armor for cleaning and polishing, leaving strict instructions. He'd be back later to check to make sure they'd followed through properly. They often didn't do as thorough of a job as he liked, so he picked up the armor early and polished it again himself. He liked gently rubbing the oils into the metal and imagining it was Verusha's lithe form instead. It also gave him a great deal of pleasure to know his hands had been the last to touch the metal that would cradle and protect her body the next time she fought.

As he headed back to the barracks, his mind turned again to the impossible, a life with Verusha. That meant the next order of business would be to get Stacia to accept her place on the throne. It was a tall order for a too-tall woman. But his happiness depended on it. After all, the empire would need a successor.

At the same moment, Stacia was sinking down into a just-too-hot bath, groaning as the water covered each inch of her body. Inevitably, her thoughts went down the same track. The empire needed a successor. But she wasn't thinking of the future or of a marriage or a child; she was thinking of the now. How could she convince her sister to do the most natural thing? Marry and rule.

Verusha was pacing her room wondering how her own sister could be so obstinate. Stacia was the strategist. She was much more capable of running an empire. Veru stopped in front of a family portrait and stared at the lines in her beloved father's face. Her vision blurred. They'd been young in that painting. Even then Stacia looked like their father, while Veru took after their mother. How could Verusha convince her stubborn sister that she was the one destined to rule?

The answer came to both sisters at the same time. As the two young women lifted their heads, they smiled in anticipation.

They'd fight.

And the loser would inherit the throne.

Unfortunately, the best laid plans, excellent though they may be, often go awry.

CHAPTER 2

There Are Many Fathers, but Only One Mother

The tsarina Ludmila Marianka Sashenka Stepanov set the list of potential suitors on the side table and allowed herself the tiniest moment to ease back into the plush settee and close her eyes. Her tightly laced corset and voluminous skirts didn't permit her to completely relax, but that was for the best anyway. It wouldn't do to show weakness. Not even to her daughters, as much as they loved her.

As her heavy eyelids closed, she smiled, thinking of how proud her husband would have been to see the twins now. Both of them were developing into intelligent, gifted, beautiful young women. Either one of them would be able to rule the empire. Truly it didn't matter which one of them had been born first. It never had mattered to her or her husband anyway. In a perfect world, Mila would like them to rule together, side by side. But she was a realist. It would be very special siblings indeed who could share a throne, and that was only if the people could allow such a thing.

Mila knew power easily corrupted those who wielded it. Truthfully, she was proud that neither of her daughters felt ready or desired to take over. It meant they'd prepared them well. Taught them the importance of caring for the people and working for them and with them to better their lives. Being a leader meant much, much more than levying taxes, fine dining, and lining one's pockets. A royal family needed to hold themselves to a much higher standard. They needed to set an example for others to follow.

How could she expect her young daughters to sacrifice so much when they'd barely begun to know who they were themselves? They were still finding their way, growing into the young women they wanted to become, developing their identities and gifts. Then to expect them to select a match at such a young age? How could she, or they, know for certain the one they chose would still fit in the years to come? Such a weighty, long-lasting decision should be given careful consideration. It wasn't something to be rushed. Love comes or it doesn't.

Mila had never believed in a perfect match. Not until she'd met the twins' father. She'd observed that in most cases couples were somewhat mismatched. They were *right enough* to work. Only a very, very few were perfect matches. Mila had been lucky in love. She just wished she could give her daughters more time.

She sighed. Whichever daughter was willing and able to marry and produce heirs based on the very short list of matches she'd found was the one who would take over. She knew either of them would do just fine.

Yes, she realized it was too early to lay such a heavy burden at their feet. Still, Mila knew they'd be able to rise to the occasion. Her hope was that they would quickly set aside their childish squabbles and lean on one another for strength. It was the only thing she wanted, hoped—no, *needed*—to arrange before . . . well . . . Mila just wasn't going to allow herself to dwell on the *after*. Only the *now* mattered.

Mila knew her daughters might balk at the idea of courting. But despite their many reforms, the people still expected a tsar to sit next to the tsarina, even if she and her husband had carefully prepared for the balance of power to be shifted to their daughters. And besides, a match didn't necessarily mean a wedding was imminent. A betrothal just meant stability, not only for her daughters but for the empire itself. She couldn't bear to think that it would be an act or an inaction on her part that would potentially cause the collapse of her dearly departed husband's carefully built Kievian Empire.

There were many who had accused her of destroying both the empire and the tsar on the day her husband announced their own match, but Mila worked hard to prove all the skeptics wrong. In fact, the empire became stronger than it had even been after Mila's union with the tsar, and she would be damned before she let it fall apart now. Not while there was still breath left in her body.

Names and renderings of potential matches and alliances between the empire and other countries danced across the insides of her eyelids. The faces blurred and then organized themselves in neat little rows like soldiers with details emblazoned on their uniforms like insignia. That was better. Mila liked things working in proper order. It was what first drew her to admire her husband, her very own match.

When she first met the tsar, Andrey Mikhail Stepanov II, the famed high commander of the feared Royal Guard, the young military strategist who conquered kingdoms, crushed insurgency, then smoothly charmed politically connected daughters as he twirled them around one by one at lavish parties, never committing himself to wed, but always managing to keep dozens of them trailing him by the coattails like a loyal pack of wolfhounds, she wasn't sure she liked him.

He was too sure of himself. Too charming. Too closed off. And worse, he was far too clever. That frightened Mila. She was used to being dismissed, or simply paraded around to be stared at and then promptly tucked into a corner, which gave her ample opportunity to study people. But as she studied the tsar, she found him a particularly difficult man to read.

The man she did see though, the one effortlessly enchanting every lady he saw and sweet-talking every diplomat he came across, was the type of man Mila knew she couldn't trust, let alone marry, not that marriage was probable with her father's connections. Still, with her beauty, it was best not to take a risk.

What she knew about the tsar was little. Mila was aware that he had taken over the military while his father had still been alive, and it had been through his efforts that the empire had expanded to twice the size it had been in the time of his grandfather. It was the tradition of the royal family for the second- and third-born sons (and so forth) to head the vast far-off sections of the empire, studying the local languages and peoples and commanding the military in those areas to gain experience in strategy, warfare, and diplomacy.

In the case of the current tsar, he was an only child and would have normally been kept safely close to home. But apparently, this tsar-to-be wouldn't be kept home. Not only did he head the vast legions of the empire's military alone but he traveled to not one but all the far reaches of the empire, studying all the peoples and languages from a young age, becoming very skilled in a variety of strategies and subjects and tongues.

If only she had been born a man. A beautiful man who was a seventh son could make something of himself. That would have been preferable. Even a homely woman had a chance to live happily as a spinster in her brother's house. But a pretty girl was sold off to the highest bidder. It was the way of things. The lucky daughters were wed to kind men. The very fortunate might even grow to love their husbands.

Mila didn't hold out such hope for herself. So she carefully watched and waited and used her gift of assessment to frighten off those who were interested, saying just the wrong thing to turn them away. But despite her considerable abilities, she didn't know what to say to this one. Honestly, she couldn't even tell what interested him. He appeared to be terribly fascinated with each person he spent time with, which was a feat she knew wasn't possible.

What she did know was that this man made her uneasy. And that he was powerful. And because powerful men tended to take what they wanted despite protocol, Mila knew she'd have to be very, very careful and assume the worst when he turned his eyes in her direction. The worst being that he'd be just as interested in her as he seemed to be in every other female in the room. Her only hope was that she'd get lucky, and his attentive gaze would be as feigned with her as she believed it was with everyone else.

Still utterly unable to read the tsar by the time he made his way over to her, Mila decided to try something she'd never done with any other would-be suitor. It was risky, in that it was nearly guaranteed to wipe the self-satisfied smile from the tsar's face and therefore anger both him and her father, but it would also serve to send him off quickly, seeking the next pretty young lady in whom to pay favor.

She decided to reveal her full self, show the tsar Milena Mariani Dalle, in all her cunning glory. Playing all her cards at once, Mila set each one deliberately and purposely on the table, a thing that should frighten any male easily intimidated by an intelligent female. She looked him in the eye, confidently assessing him as one would an enemy. When they spoke, she countered each of his queries with one of her own.

Mila didn't bat her lashes, simper, faint, or fan her face. She was bold as brass, daring him to defend his stances on recent political decisions, then she brought up the blight affecting the recent harvest, and finally, she questioned his intentions regarding a series of new immigration laws applicable to peoples petitioning to join the empire, relocating from the other side of the Ural Mountains to their own lands. There were many issues to consider, including culture, language, and what to do about the abandonment of long-held traditions. The Native Alliance was a very new and fragile government and would have to be treated gently and . . .

And . . . he didn't leave.

So Mila finally learned something about the tsar.

Andrey loved a challenge.

—

It was true.

Andrey *did* love a challenge.

And Mila was a puzzle to him.

It was her scrutiny that interested him at first. No one had ever questioned him before.

As for Andrey, he'd known it was time for him to wed, but none of the women presented to him as potential brides were interesting enough. They were lovely. At least some of them had been. There were definitely a few who were strategically excellent options. Mila wasn't one of those. She was the youngest but extraordinarily lovely daughter of an insignificant diplomat from an even more insignificant country to the far west.

Mila's remarkable face was the only reason her father even dared offer a seventh daughter as a potential match. Others tried to persuade her father to leave the party early, but the man was stubborn to a fault. Even Mila had seemed embarrassed. But Andrey, used to such attempts, laughed off the gossip and approached the young woman, ignoring her father, who, seeing his only opportunity for advancement, bowed quickly and then rather awkwardly introduced his daughter along with poorly timed, unsubtle comments about the benefits of allying with his country and the merits of his family tree.

The young tsar waved a hand, and skilled servants, always standing at the ready, smoothly guided the father away, distracting him with food and drink and, seeing the tsar's interest in the young woman, even more food. When the parental guard was sufficiently occupied, Andrey bent over the young lady's gloved hand and, with only half of his usual charm and enthusiasm, asked, "Shall we take a turn on the dance floor, then, Miss Dalle?"

As he stood, he automatically turned, extending his elbow, expecting to hear her simpering response in the affirmative and the instant female chatter that immediately followed as the young woman used the dance as the opportunity to win his affection. He didn't mind it, truth be told. He liked women. Andrey found it wasn't too difficult to listen and respond noncommittally, and yet, in a way, that kept them happy. It was much like working with diplomats. They, too, often prattled about nothing of substance.

But with women, the chatter relaxed him. They spoke of family, of friends, of favorite dishes, or horses and hounds. It didn't take much to keep them talking—a nod here or there or a simple question or two and they'd be off again, telling him everything he could ever want to know.

Andrey had found, at a very young age, that almost everyone gave up their secrets if you just listened. Sure, occasionally, he needed to make more of an effort. There were some who posed a challenge, but not many. By and large, the greater population was desperate for acceptance and friendship. All he had to do was offer one of those and the masses fell over themselves trying to please him.

But not Mila.

It wasn't even that she'd said no. Others had tried that before. They'd teased him by attempting coyness, playing hard to get, but Andrey had seen the easy *yes* hiding behind their masked expressions. He liked games, so he'd play with those women for a while.

It was so easy. All he had to do was shrug and walk away. Most would panic and chase after him almost immediately. Some of them carried the game through. They were a mildly entertaining distraction, lasting a week, or sometimes two, depending on their tenacity and the fervency of their parents.

There'd only been one who'd posed a challenge of any sort. He'd thought something might come of that one. She'd lasted for several months. But in the end, he walked away from her too. Andrey found it curious that he felt melancholy when the game was over. When he finally won, and she was his at last, he thought he'd feel a sense of victory, much like he did after defeating a particularly clever commander in battle.

Instead of buoyant jubilance, the typical swelling itch to crow that comes when moved by male pride, or even the sweet stirrings of dewy love, Andrey felt . . . nothing. No. Nothing wasn't quite right. He felt something for the girl. And that something made him want to send her immediately packing.

It was distaste. Andrey just plain didn't like her. He respected her well enough; she was calculating, cold, and clever. Wrongly, he'd believed the coldness would disappear after they were together, but if anything it became worse. Then he quickly discovered that when his eyes were turned away, her eyes went roving. She also possessed a streak of cruelty, especially toward the staff or anyone else she deemed as being of a lesser station. Her viciousness was the bag of grain that upset the boat. Admire her, he did. Like her, he didn't. All those undesirable traits made up his mind for him, and she was discreetly shown the door.

For a time, despondency took him. He was surprised to learn that he'd been looking forward to the new challenges that would come with cultivating a relationship, and he began truly seeking out a bride for the first time in his young life after that. But all too quickly, enthusiasm turned once again to boredom and then despair. That was until he met Mila. When he'd asked her to dance, there was no reply at all.

At first, when no gloved fingers clutched his arm and no warm body pressed up against his, he assumed something was wrong. Andrey twisted his head to glance back at the lovely young woman, expecting to either handle a problem or see a coy expression. Instead, he looked behind those long, dark lashes and storm-gray eyes and recognized that she was assessing him. *Him! The tsar!*

Such a thing had never happened to him before. Andrey found himself straightening, turning back to her fully as if to present himself to a queen. The seconds dragged on, adding up to a full minute. He looked into her face for that entire minute, searching for her purpose. *What is she looking for?* he wondered.

His mouth quirked ever so slightly as he anticipated a new game with an exciting new opponent. But as another minute passed, and a charming little line appeared between her delicate eyebrows, indicating she was still deep in thought, he heard the crowd stirring, their whispering escalating in volume, her own father among them, growing ever more desperate to intervene, and the tsar found he wasn't ready for their encounter to be over yet.

"My lady," he said, dipping his head respectfully. "If a dance is not to your liking, perhaps you would do me the honor of taking some refreshment together?"

She seemed to consider his offer very briefly, then shook her head. "I'm not hungry at present. Perhaps a walk instead?"

"A w . . . walk?" he sputtered, but then quickly acquiesced. "If that is your desire."

"It is."

Andrey took her hand and tucked it around his arm. The pair began to stroll about the room, and as they did, she relaxed. Though she was at least a foot shorter than him, her stride was purposeful and strong. She didn't flounce about to preen for others or show off the sway of her full hips or the swish of her skirts. He liked that she kept pace with him and was solely focused on the conversation.

As they turned around the ballroom, she launched into a barrage of questions regarding everything from his stances on the newly passed laws governing the lands to the east, to farming, to how he managed the recruitment of new soldiers from groups of orphaned children, to suggesting visiting dignitaries he should keep a watchful eye on.

Andrey answered each query as succinctly as possible, amazed and sometimes even embarrassed that he or his advisors hadn't considered some of the items she already had.

Then, out of nowhere, she added, "I should like to see your gardens, if at all possible."

Almost grateful for the change in subject, he replied, "Of course. My gardens are at your disposal at any time."

Her eyes dropped from his then, and she clasped her hands in front of her, not in a nervous way, but in a way that spoke to him of steadiness and surety. "May I be candid?" she asked quietly.

"Yes," he replied, taking a step closer, wishing the two of them were alone and not currently being stared at and whispered about by everyone in the lavishly appointed ballroom.

"I believe a garden shows the heart of a man. That and how he cares for his uniform. If I am to marry you, I first desire to judge your character. I've determined that your uniform is well cared for; therefore I'd like to move on to the garden. My apologies if I've offended you, and if you aren't interested in me in that way, you are free to move on to the next young lady. I just loathe wasting time, and I can't imagine a tsar such as yourself would appreciate his time being wasted either."

Andrey blinked not once but twice before he replied, but when he did, a genuine smile lit his face. Mila had thought her blunt comments about marriage, the garden and the uniform, and her barrage of questions would irritate him at the least, but when he smiled, and she saw the mask lift from his face and warmth light his eyes, her heart actually skipped. For the first time in her life, Mila's breath caught, and she chided herself for being distracted by the tsar's handsome face and silky demeanor. Apparently, she was as easily charmed by him as everyone else, and she didn't like it. Not one bit.

"My dear Miss Dalle, I appreciate your candor. However, I find fault with your judging criteria. Though I, too, favor a well-pressed uniform, I must ask you how you can assume one such as I, as important as I am, cares for his own uniform? Surely you would prefer to wed my dresser or perhaps my launderer rather than myself if that is your criteria. As to my gardens, the same principle applies. A man such as I would not have time to work in a garden or care for it. So how would you judge me worthy?"

"I know you care for your uniform yourself," she began, slightly distracted by the hard muscles beneath her palm. The very uniform she was speaking about suddenly became a very tangible, weighty thing.

"Indeed?" he prompted, retreating into old tricks to say as little as possible so as to get her to talk of herself and spill her secrets.

Indeed? Indeed? Her tongue felt thick. Her skin hot. The brush of skirts hit her legs, and her pulse sounded in her ears. Was she ill? What was happening to her?

When she didn't immediately chime in, Andrey became frustrated. He wanted to see her face. His body began to hum in anticipation, like it did the night before a battle. This was a game unlike any he had played before. He felt almost as if he didn't understand the rules. Before he could stop himself, he pled, "Tell me: How do you know this?"

She glanced up at him with a distracted expression. Was she not even paying attention? What was going on in that mind?

"Oh. About your uniform?" she asked.

Andrey nodded, encouraging her to talk.

Mila shook her head as if to clear it. "That was easy. The soldiers guarding you care for their own uniforms. Each one of them is mussed in a slightly different way. Not enough polish on one pair of boots or a torn sleeve or collar here or there. Perhaps a button is missing on one or a thread is dangling from a hem. Your personal guards' uniforms are all cared for by the same man. He is very good but not as good as you. The lint is brushed away, the fabric is pressed, the buckles are gleaming, and the boots are evenly polished."

That was better. When Mila focused on details, her thoughts cleared. Her skin was still warm, however. Perhaps some cold air would help.

They reached the end of the ballroom, and Andrey led her around the edge and toward a door that led to a balcony overlooking the estate. "Go on," he said.

"Though each man, I assume, dresses himself, accounting for the slight differences in insignia placement, the skew or bend of a hat, the laces of a boot, or the wear of a belt, your uniform shows that someone has blackened and carefully polished your boots to a high gloss. I suspect that the blackening is of a different type than that used on the boots of the others. Either that or there might be something added to it such as extra beeswax or lanolin or perhaps you simply allowed the polish to dry longer or took more care in the buffing. Regardless, I can see that you have also meticulously cared for the exposed side indentations. This is something not found on any of the other pairs of boots.

"Then there are the buttons. They have been polished, yes, but the carved details have also been meticulously cleaned with a tiny tool. This also was not done on the other uniforms."

Andrey didn't realize he'd stopped walking. When he saw that she simply clasped her hands behind her back, shrugged, and continued on to the balcony doors without him, he hurried to catch up, desperate to hear more details of how her incredible mind worked.

"Please forgive me," he said, taking her hand and tucking it under his arm again as they proceeded to the doors that were immediately opened by guards. The crisp, cold night air of St. Rostislav swirled around them, promising a dusting of snow by morning, but where other women would have called for furs or used the weather as an excuse to paw at him, Mila inhaled deeply and seemed to derive strength from the brisk breeze.

For the first time, Andrey found he desired to draw a woman closer simply because he wanted to, because he liked her, because she interested him. At the same time, he wanted to relish every single moment and discovery of her. He began studying her, truly seeing her then, considering her as a serious match.

There was no advantage for him politically. But she was clever, strong, and capable. He shrugged off such thoughts. There was plenty of time to think about her later. Right now he wanted to hear more. Learn everything he could.

Mila thought the cool night air would help with whatever was ailing her, but if anything she felt the heat of the tsar's body behind her even more intensely. She trembled, but not with cold. He wasn't responding to her like any man before her had or like she had expected.

"Will you continue?" he asked softly as they stood at the balcony, side by side.

His voice was quiet. Smooth. Silky. As warm as a fur-lined cloak. At once she wanted to hear that voice murmur in her ear and have it wrap around her on a cold winter night.

"Yes. But first, your guards are cold. Perhaps someone can fetch their coats? And I'd hate to let the night air disturb your other guests. One or two can serve as chaperones, can they not?"

Surprised, Andrey turned and gave a quick nod. The doors were shut and only one guard, a very discreet one, was left to watch over them. It was a great relief to know she was kind. It was rare for one of her station to be concerned about those who served beneath her. She was also observant of protocol and her reputation. He was pondering that and other things and missed the first part of what she said.

"Where I noticed a small flaw in the fabric—perhaps left in by the weaver due to a catch in the loom, repeated on each officer's uniform—I found no trace of it on yours. That is how I know you take care of your own uniform."

"What was that?" he asked. "A flaw?"

"Yes."

"Show me."

She turned to face him then and took his hand, turning his arm so the sleeve was exposed on the underside. When she traced her finger up the sleeve and found a tiny stitch, she said, "This is the first repair. The second should be somewhere . . ."

Andrey took her trembling hand from his sleeve and slid it to his chest, pressing it below his medals and insignia until it rested just against his beating heart. He wore far too many layers to feel much more than the pressure of her gloved hand, and yet, for just a fraction of a moment, he thought he imagined the uptick of her pulse.

"It was here," the tsar said softly, cupping her gloved hand, unable to resist moving his body closer to hers. He told himself it was just to keep her warm, but he knew it was a lie. He wanted to feel her against him.

When she looked up at him, her beautiful face lit by cold moonlight, strands of hair dancing about her delicate neck in the crisp breeze, and a spark of awareness slowly blossoming into interest, he smiled.

Lowering his head closer, Andrey was rewarded with a hitch in her breathing, but instead of touching his lips to hers as he so desperately wished to, or nuzzling her soft neckline, he murmured, "Perhaps I can arrange a personal tour of the gardens tomorrow?"

"Y . . . yes, that . . . that would be acceptable," she said. And Mila was surprised to note that she was anticipating seeing him again.

"Good. I very much look forward to it. Now, as I am certain we are causing the wagging of many, many tongues, despite the fact we aren't doing anything interesting with ours . . ." Though it was dark, the windows offered sufficient enough light for Andrey to see a very pretty blush stain her cheeks. The sight warmed him. "As much as I wish we could linger here, I feel it might be better for us to head back inside."

"Of course, you're right," she said immediately, then turned to the soldier guarding them. "We appreciate your acting as our chaperone. Perhaps you wouldn't mind escorting me back in. It wouldn't do for the tsar to show . . . favoritism."

The soldier sputtered, but at seeing the nod from the tsar, offered his arm, and without a glance back in his direction, Mila took her leave.

As they parted, both Mila and Andrey had the same thought.

That was . . . unexpected.

Her given name, Milena Mariani Dalle, was changed on their wedding day, representing her complete transformation not only as a wife but as a newly baptized and utterly loyal citizen of the empire. When the crown was lowered onto her head, and the cardinal pronounced her tsarina, the woman who was Milena Mariani Dalle was indeed gone forever, replaced by the regal, the new Ludmila Marianka Sashenka Stepanov.

Despite her reservations, Mila not only liked her new husband, the tsar and high commander of the Royal Guard; she quickly came to love him. It was obvious to all that the tsar was enamored of his beautiful new wife as well. That she brought no wealth or connections to the empire was soon forgotten as the tsar and tsarina embarked on a tour around the empire and he introduced diplomats, kings, and ambassadors, young and old, to the tsarina, stepping back and allowing her center stage as she impressed them with her poise, wisdom, beauty, and keen eye.

When the tsar was congratulated on his rare find in a wife, he circled an arm around her waist, thickening with their soon-to-be firstborn and proudly said, "But I didn't find her. She found me. I am a lucky man, indeed."

So effective was their co-rule and the changes made in the empire—thanks to policy reforms drafted by Mila—that the roles of women, even those elite born, shifted dramatically in the span of just a few years. Opportunities in education, the military, and politics were suddenly opened to females where they had been closed before, and the economic boon converted those few who remained tied to the old ways.

When the twins were born, both female, and doctors told Mila and Andrey they would not be able to have any other children—specifically and somewhat unkindly pointing out there would be no forthcoming male heirs, something that might have devastated royal predecessors—they were saddened, of course, but the young couple knew they could fashion an empire their daughters could someday rule. Together they worked to build a society that not only relied on women but embraced them and encouraged the growth of their twins in every possible way.

Then, when the girls were only just past a decade of age, Andrey died, and a part of Mila died with him. Though by then all considered her perfectly capable of running the empire, at least until her daughters came of age, and she had trusted generals to take over the Royal Guard, it wasn't the same without the tsar. The light was gone from Mila's life. The empire came to a standstill.

All were waiting for the twins to rise to power. Mila could almost taste the anticipation. If only they could see how much good they could accomplish, for women, for the world. If they only knew how much had been done on their behalf. But the younger never did. They never appreciated the sacrifices of their elders. Not until they learned their own life lessons.

If Mila could just get them ready . . .

Her dreams shifted away from the past and her own true love.

If only her daughters could find happiness as she had. But who among all these choices would be right? There were so many options. So many paths. Which one was right? How could she protect her children and the empire she and her husband had built when she couldn't see all the pieces? No matter what she did, she'd have to leave everything on the table, the result of the game unknown, cards still in play.

Would her daughters even take her seat? Pick up her hand? Would they notice how she'd stacked the deck for them? How everything they loved, everything that meant anything to them, had been risked and tossed into the game? Did they know how much she loved them? Did they understand how much they could lose?

Men's faces danced again behind her closed eyelids.

Together they bowed, but there was something shifty in their eyes. They began to move as one, clasping shoulders and dancing with spirited kicks, claps, stomps, and slaps around a small bonfire. As they whirled, the bonfire grew brighter, burning and licking their black, scuffed boots.

The tsarina frowned in her sleep. She didn't like scuffed boots. *They should be polished.*

Pain twisted her gut.

Who was in charge of those boots? They weren't done properly. She'd have to speak to someone. Her husband wouldn't like it. Threads dangled from sleeves and buttons popped off jackets, melting in the blaze. The fire burned. She cried out as it touched her, catching her skirts. *When had she joined the dance?*

Mila tugged, trying to escape the clutches of the men, but they pulled her closer to the hot flames. Their skin popped into blisters, the wetness trickling down blackened cheeks, then the crispy skin peeled away from white grinning skulls. She screamed, and the laughing suitors dragged her along with them into the inferno.

CHAPTER 3

Death Answers Before It Is Asked

The twins found their mother collapsed on the floor and immediately summoned the doctor. At his insistence, the tsarina finally broke the news of her illness to her beloved girls. To say their mother's secret hit them hard was an understatement. Though neither twin despaired outwardly at the announcement, as both of them had trained extensively as soldiers and had become accustomed to death and saving grief for private moments, Mila could see the distracted stumbling in Stacia's pacing and the telltale trembling in Veru's hands.

After she dismissed the vrach, sending the physician to procure her various medicines, her daughters quickly took places at her side. Despite her best efforts to hold them back, tiny glistening tears began leaking from the corners of her eyes. Oh, how she had wanted it to go differently. If she had only been able to hold out just a bit longer. *What a terrible mess I've made of things,* she thought. But then she could almost hear her husband's voice, soothing her. *Now, now, Mila*, he'd say. *There's nothing the two of us can't twist to our favor when we put our minds to it now, is there?*

No, she admitted back to the ghost of her departed husband. *There is not. Perhaps this will bring the two of them together in a way nothing I said or did before ever could.*

There's my girl, he replied. *Now summon your strength, maya radnaya. You have work to do.*

Mila stretched out one of her hands to touch each of her girls, just as she often did when they were babies sleeping near her bed. "Do not mourn, moi umnyye devochki, for I do not."

At this, tears finally began seeping from Veru's lovely eyes, just a shade darker gray than her own, but Stacia's face hardened. "How can you say this, Mama?" Stacia chided. "Do you think we celebrate the loss of both parents before we come of age? Are we so terrible? Are the pressures of rule so great you can't wait to leave us?"

Managing a weak smile, Mila softly stroked Stacia's hand. She saw so much of her darling husband in this proud daughter. How she wished she could have been by his side when he passed from this world into the next. At least their reunion would be soon. It was her only comfort now. Especially when the pain became unbearable.

"Of course not," Mila answered. "You must know, my only desire is that a cure could be found so that I might grow old and live long enough to see the two of you happily set on your life's journey. I'd like nothing more than to tell my grandchildren stories of their dedushka and turn the diplomatic matters over to the two of you when you're ready so that I can focus more on my gardening. Rest assured: I have no wish to leave you. But none of us can choose our fate. As your old amah often said, 'Fortune and misfortune live in the same courtyard.'"

"Then let us help," Verusha said. "We'll search the empire for the best doctors and healers. Surely there's one in these lands who will have a cure for this disease."

Mila had already seen every one of repute, sought every cure. But she hated denying them the tiny light of hope that still flickered within. Even worse, she didn't want to see that spark die in their eyes. They needed it. Their people needed it. She knew she was dying, and there wasn't much time left. The sickness raged in her body like a ravenous beast, slowly devouring her from the inside out. Every day she grew weaker.

Though Mila's preference would have been to spend the remainder of her days preparing her daughters for their succession and meeting potential matches so that she might find a suitor worthy of her beloved docheri, she reluctantly agreed to meet with whatever healers they summoned and would try her best to remain optimistic, hoping such actions would heal the rift between them.

Her only stipulation was that the two of them remain at her side and work out between them, finally, who would succeed her, and how, should she suddenly pass on. At least that way she could make sure there was progress of some sort being made. Otherwise, she feared the two of them would simply mount horses and disappear, seeking healers on their own, leaving her and the empire to slowly fade away into nothing. The girls agreed, albeit reluctantly, and left their mother to rest.

Everyone knew something was amiss when the twins didn't appear in the practice field early the next morning. But most assumed it had something to do with a diplomatic affair. There was not a whisper among the ranks of the tsarina's illness, which was a credit to the loyalty of those in the palace who served her and the twins.

But despite Tsarina Mila's machinations, the twins not only did *not* reconcile in the weeks that followed; instead, they grew even more distant. When Stacia recruited ten of her best, most-trusted guards and sent one to each of the bordering lands at the far reaches of the empire, Verusha became volatile, claiming it had been her idea to send for healers, not Stacia's. She accused Stacia of trying to act as high commander of the Guard.

Stacia's response was only to stare Veru down and tell her she'd better prepare her prettiest mourning gowns. Adding that the country would want to see a lovely tsarina grieving her mother. At that, Veru punched Stacia in the jaw, hard enough, in fact, that Stacia fell to the thick carpet, slightly dazed.

Lifting a hand to her tender jaw, Stacia said, "I'm surprised you didn't slap me, sestra." Then, instead of initiating the fight Veru was hoping for, Stacia seemed to respectfully consider her twin for just a moment, before grunting and rising to her feet. Then she quickly departed the room to continue seeing to her preparations.

Still itching in every cell of her body to destroy something, Veru knew the first order of business was to calm herself. With Stacia assuming command in typical fashion, she gave herself permission to step aside and consider strategy. Disappearing into her chambers, she first cursed the fate that made her beautiful. In that initial hour, she took her favorite knife to her hair, lopping off several inches. But when that wasn't enough, she considered giving herself a wicked scar along her cheekbone. Nothing deep enough to cause infection, but definitely enough to make suitors think twice. She paused with the weapon lifted.

Veru was a practical woman, and despite the fact she often hated how she manipulated others with her beauty, she could also see the benefit of it. Damaging her looks would be akin to destroying a piece of armor or wounding a prized horse. It would be foolish to throw away an asset in a moment of distress.

Though inheriting the throne had always been something open to either Veru or Stacia, Veru had been told from a young age that her winning looks would open so many doors. This had been said much too often in Stacia's presence for her not to have heard. She was sure Stacia resented her for it too. It was probably why they'd never been close.

Though her parents had always been careful to say that looks didn't matter and intelligence counted for so much more—and they were always certain to emphasize that they found *both* of their daughters beautiful and bright—Veru knew that many, if not all, the people in the empire considered Stacia the smart twin and her the beautiful twin. What that meant in terms of securing the best match to stabilize the empire, or who was best to rule, Veru didn't exactly understand.

Her parents were always fastidious when it came to saying leadership was a tricky business. But even if Stacia *was* the smart one, Veru was clever enough to realize when she was being subtly pushed. And if there was one thing that never worked with Veru, it was when anyone tried to manipulate her to do something she didn't want to do. It triggered an automatic rebellion.

That was part of the reason why she hated her looks. Whenever a diplomat fawned over her, it made her want to do something awful, like lean over and vomit on his shoes or burp loudly at the dinner table. She hated the predictability of it. Meeting the expectations of others. Above all, she wanted to be herself. And be loved for who she was—her ugly bits as well as the comely parts.

She'd seen a pretty serving girl fall for a man once. He was handsome and had a way with words that made every woman he took notice of go weak in the knees. They were a good match, or so she'd thought. They married and had a son. He doted on her and appeared to be as smitten as his new bride. But after a few years, she became ill when they lost a second child.

A short time later, when riding together, she was thrown from a horse and broke her foot. It healed, but she developed a limp and never walked the same. The man's affection waned, and he sought comfort elsewhere. Veru's maid lost her joy and left her work. She wasn't surprised to learn she'd passed away one winter from a common sickness—one she should have easily recovered from. Her husband had gone away. There was no one to care for her during her illness.

Her beauty was one of the reasons she preferred hiding behind a helmet. Veru could blend in with everyone else. She wanted to be seen and appreciated for her talents, her skills, and her personality. Not for her appearance. Her biggest fear was being matched with someone who loved what she looked like, only to despise her as she grew old and toss her aside the moment he was disaffected. She could not—would not—tolerate such a thing. But how did one guarantee love was true and lasting?

Placing the knife back into the hidden place in her custom-made palace dressing shoes, she satisfied herself instead with the large map of the empire she kept tucked in the back of her closet. If, by some miracle she feared was slipping further and further from her by the moment, she *did not* become the tsarina but the high commander of the Royal Guard, as she wished, she had a carefully plotted campaign for expansion. To calm herself, she updated once again the territories she felt were open to diplomatic approaches versus those that would go to war to protect their borders. She only stopped when her tears over the loss of her mother threatened to blur the marked lines.

Meanwhile, Stacia met with her men. Their instructions were to seek out the most renowned, the most skilled healer in the country, and then whatever the cost, whatever trade was required, they were given permission to quickly secure the service and escort the healer back with as little fanfare and information as possible. In truth, even the guards were not told for whom they were obtaining help, though all of them could guess.

They departed within the hour.

Once Stacia sent the ten, she sent another fifty within the empire itself. Their task was to round up every doctor, every shaman, every herbalist, no matter how skilled or insignificant. Upon their immediate return, they would analyze the patient, prescribe treatment, and the tsarina had agreed to try it, no matter how strange. Now all they could do was wait for the first of Stacia's men to return with help.

After an hour or two, her temper soothed, but unable to come up with anything new, Veru approached her sister, demanding an update, only to find that Stacia had exhausted all possibilities. It left nothing for Veru to do except worry, wallow, and wait. Worry she did. Wallow, she did for a while. But wait, she could not.

She had to think of something Stacia hadn't. Otherwise, one of her sister's methods would work in healing her mother, and Stacia would be known as the savior of the tsarina, leading the Guard in a victorious result, while she had effectively sat on her hands.

Once again, she returned to her rooms.

It took three long days before Veru called for Nikolai, but when she did, she summoned him to her chambers, something she had never ever done. The gesture almost soothed Nikolai's ruffled nerves. Almost. He'd heard the alarmed whispers around the camp and watched in concern as the numbers of trusted Guardsmen dwindled to mere dozens.

The doctor he trained with was beckoned to the palace and remained there, while Nikolai was told to stay and help any injured Guardsmen.

Ha! As if there were any injuries. No one could train under such conditions.

The camp surgeon was gone for too many hours, according to Nikolai's thinking, and when he returned to his cot, late at night, his face white, his lips tight with concern, and even tighter with secrets he refused to share, no matter how cleverly Nikolai questioned him, it was all the young man could do not to rush to the palace and pound on the thick doors, demanding to see if his beloved tsarevna had taken ill. Nik tossed and turned, unable to sleep with worry.

The first night, he snuck out and climbed the old tree, the one that nearly touched her balcony. If he was lucky, within a year or so, the limb would be strong enough to hold his weight, allowing him access to her room. He'd been carefully watering and fertilizing the tree over the last few years and grooming the branches just so, to encourage the growth where he wanted it, and his vigilant nurturing was finally paying off.

Unfortunately, it was winter, and there were no leaves to hide his form. He'd have to go very carefully and slowly so the palace guard wouldn't catch him, and even then he'd have to leave no indication of his footsteps. If it was discovered that he spied on the tsarevna, at the very least his tree might be cut down, and all his work over the years would be burned up in the course of a few hours due to recklessness—and that was only if he got away unseen.

If he was caught, he'd be punished, possibly even put to death, depending on how his actions were interpreted and how much Veru might be inclined to intervene on his behalf. Even if she did stick her neck out for him, there would be consequences for her. There was no sense in both of them being punished. But then again, Nik knew he likely wouldn't get caught. Besides, he had to know if she was well. If she wasn't . . . well, then a tree didn't much matter, then, did it?

Nikolai went slow. Very slow, and fortune favored him. It wasn't the first time, nor did he think it would be the last he'd have to use the gifts he'd come by so very dearly.

A storm blew in. He sighed in relief, though the cold was uncomfortable. He'd been saved by weather before, and he was glad it was helping him once again.

The stinging snow made it difficult for him to see, but it also meant that others hunkered down and weren't paying much attention to him. He considered it a sign from the heavens that he was being watched over. Then the second sign came. His beloved was standing at the window. It soon became clear to him it was not her the doctor was worried over. She paced, her arms behind her back, her stride just as strong as ever.

Letting out a sigh of relief, Nikolai settled back against the trunk of the cold tree. He let the sight of her strong, curvy body, which was outlined in her nightdress from the lamplight behind her, warm him when she passed the window. In fact, the biting bits of slush that hit his hot skin melted at once, and his eyes burned like fiery coals in the night. He didn't move until her light extinguished.

But then the next day passed, and she didn't come to him, nor the next. Guardsmen had been summoned and left quickly, but everything was kept quiet. The doctor had also been summoned but wouldn't tell him what was wrong, no matter how he tried to convince him to share the news. Nik suspected the worst. He didn't understand. Had he done something to upset her? He became angry. If she was healthy, then why wasn't she calling for him?

Then he became distressed. What if she really was the one who was ill? His worried mind killed his appetite and left him restless. Suppose she was calling for him, and he wasn't with her?

Finally, she did. Nik calmed himself then, by repeating that he didn't know what was happening. He'd hear her out. Show her again that she could trust him.

Then he was escorted to her chamber. Hope blossomed. Perhaps something had changed between them for the better.

Once there, Nikolai thrilled even more when she dismissed the guard, and the two of them were left alone. But his elation changed when he realized his beloved tsarevna was troubled in a way he'd never seen before. She paced the room again, like the caged beast he'd seen in the window. Her normally meticulously groomed appearance was unkempt.

There were dark circles under her eyes. Her soft, moist lips were cracked and bitten. And her lovely hair was tangled and unbrushed. She looked like . . . she looked much like her sister after battle, and the sight bothered Nik more than he could say.

"What has happened?" Nik asked hesitantly, fearing the worst. "Has . . . has your mother announced an engagement?"

"An engagement?" she barked a laugh, and it sounded ugly and strange to him. *For just a moment, it reminded him of . . .*

A deep tremor reverberated in his soul. Something was very, very wrong, but it wasn't what he was thinking. He reached out and took hold of Veru's arms, shaking her hard. Too hard. He needed to bring her back to herself. "Veru! Tell me. What is wrong?"

His beloved tsarevna began crying then. No. Not just crying. Her sobbing was terrible. It was repellently wet. Full of phlegm-filled heaving. But then she reached out for him and buried her streaming face in his neck, and his whole body warmed with the weight of her in his arms. *At last*, he thought. *At last, she can see that we belong together.*

Holding her close, he rocked her and murmured, "Ne plach, kukolka. Don't cry, little one. You know, they say that tears that fall so readily often come from only the eyes and not the heart."

Verusha gasped and wrenched herself away from him then, wiping her running nose and eyes on her shirtsleeve. "How dare you say that I don't love my mother," she accused.

"Your mother? When were we speaking of your mother? I assumed we were speaking of your impending nuptials."

"No, you bolvan. Haven't you been listening? My mother is ill. I think she's dying. And Stacia sent out the Guard. As much as I've tried, I can't come up with a course of action on my own."

"I see. And the problem?" Nikolai asked stiffly.

"The problem?" Veru sputtered, wondering how her best friend could be so cold.

As for Nikolai, he was fixated on the fact that she'd called him a bolvan. It was what his father had called him every day of his life, every time he'd beaten him. For just a moment, he was back in that hovel, his frail, cowardly mother watching with her newest spindly babe pressed to her breast as his father backhanded her oldest son hard enough that the cords of wood he carried spilled from his arms.

—

"You stupid bolvan," the man spat, already drunk, though the hour was still early. "Didn't I ask you to muck the horse stall this morning?"

"I did," Nik mumbled through the blossoming pain in his jaw as he crouched down to pick up the newly split logs. He heard the soft intake of breath from his mother, and the tiny sunken sets of eyes that had been peeking out from behind her skirts suddenly disappeared. Nikolai winced, realizing his mistake almost as he uttered it.

"What?" his father asked. "What did you say?"

Knowing it was coming and that it was better not to give him a weapon, Nik dropped the wood and stood. "I said, 'I did,'" Nik repeated, louder this time.

"Is that right?"

When his father raised his hand again, Nik flinched, much as he was used to it. But instead of another blow across the cheek, the heavy hand clapped down on the back of his shirt, and he felt the thin fabric tear as he was manhandled into the ramshackle building his father had erected once upon a time that served as a barn.

The old horse stood in her stall, munching on the meager fare Nik had rustled up for her that morning. The straw beneath her hooves was still as fresh as it had been when he'd mucked it out just as dawn crept over the frigid horizon, with the exception of a very large, very new, pile of steaming dung.

Sighing, Nik said, "I'll take care of it."

"That's right," his ox of a father said. "Get yourself in there and take care of it." With that, the man opened the stall and shoved Nik inside. "On your knees, boy."

Nik couldn't imagine what the man was going to do. It would be dangerous to whip him near the mare. Not that he hadn't taken the crop to the beast enough times for her to shy and crowd herself into the corner of the stall as well, already neighing in protest to his father's arrival. But no, his father had more terrible things than a simple whipping in mind. For a moment, he feared the man would shove him facedown into the pile of navoz, but instead, he had a worse fate in store for his boy.

"Eat it." Nik heard him say. "Eat it while I watch."

When Nik hesitated, uncertain at first that he'd understood correctly, his father bent down and added, "You know what I'll do if you don't."

So Nik ate it.

When he vomited, his father made him eat that too. But he vomited again. As he did, his father laughed and kept laughing, lifting a bottle to his lips that he must have kept hidden in the barn.

Nik went about the business of eating navoz and retching navoz and then lifting the disgusting mass back to his lips, repeating the cycle until sweat slicked his entire body and tears blurred his vision. The protesting horse danced nervously beside him, and the thought occurred to him that he envied the beast. All she had to worry about was physical punishment and eventual death, something that sounded more and more peaceful to him as the long, agonizing moments stretched on.

As Nik was well aware, there were more terrible things in the world than death or pain. Many more terrible things. Finally, the anxious mare kicked him in the arm, dislocating his shoulder, then a second strike to the head was hard enough to put him out of his misery until nightfall.

When he awoke covered in his own vomit, horse dung, straw, and blood, the sound of a night owl hooting from the rafters, Nikolai cursed the fact he still lived. The mare's soft lips gummed his hair, leaving a trail of saliva as she sought the rotten apple he often saved for her when he found them beneath the old tree on the edge of the property. Nik's shoulder spasmed as he tried to sit up, and his jaw and head ached.

"You should have killed me," he said thickly as he pushed her head away and assessed the deep cut her sharp hoof had made on his scalp. "It would have been kinder."

Struggling, he got to his feet and used the water from the trough to clean his face and wound as best he could. It would need stitching. He could feel with gentle probing how deep it was. But to ask for help meant waking his mother, and once she was in bed with their father, there was no disturbing her. There was no other option. He'd have to stitch it as best he could himself.

Abandoning his filthy but warm winter outerwear, he made his way back to the tiny home in just his threadbare undershirt and boots, forging a path through new-fallen snow. Without a lamp to light his way, he used the light from the crescent moon to guide him to the shadowy house. Once inside, he lit the stump of a candle and located the tiny tin box where his mother kept the needles.

He was in the middle of stitching, using the inside of the tin box as a mirror and his hunting knife to cut the strings, when he saw the reflection of something in the darkness approaching behind him. He didn't know what came over him. When the hot breath of the person behind him hit the back of his neck, and the stink of his own vomit mixed with blood and horse dung wafted over him, he clutched the knife in his fist, spun, and sunk it deep into the belly of the dark form lurking in the shadows.

Nik heard a soft gasp and fingers clasped his where he still held the knife, hot blood wetting his fingers. A body thumped to the floor, but it wasn't as heavy as it should have been. Nik grabbed the stub of the candle and frantically relit it. The flame had sputtered out when he'd spun around. When he turned, lifting the meager light, who he saw on the floor was not the father who'd abused him all his life but the thin form of his nearly equally abused, once beautiful mother.

As she lay dying at his feet, hand stretched up to him with blood trickling from her lips, Nik tried to summon empathy for her, but found he had none. The only emotion he felt in that moment was sheer panic. He sat immobile, listening intently for the sound of his father's waking, the man's angry grunt as he roused himself from slumber. But all he heard was the deep, drunken snoring that soothed all of them enough so they could close their eyes, at least for a short while.

When the spark of life faded from her dull eyes, Nik thought, for just a moment, he glimpsed relief. The lingering tenderness he felt for his mother turned to stinging betrayal, as it often did. How could she? She was leaving him unprotected, again! Then he realized the only champion he had, the only friend he'd ever known, was gone forever, and it was his fault. Tears slipped down his cheeks as he inaudibly mouthed, "Mama! Don't leave me! Please! I'm so sorry!"

His body heaved in silent shudders as he clasped her hands to his chest, kneeling next to her in the growing puddle of blood. Whatever mixed feelings he had about his mother, he'd loved her, and her death was something he'd need to atone for. Nik hoped wherever she was now, she could grasp on to happiness and somehow find peace. At the same time, Nik knew peace and happiness weren't something waiting for him in his immediate future, not with the monster he'd soon have to face. Then a terrible thought came, one that would make him as terrible a villain as the one sleeping in the other room.

Gently, he folded his mother's hands across her chest and bent to kiss her forehead, whispering an apology for what he was about to do to her children. He wasn't asking for forgiveness, but just expressed his sorrow for what he viewed as unavoidable.

After packing a sack with the few foodstuffs they had in the house, Nik dressed in silence, taking the too-small clothing of his younger brother. He knew he needed to hurry. The babe would wake soon and demand his mother's breast, which would rouse his father. Grabbing his rucksack, Nik said a silent farewell to his siblings and left, barricading the door behind him.

Later, Nik sat on the mare, considering his work as he watched the flames lick at the barn and the house. The screams had quieted long since. A storm was blowing in which would help cover his tracks. He didn't think anyone would believe the fire had been intentionally lit, and they were isolated enough that it was unlikely the family would be found for quite some time.

Nik didn't regret the deaths of his siblings. He surmised that they had now discovered the same peace his mother had found. In fact, he considered himself something of a hero to them. As he rode west, Nikolai vowed he would never let a man take advantage of him again. That was why he decided to join the Guard.

—

"Come on, Nik," Veru said. "Snap out of it. Don't you see I need you?"

Nik shook his head, relegating thoughts of his past to the past, where they belonged. "Forgive me," he said, bowing his head deferentially. "What can I do to help?"

"Stacia is outthinking me. I need your brain."

This was why he loved Veru. She was powerful and strong, but more than that, she was clever. He'd seen her handle all sorts of men, even men who were abusive like his father had been. Men like that made Nik's blood go cold, but not Veru. She'd smile at them with cat's eyes and bat her lashes, all the while she'd have a knife aimed at their ribs. No one would ever corner Veru. He admired that. She never gave up, no matter what. Sometimes he thought if he'd been a bit more like Veru, then maybe his mother . . .

Nik blinked rapidly. It was best not to let his thoughts drift down that road. "Tell me everything that has happened," he said. "Start at the beginning."

By the time he left, they had a plan. Stacia might have sent the Guard to the four corners of the earth, but he had a note from Tsarevna Verusha, one that would open doors for him anywhere and everywhere in the empire. And Nik knew places and people the Guard wouldn't dare seek out. In fact, there was one man who immediately came to mind.

As he left, he reassured Veru that Stacia, for all her efforts, wouldn't accomplish much on a crooked goat, managing to garner the laugh he'd been hoping to hear. He told her to rely on him, and he would find the one person who could fix everything. If he was right, Nik just might indeed be able to fix everything, setting himself and his tsarevna up for a future beyond even his own dreams.

Buoyed by her confidence in him, Nikolai mounted his horse and departed that very hour, setting down a path that would lead him to a dark forest rumored to be the home of an outcast monk who practiced a dark mysticism.

Some said he was a religious man, a healer. Others called him a monster who awakened the dead and refashioned them into monsters that terrorized the forest. Whatever the case, Nik knew the man's powers were real indeed. For he had met one of the man's monsters.

It had been his own father.

And Nik had been afforded the unique opportunity to take the life of his own father twice.

CHAPTER 4

An Affectionate Calf May Drink from Two Mothers

It had been about five years since Nik had barely escaped with his life, and only great desperation would make him seek out the man who nearly destroyed him. Years before, after watching his home burn, he had been traveling to St. Rostislav and passed through the small town of Pyrs, where he stopped for the night.

A kindly widow took him in, fed him a hot meal, and asked him to stay on for a few days during the harvest to help set her up before winter. In exchange, she would pay him in food; fit him with clothes left behind by her son, who had also joined the Guard but perished in a long-ago battle; and gift him with a heavy fur-lined pair of winter boots, made by her brother who lived nearby.

The work was easy. The town was small and sleepy. And the old widow kept his plate full of more delicious home-cooked food than he could possibly eat and his mug brimming with hot, sense-dulling, sleep-inducing drink every evening. Soon thoughts of joining the Guard became distant.

The widow was more than happy to keep him for as long as he wanted to stay. Having a son again filled her lonely home with happiness, she assured him, as she darned his socks, knitted him woolen caps, and began embroidering him a beautiful new tunic on crisp white linen should he be inclined to stay through the Christmastide season, long enough for the arrival of Grandfather Frost and his granddaughter the Snow Maiden.

Nik didn't say as much, but he was inclined.

As the days turned to weeks and the weeks to months, Nik's gaunt frame began to take on flesh, and he noticed the cupboards were beginning to run low on supplies, especially with the way the kindly widow stuffed him with food. After feeding the humpbacked pony and milking the goat, he offered to go to town in his newly acquired fur-lined boots and trade for some items to get them through winter.

"Spasibo but nyet, my son," the old widow said, setting down his heaped plate of breakfast and mug of goat milk. "I shall go myself when the mood strikes me."

"Please, let me," Nik insisted. "Your back pains you overmuch. I don't want you to suffer needlessly."

"You're a sweet boy," she said, patting his cheek. Her rheumy eyes peered into his for a long moment, and he wondered what it was she was looking for. Perhaps it was her lost son or a lost memory. Finally, almost sadly, she said, "I can't stop you if you want to go, but I'll ask you not to. At least wait until tomorrow, won't you? You're safe here."

Nik frowned at the last, but said, "I know I'm safe with you, babushka. Yes. I suppose I can wait until tomorrow."

"Very good." She cackled and gave him a gap-toothed grin. "Then let me work on your tunic today. Perhaps I'll have it ready for you in time."

"In time? Christmastide is a month from now. I won't need it just yet."

She replied with a distracted, "Yes. Must hurry, then. Must hurry."

The old widow worked so hard on his tunic that even when it became dark, she refused to stop. Nik lit a candle, set it by her rocking chair with a plate of stew and a slice of toasted bread slathered with fresh butter, and went to bed.

When he woke the next morning, he found her still in the chair, slumped down, deep in sleep, the tunic clutched in her gnarled fingers, and a tiny bit of drool escaping from her slack mouth. Gently, he tried to wake her and coax her to her bed, attempting to take the tunic from her hands and set it aside, but when he pulled, it came away attached to her palms with sticky fibers. The old woman startled and blinked, and Nik swore for a moment that he saw not one pair of eyelids but two.

"What? What is it, dear?" she asked, sitting up and adjusting her shawl around her shoulders.

Why hadn't he noticed the bump between her shoulders before? The poor woman needed a physician. She was likely in great pain.

"Won't you take to your bed this morning?" he asked. "You've had a long night."

"Nyet. I'll be fine. Just let me get my feet under me. I'll see to your breakfast." As she lumbered over to the table, her knees and joints cracking like heavy-laden tree branches in an ice storm with every step, and set down the tunic, she asked hesitantly, "Will you be leaving this morning? I wasn't able to finish your tunic, I'm afraid."

Nik saw her hands tremble as she took his mug and plate from the cupboard. "No," he answered slowly. "It looks as if bad weather is approaching. I think I'll hold off another day."

"Does it?" she replied, not even bothering to look out the cottage window already lit with the rosy promise of winter sunshine. "I'll keep on, then."

They played the game every day for a week, with her working late into the night, her eyes straining to see the thread and the needle, and him postponing heading to town due to some reason or another, until the seventh night. That evening there were no more candles left for him to light, and they'd scraped together a meager dinner using the last of the mash and a bit of goat's milk. By the light of the fire, they sat together as she sewed. Both of them knew there was no more time to spare. He'd have to go to town for supplies in the morning.

Finally, just as he was preparing to rise for bed, about to caution her to do the same, she carefully folded and set aside the tunic, then announced, "It's complete."

Nik thought she'd be happy, and he was ready to lavish great praise upon the garment, but then he saw how heavy tears filled the widow's eyes, and she rubbed them until they appeared quite swollen indeed.

"Please don't cry, babushka," Nikolai said, taking her sticky hand in his and patting it. "If you really don't want me to leave, I won't. I'll go hunting instead. We'll make do, somehow."

"It's not that. Ty khoroshiy mal'chik. You're a good boy." With that, she burst into a fresh set of tears. "If only you weren't. Now my husband and I will have no Christmastide feast."

"What? Your husband? Don't you mean your brother? I think you're confused."

"No," the old widow said, then sighed and shrugged off her shawl. "I'm afraid you're the one confused, my dear."

As she spoke, her voice changed. It deepened into something sinister. More like a growl than the sound of an elderly woman. Then, to his horror, her head lifted, and her jaw unhinged. Before he could scream, the bottom of it elongated, and Nik found he lost his own voice entirely as his mouth went dry. The widow's weepy eyes widened, and two sets of lids appeared, which was fortunate, because her eyeballs grew larger and larger until they finally popped out from the woman's head and hung like bulbous white radishes on coarse stalks.

It was then that Nik realized the orbs gazing and blinking at him as they danced on either side of her cheekbones no longer contained a single eye hanging on the end of the fibrous crimson stalks, but a cluster of jellied, winking pustules. It reminded him of a monstrous arachnid, especially when thick black bristles erupted from her neck and arms.

Gooseflesh stood out on his own arms, and he felt the cold whisper of death dampen the backs of his ears. A bad omen, indeed. Nik scrambled away from her to a far corner of the room, but she lifted a hand and thin filaments shot from her palms. As she twisted her hands in the air, murmuring an incantation, the fibers wove together into a rope that shot toward him, quickly binding his feet, hands, and torso.

"I don't want you to leave just yet," the creature he'd lived with for months said in her new voice, one that gurgled and rasped as if she were speaking underwater.

"What . . . what are you?" Nik asked as she stood, her rickety knees unlocking and bending unnaturally, the joints turning backward as the skin on her arms bubbled and erupted in red scales.

"I am called many things," she replied as fangs swelled in her upper jaw, the sharp tips glistening with golden liquid. "Some refer to me as a sheetweaver, or a moroi. But you might know me as a kikimora."

Nik began shaking. Kikimory were nightmarish house spirits that strangled people in their sleep, kidnapped children on the road, and didn't his mother once tell him a story saying that those who saw a kikimora spinning or weaving would die soon afterward? Well . . . if that was his fate, perhaps it would be better to embrace it. In fact, he wouldn't be surprised if it had been the ghost of his departed mother who had cursed him in such an awful way.

"So"—Nik straightened his shoulders, the fear suddenly leaving him—"you've finished my burial shroud, then. I suppose I deserve it. What happens first? Should I put on my new tunic? Do you put that shroud on me, then drink me dry? Will you and your—your husband, is it? Will the two of you simply deprive me of my lifeblood, or will you consume my flesh as well? Shall I confess my sins first? That is the least you could let me do before putting me out of misery, don't you think, babushka?"

The spider woman stopped advancing when she saw Nik's lack of fear and heard the tone of resignation in his voice. "Why do you wish to confess your sins?" the new creature asked him, sliding a foot to the side so a third and fourth leg could free themselves from the waistband of her dress and deposit themselves on either side of her body. She sighed with relief, and Nik realized she was neither as old as he once believed nor as fat.

Twisting her strange head, she waited for his reply, and added, "I did not lie when I said I believe you are a good boy. I will regret eating you. But I am hungry. If you wish to tell me of your sins, I will listen. Perhaps hearing of your sins will soothe my conscience. Or possibly it will ease your journey to the next life. Either way, I think it is a good thing."

"You are right," Nik said, after a moment. "I know it will change nothing. Still. If you can manage your hunger for a while, I will tell you of my sins and of the terrible monster I destroyed."

"It must have been a terrible monster, indeed, if you have no fear of me."

"Yes. He was. The terrifying monster was my father. And though I killed him, he still haunts me. But please, won't you first make yourself comfortable? You don't need to keep your human form for me. Let me get you a bit of bread and some tea to ease your hunger while I speak."

The clusters of eyes blinked shrewdly once, then twice. There was a shudder, and then what was left of the grandmother he knew dissolved before him as her limbs grew and shifted, hardening and transforming into a nightmarish being that would disturb his dreams if he was ever lucky enough to have a dream again.

Where the old woman was slow, her body creaking and stiff, the new thing that replaced her was deadly silent other than a clicking of teeth and a scraping of bristles. It settled itself, not on the chair as it once did, but hanging from the ceiling with one long limb, its body draped across the door so there was no escape. The temperature in the room cooled, despite the crackling logs in the fireplace. Nik could feel the rime of bitter winter seeping through gaps of the poorly sealed window.

To distract himself while he boiled water for tea, he asked about her husband. "Before I begin, will you tell me—is your husband a being like you?"

"He is not," she replied, in her rasping new voice. "I am of the swamp, and he is of the forest. My husband is a leshi."

"Leshi?"

"Da. A wood spirit who casts no shadow as he walks. When he stands quietly, he is mistaken for a tree. Those who are lost follow his voice until he leads them to me. Then I capture and slowly drain them. It is our way. He doesn't like trespassers, and I keep that green nest he calls a beard clean and rodent-free. Sometimes he'd let me hide beneath it, and the two of us would wait for a stranger to pass beneath his tall legs. That's when I'd pounce and . . ." She licked her black lips hungrily. "Well, it's been a while since we've enjoyed being together in our forest."

"But I don't understand," Nik said. "If you are of the swamp and he of the forest, what are the two of you doing in Pyrs?"

The creature shifted uneasily and spat on the floor. The liquid that came from her mouth was black, and it smoked and hissed, bubbling until it ate a hole in the floor. "Bah! See what you made me do? Now I shall have to summon my husband to repair the wood before he brings me the next boy. Assuming he'll find another one before I starve. We don't get as many wanderers as we used to, thanks to *him*. He takes all the nomads to build up his ranks. You're the first one we've seen in a long time."

"Him?"

"If you can call such a thing that."

"Who are you referring to?"

"The one who took over our forest and cast us out. We don't know his true name. He is known to us only as the Black Bies or the Death Draughtsman."

Nik's hands shook as he poured the tea into two mugs. Whoever this Death Draughtsman might be, he was powerful enough to cause this terrifying creature and her husband, who were holding him prisoner, to leave their home and risk living in a town inhabited by humans. He slid the bit of bread and the mug of tea to the edge of the small table near her outstretched leg, only then noticing she no longer had fingers, but a thick, blackened stump covered with what looked like leather on one side and hairs on the other. It was far too bulbous to use the mug handle.

Opening his mouth, Nik was about to offer to hold the mug for her when she touched her hairy limb to the side of the hot mug and a sticky substance enveloped the entire thing. When she brought it close to her face, a long, writhing proboscis uncoiled from her mouth and dipped into the cup. It quivered as she sipped and changed color from pink to nearly white. Nik gulped his tea wrong and choked, sputtering and coughing, imagining that long tongue piercing and lapping at his neck.

"Right," he said, clearing his throat. "I suppose I'll get on with my confession, then." When there was no response from the creature, he forged ahead, regaling her with a tale that needed no exaggeration, painting his father in all the vivid monstrous colors he recalled, while minimizing his own reprehensible acts and instead rendering himself as the hero.

"In fact," he added, after telling her of how he rode off with the blaze of the house burning brightly behind him, "I'd like to be able to do the same thing for you."

"What do you mean?" she asked suspiciously.

"I mean, I've rid the world of my monster. Perhaps I can rid your forest of yours."

There was a dark pause and then an even darker cackle followed. When she caught her breath, the creature said, "You? You think you'll be able to do away with an evil as great as the Death Draughtsman? Nyet, you fatuous boy. He is no simple human for you to vanquish. It is folly to even consider it."

She denied the possibility, and yet Nikolai could hear the tiniest tinge of longing in her voice. Furrowing his brow, Nik nodded in agreement. "I'm sure you're right. It was foolish for me to hope. It's just that I can't help but desire a final wish to serve my ailing grandmother in more than a temporary sustaining of body. Don't you see? If I could defeat this villain, there would be plenty for you. I would not have to worry about you starving after I am gone."

Nik's earnest expression and utter sangfroid were skills he had developed at a very young age, after living with his abusive father and a mother too weak to fight back. He was almost grateful now for the skills. *Almost.* That he could use them to negotiate for his life with a monster was incredible. Still, he wouldn't thank either of his parents had they been there at that moment. No. What he had was his own. It was no thanks to them.

"Oh. You *are* a sweet boy," the creature said.

He might have been mistaken, but Nik thought in that moment that tears were leaking from her bulbous eyes.

"Let me summon my husband and see what he thinks of the idea." This was followed by an otherworldly screech that sounded something like the hoot of an owl crossed with that of a giant bat. Nik wanted to cover his ears, but he didn't think that would go over well. It wasn't a few moments later that a resounding thump landed on the door, so thunderous that the walls shook. The spider woman shifted away from the entry, and it slammed open.

At first all Nik could see were long legs covered by enormous boots. Then the man, who bent over nearly halfway to enter the house, came inside and sat on the floor. His body was large, but not fat. He was thick, solid, built like a tree. The brown skin was wrinkled deeply on his face and arms, almost like tree bark, and his beard, which narrowed to a point at his waist, looked like moss.

"What is this, Escovina? Do you not find this one to your liking?"

"Nyet, Larix. Nyet. He was a good find."

"Then why have you not consumed him? You are hungry. The winter will be long. You cannot sustain yourself from the ground as I can. I've already lost too much. I will not lose you as well. If you cannot bring yourself to kill him, I will do it for you."

The large tree spirit lifted his long arm, ready to backhand Nik, but the other creature shot a web out and captured his hand so it couldn't move. "Wait," she said, almost gently for a being so monstrous. "He wishes to help us."

"Help us?" he replied with a stoic incredulity befitting a tree. "He is deceiving you in an attempt to save his own life."

"I do not believe so," she retorted softly. "I wish to let him try. Will you help him on his journey?"

"Even should he be sincere, he won't survive the endeavor. Then what will happen to you?"

"If he succeeds, then there will be plenty."

"And if he doesn't?"

There was a pause. Then the spider creature sighed and said, "If he doesn't, then there wasn't much hope for me anyway."

The green tree man pounded a fist through the floor, making a hole. Immediately, he placed a hand over it and the wood came alive, regrowing itself, filling the gap. "We've talked about this. You can take a townsperson."

"No. I won't cause unnecessary pain to a family. It's not our way."

Nik raised an eyebrow. This was an interesting turn of events. He found he now genuinely wanted to help the two strange creatures. Finally speaking up, he said, "If you'll point me in the right direction and give me a few tips, I promise to do my best to defeat the Death Draughtsman and thereby return you to the forest."

The tree man looked Nik over for what seemed like a very long time indeed, then gave a slight nod. "Escovina, I will agree to this, though I do not have high hopes for the outcome."

"Spasibo," Nik and the spider creature said at the same time.

"Do not thank me just yet, little man child," Larix said. "You're still likely to die, in a much less pleasant fashion, and this time it will only be temporary."

"Temporary? What does that mean?"

"You'll see. Now grab a satchel and put the last of the bread and the salt inside. Hurry."

"Yes, da, Nikolai. You must follow each of Larix's instructions exactly. Promise me you will."

"I promise, babushka. Dedushka," he added, nodding to the tree man, hoping to gain his favor.

"Yes, yes," he said, waving a wrinkled hand impatiently. "Now take off your clothes and put them back on inside out. He'll need all your magic, Escovina."

"Yours too, Larix?"

"Yes. He'll need all the magic he can muster."

"Very well," she said.

Nik watched in fascination as his "babushka" began twirling and spinning, but this time it wasn't with thread but with light. The tunic she'd created began to glow.

As she worked, her husband explained, "She created a death shroud for each boy. It's a wrapping, essentially. It preserves their body as she drains it of life over time. That way it can sustain her as long as possible."

Gulping, Nik asked, "You . . . you mean they're still alive?"

"The shroud suspends them in a sleeplike state."

"They are happy and dreaming. I make sure of it," she said as she continued working.

"Still, they don't last long," Larix said. "Then, after they die, she buries them in the shroud."

"How . . . lovely," Nik managed, now wondering what they meant for him to do. "Is the tunic going to make me dream?"

"Not now," Escovina said. "I've imbued it with light magic. Now it's a gift. Larix has a gift for you as well. Here, I'm done. You can put it on now."

He hesitated only a moment but then lifted the glowing tunic over his head and slid it over his chest. It crackled with energy.

When he turned about, gaining a nod of approval from his two strange and deadly adopted grandparents, Larix said, "Perfect. Now we need to visit the goat and the horse."

"Why?" Nik asked, following the large tree man out the door.

"Because we need the goat to kick you and the horse to butt you."

CHAPTER 5

Beware of the Goat from Its Front Side, of the Horse from Its Back Side, and a Monk from Any Side

Quickly, Nik trailed behind the leshi, trying to ignore his irritation as he walked in clothing that was inside out and backward and twisting uncomfortably in places he'd prefer the fabric not be bunched. He tugged at the neckline. "Don't you mean you want the horse to kick me and the goat to butt me?" he asked the tree man.

Nik had been kicked by horses enough to know such a thing rarely if ever brought luck, but he wasn't going to complain. Better to be kicked than eaten.

The tree spirit called Larix turned suddenly and lowered his head, pointing a gnarled finger nearly a foot long at Nik's nose. Nik swallowed when he saw glowing yellow eyes blinking from the depths of the mossy green beard and remembered the spider creature saying how much she'd enjoyed hiding behind it and springing out on unsuspecting victims.

"If you want to survive," he cautioned in a gravelly voice, "I'd suggest trying to be more like a tree."

"I don't understand," Nik said in reply.

"Exactly. Humans are nearly incapable of remaining silent. They are too desperate to be seen. Too anxious to be adored. They don't realize that the ones who are watched and admired are the ones who are cut down in their prime. How much better is it, then, to go unnoticed? To hide within a copse? Animals understand this. They are camouflaged from those that prey on them. Or they hide among large herds.

"Trees only speak when there is something of grave importance to say. Wisdom takes decades to acquire. If you must speak at all, speak tacitly; otherwise, watch, observe, listen, learn. Those who live longest are the most careful and observant. If you want to survive, you must learn this skill."

Nik rehearsed in his mind the advice given many years before by the old tree spirit as he rode on, league after grueling league, back to the shadowed, dark forest near Pyrs. He no longer regretted how he was raised or the fact that he'd been nearly destroyed by monsters, both the human kind and the supernatural. Those experiences had forged him into the creature he now was: the soldier worthy of caring for a tsarevna and, someday, if he watched and waited patiently enough, the one who'd win her care in return. All his prior perils had led him to his beautiful Veru, and he'd brave any obstacle, defeat any foe, and outwit any rival to remain in her presence.

When he was a good distance outside the town and far enough away from the forest not to be in danger, he dismounted and stripped off his clothing, carefully turning all the items backward and inside out just as the tree spirit had instructed him to do many years before. Then he placed his military-issued boots in his knapsack and pulled out the boots lined with gray winter wolf fur the leshi had made for him so many years before.

After lacing them up, he walked a few steps, taking his time and practicing as the tree spirit had taught him. He was delighted to find he could still move as silently as he'd been taught. Nik had been careful not to use the skill or the illusion cast by the tunic and the boots in the camp with the soldiers unless he absolutely needed it. The Royal Guard were a suspicious lot, and they were quick to burn anyone practicing zagovory, or folk magic, not bothering to differentiate if it was black or white magic before resigning the poor wretches to an awful death.

It was that, as well as Nik's growing experience with distrusting those around him, that led him to hide his magical gifts as well as the means of escape in several places over the next few years. He made it a point to sleep with his back to the wall and in the closest spot to the door, and he never attempted to stand out in the crowd, just as the wood spirit had taught him. That particular counsel had saved his life on many an occasion. Nikolai made it a point to only achieve enough to accomplish his purpose and then quietly fade into the background, just as the leshi had taught him to do long ago.

Over the years, Nik caught wind of a few hermits and lone wanderers who supposedly held knowledge of the magical arts. He always managed to get himself assigned to the groups sent out to investigate. Most were charlatans, but a few were legitimate. When the opportunity presented itself, he'd steal their books of magic or spells, which were very probably nicked from other traveling sorcerers anyway, and practice. Most items ended up being fake or tricks, but he always learned something and held out hope he'd discover more magical relics someday.

Since he was small for his age and looked younger than he was, he shaved a few years off the calendar, which made it all too easy for others to trust him, including his beloved tsarevna. But Nik knew simple parlor tricks and lies wouldn't work this time. What he was about to attempt would require all his skill, all the artifice he could conjure, if he was going to be successful.

As he stood there on the same road he'd once escaped on, heading back to the very forest he vowed he'd never enter again, he wondered for a moment if this was the best way. He wanted to prove himself to Veru. Show he was worth not only keeping around, not only as a friend, but that he would do anything, absolutely anything, to be considered good enough for her. The problem was, deep in Nik's gut, there was a sinking feeling that there was nothing he could do that would ever make him good enough. Not for any woman. And certainly not for a tsarevna.

He worked his jaw, gritting his teeth as he considered giving up instead. Just accepting there was no hope. No redemption.

Nik had been running away from something for a long time. When he'd been with Veru in her room, it felt for the first time like he was a protector and not the victim. Like he'd been running to her all along. If he ran from her now, leaving her alone with her problems, then what did that mean? That he'd been a coward all along? That he'd deserved everything that had happened to him?

No. He refused to accept that. Nik would help his tsarevna, and in saving her, he'd also be securing his own future, his own rightful place. He had to return. There would be no more running. Not this time.

Veru was the most likely of the twins to win an alliance with a powerful leader. She'd be married, and soon, if he recognized what was ailing the tsarina. If Nik had any chance at all of attaining his dream, convincing an empire that a tsarina's consort could be a commoner instead of royalty, then it meant he had to save the tsarina. And there was only one way, as far as he knew, to do that.

Nik let out a shaky breath, not relishing what was to come. Then he centered himself, gritted his teeth, and a silent, steely resolve strengthened him. He stood still for one long moment, then another. He barely breathed. The skin on his knuckles became numb in the cold. Then he felt nothing as the magic came to life. The air hushed. He heard the scurry of a small animal digging in the snow, the call of a bird high overhead, and the wind moaning through the damp trees.

Silently, he took one step, then another. He stood next to a bush. Then in a copse of trees. The animal kept digging. It even popped out its head and looked around before ducking back down to dig again. His own horse couldn't see him. She grazed and glanced up once in a while but nickered and then went back to wandering off the road. The magic of the tunic and the boots still worked well.

After checking his bag for kalach bread and salt, he stood in front of the horse and turned his back to her. She sensed something but couldn't see him and danced away. It took several tries, but finally she butted his back lightly with her head, then she startled and took off at a brisk trot, neighing and shaking her head as if disturbed.

"Neechevo, little one," Nik said, hoisting his bag on his shoulder. "That's all right. You head to town. If I survive, I'll find you later. If I don't, it won't matter much." As he began walking down the road toward the town, Nik mumbled, "Too bad there isn't a goat around here."

The kick from the goat had hurt his shin, but he couldn't deny he'd had great luck in that he'd escaped from the dark forest with his life that first time. He wasn't convinced he'd be as fortunate this time around. What he and his tsarevna needed was a miracle. Nikolai didn't know for certain whether the force found in the trees bordered on the miraculous or the preternatural, but his intention was to harness that power to his advantage.

As he drew closer to the town, he began noticing that Pyrs was much worse than when he'd left it five years before. In fact, the town looked as if it had been abruptly abandoned. It had never been a large town, but the fat cottages that once had rosy glows in the windows and smoke coming from stone chimneys now appeared gaunt, with hollowed-out innards and creaking open-mouthed doors that barely hung on their hinges.

Hungry, golden-eyed animals now half-wild and half-domestic slunk and hid in dark shadows and crevices searching for something weak to ease the growling in their bellies. Overturned carts with ripped-open bags, boxes, and crates half filled with weeds and snow showed how long it had been since anyone had cared for anything in the now emptied streets.

Curious, Nik made his way cautiously to his old babushka's home. He stood outside it for the better part of an hour, listening . . . waiting . . . watching for some sign that she still lived. But he heard nothing, except for the sound of the wind and the rustle of leaves.

Finally, he called out her name softly. Barely a sound.

"Babushka?" he said, a whisper that carried.

There was no reply.

"Escovina?" he tried.

Something snapped near the home, and he peered in that direction, but could see nothing. He was quiet for an hour. Unmoving. His time in the forest before had taught him how to be still. Another hour passed, and even then Nik didn't stir. Finally, his patience paid off.

"She's gone," a familiar voice said.

The old tree spirit stepped away from the large fir near the old house and made himself visible. "I can see you've grown, lad. Kept up with the lessons I've taught you. Too bad you didn't honor your promise."

"I tried. He's too powerful."

"He's grown even more so, I'm afraid."

"Has he?"

The two stared at each other for several long moments, saying nothing.

"Why are you here?" the leshi asked. "You don't mourn her."

"No," Nik admitted. "I need to enter the forest again."

"Why?"

"I need his help."

There was a hiss. "Help? He helps no one. Are you addled in the brain or simply possessed of an unctuous fervor?"

"Perhaps it is a bit of both. I must save my love."

"There is no saving in what he does." The tree spirit shifted his great head, considering him. "I'm surprised to hear you have found a love . . . that dear."

Not bothering to remark on the last comment, Nik said, "I know he doesn't use his power to assist others. To be clear, it is the mother of the one I love who must be saved. I care not about the means."

There was a long moment of silence.

Nik was about to take his leave when the leshi said, "You mean to take him from this forest, then?"

"I do."

"Then I will help you."

"I'm not here to ask that."

"Yes. You are. You would have asked her."

"Yes. Passage through the swamp would have made it easier."

"You don't need her for that. Come. Pay your respects. Then I'll take you as far as I can."

The tree spirit took him behind the cottage, showing Nik where he'd buried his kikimora wife. He'd fashioned for her a beautiful coffin made of polished mahogany. A large tree had sprung up nearby and overshadowed it with its leaves. Despite the fact it was nearing winter, the tree was in full summer leaf, though the green leaves were quivering in the fall winds.

Nik knelt on the cold ground and said a prayer for his old babushka, thanking her for the gift of his tunic, surprised when he found he meant the words sincerely. Then he turned to the tree spirit and showed him the bag with the bread and salt.

"It's not enough," the leshi said, after his own moment of silent contemplation. "Come with me, boy," he added, stirring much too slowly for Nik's liking.

They entered the barn and Nik found, to his delight, the same nanny goat he used to milk. "You're still alive, then, old girl?"

"She is. Stand behind her and give her teat a hard tug. You need a kick."

"Right." He winced, and said, "Sorry, girl," more due to anticipating his own pain than feeling empathy for the old goat.

Baaa!

"Ow! Right in the knee! That'll leave a weal."

"Let's hope it does. You'll need it. Have you eaten?"

"Not much."

"Good. You'll blend better with nothing in the belly. It'll keep your eyes sharp and your mind natty."

As they moved from one group of trees to another, the tall creature warned, "Once you enter the edge of the forest, you'll be tempted by viands of every type you can imagine. You'll see pools of kefir, sbiten, kvass, or vzvar in cavities of rocks, borscht and ukha swelling up in tree stumps, stuffed blintzes and pierogi mushrooming in flower clusters or out of tree bark or hanging from leaves, and cream-covered smetannik adorning trees like snow. Do not be tempted by this. Don't even touch this food. Itis a wurdulac trick. This is how they find you. Tell me you understand this."

Nik nodded gravely just as his stomach growled at the mere mention of such delicacies.

The leshi ignored it.

"Why didn't I notice those things before?" Nik asked.

"Because they weren't there before. It's as I said—he's grown more powerful in the time you've been away. More desperate too. He wishes to draw others to him. It's safer for him that way." Before Nik could even begin to process that, the leshi moved forward, saying, "Let's get on with it, then."

Silently, they walked together to the edge of the forest, and they stood there until the leshi gave a twist of his long limb, signaling that it was finally safe to move into the tree line.

When Nik entered the hushed shadows of the trees, he'd expected the sinister prickly sensation of crawling things seeking refuge beneath the layers of his clothing, their tickling feet tracking a course along the bones of his spine and making the fine hairs on his body stand stiff, while his own slick sweat added to the swamp sweet perfume that rose up to bewitch his nostrils. What he hadn't anticipated was the eerie quiet, the unnatural stillness of death that masqueraded as life.

Even the trees and underbrush felt wrong. When he placed his hand on the old, stiff trunk of a beech tree, Nik noticed that instead of the wide canopy with heavy, low branches and a silvery-gray color to the wood, the tree appeared spindly and thin, its trunk ghostly white. When he pulled his hand away, sticky syrup pooled in the cracks and dribbled down the bulging sides like fat tears, and dusty chalk clung to his hands as if he'd not touched a tree at all, but an artist's rendering.

When he glanced up at the leshi, he saw similar tears leaking down the cracks in the tree spirit's face and disappearing into his long, moss-green beard. They moved on, and Nik spotted a well-worn trail with a sign. It read . . .

бесплатная водка
предстоящий

. . . or

Free Vodka
Ahead

Nik stopped and pointed out the sign to Larix, who shook his head sadly, ignored the trail, and continued through the trees, cutting his own path yet moving soundlessly. Nik followed, moving not as quickly or as quietly as the leshi, but he was still proud of the fact that he was much faster and more skilled than the first time he'd been in the forest. This was made clear to him when he earned not just one but several surprised looks from the tree spirit as they walked through the trees without so much as cracking a dried branch underfoot or stirring a leaf.

They made good time, not stopping until dusk, which was about the time Nik began noticing the strange temptations Larix had warned him about. Clusters of cheese blintzes winked at him from green stalks, tiny round cakes surrounded by glistening fruit petals, the inside of the edible flowers full of candied glaze bounced on leafy vines, and he even passed a hollowed rock with steaming soup bubbling inside, fat sausages rolling to the top, making his mouth water.

He resisted the temptation, though the smell alone nearly did him in. Once he even caught himself reaching for a blintze that burst open just over his head. It was shaped like a large flower and mounded in the middle with fluffy farmer's cheese. Around the warm, doughy, fragrant petals, he spied thick berry sauce that pooled until it dripped down the tree branch. Nik knew that if he stood just beneath the blossom and opened his mouth, he'd catch some. He could almost taste it. Closing his eyes, Nik steeled his resolve and was about to push the branch out of reach when the leshi smacked his arm hard enough that he lost his balance and fell.

"I told you not to even touch it," the leshi snapped at the cross young man.

"You didn't need to hit me," Nik replied, scowling as he climbed to his feet. "A verbal reminder is sufficient."

"We are in their territory," Larix said. "Resent my censure if you will. My only aim is to preserve your life."

After climbing to his feet, Nik took a long look at the tree spirit, who seemed to have shrunk in size and appeared even more wrinkled than usual. "What's wrong?" he asked.

The creature hesitated momentarily but then let out a deep sigh of resignation and admitted, "The same blight that kills the forest affects me as well. The monster who lives here uses his power to drain the life from the trees and the animals to give false life to dead things. The longer I stay, the more likely I will die—that is, unless you are successful in evicting him or convincing him to follow you."

"I see." Nik placed a hand on the bark of a nearby tree, and it sloughed off, collapsing into a pile of dusty pink powder at the base. "We'd better hurry, then."

"Yes. We should."

They pressed forward until they finally arrived at the swamp of the kikimory. Uncertain, Larix hung back at the edge, his still-large feet sinking into the mud, the murky waters enfolding them like lover's hands beckoning him into a dark, eternal embrace.

"What is it?" Nik asked, standing higher on solid ground, searching for monstrous spider creatures lurking beneath the exposed roots and moss-covered branches.

"I was larger before. I planned to carry you across my shoulders and wade through, but I'm shrinking quickly. The bog is vast. I do not think we can span the distance safely while my legs are still long enough to do such a thing. A raft might be possible, but in my weakened condition . . ."

His words dropped off, and different possibilities of how Nik could perish lapped thickly in his mind just like the heavy water rolled over Larix's wooden ankles. Whatever they decided, time was running out, and the longer they hesitated, the worse off they'd be. A decision needed to be made, and quickly.

"Carry me for now and construct a raft when that no longer works. We won't worry about the kikimory," Nik said. "If we run into them, it's likely they're being drained just as you are."

"Very well. Come."

Larix offered Nik one of his very long arms, and Nik climbed up and up until he settled on the tree spirit's shoulders. Branches grew around his body to give him a place to rest, and then the creature set out across the bog, his legs and feet sinking deep into the water, stirring bugs and iridescent green globules to the surface.

For the span of a few hours, they met little resistance other than frogs, snakes, and tree roots. Snakes moved quickly out of the way, unless they were large. Bigger ones hissed angrily and occasionally attacked, but their bites did nothing to Larix, and they just assumed he was a large floating tree, so they moved on. Only once did a large snake cause trouble, wrapping itself around the tree spirit and impeding their progress.

It was angry and hungry, and it sensed Nik up in the "tree's" branches even with the magic of the tunic and his boots. Nik had to climb down Larix's arm and hang by his legs, upside down, then use his soldier's sword to cut off the head of the large reptile. After that, it still took the better part of an hour to untwist the heavy, muscled body from its death grip on the tree spirit's body. Fortunately, Larix shrunk during that time, making the job easier; unfortunately, he found he could no longer support the weight of himself and his passenger as well. It was time to build a raft.

Larix channeled more of his power into shaping branches into a raft complete with a long pushing pole. By the time he was done, he'd shrunk even more. He was now just the size of a large human man and no longer had the ability to expand his form. Together the tree spirit and Nik climbed aboard the newly constructed raft and continued their journey. They'd traversed nearly three-quarters of the swamp. Only a bit more to go. They hadn't encountered a single kikimora yet, either, and wondered if perhaps they were all dead.

In fact, they were just congratulating each other on the success of their journey when they spotted a ripple in the water. They quieted, watching as it diverted toward them, accelerating at a steady pace. Then an arced shape broke the water, and suddenly a huge arachnid body burst upward and landed on the surface, stretching out its eight hairy legs so each one made a puckered dimple atop the dark bog, allowing it to float.

It considered them for a moment, blinking its many eyes. Then it opened its black mouth, and Nik could see the sharp, glistening fangs. "Have you come seeking your exculpation for the death of my sister, Larix? Do you think this gift of blood, organs, and adipose is enough to shrink my fangs? I promise you—it is not. When she left our swamp hidden in your beard, you swore she would be safe. Now I will not rest until your beard is trampled beneath my eight legs and lies at the bottom of my swamp, where I will use it as a nest."

Nik was surprised that the monstrous tree spirit beside him began to cry.

"I didn't know," he proclaimed bitterly to the angry kikimora.

"Your ignorance is no excuse. Come and let me kill you. Then I can die in peace at last after having built our final resting place. A nest in which to lay all my dead children. And all the eggs that will never hatch. I will use your bones to build a memorial to all the kikimory who have died, and then I will lay down next to it and pass from this world to a greater."

With that, she pressed her legs into the water and rose up, then did it again and again, coming toward them faster and faster, running atop the water on eight spider legs at a gallop that was at once monstrous and beautiful. Nik didn't know if he should describe it as flying, natation, or silk spinning, but whatever it was, however she moved, it was a type of magic all its own.

Before he could prepare himself for her attack—not that there was any way he could have prepared—the kikimora was on them, and she wrapped all her spidery limbs around Larix and upset the raft, dragging the tree spirit beneath the dark water. Nik went overboard as well but quickly scrambled back on top and managed to grab hold of the push pole. He waited for a moment, but he couldn't hear any struggle between the two large beings. Figuring Larix had given in to fate, and knowing there wasn't much he could do to help other than wishing the tree spirit luck with his sister-in-law, Nik pushed ahead.

As luck would have it, he met with no other opposition and finally found the end of the swamp a few hours later. He'd just located a cavity formed by some large rocks and was ready to sink into a deep, much-needed sleep when something hit him hard on the back of the head. The last thought he had as he slumped to the ground was that he must have been more tired than he'd thought.

Later, when he opened his eyes, he tried to swallow, but his mouth was too dry to let him do much more than just press his tacky lips together. The light was far too bright to see anything clearly, and his head hurt badly. There was a sticky, metallic taste in his mouth, and he couldn't move his hands or his head for some reason. That's when he heard the laugh. The one he recognized. The light moved, and he blinked. If he was an optimist, he'd say that the good news was that he'd ended up where he'd meant to be. He just didn't have the upper hand. At least not yet. Nik tried to say something, and it came out a jumbled mess.

"What? What was that?" the man said. "Speak up. Get him some water."

A cup of water was lifted to his mouth. Nik swished it around and spat. Then he took one deep swallow and another. "Thank you. I . . . I've come to make you an offer," he said.

"An offer?" The man laughed. "What would a soldier have that I couldn't just take for myself?" he asked.

Nik became alert enough to recognize that his hands were tied behind his back. Wincing, he shifted to his knees and then awkwardly stood. "The offer doesn't come from me but from the royal tsarevna."

“The tsarevna?” the man asked, sitting forward, the interest clear on his face.

“Yes. She offers a position in the government and a title of honorary boyar in exchange for saving her mother . . . *from death.*”

At those words, the Death Draughtsman smiled and summoned his underlings, saying, “Make preparations. It seems we’re going on a journey.”

Chapter 6

Don't Enter Another Monk's Monastery and Start Changing the Rules

Grigor was born the eighth child of nine to wheat farmers. Of all his siblings, he was the only one to survive to adulthood. It had been a long time since he'd seen the lands of his native country, the Great Khanate State or the Golden Khanate, not that he felt any particular allegiance or patriotic feelings for his homeland.

His family had never set foot in the city of the Golden Spires or worshipped at any of the temples there. Never once to his knowledge had any of his ancestors pilgrimaged to sit at the feet of the Learned Ones to hear a reading or sipped tea and traded spices at any of the famed teahouses or markets.

No. Grigor's parents and theirs before them and so on and so forth had always been simple folk who lived off the land. They had no ambition. No care for politics. No mind for diplomacy. Little need for coin. What they needed, they grew or raised. They were a hardened people living a hard life. Grigor was forged from the lessons he learned there.

As he worked alongside his siblings, scraping a living from the soil, sleeping in close quarters in their yurt, and watching as illness and the specter of death took them one by one, Grigor realized how quickly the candle of life could be snuffed out. When he saw exhausted acceptance on the faces of his parents as they dealt with the loss of each child, he became angry and bitter. As the years passed, those feelings of resentment turned to hatred.

For a time, it seemed to him that he was doomed to the life in which he'd been born. Then, finally, providence smiled upon him in the form of a traveling stranger.

Reflecting on the experience now, Grigor supposed he was grateful to the traveler who tempted him with a wink and wish in exchange for a day's rations. When he passed the man his flagon of water and his wrapped lunch, asking for a stallion worthy of a prince for his wish, he didn't expect the immediate snort and wicker coming from behind him.

When he spun at the feel of hot breath blowing on his neck and saw the most beautiful black Arabian stallion, one looking just like the dream horse he'd always imagined, he didn't even know what to say. The horse shook its head and pawed a hoof at the ground as if impatient to be ridden. Grigor reached up to stroke its silken mane. "He's . . . he's mine? Are you sure?" he asked the stranger excitedly.

"Yes. All yours," the man replied with a contented smile as he sucked sauce from his thumb, enjoying the boy's lunch. He raised the sack, his mouth still full. "Thanks for the trade."

Grigor had always been a quick child. He'd caught the man clutching the chain at his neck on more than one occasion. So very quickly, he offered, "Wouldn't you like to have supper with us too? Perhaps you could stay over tonight? It's a very long walk to town. It's such a fine horse. I'd like to offer a bit more in exchange. It doesn't seem like much of a fair trade."

The man stood for a moment, considering the horse and the food, which was now gone. "Very well. I suppose a good meal couldn't hurt." He smiled amiably at Grigor. "Lead on, then, lad. Let's get that new stallion of yours in a barn and then introduce me to the wonderful woman who makes these little cakes. They're delicious."

Grigor worried that his parents weren't going to cooperate at first, but they remained as indifferent over the stranger as they were with most things in their lives. His mother reacted to the news of the horse and the stranger as she did to news of another baby—with a mixture of ambivalence, anxiety, fear, and vulnerability but ultimately with acceptance. She placed the same plateful of food before him that she did in front of Grigor and her husband and then ate her own food and headed to the curtained-off area where she and her husband slept.

As for Grigor's father, the stranger quickly discovered the farmer to be a man of few words, who was largely uninterested in both him, his gift of a beautiful horse, and his only remaining son. It was young Grigor who continued plying the stranger with questions and with tea long into the night. And when the stranger finally slept deeply, thanks to the draught of pain powder Grigor mixed into his tea, the young boy peeled back the man's collar and found the sliver of gold attached to the chain on his neck.

It didn't take Grigor long to pocket that slip of gold, place a few day's rations in a bag along with a skein of water, and climb onto the back of his new stallion. Without even thinking of the parents or the stranger he left behind, he pressed his knees into the sides of the black stallion, who trotted off through the waves of undulating wheat, the full stalks shushing softly against one another in the moonlight, and finally allowed himself to imagine an entirely different future than the one fate had given him.

When he arrived at the dirt road, he urged the horse to a gallop, holding on to the mane tightly and clutching the horse's flanks with his legs until they grew sore and tired. When the horse slowed to a walk, he let the animal have his head and was happy when the horse came to a stop by a small, bubbling creek. Grigor slid off the stallion's back then, stooping down to stretch and to cup his hands in the cool water for a drink himself.

Only then as he sat down by a fallen log to rest, dawn just a flicker on the horizon, did he attempt to copy the man's actions by rubbing his fingers over the gold. As he did, he repeated in his mind a new wish for himself. This time he wanted to be a man of power, a man of influence, very different from his farmer father.

Before he could finish his wish, the creek, the Arabian stallion grazing near his feet, and the dark land surrounding him disappeared. Grigor found himself in a place utterly unlike his wheat farm and the nearby dusty road. In fact, the place he found himself was unlike anything he'd ever experienced before.

Grigor didn't know how long he stayed in that other place, but while he was there he encountered magic and fantastical beings unlike anything he'd ever seen before. He learned very quickly that when he overcame demons or monsters or watched them long enough, he could, in most cases, learn how to steal or harness their gifts.

Only one eluded him. Outwitted him at every turn. It stalked him at night with claw and fang, but try as he might, he couldn't find a way to trap or kill it, and somehow Grigor knew that the powers he collected from his nightmare visitor would be the most lethal of all.

When he'd finished destroying everything he'd discovered in the other place, it responded by collapsing entirely, and thrust him out. He came to himself realizing he was still near the same creek of long ago, though it now was substantially larger, as was the road.

Grigor immediately set off for home to search for the stranger, desperate to discover more about the charm, find out if there were more pieces, more lands to plunder for hidden powers and magics. But when he arrived at what was once his family farm, he didn't see his new horse, his farmstead, or even his homeland. Instead, Grigor discovered that he'd been gone more than ten years.

Though Grigor had indeed gained much in the way of new magics and dark powers from stealing the slip of gold, he realized it had come at a cost. First, he'd lost a great deal of time—the rest of his childhood, in fact. Not that Grigor felt any remorse over that or even the loss of his family. He didn't harbor any sentimental feelings in that regard. Nor did he mourn the demise of his country, though he wouldn't have minded visiting the large cities before they had been changed too much by the empire.

What he did regret was the demise of the stranger. When he returned to the farm, or what had once been the old wheat farm, he found four graves that hadn't been there before. Two belonged to his parents. His mother's marker indicated she died in childbirth five years after he'd left. One to another sibling that was stillborn two years after he left. His father passed just a few months after his mother.

The other marker simply said "Unknown," and the date indicated the same approximate time of his disappearance.

If that was the grave of the stranger, then he surmised it was possible that in taking the charm, he'd himself relegated the stranger to death. He wondered if the charm somehow kept the stranger alive, and made a mental note to always, always keep it on his person. Without the stranger, how was he to discover more about the charm, its origins, and find out if there were more of them?

Acquiring magics and powers had left him . . . hungry. He wanted more. Grigor craved it like a starving beast slavering after flesh. He slept in the ruins of the old farmstead that first evening, and when the moon rose and the wind whistled through the cracks between the posts, he heard a familiar rumble.

His eyes flew open, and he dashed to a window and looked outside. There was a flash of a tail that disappeared into the brush and a glint of moonlight on sharp teeth. A growl rattled the pebbles on the old window frame, and his heart jostled in time with them.

How did it follow him from the other place, he wondered. Grigor had no weapons. He knew magic wouldn't kill the creature. It was a demon of shadows and nightmares. It hunted him just as surely as Grigor hunted everything else. He knew that if he was to become the truly powerful being he wanted to be, he'd first need to learn how to slay the monster that hunted him at night. To do that, he'd need to collect more magic, more power, more charms. He sat up watching all night and fell into a fitful sleep in the early morning hours.

The next day he made it his mission to learn everything he could about the stranger's charm on his own. Instinct told him that gaining the stranger's power was only a small piece of a very big puzzle, and that there was much, much more in store for Grigor. The idea that he could uncover, overcome, and absorb and become even greater than he was buzzed life through his blood. So his hunt began.

The first step was to explore the limitations of the "wishing" power.

He quickly learned it could not be used for himself. It could only be granted in trade and to those of a good heart who gave of their own free will. The charm seemed to have a mind of its own and almost led him to those who needed a wish. Try as he might, he could not manipulate or fabricate wishes for himself. However, that did not mean he could not "lead" the wishes of the pure in heart or manipulate the trade in some way.

He became particularly gifted with language over the years, and once he found a person to whom the charm wanted to grant a wish, it was fairly simple for him to take his time and study the person and the people surrounding them. He'd make a big show about how he was looking for a worthy specimen. Someone to whom Shangti, or Allah, or Zeus, Ra, or Baal, or Vishnu wanted to show a miracle or give a blessing. Others would come forward; many would seek him out then, showering him with gold, precious gems, even sneaking daughters or beautiful handmaidens into his tent just to gain his favor.

Grigor would always accept these gifts graciously. Some he would even share with the townspeople. Subtly, though, he'd send word that what the god they worshipped was really seeking was a set of old hidden artifacts—worthless charms that were just tokens passed down in certain families that were signs of their god's favor. Any family in possession of such would surely gain any blessing they sought.

As he traveled from town to town performing his "miracles," his fame grew. His followers considered him a holy man, and why not? Wasn't he a saint? Wasn't he helping others? Wasn't he performing miracles?

Years passed, and he traveled from one city to another and then from one country to another. He saw the Kievian Empire expand and grow until it was so large it touched both great seas. It didn't matter much to him. Politics and armies were nothing to Grigor. They came and went like waves on the sand. Then, almost as if his own wish came true, a tiny woman brought him a genuine charm, a second piece. Many had tried to fool him before with false pieces, but he could feel it when she came near. It hummed through his blood. The piece was genuine.

To his surprise and delight, the old woman had no idea what she possessed. To her, it was a mere heirloom passed down from her ancestors. She was willing to give it up in exchange for a miracle. Grigor was more than happy to oblige, willing to part with whatever wealth or gems he had accumulated in exchange for the powerful object she'd granted him.

Unfortunately, the woman didn't desire wealth or gems. What she wanted was to regain her youth, and what was doubly unlucky for her was the fact that his particular charm didn't seem inclined to grant her a boon. Still, that didn't stop Grigor from assuring her that he'd do his best, nor did it hinder him from proclaiming as much to his devotees.

All it took was finding a street urchin, a girl orphaned and unattached to anyone in particular, one young enough not to be particularly fond of a name. With great fanfare before the crowds, he took the star-struck woman into his spacious tent and made her comfortable on his very own silk pillows, then graciously took the charm and slipped it into a secret pocket sewn into his elaborate floor-length coat.

Then he read several verses from mysterious, undecipherable scrolls recovered from distant caves written by dead prophets no one had ever heard of before. Quoting from the strange ciphers, he promised the devoted and the pious blessings and treasures more numerous than the stars. When she was utterly transfixed, he smiled most graciously, proclaimed her ready, and plied her with spiced wine laced with enough sleeping draughts to knock out an elephant.

When her heart stopped, he summoned one trusted servant, who wrapped her dead body in fabric, placed her in a crate, and nailed it shut. Then he produced the orphaned child and called in other servants to cart out the box containing the body, telling them to bury it outside the city, far enough away that no one would find it.

Grigor knew none of them would talk. Even if they suspected, they wouldn't dare. They all hoped to be granted a wish themselves, and they had seen enough to believe in his powers. Grigor was also very careful to keep up the act, reassuring all that the woman's old form had been reinvigorated. The young child was presented to the world outside as the new version of the old woman. She was quickly accepted by the family, and the whole town celebrated the miracle, even throwing a feast for Grigor.

Grigor smiled his oily smile and went through the motions of feasting, waving a dismissive at all the new requests for favors and invitations for dining and so forth, passing off such things to his minions. He had more important concerns on his mind. That evening, he retired early and, careful to make certain he was completely alone, pulled the new golden charm from his secret pocket.

He turned it over and over between his fingertips, comparing it to the one he'd had for so many years. Both pieces warmed under the pads of his thumbs. He could just make out writing on each piece. *Was it possible?* he thought.

Carefully, he touched the two pieces together. They fit with a snap, and a burst of energy shot out through the tent and slammed into his body, knocking him back onto his silken pillows. He was aware of falling and his head hitting the silk, and then, just like before, he was in a different place altogether. A new place. A place that offered a test. He went through the trials again, showing the new piece that he could face any challenge, defeat any enemy. Again he defeated all, seizing each new ability except one. His enemy with fang and claw had gained more power, but so had he. Still, the monster eluded him. He knew that to win he must defeat the beast once and for all. Again he was released back to the mortal world, victorious, even more powerful than before. He became obsessed with finding more pieces, collecting more power, and defeating his enemy.

Since the time of his youth, he'd discovered four of the seven pieces. It had taken him the better part of four centuries, according to his time, but the weeks, hours, and days spent lost in the tests prepared by the amulet—for that is what he now knew it to be—were nothing to Grigor's body. The trials he passed were helping him prepare for what was coming.

Now Grigor understood that it was his destiny to walk as a true god among mortals, not a charlatan who impressed those who were beneath him. Already he had conquered each of the terrible tasks assigned to him, slaying each monster hidden in the amulet, getting it to release its power to him, and in return he had been granted beautiful gifts. But try as he might, he could not seem to find the last three pieces of the amulet, or defeat the ever-growing brute that haunted him in the night.

Grigor knew his best hope would be to continue traveling the world, offering miracles in return for "gifts," pretending to seek "religious relics" as he did so. Unfortunately, those in power were always suspicious of those who attracted a following. It had always been so, no matter what century one lived in.

To stave off those who would do him harm, he sought refuge in monasteries, thinking to impress the growing new church with favors, followers, his abilities, and godlike powers, but instead of finding in Grigor the spark of divine, or recommending him to the archimandrite inspectors, the church officials, bishops, and rectors found his actions were altogether "too eccentric," "self-serving," and "of a supernatural nature rather than spiritual."

Though Grigor insisted he was a starets, a holy man, they questioned his background, his parentage, his education, and above all, would consider him no such thing. Then, when he thought to prove his worth and used his newfound ability—thanks to the fourth piece of the amulet—to raise the recently deceased Bishop Alexandrovna, proclaiming he had been given the power to resurrect, they cried, "Heresy!" "Blasphemy!" and "Put him to death!"

So he took the now malleable raised-from-the-dead Bishop Alexandrovna with him and left. It wasn't like they had the power to stop him. Still . . . he tried the same thing again at another monastery and another. It was the same at each one. He even tried a mosque or two outside the Kievian Empire but received the same fearful reaction.

Grigor realized he just wasn't going to be appreciated in his time. So instead, he decided to simply bide his time and wait. He wondered if he'd been going about things all wrong. Perhaps instead of seeking the adoration and devotion of religious fanatics, he might gain more from fear. He decided then to seek out a small town and experiment by building up his own undead army instead and use them to look for the other pieces of the amulet.

He started with his own minions, killing them first and then bringing them back. It was easier than he'd thought it would be and doing so carried with it the added benefit of saving the cost of feeding or housing the living. After them, it was easy enough to recruit others. The only negative side effect was that the undead army didn't move about in the sun, thus their taking up residence in a deep, dark forest.

Now he had adopted the same hours practiced by his army. It was simply easier to remain awake when they were. And instead of being honored, he was now feared, which he didn't really mind. The townspeople had called him and his followers wurdulac, upyr, or the undead.

While he supposed that technically "undead" was a fitting description, he wasn't fond of the other two terms. One of them implied that he drank the blood of the living, which simply wasn't the case. The other meant he'd been excommunicated from the church, which was also wrong. Technically, he'd never been a baptized member of the church.

What that meant as far as him being sinful or having a soul, he didn't know, but he did know you couldn't be cast out of a place you'd never been invited into, so excommunication was impossible. Truthfully, he didn't know what he was now. *Am I immortal?* Maybe. *Do I still have an appetite?* Yes. *Can I be hurt?* Yes. Though he did heal rather quickly. It was one of the side effects of the amulet. He also noticed that those he raised didn't experience pain. They did not, however, heal. Perhaps it was because they were no longer alive.

He'd experimented on a few of them before, cutting off arms or hands and fingers and the like. It didn't seem to bother them in any way. They didn't bleed either. Or eat. But cutting off their heads did them in permanently. There was no bringing them back again after that. Once the brain was detached from the body, they were gone.

Grigor's ability even worked on animals. He'd brought back birds, reptiles, horses, even pigs and cows. As long as there was enough of a brain left to work with, they came back. He'd rather enjoyed experimenting with each of his new powers as he'd acquired them.

Now it was time for a new experiment, and this boy had brought an intriguing proposal. He'd been in the forest building an army long enough. It was time to flex his muscles, as it were, and shake the tree to see what fell out. It had been too long since he'd heard word of any new pieces of the amulet. Perhaps it was time to rule from a larger throne.

As he instructed his undead minions to prepare to move out, to march out of the forest toward the Kievian capital city, he kicked his horse, spurring it on, and thought about that black Arabian stallion for the first time in many centuries. He *had* loved that horse. If he had a chance to bring it back, he wondered if he would. He'd certainly love to ride that beauty right up to the palace gates. But he also knew it wouldn't be the same.

And what would his parents think if they could see him now? Being personally invited to the palace of the empire itself? Would they be proud? Probably not. It didn't matter. Grigor could feel it in his blood, just like he did when he found the other pieces. It was time. Something was coming. His destiny. The throne itself was waiting for him.

Those days on the farm were far behind him now. His country, his people, and even his old language were gone—absorbed by the ever-expanding Kievian Empire. That wheat field, if any part of it remained, was now farmed by someone else. His family had long since vanished into the dust where they had once dug out a meager living. Even their graves were likely gone.

Grigor whistled, and his undead army advanced, following the human soldier. He wondered: If he had the ability to draw his parents, his siblings, from the dust, would he? *Would I feel some sense of justification, or liberation to have them serve me as I served them?* he thought. The answer came to Grigor swiftly. *No.* He decided that even if he could raise them, making them undead, he wouldn't. In the case of his blood family, he was surprised to note that like that beautiful stallion, he was content to let them enjoy their hard-earned respite.

Chapter 7

Lie Down to Sleep: The Morning Is Wiser Than the Evening

To say Nikolai was uncomfortable leading this entourage of the undead was an understatement. Nik glanced back at the man briefly and caught him staring at him, transfixed. He shuddered involuntarily and reined in his horse. "Dawn is coming," he said. "It's time to break."

"Very well," the man replied. The Death Draughtsman pulled up, stopping his horse, then closed his eyes, silently communicating with his army who were traveling not on the road but through the woods on either side of them. Try as he might, Nik could see no more than a shadow or hear anything louder than rustling in the underbrush, which might as easily be mistaken for an animal. Any passerby would never know there was an undead horde lurking within striking distance.

"There," their leader said, distracting Nik from his thoughts. "They will find shelter from the sun and meet us at dusk. Shall we proceed to make camp, then?"

Nik nodded, tearing his eyes from the gloomy trees. "There's a small creek, not too far from here. We can water the horses there. I can hunt. Fish, too, perhaps."

"No need," the strange man said. "My army will leave game by the river."

Tilting his head quizzically, Nik asked with barely disguised revulsion, "Do they . . . eat animals?"

"Not at all," the Death Draughtsman answered with a wide, white grin. "The animals simply run from them." He leaned forward in the saddle. "They sense death coming, you see." He kicked the sides of his horse, causing it to skirt ahead of Nik. "Animals are usually smarter than people."

"Right." Nik nudged his own horse, following the frightening man, and had a difficult time sleeping after they made camp, not only because he was trying to sleep in broad daylight but because he couldn't trust the man across the fire. When he did nod off, he had nightmares about being chased by the undead. He ran but was eventually caught by them and then . . . consumed. His dreams shifted then to their leader and of how the man had used his power on him in the forest.

He was back in the gloomy forest, a prisoner. Standing there in front of the Death Draughtsman, his arms held fixed by animated corpses, their stench filling his nostrils, Nik prepared for death, either that or to join the legions of the undead surrounding him. He mourned the loss of his beautiful tsarevna and wondered if the leshi had survived the swamp.

Then, when he wasn't immediately killed or transformed, he opened his mouth to speak but found he couldn't. Instead, the Death Draughtsman used a great power, one he could neither see nor hear, one that didn't seem to depend upon any spell or magic of any kind, and yet Nik knew it was embodied in the man. He was at once terrified, fascinated, and bitterly envious.

With a simple penetrating gaze, the man slipped into Nikolai's mind as easily as he would slip into another man's pair of boots. Nik's vision darkened, and then everything went white. He could feel the cold fingers of the man probing his mind, pulling his secrets out and examining them one by one, discarding the images he cared nothing for and then squeezing the one he sought until it popped into life.

The forceful man chuckled when Nik sobbed in pain, and he heard him say, "Don't struggle. It hurts more when you do."

Suddenly, the raw ache swelled and burst like a blister, oozing throbbing memories that lapped through him like boiling acid. He was back in the forest again but for the first time, years before. It wasn't as diseased then as it was now. There weren't as many undead to avoid. In fact, the man who found him wasn't undead, not yet. Not that one could tell. Nik wouldn't have recognized the man at all if he hadn't spoken to him first.

Nik had been caught in a trap. Not one of the food traps. They didn't exist back then. This trap was a simple rope snare meant to catch game. It was a well-made one, too, seizing him by the ankle and hoisting him ten feet off the ground. He hung in midair for the better part of three hours before someone came along, and by then he had lost all feeling in his lower extremities.

"Well, well, well. What have we here?" two men said as they walked noisily through the leaves down the trail. "Looks like we caught ourselves something good to take to the boss."

"Shut up," the bigger, uglier one replied.

He wore a large hat over his head. His voice was gruff and broken, and he was missing part of his arm, but there was something familiar about him. Prickles stood out on Nik's neck and arms. *It couldn't be.*

"Here. You watch him while I let him down."

The big one pulled a wicked blade from his belt, and Nik braced himself for a hard fall, wondering if he could time it well enough to knock the big fellow to the ground without gutting himself, yet knock the knife from his opponent's hand so he could saw off the rope before the other man returned. It wasn't likely.

He felt the rope give, then he dropped several inches. Deciding to take a risk, he swung. The timing was good. He fell just at the right time and landed right on top of the larger man. The knife came up, but only nicked him on the shoulder and then got stuck in the tunic made by the kikimora.

While the big man scrambled, Nik quickly reached up and grabbed the knife and threw it at the other man coming around the tree. It was a lucky strike, sinking into the man's throat. He died with hot blood gurgling from the wound and dribbling from his mouth. Swiftly, Nik slipped his foot from the thick boot and yanked the rope from it while the man went to inspect his friend's wound and retrieve his knife.

By the time he turned back to his prisoner, Nik was gone, made invisible by his magic tunic and the boots made for him by the tree spirit. But what Nik didn't know was that his attacker was mostly blind and had developed a good ear and strong instincts.

"I hear you, boy," he said. "There's no hiding from me. You might as well come out and save me the trouble of searching for you and yourself the pain of further punishment. Trust me—you won't like what'll happen to you when I find you if you make me look."

If Nik hadn't already been frozen in place, those words would have made his blood freeze in his veins. He might not have recognized the man before, so disfigured he was now, but those words left no mistaking him. The man standing before him was Nik's very own father.

How had he survived? Nik wondered. *It should have been impossible.* As the man swished the knife back and forth through the air, trying to find his escaped quarry, Nikolai took a good, long look at the man who he'd left for dead in the inferno that had once been his home, with his lifeless mother and sleeping siblings.

Obviously, survival hadn't been easy. He wondered if the man had tried to save anyone other than himself. It was unlikely. Nik snorted, a sound that didn't escape the man.

He stalked closer. Nik didn't care. Let him come. He wanted to see the damage he'd done up close. It wasn't fair. It wasn't right. That this man had lived while his mother and siblings died. He looked closely at what had been raw, burned skin now healed over and scarred. The dead eye and teeth bared on one side of his face where lips should have been. Nik studied the stump of an arm, wondering if it had been too damaged to save, and thought, *Good. I hope he suffered and suffers still with the loss of it.* Feeling a smirk lift the corner of his mouth, Nik wondered if perhaps providence had given him a second chance to make things right. *To make him feel pain once more.*

Waiting until the man turned away, he kicked him hard in the backs of his knees, laughing when he crashed down, dropping the knife. Nik scooped it up and leaned over, ripped off the man's hat, revealing a hole where his father's ear should have been. "Hello, Dad," he said, before putting the knife to his throat.

The man swallowed, choked, then said, "Nikolai? Is it you?" Then he began laughing. "I've been looking for you, you sniveling little . . ." Then he sputtered and said nothing else.

"What was that, otets?" Nik clucked his tongue. "It seems you won't be able to speak any longer," he said as blood gushed from his father's cut throat. Leaning down, he added. "Let's hope this is the last time I have to kill you," he said before sinking the knife deep in the man's kidneys once, twice, three times, and then pushing his father's now limp form over, letting it bleed out on the forest floor.

He took a long moment to stare at his father's ruined face, the dead eye staring up at the trees and the damaged ear gaping as if scavenger birds had already begun tearing him open. With a grunt of satisfaction, he wiped the bloody knife on the man's coat, slid it into his belt, and turned back, keeping a careful eye on where he stepped to avoid any other traps.

Unfortunately, that wasn't the last time Nikolai would meet his father. Days later, Nik had just reached the edge of the dark forest when the reanimated corpse of his father caught up with him. At least this time the man didn't speak. That was something of a positive change. But he was supernaturally strong, and despite Nik's repeated stabbing, and the gaping wound at his throat, he refused to die a third time.

Only a lucky strike with a nearby axe that took off his head finally stopped the advances of his undead father. After his father's third and, he hoped, final death, Nik set out for the Kievian Empire's capital, hoping to get away from monsters and madness and find a life of normalcy as a soldier. Still, magic had grabbed hold of him and refused to let go.

Now he was back in its clutches again.

Nik woke from his dream sweating and chilled at the same time, and bile rose to his throat. *Had the Death Draughtsman conjured the dream?* He shivered. It was almost as if he were back in the old barn of his childhood home, his father standing behind him, forcing him to swallow his own vomit and horse dung once again. Leaning forward, he spat into the smoking ashes of the dying fire and grabbed his water skein, swishing the liquid in his mouth before spitting again.

After wetting his palms and wiping the remains of the dream from his eyes and face, he looked across the fire and found the Death Draughtsman wide awake on his side, watching him.

"Is sleep evading you, droog?" Nik asked nervously.

"I do not need as much as the typical man," he answered, sitting up. "You do not need to waste time in flattery. I know you do not consider me a friend." He began rolling up his blankets and added softly, "No man should."

Nik nodded more to himself than to the powerful man across from him and rose, collecting his few belongings. "Can I ask, then—"

"Why do I go?"

"Yes. You are already very powerful."

"That is not the question you really want to ask. Be brave enough to say what you truly wish. Nothing you voice will shock me. I've already been in your mind."

Suppressing a shudder, Nik said, "Very well. The truth, then. I don't care what happens to the queen or even the tsarevna Stacia or to the empire itself. You can do whatever you like with them. All I want is Veru. They believe I'm bringing you back so you can heal their mother, the tsarina. I don't know if you can heal her truly or just reanimate her body, and I don't really want to know. You can make an army of the entire empire if you want. It makes no difference to me as long as Veru is mine."

Nik heard the snort first, then it was followed by another and another. They grew in depth and volume until dark, deliberate chuckles filled the twilight air with a sinister foreboding that made Nikolai twitch like an unschooled rube before a master. When the laughter died, the man skirted the embers of the fire, uncaring of the edges of his robe.

"You have given me the truth, and I will return it to you in kind. Understand this, young soldier," he said. "I care not for you or your tsarevna or even the tsarina or the army. There is only one power I seek, and it is found within a few simple relics that have been difficult for me to locate. Help me find them and you shall be rewarded beyond your wildest dreams. In fact, I will make certain you obtain"—he placed his long, knobby-knuckled finger on Nik's chest, punctuating each word—"*every . . . single . . . wish* your black little heart desires, even including the undying love of your tsarevna."

Nik's heart beat wildly, partly in fear and partly in hope that he could find what the man sought and thereby win the heart of the woman he loved. He swallowed and wet his dry lips. To have everything he desired. To be able to forget the vile and ugly things of his past and live surrounded by plenty, peace, and beauty. That was what he craved above all else. "What artifacts are you seeking?" he asked.

The man smiled. "I'm happy you asked. Come. Let me draw them for you."

As they neared the palace, Nik went over the story in his mind. He was to introduce the Death Draughtsman as a traveling monk, a wandering strannik, named Grigor Sobol Petrovsky. He was to help ensconce the man in the palace where he would use his various abilities to attempt to actually heal the tsarina. In return, the tsarevnas and their mother would show undying gratitude, ply him gifts and treasures, which he would graciously refuse.

Nik would then describe what the monk was truly seeking, relics lost by the church long ago. His only purpose now was to locate and return them. If they could use their vast resources and incredible reach to help him find such items, he would be eternally grateful. Veru and Stacia would be so pleased that their mother could still manage the empire, staving off the need for either of them to ascend to the throne, that both of them would immediately head out in search of the items, Veru with

Nik, of course, and the monk would use his ability to prompt Veru to fall in love with Nik, cementing his place in her life.

The plan would work; everything would be perfect. The undead army would stay at a distance, too far away to cause any harm. The soldiers wouldn't even notice them. Most of their patrols occurred during the daylight hours when they slept anyway. Nothing would go wrong. At least that's what Nik kept telling himself as he signaled the guards to let them pass the main gates.

At first everything did go according to plan. He was welcomed, just as he'd expected he'd be. Veru was happy to see him, but the concern etched on her face was more pronounced than usual. Even Stacia didn't bother to raise an eyebrow when he immediately sought out her sister, and neither of them blinked an eye when he introduced the "monk."

They didn't even care what name passed his lips or look in the man's direction. *Do they not sense the same danger I do when it comes to the man?*

The two of them were immediately ushered in to see the tsarina, which was also telling. Their mother must be in very grave condition if they were immediately led on through. It only took a moment after entering the royal chambers for his suspicions to be confirmed.

To Nik, it appeared as if they'd arrived too late. Their mother, the tsarina, looked dead already. Her body was small and completely still beneath the silken sheets; her tiny, white hands were crossed upon her chest, and though her dark hair was perfectly coiffed, and her pillow fluffed, she was as pale and lifeless as a plucked rose. Then he saw the merest flicker of movement where her breath stirred a ribbon tied at her neck.

Turning to the man beside him, Nik implored, "Is there anything you can do for her?"

The Death Draughtsman narrowed his eyes. "Let me pass."

He approached the bed and studied the form lying upon it as he might a painting or a statue. Without looking up, he spoke, addressing the various men of religion keeping vigil at the tsarina's side. "Leave the room. All of you."

The men started, jowls quivering, incense wafting around their voluminous robes as their soft chanting ceased and they looked at one another and then at the tsarevnas across the vast room. She nodded in consent. One by one they shuffled out through a side door, and it snicked shut.

"Can you help our mother?" Tsarevna Stacia asked.

"Quiet," he commanded.

Stacia obeyed—which surprised everyone, Stacia included.

Sweat broke out on the man's face as he concentrated. He held the tsarina's palm in his hand, pressing it between both of his and remained that way for some time; then he opened his eyes, gasping hard, and placed shaking hands on her temples. Remaining fixed in place, he began murmuring words none of them understood, and the room filled with clouds of color—pink, blue, purple, and gold, all roiling and undulating. Lightning snapped and sizzled and then dissipated.

Finally, the man sat back, away from the tsarina, resigned and with a somewhat stunned expression on his face. Turning to the tsarevna, he said, "She . . . she does not wish to be healed. And it would *appear* that . . . despite my considerable abilities, I cannot force the issue."

The sisters stepped forward, about to protest, when he held up a hand. "However, she has agreed to allow me to 'facilitate' a final conversation between you, assuming the two of you are agreeable."

"We agree," Veru said immediately while Stacia nodded stiffly.

"Very well," the Death Draughtman said. "Come, then. Take your places on either side of her, and each of you take one of her hands."

The twins sat down, and when they took their mother's hands in theirs, the strange man touched their mother's forehead again. When he did, they were suddenly thrown into a dream, and they heard their mother's voice.

"My darling girls!"

They spun around, and there was their lovely mother, dressed for a party, with her hair coiled up beautifully and pinned in place by a diamond tiara. Crying, both young women threw themselves into her outstretched arms.

"There, there. Now stop that, you two. Enough of tears. Not now. There isn't enough time."

"There would have been enough time if you'd let that man heal you," Stacia accused.

Mila frowned but cupped her daughter's cheek and patted it gently. "What that man offered wasn't healing, my sweet."

"If Nik trusts him, then I do," Veru insisted.

Clasping Veru's hands tightly, the tsarina said, "I know you miss your father. And I know you're upset with me for leaving you too. But don't be so afraid of being alone that you give your heart and your trust to just anyone. That goes for both of you," she said, kissing both girls on their cheeks.

She sighed. "I'd hoped the two of you would be able to work out your differences before it came to this, but if there's one thing I've learned as a leader and as a mother, it's that you don't always get to see the fruits of your labor. Still, you plant in the spring and look forward with faith in the summer that the rains will come and the sun will warm the ground and that there will be a harvest in the fall."

Mila placed her hands on her daughters' hearts, and the girls reached up to clasp her fingers. "The seeds of leadership have been planted. Let them take root. But be on guard. There are enemies all about you trying to sow corruption. Shore up your defenses. Promise me that above all else you'll listen to your good hearts and minds. They'll always lead you in the right direction."

"We promise, Mother," both girls echoed.

"And if you need to trust in someone, trust in one another. You've had your disagreements over the years, but the two of you can rely on each other. Help each other when you're in trouble."

Stacia and Veru eyed one another but nodded. "We will."

"And the last thing. Your father and I will always be with you. We'll watch over you. Do you remember the charm he always wore in battle, the one I wear now?"

"Yes," Veru said. "It was supposed to protect him."

"It did, in its own way. What I didn't tell you is that we have two of them. One is mine and one is his. I've carried both of them since his death. Now I'd like each of you to take one. It will ease my mind if the two of you promise me you will always wear them. Tell me you will do this. Do you agree?"

"Yes," Stacia said.

"I will," Veru answered.

"Good. They're hidden in the secret pocket of my skirt. Now . . . come here and give your old mother a tight hug. It will have to last me awhile."

They did, and as she squeezed them extra hard, whispering she wanted white gardenias planted where she'd be buried, making the girls sob anew, the dream vanished, and they opened their eyes to see their mother exhale her final breath.

CHAPTER 8

Every Blade Has Its Billet: Fate Cannot Be Sidestepped

The funeral of the beloved tsarina, Ludmila Marianka Sashenka Stepanov, was even grander than that of her late husband, buried only a few years prior. The entire empire mourned. Heads of state, diplomats, lords and their ladies, scholars, clergy, burghers, and even the impoverished, pressed their way to the capital to pay their final respects.

Those not invited to the ceremony left tokens of affection at the gates, palmed thoughtfully written notes with descriptions of kind words or acts the tsarina had done for their town or family into the hands of the Royal Guardsmen, or simply placed bunches of gathered fall wildflowers or left handmade gifts in baskets along the road nearby.

Stacia and Veru had the flowers, notes, and gifts gathered daily, sifted through them personally, and shared them with the staff. Those were the items that would have held the most meaning for their mother. Their mother's favorite flowers, specially grown year-round in her greenhouse, were brought into their mother's gardens, where they were placed on display along with the simple arrangements produced by their own servants and the commoners for the three days of viewing that took place before their mother was interred in the family crypt.

The nations loyal to the empire sent dignitaries along with more lavish gifts, each trying to show their devotion by the extravagance of the items or for the attention to detail given to the token. These were, of course, accepted as well with the grace and decorum expected for such an occasion. The twins were, after all, their parents' daughters. Though they still postponed all major decisions, they stiffened their shoulders, bearing the burdens of leadership together, just as their mother had wanted. They knew what was expected of them, even during a time of intense mourning.

Rival nations' responses varied. Some sent condolences while others quietly schemed, planning how they might use the tsarina's death to their own advantage. The twins knew this, but there was nothing to be done about it at present. They had learned, above all else, to deal with the matter at hand first, and save other matters for tomorrow. Compartmentalizing concerns had been a large part of their training, but they were still very, very young. And now the two of them were orphans in truth with the weight of a vast empire and all the peoples living in it resting on their very narrow shoulders.

One thing all the people both rich and poor, royal and peasant, loyal to the empire and those scheming against it, had in common, the emotion underlaying the sorrow or greed or empathy or plotting, was unease. Everyone sensed change was coming. Each person wondered what would happen next. *Would the tsarevnas rise up and rule seamlessly as their parents had before them? Would one or both of them marry advantageously, and would that man lead or let his wife rule? Would one of the twins choose a man from their own country, or would he hail from a rival kingdom? Would it be a political marriage? Were the twins even ready to take on such a challenge?*

There were so many questions. So much speculation. It was all anyone could consider. Hushed whispers abounded in every corner of every town and every hollow touched by the empire's reach.

It was only a matter of time until those whispers became shouts. Until voices demanded that they knew better. That their ideas were stronger. More viable.

But for now, the people knew the respectful and appropriate thing would be to at least wait until the tsarina was properly laid to rest before voicing their concerns. They would then let the twins make an announcement before making any hasty decisions. After all, the girls had the backing of the Royal Guard, did they not? Of course, there were those who favored Stacia while others preferred Veru, but most everyone agreed they'd feel much better about either one of the twins if they announced an engagement to a suitable match.

The people weren't the only ones with matchmaking on their minds. Grigor himself was considering the idea. He wasn't a particularly amorous fellow by nature, and he wasn't exactly enamored with all the work that came with leading an empire. However, both girls appeared to be adept at the job, which would leave him free to do what he wanted. He'd then have the resources he needed to continue his search.

Even if they denied his suit, so long as he ensconced himself as a counselor, a healer, or even as a religious zealot, thereby gaining the favor of either young lady, it might be possible to attain his aims. He'd have to rid himself of the lovestruck soldier boy first. That one would cause trouble.

He could use him as a minion, Grigor supposed, but he had plenty of those already. True, there was something . . . *different* about the boy. It wasn't his past abuse. No. He'd seen plenty of those cases over the years and had been inundated with enough sad little fellows in need of a mamenka. It wasn't that. Surely it wasn't that he *identified* with him.

Grigor *loathed* the very thought. The idea that he could have something in common with a young man who would risk his own life, the little power and freedom he possessed, for the mere possibility of obtaining the attentions of a beautiful woman sickened him. And yet . . . he couldn't deny there was a depth of character that went unseen by most, a ruthless quality hidden just beneath that flaccid surface.

It was that spark that made the boy interesting. Otherwise, he would have been dead already. Like everyone else, Grigor lurked, watching and waiting for just the right moment to present his own proposal to the royal twins. It would have to be timed to perfection.

Interestingly enough, it turned out that the lad was more useful alive than dead. After the tsarina's death, Grigor had been thanked, given a bag of coin, but then was summarily dismissed and shuffled quickly out of the palace. When he had requested a week's lodging, he'd been reluctantly shown to the boy's own bunk, where he slept as a medic's apprentice in the soldier barracks.

Grigor was only aware of the goings-on in the palace thanks to his connection to the boy's mind. It seemed the young man had indeed caught the favor of the tsarevna, at least in the way of camaraderie. After the tsarina's death, he was relocated to rooms nearby his beloved, though, as far as Grigor could discern, the relationship was still completely platonic.

As Grigor watched their connection cement during the time of mourning, he knew this was his chance. After waiting the appropriate number of days for the funeral rites to be accomplished and for the visiting dignitaries to leave, he caught a mental glimpse of the young man heading to the royal stables. He quickly set off to intercept him.

"Hello," said the Death Draughtsman from the shadowed corner of the stable.

Startled, Nik dropped the bristle brush. He'd been preparing Veru's favorite horse for a ride. It had been Nik's hope that he and his tsarevna riding together through the countryside might lift her spirits. Truthfully, he'd also hoped he'd seen the last of the frightening man who had just made a sudden appearance in the barn. Apparently, he wasn't so lucky.

"You're still here, then?" Nik asked, stooping to pick up the brush. "I thought you'd given up."

"Not at all." The man smiled, and Nik shivered at the sight of those white teeth in the shadows. "I wonder," he said, coming closer, "if the two of us might help one another."

"Oh?" Nik said, brushing the horse a little too hard. It danced away from him, neighing in protest. "How's that?"

"You know, you and I are much the same."

"Is that right?"

"Yes. We are wolves, living among men. To hide, we fool them. They think we are tame, like loyal dogs who play fetch. But we are wild at heart, aren't we? You have this same quality. I have seen it in your mind."

"What's your point?" Nik asked.

"My point, boy . . ." the Death Draughtsman said, placing his hands on the door of the stall, his long fingers wrapping around the wood.

Nik swallowed, noticing that the man's fingernails were jagged, broken, and too long. They were crusted beneath with dirt, like he'd been sleeping beneath the ground with his undead army and had recently exhumed himself from the soil.

". . . is that, though sometimes solitary, wolves are also known to run in packs, to take down larger prey. I propose that we do the same. Perhaps you've heard the saying that goes, 'A wolf doesn't claw its own kind'?"

"Yes," Nik answered slowly. "And . . . what is it we're hunting, exactly?"

Grigor smiled; reached into the inside pocket of his floor-length, voluminous robe; and pulled out the largest, gaudiest, ornate emerald ring he had ever seen. As Nik gaped, Grigor answered, "My dear boy, we are hunting brides."

It was that very evening after having sent word to Veru that he'd canceled plans for their morning ride, claiming he'd fallen suddenly ill, that they arranged to meet with the sisters. To say Nik was nervous was an understatement of the worst kind. He actually felt physically ill. He was in it now. Either Veru was going to go along with this farce and marry him, or she was going to banish him from her side forever. It was the worst kind of risk he could possibly take, and yet he felt he had to do it. He was sick of doing nothing. That much was true. It was time to move forward, one way or another.

"Sit back, boy. Relax. Everything is going to go according to plan. Remember: it's the best thing for the empire. Everyone gets what they want. The empire will be stable with two tsarinas engaged to be married to very worthy, eligible, and wealthy suitors. They will have plenty of time to decide which of them wants to rule, as neither of us desires such. And should Stacia wish to marry another at some point, we can arrange a dissolution with some sort of contract. As for you and Veru, the two of you can arrange your union as you wish. Trust me. It will work."

"How can I relax when all I care about in the world is at stake?"

"You know what I can do. Even should they not want to listen to reason, they will not be able to resist the powers I possess. It's for their own good and the good of the empire. When it comes to that, how can you doubt me?"

"I knew what you could do for their mother, and yet I saw you falter."

"I told you; I did not falter. There was no hesitation or lack of skill on my part. The woman simply refused to live. Most beings reach for some semblance of life. She wouldn't. It was a first for me." He waved a hand in dismissal. Nik noticed that even though he'd cleaned up, slicked oil through his long, wiry hair, changed his heavy robes for more lavish clothing, and wore expensive jewels, he still looked . . . *old*. There was nothing modern about his selections. The jewels were garish and unattractive, his beard unkempt, his eyes wild, and there was still dirt beneath his too-long and cracked, broken fingernails. He brushed something from his fur-lined robe. "It was for the best anyway. Now we are in a better place to take what we want. No?"

"I guess," Nik said, looking away from the man, trying to hide the disgust.

"What is with the guessing? Tonight you will be accepted. Tonight you will celebrate your engagement to your lyubit, the beauty of the empire. Enjoy this moment."

"They aren't duraki or simple nesting dolls you can shuffle around. It's very likely they'll see through all this." Sweat broke out on Nik's temple as he plucked at his vest. He yanked on the tight collar circling his neck. *Why did the wealthy wear so many clothes?* He longed to remove the tight jacket. "Where did you get these clothes anyway?" he asked, shifting in the bouncing carriage.

"Do you really want to know?" the man asked, his eyes gleaming in the darkness.

Nik could only imagine. He could almost smell the vague stench of the undead on the clothing despite the heavy splash of cologne the Death Draughtsman patted on Nik's person when he climbed into the fancy vehicle. It was too much. He couldn't even stand to be around himself. How could he expect a tsarevna to like it?

"No," he admitted. "I don't want to know." Nor did he want to know how he and his newfound "father" had ended up being the exiled royals of a small island kingdom, along with the paperwork and enough wealth in the form of rubles, gold, and gems to prove it, *and* the sworn testimonies on paper from dozens of neighboring countries, dignitaries, and clergy.

That the papers were forgeries was certain since they'd only hatched the plan that morning, but the rolled and sealed forms were cleverly done, created by an expert. It was the wealth that boggled Nik's mind. With all the treasure he had at his disposal, why in the world was a man that powerful searching for simple charms? It made no sense. Then to seek the hand in marriage of the tsarevna? Did he want to be the tsar? Was that his aim all along?

Truthfully, Nik was the one who felt like a durak. He was missing something. Biting his lip, he thought that he didn't even care if Veru agreed to the marriage or not. If he could simply steal her away, even for a moment, then perhaps he could explain how he'd brought a viper into their home. Maybe she'd forgive him. Maybe she'd kill him. He probably deserved it.

But then what if she said yes? Then what would he do? Continue to play the man's game? Pretend he was something he wasn't? Watch as the man likely killed Stacia or, at the very least, controlled her like a puppet? Nik didn't particularly like Stacia, but he didn't hate her. He thought she'd make a very good tsarina, in fact. The empire needed *someone* to rule, after all. And Stacia was a good sort of person for that.

The thing was, if he could take the man at his word, the plan didn't actually sound all that bad. Giving the twins more time wasn't a *bad* thing. The empire *did* need stability. But anyone who promised to give you everything you ever wanted at no cost to you was lying. Making a deal with the devil always ended with regret.

Then there was no more thinking. They'd arrived. Whatever power the Death Draughtsman used to control those around him still worked on the soldiers, because they mindlessly opened the gate for their carriage, not even asking who they were. Then, when they pulled up at the front door of the palace, other servants, their eyes glazed over, opened the carriage and guided them up the steps and into the lavish front hall, taking them all the way into the receiving room, a place reserved for only the top dignitaries. Nik had never set foot in that room before.

Inside the opulent room with floors polished to a sheen that sparkled so brightly it was almost mirrorlike, the two of them were left, the heavy doors closing with a thump behind them. Above, sparkling chandeliers were lit with dozens of candles, their light reflecting from crystals dangling from the delicate gold-filigreed candleholders that were mimicked by other ornate candlelit sconces placed around the room at intervals, bathing the entire room in warm light.

At one end of the room was a raised dais with two gilded thrones and several padded benches flanking them on either side. Nik assumed these were reserved for Royal Counselors or other ranking officials. At the moment the thrones were empty. It appeared they were in a ballroom of some type. He was studying his image in the large mirrors that cast an "infinity" reflection since they were set on opposing sides of the room and frowning at his clothing, attempting to adjust the ill-fitting jacket and vest, when his "father" elbowed him.

The heavy red curtains behind the matching thrones shifted as if moved by the wind and then parted as the twins, dressed in courtly apparel, entered the room and were seated, accompanied by four Royal Guardsman wearing highly polished court armor, their swords at the ready. They took up positions on either side of the twins, and Nik, looking into the hard faces of the soldiers, knew instantly that these were not trainees but experienced men of war who had been recalled. He didn't recognize a single one of them, which was probably both a good and a bad thing. It meant they didn't automatically know him either.

He could see the shock register on the twins' faces when they realized the two men standing before them were not, in fact, a king and a prince from a distant land but the monk who'd tried and failed to heal their mother, and Nik, the soldier they'd trained with for years, dressed up in new clothing.

Stacia spoke first. "What is the meaning of this?"

"Is this some sort of joke, Nik?" Veru asked. "Because I don't find it funny."

Almost in perfect synchrony, the soldiers stepped off the dais, their armor clinking in harmony, and they drew their swords.

Stacia held up a hand. "Captain Kostya, hold. Don't throw them out just yet. I want to hear what they have to say for themselves."

Thankfully for Nik, the Death Draughtsman stepped forward to speak first. As for him, he was speechless. He knew Veru, and she was livid. He'd betrayed her, and he wouldn't be forgiven—he could read it on her face. There would be no accepting of his proposal today. The blood in his veins turned to ice. Frantically, he searched his mind for a way out, a way to save himself from the terrible mistake he'd made. If he was very, very lucky, she wouldn't have him sent to the northernmost border to freeze to death.

"I understand your confusion," the Death Draughtsman began. "My son has lived with you for many years in disguise, and this must seem like a terrible deception on his part. But I ask you please to bear him no malice. We were in hiding, you see. Something, as royals, I'm sure you can understand, even though you are still young girls in your tender years."

Nik would have groaned and slapped his face if he could. Did he not hear how he was talking down to the tsarevnas? Just because they were female, and young, did not mean they were ignorant or needed a man to explain the way of things. The best thing for Nik to do would be to prostrate himself before them. He was about to do just that when he noticed how the four soldiers had lowered their swords and stood erect, staring into nothing, their eyes glazed over.

He started sweating again, wondering if the man was going to hurt the twins. Quickly he turned his attention to them, trying to warn them with a glance, but they weren't paying him any mind. Were they also falling victim to the same spell? Nik inhaled, smelling magic at work. What could he do? His magic was nothing compared to this man's. *Would he kill them while they sat there on their thrones?* Perhaps he would just mesmerize them like he was doing with the soldiers.

Nik wondered how long such a thing worked. Was it permanent? Maybe it only lasted as long as he was in the same room. He narrowed his eyes then, no longer sweating but curious, trying to figure out how the man was using his power. Trying to discern its limitations. Would he use his magic to force them to obey? To marry them? Nik was sick at the very thought. He wanted Veru, yes. But not that way.

As he watched the sisters, half-listening to the dialogue of the Death Draughtsman as he went on fabricating his falsehoods about their past and heard their questions coupled with his answers, he studied them for any signs of falling under his thrall and found none. The soldiers, on the other hand, not only appeared to be completely senseless but entirely unaware of their surroundings. What's more, his new "father" didn't seem to be paying the soldiers any further attention whatsoever, instead focusing all his efforts on the twins.

The more the man talked, the more frustrated he appeared to become. Nik tuned back in to their conversation and heard Veru say, "So you're proposing we marry the two of you? And the benefit to us would be *what*, exactly?"

Stacia snorted. "Why are you even asking? There *is* no benefit to us. We don't need your money, such as it is. You think we are donkeys to lead us out onto the ice? Nyet."

"Perhaps the young lady is forgetting my considerable powers and the favors granted that allowed a final farewell to occur between her and her mama? Also, keep in mind an alliance with us will be favorable in other ways. Remember: neither of us possess a desire to rule. We are both in agreement that the two of you are as perspicacious as you are lovely and are therefore much more apt to leadership. Should you choose us for mates, we are prepared to sign over all rights and responsibilities to the empire as well as all decision-making to the two of you."

Stacia sat back in her chair and crossed a long leg. Apparently, that statement had caught her attention. But Nik could see the naked doubt on her face. He didn't blame her. After removing an invisible speck from her skirt, she said, "Is that so?"

"Absolutely," the man mumbled distractedly.

Magic swirled in the room so thickly that Nik could almost taste it. The soldiers swayed in danger of falling over. Nik took a step toward the man and saw his eyes had gone black and beads of sweat dotted his brow.

"Are . . . are you quite well?" Nik asked him.

The man turned to Nik, tearing his eyes from the sisters. "I don't understand," he said. "There's something about this family. They resist my powers."

Nik nodded and took a few steps back, watching the man closely as he clutched at a token hanging about his neck and sputtering, continued. "In . . . in addition, should the coffers ever need filling to fund various wars, pay wages, feed the hungry or the winter-stricken, or whatever pet project the two of you decide to take under your wing"—Nik saw both the twins tense up at his words again—"you need never worry over funding. I will set no limit to the bounds of your cupidity. As your husbands, it will be within our power to grant you any amount of coin for any purchases you choose to make. The fact is, you need husbands to stabilize the empire, and we are offering you an option you might be able to live with. All we ask is that you consider us."

Veru leaned forward then and simpered, blinking her long lashes. She sighed dreamily. "Could I wear a golden train? I've always wanted to have a golden train on my wedding dress."

Nik knew they were in serious trouble if she was putting on a show.

"Absolutely, my dear. Anything you like. All I ask in return . . ." He glanced over at Nik, who had been continuously edging away from the man little by little. "All *we* ask in return," he continued, "is that you help us attempt to locate these three charms."

He held up a copy of the drawing he'd made for Nik. It was very detailed. Nik still had his own copy that he kept with his magical items in his hidden stash in the woods.

"Charms?" Stacia asked, her interest revived. "May we see your drawing?"

"Of course," the man replied with a winning smile.

He approached the thrones, and that's when the sisters finally noticed that their Royal Guard were frozen in place. But soldiers themselves, they simply gave one another a slight nod. Inside the thrones were hidden compartments. They pressed a button to ring a secret bell for other Guardsmen, and, at the same time, knives dropped from beneath the arms of the chairs and were quickly hidden behind their voluminous skirts or slipped into their boots.

Stacia took the paper from the man, who bowed and stepped back down from the dais, staring hopefully into the faces of the tsarevnas for any sign of recognition. Gazing long and hard at each charm, Stacia took in each one, nodded to the man, and then passed it along to Veru, who added comments such as, "Aren't they so pretty?" and "Are they made of gold or silver?"

Though the twins were very good actresses and adept at hiding information from those they did not wish to share it with, the knowledge of the charms wasn't something they could keep secret, at least not for long. Nik knew both of them far too well. It would only be a matter of time before he found out what they were hiding. The question then would be: Where did his loyalty lie?

Attempting to dismiss the man, Stacia said, "You have given us much to think about. May we keep a copy of this, consult with one another, and give you our answer within the week? You may, of course, remain here if you wish. Arrangements can be made for the two of you to stay in our guesthouse."

The Death Draughtsman smiled, bowed, and replied, "That would be very acceptable. Isn't that right, son?" He walked up to Nik and clapped him on the shoulder. The twins rose and turned, parting the curtain to leave. It was Veru who touched the charm hidden on a chain under the neckline of her dress. When she did, the shadow man felt the magic of the amulet like a wave.

The smile slowly died on his face, and his hand tightened on Nik's shoulder until the younger man cried out. Whipping around, the Death Draughtsman laughed, and the sound was terrible indeed. Nik could almost see darkness gathering around the man as he whipped off the heavy fur-lined cloak. "You!" he said, in a seething voice, half mad, half gleeful. "You thought you could hide it from me!"

"Veru!" Nik pled, ripping a knife from his own vest. "Run!"

He plunged the dagger into the man's chest. Blood spurt out from the wound, sliding across the knife and onto Nik's hands. The man screamed in rage and pulled out the knife, tossing it to the floor before using his power to throw Nik across the room. The younger man thumped into the wall, hitting his head hard. The twins ran back into the room along with several new soldiers. Swords drawn, the soldiers engaged the Death Draughtsman but fell under his stupor one by one.

Only Stacia and Veru were left to battle. They fought hard, but their would-be suitor used his power to hide in a fog, only reappearing to grab hold of one sister and then the other. The twins, instinctively, turned back-to-back, protecting one another. They spun slowly, circling, and waiting for an attack that didn't come. Sweat broke out on Stacia's forehead, and she cursed the skirts that constantly threatened to trip her. Veru nervously passed her deadly sharp knife between one hand and the other, her eyes equally as sharp, waiting for the moment to strike, but it never came.

When the chanting of the monk-turned-suitor began, they froze. The voice seemed to come from everywhere and nowhere. Light suddenly filled the room, and a beam of it shot out from the fog, then it split in two, hitting the twins right in the chest. They screamed, and each one clutched the pendant they wore around their necks. Then they dropped to the polished floor on their hands and knees, their carefully coiffed hair tumbling around their faces.

Pain filled both Stacia and Veru as the blood pounded in their veins.

Nik, groaning and stumbling as he tried to stand, dashed the blood dripping from a cut over his eyes and gasped in horror as the two young women he knew, one he loved more than anything, the twins who were to rule an empire, changed into something monstrous and terrifying, something nightmarish made of teeth and claw.

The beasts rose and attacked. Then came the smell of blood and fur and magic mixed with his own vomit. The hot stench of his own death and fear hit his face, the warmth exploding over his skin until it was all he could smell and taste. Bile rose again, and then he knew no more.

CHAPTER 9

Luck Rarely Appears without Misfortune's Help

"Snap out of it, you fool!" Water was thrown on his face, and Nik struggled to rise from the nightmare, knowing the moment he opened his eyes, he'd be facing a worse one. A rough hand shook his shoulder. "Come on, durak! Hurry. The tsarevnas need you."

"Wh . . . what?" That did it. For a moment he'd been back in the barn with his old horse, him covered in his own vomit, his father waiting for him to wake up for another beating. Now he remembered: he was in the capital, and he'd made a terrible mistake. "Where's Veru?"

"She's here. She needs your help." The hussar trying to wake him shook his head in disgust, yanked off his own cloak, and tossed it to Nik. "Here. Clean your own sick off yourself and get up." When Nik didn't immediately move, the older man took hold of his arm and yanked him to his feet. "We need to get them out of here before he comes back. They managed to chase the sorcerer off for the moment, but he's powerful, and the others have sighted his army."

"His army? His undead army?" Nik paused in his wiping. "They're coming? We've got to hide. They'll kill everyone!"

"I know, boy. What were you thinking leading a wurdulac to our tsarevnas? He could have destroyed them. He still might."

"What do we do? He's too powerful. There's no way to stop him."

"We must preserve the tsarevnas at all costs. Despite what you've done, they seem to trust you. The question is, can I?"

Nik nodded furiously. "I'll do anything to protect them. I swear it. I'll even fight the beasts if I have to."

The older man gave Nik a strange look, then shook his head. "Very well. Do you know any hidden ways out of the palace and into the woods?"

"Yes. Give me your sword. I'll lead them out. I can protect them."

The man grunted. "I think they're fairly capable of protecting themselves. They'll just need a little help with the doors."

Nik grimaced. "Right. They're fighters. Better than myself. We'll head to the stables, get horses."

"No. You'll go on foot."

"On foot? Why? Riding is faster."

That's when Nik heard the clicking of claws behind him. His heart leapt in his chest. Patting his vest and reaching at his hip for a sword that wasn't there, he cried out and spun, hands out. He couldn't help the scream that leaked from his mouth when he saw them, the two huge beasts from his nightmare. They were real. And almost more frightening than the undead, with huge fangs protruding from their jaws and powerful striped bodies. They paced back and forth, watching him carefully.

One sat and began licking its paw but kept a close eye on him like a large cat teasing a mouse. He darted behind the older man and trembled, placing his hands on the man's shoulders, saying in a whisper, "If we back up very slowly, we can find the twins and escape. Maybe we can seal these two . . . whatever they are, in the room so they can't follow, and then let them deal with the undead army when they arrive, yes?"

"I don't think so," the older soldier replied, shrugging off Nik's hands and turning his back to the beasts.

Gaping at his nonchalance, Nik slid one foot and then a second one slowly behind him, thinking that at least the soldier would be likely to lose his life first. It didn't make sense. His demeanor was as calm as if he were simply having a meeting. Nikolai thought him crazed.

"I'm afraid you don't understand," the older soldier said, gesturing to the large animals behind him. "These two beasts, as you call them, *are* the tsarevnas. They are not, in fact, monsters, or nightmares, but in this form, they are the bol'shoy kot, or *tigers*. Have you never heard of them?"

Nik swallowed. "They . . . they are much bigger than wolves."

"Yes. Of course they are."

"And you're sure the tsarevnas are in there somewhere?"

"I am. I watched them change myself. I've heard stories of such a thing happening from my mother's people. That's where you need to take them. My mother's clan can help."

"Your mother's people? But I don't understand. If they're in there, can't they change back?"

"Perhaps, but perhaps not. I would think if they could, they would have already. My mother's people, the Evenki, will know what to do. They live on the other side of the great mountains. The tsarina established several laws protecting them, and free trade has been the policy for some years now. My father was stationed at one of the highland outposts as a young man. That's where he met my mother. Her people are reindeer herders. They migrate in the hinterland, so you'll have to find them, but if you head to one of the outposts at the borders of the taiga lands, they'll direct you to the nearest settlement. Tell them you need to speak directly with a shaman. Hunt before you arrive and offer them meat or pelts in exchange for their help."

"But I don't understand. How did this happen? Was it the monk's black magic?"

"No. It couldn't be. This is very powerful magic, but it isn't black. It's a different sort. Do you understand? Tell me you understand."

Nik looked at the beasts seated near him and at the hussar speaking earnestly about the magic of his people. If there was anyone who understood magic, it was Nik. "Yes," he said. "I understand. It's special to your people."

"Good." The older man looked relieved. "Once you arrive, you can talk with them openly about the tsarevnas and the tigers. They'll believe you and the tigers will be protected once they're on Evenki lands. But don't mention anything about what happened to others in the empire.

They'll kill the tsarevnas on sight and likely string you up for heresy or lock you away. According to the law, farmers are still allowed to trap and kill wolves, bears, lynx, and tigers whether they're threatening herds or not, so long as they use the skins or meat. Now, do you understand my instructions?"

Nik nodded, still wary but less nervous, having watched the large creatures and seeing that not only had they not attacked but that some of their mannerisms were indeed similar to the twin tsarevnas he'd come to know. "I do," he said.

"Good. Then take my knife and sword. I'll grab others from the armory. There isn't much time. Out with you now." He crouched down to the large cats and patted each of them cautiously on the shoulder. "Goodbye and good luck to both of you. May the souls of your good parents watch over us all. I promise we'll do our best to guard your empire until your return."

With that, he slipped out the door and was gone.

A bit awkwardly, Nik murmured, "Well then, now that it's just the three of us, I wanted to take a moment to apologize for the display from before. Obviously, that man is *not* my father. And I—"

The larger red tiger with black stripes growled softly, cutting off Nik's words.

"Right. Let's be off, then, shall we? Apologies can wait for a better time." He leapt up to the dais, circled the thrones, and found a dropped knife. Quickly he pocketed it and discovered the hidden panel that allowed them to exit through the back of the room. Checking for passersby and finding none, he gestured to the cats, who padded quietly behind him, stopping to sniff the air. They clearly wanted to head to the left, but he hissed that they should follow him to the right instead, and reluctantly, they did.

That way led to the kitchen. There was the sound of items breaking outside, coupled with screams and shouting. Pots were left boiling over with no one watching, and bread was burning in a hot oven. Nik quickly grabbed a sack and stuffed it full of anything he could find—bags of preserved apples, a half-burned loaf of bread, some goat cheese, and strips of dried meat—and then he took two bladders from a hook and dipped each into a large barrel of water, filling it to the brim and capping it off, slinging both over his shoulder, before checking the door that led outside.

Servants and soldiers ran in every direction. There would be no easy means of escape from that exit. He turned back and went down one hall and another until he came up to a wall and felt along the top until he heard a click. A pocket opened, and he pushed, revealing a black opening that descended down a staircase into darkness. He was about to turn to the tigers and beckon them forward when the large red one pushed past him. He figured that one was Stacia.

As for him, he was nearly blind in the dark passageway and had to hold his hands out to feel along the sides as he walked down step by careful step, but the large cats bounced quickly down and were soon so far ahead of him he could no longer hear them. He cried out softly, "Stacia? Veru? Wait for me." Soon he bumped into a soft tiger body. "Er . . . sorry," he said awkwardly. "Can you just move over a bit? I need to find the latch."

When he did and the door opened, he had to push hard against the wind to get it open. He hadn't used that particular passage in too long a time, and outside of the palace too much debris had built up against the door. Once outside, they were protected by bushes since the opening led to the garden.

"Stay here for just a moment," he said in a whisper. "Let me make sure the way out is clear." Within a few minutes, he was back and gave them a signal. They followed him to the garden gate and only paused a moment at their mother's grave, sniffing at the dying gardenias they'd left outside her crypt, remembering their promise to plant living blooms when the season was right, before trotting quickly out and into the woods after Nik.

Both tigers lifted their heads, turning to look at the palace when the fire started. They growled softly and almost whined. Nik glanced back and reached out a hand as if to touch them in consolation like he would have with a horse or a dog, but then quickly pulled his hand back. *What am I doing?* They were royalty. Not dogs for him to pet as he willed.

Pressing on, he only wavered for a moment before revealing his hiding place. They watched in curiosity as he dug beneath the trunk of an old tree and pulled out a large wooden chest. From inside it, he gathered a bag of rubles, several changes of clothing, including his magical tunic and boots, and book of spells, a flint and fire striker, and some other items they might need on a long trip, including snowshoes.

He placed all the items in a sturdy waxed leather rucksack to keep everything as dry as possible. Then he took a change of clothes and headed into the woods, using a nearby icy stream to wash as much of the sick off himself as was possible. After slipping into his own clothes, he tossed the others aside, knowing he'd never again don the clothing the undead had acquired for him, and headed back to the twins.

Hoisting the bag and centering it across his shoulders, he took a long drink of water and told them they could drink at the nearby stream if they wished before starting out. They glanced at each other and headed toward the water. He followed and wondered if they could communicate with each other or not and if they still thought like humans or if they were ruled by tiger instincts. Then he supposed he already knew the answer to that question. They wouldn't be following him if they didn't have their minds intact. How must it feel to be trapped inside those cat bodies? *Powerful* was the first word that came to mind.

Ready, they left the sounds of battle and the screams of the dying and the undead behind them, heading in an easterly direction, hoping that once the tsarevnas and the charms were gone, the monk would have no reason to stay and terrorize the palace or the Guardsmen. They knew the territory well enough to realize that traveling on foot to the great mountains would take more than a month. Winter would be upon them before they arrived, which may not affect the tsarevnas in their current form, but Nik wasn't prepared for a brutal winter outdoors. Still, he thought it best not to think of that at present and only consider their escape.

He'd donned his special boots and tunic so he could walk without leaving tracks. Not that it would matter too much. It was certain the tsarevnas in their current form would be leaving obvious pugmarks for the undead to follow, but after a certain distance, he found the two large cats lifting their noses and turning toward the creek again. It was moving much faster than it was near the palace.

Leaping into the water, they strode along in the icy-cold rushing stream, leaping over fallen trees and around rocks and other barriers, always careful to stay in the water to cover their tracks. For an entire day, they marched upstream, staying in the water and catching their own dinner, a large wriggling fish for each of them. With their kill hanging from their jaws, they crouched low and launched their huge bodies up onto tree limbs that trembled with their weight but held, and there they ate, swallowing big chunks of their food until it was gone, then proceeded to bathe themselves with rasping tongues on fur as the sun sunk in the west.

Nik built himself a small fire near the large tree, ate a bit of his own hastily collected food for dinner, refilled his water bladders from the stream, and slept with his back to the tree. Once, when he woke at the sound of a branch cracking, he stared up into the dark canopy and saw a striped tail twitching in the shadows. The eyes glowed eerily in the night, and he shuddered. That night he dreamed the soul of the girl he'd loved had been replaced by a demon, and it was stalking him, a punishment for his many sins.

The next day Nik decided to try to communicate with the tsarevnas. First, he studied the tigers, much as he did when the twins fought one another in the practice field near the soldier barracks. The larger, red cat was bold, brash, quick to snarl a warning at the other for getting too close, and its vivid green eyes were a match to the redheaded twin.

By comparison, the other creature was smaller, sleeker, golden, but he could see clearly just how dangerous it was. In fact, it frightened him more than the larger cat for some reason. It seemed more unpredictable. Almost as if you could be petting it one moment, enjoying hearing it purr, and then it would just as happily run a sharp claw down your center, flaying you alive, and it would still be purring while it ate you. Nikolai had no doubt such a predator wouldn't hesitate to hunt and kill for sport.

That such a monster could be his sweet Veru shocked him. What was even more surprising for him was that he often found himself keeping the red tiger between them as if he didn't trust the tsarevna he proclaimed to love. It was so strange to see her in that way. Then again, he supposed he could be entirely wrong. Even if the golden tiger with the dark gray eyes who watched him in a strange way, as if she wanted to devour him or at least gnaw on his arm for a bit, looked like his Veru, it didn't necessarily mean she was his tsarevna. The coloring could mean nothing.

When they stopped for a midday meal, he decided to find out. Holding out a piece of dried meat to the red cat, he asked, "Are you Tsarevna Stacia, then?"

The cat took the stick of beef, chewed it awkwardly, fangs protruding as she rolled it around and around in her mouth and then just ended up swallowing it whole. Looking up at him then, she simply huffed at him, blowing out a hot breath in his face that smelled like beef and raw fish.

"Is . . . is that a yes?" he ventured.

Another huff, this one nearly making him gag. It was then he realized he'd been bent over, looking down the huge cat's throat. Probably not a good idea. He straightened abruptly and jumped to the side with a yelp when he saw the golden tiger had padded up just behind him and sat down with her jaws wide open.

"Oh. Ha. Ha," he forced an uneasy laugh. "I . . . I didn't see you there. Bet you'd like a snack too, then, eh?" Quickly he fished in his sack and came up with another stick of beef and gingerly placed it in the cat's open jaws, then yanked his hand away and scrabbled backward so fast he fell.

The golden tiger tilted her head, slowly closed her jaws, and sucked down the dried beef with a snick, while the red tiger exhaled and snorted in a way that sounded suspiciously like a tiger version of laughter. With a flick of her red tail, she turned and was gone, disappearing through the brush.

It was two days later when Nik ran out of food. They'd been sticking close to the water, following it to the source since they knew it eventually led all the way to the mountains. All of them were experienced hunters and trappers, but Nik only had a knife, and they didn't want to waste time setting traps for game. That left the hunting up to the tsarevnas, and they'd never hunted as cats before.

They'd been lucky with the fish. The huge sturgeon had been spawning very late in the season. But the twins could feel their energy being sapped. Their bodies were much bigger now, and they were traveling constantly, using the reserves they had. Instinct told them they needed to pace themselves, go slower, but they also knew that as humans they could have moved much faster, especially on horseback. They weren't used to maintaining the mass of muscle, bone, and sinew they carried now.

Stacia caught a small fish that night after Nik fell asleep by the fire. The twins stared down at the bleeding creature, and Veru batted it with a sharp claw to prevent it from bouncing its way back into the water again. Glancing up, they made eye contact with one another, and then Veru picked up the now dead fish in her mouth and padded over to Nik, dropping it near him on a grassy mound, then the two tigers turned and ran north, racing through the rushing creek to the other side, following a scent they didn't understand.

When they came upon the large musk deer, they crouched low in the grass, watching and waiting for just the right moment to strike. The twins knew the animals were solitary creatures, and this one was busy marking his territory, using his scent gland to try to attract the attention of a wandering female, utterly unaware that not one but two large predators lurked nearby, watching him hungrily.

Though Veru and Stacia were unable to talk with each other as they once had while trapped in their new forms, they knew one another well enough to guess what they were thinking, and each sister could predict the moves of her twin fairly well. Thus, when Stacia dug her paw into the ground on the left, Veru assumed that meant her sister would take the left and she should go right.

The red and gold tigers turned their tails to each other and slunk off, circling the heavy animal. When each sister was in position, they lifted their tails, twitching them in the air just enough to be visible to the other, and then they charged. However, the deer, very used to being on alert for danger, spied a movement in the brush, and bolted.

He bounced over logs and through underbrush, squealing and racing, the blood in his veins running hotter and perfuming the air in a way that made the cats salivate. Neither twin wanted to consider why or how they salivated at blood. They were much too practical for that.

It was Veru who caught up to the deer first, catching his back leg and sinking her jaws in. She took no thought for her sister. Instinct pushing her to kill and driving her muscles, fangs, and claws. But she was clumsy using her new weapons, and he quickly bounced on his front legs and kicked her in her face, and she let go. Then Stacia was on his back, her claws in his shoulders, her teeth in his neck. She bit and hot blood spurted into her mouth. Licking, she tasted salt and warmth and life. It was surprisingly delicious.

But the musk deer wasn't done yet. That was her mistake. He was also a powerful animal, and he wanted to live. He reared up and Stacia fell off. Tossing his head just when she tried to attach her jaws to him again, his long, protruding fang pierced her side. She let out a roar as he whipped his head back and forth viciously, widening the wound until it seeped blood and her skin flapped loosely around the tear.

Veru rebounded, this time aiding her sister. She knocked him away with her paw, and the deer fell. Before he could scramble to his feet, she jumped on top of his wriggling form, bit his skull, and crushed it, finally killing the animal. When she limped back over to Stacia, she could see the wound was a bad one indeed. They'd have to get Nik to sew it closed and hope infection wouldn't set in.

As for her, Veru knew it was likely she had a broken ankle, or at least a very bad sprain. She could hardly put any weight on her front leg. Still, at least now they had food. She supposed it would be better for them to rest and eat during the night and then head back to Nik with a chunk of deer meat and, if possible, have him tend to their wounds and see if they could travel.

Huffing softly to her sister, Veru encouraged her to come closer and join her at the deer's side. Together the tigers ripped into the soft belly of the animal and gorged themselves on the slightly bitter and tangy but rich offal first before ripping off chunks of steaming warm meat.

The gnawing hunger in their bellies turned to a warm sense of fullness, and the sharp ripple of pain began to dull with it. The twins, lulled by their exhaustion, placed their heads on their paws right next to their kill, and faces still bloodied, they slept.

CHAPTER 10

Beware of Silent Dogs and Still Waters

The next morning dawned bright and crisply cold, but in their tiger bodies the twins barely felt the chill. Sleeping next to one another kept them warm, and the fur covering them felt as luxurious as any fur cloak. Even better, because not an inch of them was exposed to the cold. They woke and stretched, prepared for the painful pull of torn skin or bruised ribs only to discover there was no pain.

Veru nudged Stacia in the ribs where she'd been torn the night before. Unable to twist her head well enough to see the damage, Stacia cocked her head at her sister as if in question. In reply, Veru lifted the paw that had also been damaged and then proceeded to pace back and forth, showing her sister that the injury she had received had mysteriously healed as well.

The cats rose, relishing the feeling of every strong muscle moving beneath their coats, then raked their sharp claws down the trunk of a tree, and watched in fascination as the bark peeled away in shreds. Whatever strange magic had made them cats also granted them relief from pain and injury, a gift they desperately needed if they were to navigate the strange new world of animal life. They also needed to learn to work together if they were going to learn how to catch prey.

They shook their heads and yawned widely, scraping their tongues over their new sharp teeth, and letting the natural gruff noise of a big cat huff out of heavy lungs and lift into the air, a warning to any other nearby predators who might be interested in the remains of their kill. They padded over to the dead animal, noticing the smell wasn't nearly as appetizing as it had been the night before, and played with it a bit, trying to find something interesting.

Veru laid down and began gnawing on a leg, cracking through bone, and making a happy sound when she discovered the delicious marrow inside. Stacia held the carcass down with her claws and ripped chunks of meat from the ribs, swallowing them whole, then found a nice piece she could set aside for Nik to roast later.

When she licked the bone, she realized the coarseness of her new tiger tongue nearly scraped it clean for her. It was a beneficial trick and one she thought she might like to carry over when she was a human again, assuming she ever managed to change back. The ability to swallow meat whole, forgo chewing, and carve it with just her tongue would save her not only time but from many a toothache in the future. Not to mention the fact that there wouldn't be a man alive who would dare risk a "tongue-lashing" from her. She huffed softly, laughing at her own thoughts.

Content with their morning meal, the twins flicked their tongues over their crusty jaws and then proceeded to help one another clean their faces. Stacia realized then that though their tongues were indeed rough, they could control the pressure, so they didn't tear each other's faces off. Once they were clean—or at least, clean enough—they stood panting, both needing water.

Grateful she would not be needing to solicit Nik's help in stitching her wound, nor would she need to tolerate a censure from her sestra's lovestruck sycophant, Stacia picked up the large chunk of meat meant for Nik in her jaws, and the two tigers began the journey back, easily following their own trail.

When they arrived at the tree where they'd left the young man, the fire was cold, as was the scent of any food he'd eaten. He'd been missing for several hours and was likely out searching for the two of them.

Though it wouldn't be impossible for them to find the young man, it would be more difficult than it should be under normal circumstances. The moment he donned the tunic and boots, his scent and his trail disappeared. Even as tigers the only way to track him was to keep him close, to listen for his footsteps. Sometimes, even with their enhanced hearing, they couldn't see or hear him until he removed his boots or tunic. They often depended on the scent of his food or the sound of his voice to point them in the right direction. With those boots, he didn't even leave tracks.

Prior to the awful week of their mother's death, Stacia had no idea that Nik was anything other than the bumbling young man he showed the world. As for Veru, she had always known there was more to Nik than met the eye. She was aware that there was a part of his life he hid from her, but she'd always assumed that he'd share that with her someday. He had a difficult time with trust, but then so did she. When he arrived at the palace with the dangerous monk in tow, to say they were shocked would have been an understatement.

When the twins had demanded that Nik explain where and how he'd met the man just after their mother's funeral, he'd been truthful, but they both knew he wasn't telling them everything. The doctor had informed them that the mysterious man remained nearby, and it worried them.

Then after it was announced that a new king and his son were arriving from a place neither of them had ever heard of before and at such an inauspicious time, they prepared for the worst. They recalled their top advisors and surrounded the palace with guards. When the king and his son got through all the checkpoints with their trusted men unable to answer the most basic of questions about them, the twins knew something was very, very wrong.

The odd thing was, there were no signs of revolution. There was no army accompanying the so-called king's entourage. He flew no banners of any kind. Nothing added up. They had never seen anything like it before. After consulting with their mother's closest advisor, they decided to allow the man and his son entry, knowing the two of them and their guard could handle themselves well enough.

Their parents had taught them that in matters of diplomacy, trust was never given outright. Not to anyone. Betrayal was the expectation. You prepared for it. You planned for it. And if it didn't happen, you counted yourself lucky. Despite this fact, a royal was never allowed to show distrust outright. Instead, royals needed to become skillful at hiding their true thoughts and feelings. They were taught to play a dangerous game in which they appeared on the surface to trust everyone and take them at their word.

Comparing it to the sea, their parents taught them that a skilled mariner considers everything—the dangers above and the possible threats below the water. They must plan for every contingency they see in the sky above, which might come from storm clouds or thundering waves, as well as those they don't see, such as icebergs or deadly sea creatures.

It doesn't matter how much a person loves the sea or even how expertly they navigate its waves. The moment they are wrapped up in its beauty or lulled by its calm waters is the moment it will reach up and destroy you. The same is true when working in politics. Every negotiation, every meeting, every discussion and interaction were like those ocean waves. Always be on alert. Remain focused. Take your eyes away or allow yourself to trust and lean upon others and you will find yourself sinking in the depths with no one to save you.

Both of the tsarevnas were thinking of this when they entered the room and sat before the king and his son. They had been prepared for a shock, but what neither of them had expected was to see Nik. Still, they schooled their expressions and allowed them to pitch their proposal.

The two sisters watched Nik closely for signs of betrayal, listening as the man began weaving his lies. They could both tell that none of it was Nik's doing. It was easy to see the naked fear on his face and his distrust of the man. It pained him to be there, and he was obviously uncomfortable in the clothing he wore. Nik was no prince. That much was obvious.

What they didn't know was why. Why did Nik go along with the man's plans? Why didn't he come to them in the first place? What power did the man have over him? More than anything, they wished they could talk to him, especially seeing as how there was much more going on with Nik than they ever suspected.

Maybe it was the magic that tied him to the other man. But it was certain that Nikolai possessed a magic all his own. If they hadn't seen his reaction to them when they'd turned into tigers, they might have thought it had been him who had cursed them to their current form. The fact that he was more frightened of them than anyone else assured them that he hadn't. Nor did they believe it had been the stranger impersonating Nik's father. He seemed almost as shocked by their transformation as Nikolai.

Truthfully, they didn't know what to make of it. If it hadn't been for that hussar, the older soldier with Evenki heritage, they wouldn't have been able to form a plan of any kind. He seemed to think it was some sort of spirit possession or animal protection. Perhaps he was right. Whatever it was, the twins were trapped. And now Nikolai was gone. And with no scent of food or tracks, they had no idea where to go other than the direction they'd been headed—the great mountains.

Stacia dropped the hunk of meat, wishing, above all else, she could talk to her sister. How ironic. They'd fought each other most of their lives, and now that they couldn't communicate, what wouldn't she give just to share a few words with her twin? She growled softly into the air, hoping that if Nik was somewhere nearby, he'd hear. Trying again, a bit louder, she stopped, listening, but heard nothing in reply.

Verusha had certainly thought she'd like to talk with her sister as well since their transformation, but at the moment she was circling the tree, searching for some sign or signal left behind by her friend. At last she found it. Letting out a snort, she pawed the tree and huffed until her sister joined her. Carved into the bark was a small arrow pointing east.

With a happy sort of chuff, Veru took off at a leap, almost galloping along the creek, only stopping long enough to drink deeply first. Stacia was about to follow but turned to look at the hunk of meat she'd dropped. It was really too big to bring along for any distance and too big to swallow, not to mention that she was still full of her dinner and hasty breakfast. With a small growl at the stupidity of the young man for heading off without them, she hurriedly stuffed the morsel under a raised root and scraped some leaves over it with a paw.

The human part of her knew it was highly unlikely they'd be back before the meat spoiled, but there was a cat instinct that told her to save the meal for later, that she just didn't know when the next kill was likely to happen. With a quiet growl, she darted off after her sister, easily following her trail, and splashed through the water, cold droplets running down her red coat.

—

It took two days for Nik to find them, and during that time he learned something very interesting. Two things, really. First, he'd assumed the twins, as tigers, could track him. It seemed they couldn't. Even though they were magical creatures, they appeared to be unable to find him when he was wearing his boots and tunic. That was a good thing, he supposed. It meant the Death Draughtsman wouldn't be able to find him either.

The second thing he discovered was that as he tried to hurry ahead to find Veru, since he'd decided that she must have gone ahead without him, his speed increased and increased, to the point where the things around him became a blur. He also found he didn't need to stop for rest or food, and within just a day he'd reached the foothills of the mountains, something that should have taken him more than month.

Turning around, he headed back, careful to listen for the sound of a tiger's cry. Luckily for him, he heard them from quite a distance off and was able to slow himself in time to find them facing down a lone wolf. Their roars had scared off the poor creature and served as a signal to him. It took only a few minutes to race into the glade where they'd cornered the creature, and he arrived in time to watch him run in the other direction.

Nik realized by then that it was the boots and tunic causing the problem for them and hastily sat on a log, removing the tunic. "There you are," he cried as he tugged off the boots that showed no signs of wear, despite how far he'd traveled. "I've been looking for the two of you. You'll never guess where I've been."

Quickly the two tigers chuffed and trotted over to him. The golden one pressed her face into his chest, nudging him so hard he fell over the back side of the log. He laughed, but it sounded nervous even to his own ears as he climbed back up and sat again. "All right, Veru. Calm down. I'm here. Sorry I took off like that. I didn't realize you couldn't follow me. I'll be more careful from now on. I've got good news though."

The golden tiger laid down next to him with paws outstretched in his direction while the red tiger merely sat on her haunches, watching him intently.

"I've been to the mountains," he exclaimed. "I know. It sounds crazy, but it's true. These boots can travel fast. Quicker than horseback or by carriage, or even water. As far as I can tell, I spanned leagues in just a few moments."

Nik paused. He wasn't certain why. He knew the sisters couldn't talk back, and yet he felt like he needed their approval somehow. "The thing is," he said. "I don't know if there's a way to make them work for all three of us. Maybe if I touch you at the same time, or something?"

He rubbed his stomach. "Huh. I wasn't hungry before, but suddenly I'm starving." Nik licked his lips. "Thirsty too. I haven't eaten or drank anything in the last two days. You two wouldn't happen to know where there's any food nearby, would you?"

The tigers looked at one another, and both cats rose to their feet. Nik reached into his bag and slipped on a different pair of shoes. "Guess I'll use these for now, so you'll know where I am. We'll try out the other pair after we eat. Da?"

When a rumble came from the red tiger, Nik grunted in reply and slung his bag over his shoulder, wobbling a little when he stood up to follow them. They didn't walk too far. Nik was grateful for that. He was starting to feel dizzy and very, very weak.

They stopped at what appeared to be a little farm complete with sheep, a few cattle, and some pigs. It was dusk and Nik figured he could probably scare up some milk, eggs, or cheese, or maybe find something saved for the animals in the barn. "You two stay here out of sight. Remember what the soldier said. Farmers are allowed to kill tigers. Poachers, too, I imagine, assuming they can catch me. But they might think twice about it at least. I'll be back soon."

Stacia and Veru crouched in the brush watching and waiting as the setting sun disappeared and the stars filled the sky. When the moon rose over the horizon, filling the little farm with pale rays of limpid light, they heard a dog bark. A second dog echoed the first. Quickly the bark was silenced. Then they heard a shout and a scream. They stood, hackles rising as they caught sight of a man running with a torch toward the barn. Another followed with a long, sharp sickle in hand. They heard a stamping sound nearby, and soon Nik had returned.

"Hurry—this way. They'll be upon us soon," he said.

They ran together, but Nik was slow, and the bright moon made hiding difficult. They heard the bark of not one but many dogs, and both Stacia and Veru knew the moment when the pack had caught their scent. The pursuing animals nearly erupted in a frenzy of yips and baying. The shouts of men followed as they crashed through the brush after them.

Continuing to run, the twins keeping slow pace with Nik, they could hear the pack quickly overtaking them. Veru glanced at her sister and with a gruff growl, whipped in a quick circle.

"Veru!" Nik whispered in alarm. "Don't! You'll get hurt!" He stumbled then and fell. Stacia stopped and pressed a paw on his chest, peering into his face in the moonlight, trying to convey to him to hide, then she was off, moving like lightning through the brush. Nik scurried backward, hiding himself behind a large rock, and stuffed a large hunk of rye bread in his mouth, chewing quickly, and then pulled the stopper from the leather.

He drank down half the bag—delighted to find it was spiced cider—and tore off another piece of bread when he heard a terrible roar and a scream of pain. Nik dropped his loaf of bread and grabbed his head, rocking back and forth, praying it wasn't Veru. He didn't know what he'd do if she was hurt. Tears pricked his eyes when he heard a yelp and a large body hit the ground. Quickly he rose, stuffing the bread in his bag. Putting on his boots, he centered himself, pulling the magic to him, and began moving toward the sound, not quickly but quietly.

When he arrived, he found some of the dogs dead and two people injured. The tigers were circling the remaining humans, two of which carried huge scythes, and they looked like they had the muscles to use them. Even from his hiding place and with the moon now hidden in the clouds, he could see both the tigers were injured with dog bites and long cuts on their shoulders and sides.

They'd need to heal. Could they even travel with injuries that bad? At least most of the dogs looked like they were in worse condition, if not dead. They wouldn't be chasing them anytime soon. He thought they might be able to outpace the men, at least for a while. Softly, Nik cursed himself. He *was* a duraki. This was all his fault. Well, then the least he could do was get them to safety.

Racing back to the farm, he started a fire not at the barn but in a pile of hay outside it, near enough for them to be alarmed but far enough away that they'd likely be able to stop it before it spread. Then he shouted, "Pozhar! Fire!" until he was certain the cry had been picked up by others.

Once the men headed back to the farm and the growing blaze, he hurried back to the two tigers who had just dispatched the last snarling dog. Stacia was limping but she froze when he put a hand on her back. He asked, "Can you walk?"

She huffed in response.

"Come with me."

Walking beside him, his hand still touching her neck, he crouched down next to Veru who was licking her bitten hind leg. She turned abruptly at his touch and snarled, baring her bloody fangs. "It's me, Veru," Nik said, backing away but then returning when she closed her mouth. "Can you walk on it for a bit? I want to try walking with my boots on while touching both of you to see if we can go a distance away."

She returned to licking her back leg and growled when he touched her head but didn't attack. He waited impatiently for her to finish seeing to her wound, keeping a hand on both tigers. Stacia sat next to him, waiting, and when Veru finally stood and the three of them began to move forward, walking slowly, both Stacia and Veru limping, their gaits moving in strange opposing ways, he wasn't sure the magic boots were working.

They continued their slow progress, tracking time by the movement of the moon, and when it had gone halfway across the sky, they finally stopped. Nik didn't sense a blur or feel as if the boots had created any speed for the three of them, but at least the farm had fallen behind them. When he stopped and pulled off the boots, he crouched down to examine the wounds on the tigers as best as he could in the dim light and was surprised to see they had fully healed during their walk.

"The boots created another miracle!" he exclaimed. "Your injuries are gone. I don't know how far we've come, but that in and of itself is exceptional! Do you want to continue on, or would you like to rest for a time?"

Stacia stared at him for a moment, blinked, and then headed off to a patch of grass and then slumped down, laying her head on her paws, shutting her eyes almost instantly. Veru blew a hot breath on Nik's hands and then moved over by her sister, yawning hugely and stretching before she, too, laid down to sleep.

"Okay, sleep it is," Nik said. He didn't bother making a fire at all but drank several swallows of the cider, then, using his bag as a pillow, made a bed for himself near the two tigers and fell asleep almost instantly.

The sun was well above the horizon when Nik woke, and the only reason he did was the unpleasant sensation of his body being saturated with a spray of water. He rose with a start, the hard sleep making his eyes sticky. "Gah!" he said, wiping the damp from his face. "Hey!"

Stacia guffawed and stalked away, her body still wet from her bath. Bending her upper body low to the ground, she lifted her rear in the air, twitching her tail. She relished the feeling of her entire spine stretching out.

Nik, seeing her tiger rear aimed at his face, reddened and looked away, just in time for him to get his face flicked with her red-and-black-striped tail. He rolled to the side and stood. "Keep your tail out of my face, would you?"

The red tiger wrinkled her nose and sneezed.

He pointed his finger at her. "You'd better not be laughing at me, Stacia." Sitting on a log, he pulled out the magic boots and the crumbling rye bread. Taking a bite and chewing, he studied their surroundings. They'd walked in a southeasterly direction from the farm the night before, and though they hadn't run, it was obvious they had indeed been moving faster than normal. Not as quickly as he'd been moving on his own, but much quicker than they could walk before.

When Veru walked up to him, he reached out and stroked the golden tiger on the head, not noticing when she pulled away and sat down. "Look, Veru. See those mountains? They're closer. If we walk the same way or even try to run in tandem, I'll bet we could make it there in a day or two."

He looked at her. Even as a tiger she was prettier than her sister. "Are you hungry?" He tore off a piece of bread. "Want some?"

Holding it out on his palm, he smiled in a way he hoped looked charming, but the gold cat just looked at the meager offering and then up at him and turned and walked off. He heard a noise from behind and turned to see the red tiger. "I don't suppose you want it?"

Growling softly, the red tiger stood and started walking after her sister, who had disappeared in the brush. Stacia then paused and waited patiently for him to follow.

"Where are we going?" he asked, shouldering his bag.

It didn't take him long to figure out. The tigers led him to a small pool, where he filled up his now empty flagon along with the other skeins he'd brought with him. He also took the time to wash his face in the ice-cold water and wished he could wash his hair, but he knew it was much too cold for that. He'd have to wait until they were back in civilization. Apparently, such concerns didn't bother Stacia and Veru; the golden tiger hopped into the pool, shook herself, then darted under and grabbed a fish for breakfast.

After they ate and drank, he donned his boots, put one hand on each tiger, and they began their journey again. They started off with a walk, then when he asked if they were ready, he increased the pace and found they could keep up, even when the speed was so fast the world around them grew hazy and distorted.

Nik was so excited by the weeks they were shaving off their journey and the new magic he'd discovered that he didn't notice immediately when his love, the tsarevna Verusha, disappeared. He'd gotten so used to the feeling of fur beneath his fingers and the play of muscles as they moved together, the three of them as one, that they'd marched in a sort of musical rhythm.

When one player left the song, the music continued, and the march kept going, so he didn't realize the fur and the tiger were missing. When he did, he grabbed hold of the ruff at Stacia's neck and cried out, "Stacia! Veru's gone!"

CHAPTER 11

Dig a Hole for Someone Else and You May Fall In

Veru didn't quite understand what had happened. One moment she was moving alongside her sister and the invisible being her friend had become, thanks to his mysterious power, her mind transfixed as the world shifted around her, and the next moment the ground fell out from beneath her. The hum of magic and the bubble of warmth that had encapsulated her burst, and she was plummeted into a dark, fetid den where the musky earth surrounded her on all four sides.

Panic set in as she bumped her nose against one wall and another. The thought came that she had been buried alive. She roared grievously for her sister again and again, but she couldn't hear or smell evidence of her. A rotten kill assailed her nostrils, though, setting off pangs of hunger like she'd never felt before in her life. Weak starlight shone down from above, and she realized she must have fallen into some sort of pit.

Gingerly, she stood on her hind legs, trying to reach the surface, but it was far too high for her to jump. *Think, think, Veru*, she lectured herself as she paced from one wall to another, unwilling to explore the dark depths at the back. The fragrant odor drifted down again when the wind rustled the long tree branches above, and peering into the darkness, she could just make out an object hanging over the center of the pit, far above her head.

It's an animal trap! she thought. *Now, how do I get out of it?* Baring her teeth and wrinkling her nose so her whiskers stood on end, she sneezed, thinking she'd been lucky there hadn't been another large predator caught in the pit with her. She could still smell the lingering stench of fear and the stink of old urine and droppings, but she couldn't catch more than a haunting trace of blood, and there wasn't the telltale scent of death she expected.

After their first kill, it was a shock to Veru that the animal transition from life to death was now a tangible thing. She could not only smell it but sense and taste it. It left a bitter tang on the back of her tongue. Never again would she take the life of an animal for granted. Though she knew it was necessary, that didn't mean she couldn't be more aware. More grateful. Even if her time as a tiger was transitory, the uniqueness of natural life was something she'd remember forever.

Carefully, she began exploring the dirt walls, looking for any place in which to dig her claws or something to grab on to and hoist her body up and over the side. For the first time, she cursed the fact that her body was so large and powerful. If she'd been smaller, say a normal-sized cat or even a mouse, climbing up a wall would have been simple. Since she'd been changed into a tiger, she enjoyed the fact that her body was finally a match for her mind.

Veru had always been envious of her sister. Stacia was tall and strong and able, and the men under her command never looked at her with lovesick cow eyes or forced her to stand back in battle, thinking her too soft or small or in need of protection. Her sister and most of the people in the empire believed that beauty was something laudable, but Veru disagreed. Beauty wasn't earned. It just was or wasn't. Their mother understood. She had suffered with the same impediment. But it was her mother who taught her to use it for her own purposes.

She did, and Veru could see how it benefited her family and aided her in spy work and diplomacy on occasion, but secretly, she despised herself for doing so. When she did agree to do such a thing, she felt shameful. Yes, there were times when it was necessary to play at being unscrupulous, or deceptive, or to mislead an opponent and win through subterfuge, but Veru wanted to beat her enemies with wit and intelligence, not by having them swoon at her feet or simply by having turned them into babbling idiots. Playing a vixen was not noble or proper to her way of thinking. As a soldier, she could at least hide behind her armor and be appreciated for her knife skills instead of her figure. Men feared her rather than fawned over her then.

It was one reason she had no interest in men. Not that she didn't like men. She did. But when a man looked at her with interest, it was never for her mind. If at any time she thought a man could actually see her and not just her body or her face or her hair, and like the woman beneath, then she might, just might, be interested. It was one reason she liked Nik. He never treated her like a fragile creature.

Oh, Veru knew he had feelings for her, but he'd never pressed her about it, at least not until the recent unpleasantness. It didn't make sense. Nik had always been observant. Too observant sometimes. He knew her weaknesses as well as her strengths. He'd always been possessive, but it never bothered her before. Now, if she wasn't in tiger form, she wouldn't know what to say to him, how to act. She didn't for a second believe he was the son of the monk or magician or whatever that man pretended to be. But she knew Nik would never hurt her either.

Like her, Nik said he'd always dreamed of the two of them heading off into the world together, leading the Guard. Stacia wanted to command the military, too, but the two sisters wanted the job for very different reasons. Veru feared being consigned to the palace, ending up the prized pet plaything for some boorish foreign prince. Her only job that of producing the next heir to inherit the throne.

As the years passed and her looks declined, so would her influence and power, until one day she'd find herself locked away somewhere, unable to help anyone, not even herself. She'd end up a prisoner, used only for her name, her womb, and the inheritance she brought to another who kept her securely beneath his thumb until she passed from this life unloved, old, an impostor who'd once had a dream.

While it was true that their parents had shared responsibility equally and, thanks to their mother's influence and their father's open-mindedness, had advanced women's rights as well as the rights of the indigenous peoples in the empire further than in any of the neighboring kingdoms or principalities, that did not mean it had been easy or that there weren't still many fixated on the "old ways" who wished to keep women consigned to the home. Never mind that over hundreds of years the majority of peaceful negotiations had women involved.

It wasn't that Veru didn't respect the work her mother and father had done or that she didn't want to continue it. The truth was, Veru was afraid. She didn't feel as confident with the counselors staring at her bosom or even her face as her mother had been. Even if she had something important to say, would they even listen? Whereas, on the battlefield, she could cover her body with armor, hide her face with a helmet, and let her knives do her speaking.

If she was lucky enough, all it would take would be one or two good blows to mar her pretty face, and then it would no longer matter. She could picture it now, a wicked scar across her eye and down her cheek to her lip, puckering her face enough so all could still recognize her but no longer desire her. Instead of lust-filled expressions, she'd see awestruck loyalty and dedicated patriotism. For who wouldn't follow the once lovely tsarevna into battle, whether that be in war or in negotiations?

She'd command their full attention then. No one would stare at her body anymore. They'd be too busy looking at her scar. In it, they'd see her perseverance, her unwavering strength, and her commitment to her people and the empire. At that point she could marry and know the man who sought her hand saw her and desired her for who she really was, not for the package.

Dirt rained down on Veru's head. She sneezed again and shook it off, roaring loudly in protest. What did it matter? There was probably not even a palace left to run. Perhaps not even an empire. She'd thought that by them leaving they might have drawn away the attention of the monk and his minions, but maybe not. They'd seen no sign of him. Maybe he'd stayed to ravage the Guard and the servants. At least it was nearing winter, and most of the villagers had returned to their countryside homes for the season. It might even take months for any of them to notice anything was amiss if the snow cut off the roads. They never held any major gatherings in the winter months.

Veru huffed softly. *Why is it taking so long for Stacia and Nik to notice I'm missing?* Her tiger stomach rolled and grumbled. Never in her life had she felt so hungry. Even the rancid meat overhead was starting to smell appealing.

Giving up on wall number two, she felt with her paw along the dark edge until she came upon wall number three. Aligning her body with the wall, she looked above, searching for a good place to try to jump. Backing up, her back paw felt a heavy piece of metal buried in the soft earth. *What's that?* she wondered, excited that she might have discovered something she might be able to use, and was about to turn around to investigate when her paw brushed across something rough—a rope.

There was a twang, and a net collapsed over her head, frightening her, and she backed away quickly, stepping over the metal ring. Hearing a click and a snap, Veru realized too late what she'd done. The trap closed around her back leg with a clang, and she screamed a roar and collapsed when she heard the sound of her hind leg crack as the bone shattered. The sharp metal teeth bit into her ankle, and the pain almost caused her to black out. Veru could smell her own blood weeping and heard it plop to the earth in steady droplets.

Suddenly, she was very sympathetic to the deer she and Stacia had killed. Her leg throbbed in waves of agony, and the net prevented her from seeing or accessing the wound. Now she understood the tendency for trapped wolves to chew off their own legs. All she could think about was freeing herself, of ending the pain.

Any minor movement proved to her that the steel trap was embedded deep into the ground. There would be no pulling it free. If there had been any hope for her to escape the pit before, there was certainly no chance now, not with the heavy trap attached to her back leg. Veru would have needed her powerful back legs to propel herself up and out of the pit. An injured back leg would make that impossible. She'd have to wait for rescue.

She laid there, whimpering quietly, and tried to quell the strong urge to contort her body so as to lick and chew on the wound or bite and work on the trap itself. Then, as the moments passed, she felt her limb healing itself. The pain lessened. The bone knit itself back together as best as it could with the trap still embedded in the leg. At least it was more bearable than it had been before.

Hours passed. Then morning broke. All day she laid there waiting for Nik and her sister to find her, but they never came. She was so thirsty. Flies buzzed overhead, attracted to the old piece of meat dangling above. Veru estimated the meat couldn't have been there more than a week.

She panted, her tongue swelling in her mouth. The sun was warm enough to cause some snowmelt, and rivulets of water streamed down the hard-packed dirt walls. Veru licked the wet puddles until they froze again at dusk, then laid on her side and slept. Her dreams were dark and nightmarish. In them, her mother warned her over and over not to trust anyone, but her mother was gone, wasn't she?

Waking just before dawn, Veru blinked and remained motionless, barely breathing. There was a sound nearby. Footsteps. Someone walking through the brush. The desire to cry out to her sister, to Nik, was almost desperate, but instinct cautioned her to be quiet. A new scent tickled her nose. It was someone she'd never smelled before. A man. He carried with him the scents of other animals—of death. Panic set in, making her heart race and her muscles warm. Veru's sharp claws dug into the soft earth, kneading the soil. She was ready to pounce on whoever tried to harm her.

With wide eyes, she turned her head quietly back and forth, watching the rim of the pit, waiting to see who would appear and look down. Her lips were peeled back in a silent snarl with fangs bared. Though she didn't relish taking the life of a man, Veru reasoned that the world could do with one less hunter.

Her own breath felt hot as it bathed her face. *Where is Stacia? Why haven't they found me by now? Don't they know I'm in danger?* Whatever was going on with Nik and Stacia, it was too late for them to help her; Veru was going to have to save herself, hurt leg and all.

The footsteps came closer. She heard humming. A snarl erupted from her throat. Veru couldn't stop it. The humming abruptly stopped, as did the footsteps. Good. Maybe she'd scared whoever he was away.

Then she heard a too-cheerful voice. "Well, hello down there. Be with you in a moment. Just need to adjust a few things up top first, if you don't mind."

There was some sawing and hammering and more stomping. Whoever the man was, he certainly wasn't making any attempt to be silent. Veru's ears pricked again and again, listening to his strange sounds, trying to figure out just what he was up to at the top of the pit. Her imagination ran wild.

Was he fashioning a spear with which to kill her? Perhaps he was making a cage in which to carry her off. If she could have laughed at that one, she would have. She heard no evidence of a horse or a cart, and Veru imagined she weighed twice as much as any of her armored soldiers. If he did want to capture her alive, it would be a difficult feat, that was certain. Then again, if he killed her and just took her fur, it would weigh much less. *I'm not going to make it easy on him*, she thought.

Veru heard his voice again. "Now then . . . what have we here?"

At first she couldn't see his face. The sun was in just the right spot to halo the back of his head, darkening his features. Crouching down, he set his bag down beside him and leaned over to see into the shadows of the pit. Veru snarled viciously in response but was surprised to see not the middle-aged hunter she expected but a younger man, very near her own age.

Bunching her injured leg beneath her, Veru instinctively pounced, clawing with her front legs desperately against the dirt wall, trying to catch the young man's bag strap that dangled over the edge. She hoped, at the very least, her efforts would serve to give him warning that she was not to be trifled with, but she collapsed in a heap. As a result, the trap tore open her skin, reinjuring her.

The young man held out his hands, obviously upset by the display. "Hush now, moya krasivaya koshechka. I did not expect to catch you. I've been hired to trap wolves. Never would I hunt one of your kind." He rubbed a hand across his cheek, and Veru could hear the light scrape of stubble against his flesh, though his beard was so pale she could not see any hair on his face.

Slipping his hand up to his forehead, he removed his woven hat, and dark blond hair fell across his face. It was longer on top and short on the sides. The nose was long and aquiline, the lips full and brooding. By men's standards, he was handsome, with high cheekbones, a square chin, and wide blue eyes, but Veru was unaffected by such things.

She'd learned long ago never to let a handsome man or a winning smile turn her head. More than anyone else, she knew better than to judge someone based on their outward appearance. Smoothing his dark blond hair back, he affixed his cap and bit his lower lip. "I must confess—I'm not quite sure what to do with you. If I let you out, you're likely to kill me. Even if you didn't, and I somehow got you out of that trap, it's going to be difficult for you to hunt."

Deciding she'd better help the young man figure out he needed to save her, Veru did her best to sit still and be quiet. She huffed quietly in response to his musings.

"I suppose the least I can do is get that net off."

For a moment he stepped away and then returned with a long staff with a hook on the end. Very carefully, he lowered it next to Veru, and within a few tries had freed her from the net. Once he did, he whistled and sat cross-legged atop the pit. "I was right. You're a beauty. Never seen the like of you before. All gold and white. What a price your fur would fetch."

Veru roared softly.

He held up a hand. "I'm not saying I would. It's just nice to think about the money once in a while, you know? Besides, I could never live with myself for doing it. Wolves are one thing, but a beauty like you is rare. My guilt is already bad enough I have to haul myself into a town with a church once a month for confession."

After hearing the chuffing sound coming from below, the young man laughed. Veru liked the sound. His laugh was relaxed. Soothing. He was at ease with himself in a way that made her jealous. Not jealous like she felt around Stacia, but an admiring sort of feeling that left her wanting to figure him out. To emulate him in a way so she could acquire the same sort of acceptance within herself.

"Now I know what you're thinking. What would an upstanding character such as me have to confess to a member of the church?" Leaning over, he grinned. "It's a mystery, isn't it?"

His grin fell away, and he quickly stood. "Let's get you some water, girl. I'm certain you're parched."

As he figured out how to get water down to her, he continued talking. Veru found she enjoyed listening to him babble. "I'm not a drinking man, so get that vice right out of your head. Nor am I cruel to women or children. Skirt-chasing isn't my thing. The truth is, I don't think there's a woman out there who'd take to my lifestyle. I like the outdoors far too much. There's too much to do and see and explore out here. I hate farming and the idea of being trapped in a small house for the rest of my life . . ."

He'd been carving a large piece of tree bark into a bowl of sorts when he paused. "Oh . . . excuse me for being indelicate. I forgot that here you are trapped in a pit while I'm up here free as a bird complaining about being stuck in a house somewhere. Where are my manners? If you'll forgive me, I'll try not to talk so much and hurry up."

Finishing his makeshift tree bark bowl, he dropped it down into the pit, and luckily it landed with the bowl angled up. It took a few tries, but eventually he was able to fill it at least halfway with water. Veru lapped greedily, draining it within one moment, and he refilled it with his remaining supply and finished his tale.

"As I was saying, the reason I have to attend confession is one you might have guessed. It has to do with my profession. I'm a trapper by trade—specializing in fox, mink, and sable. Occasionally, I accept contracts offered by area locals and create larger traps, such as the one you currently find yourself in. I know most trappers wouldn't be bothered by their work, but I can't help it."

He looked down at Veru as she lapped at the wooden bowl, trying to catch the last few drops of water. Giving up, she sat on her haunches and, tilting her head, stared back. Their eyes locked.

"That's the thing, isn't it?" he said in almost a whisper, his beautiful blue eyes bright with unshed tears. "When you've spent time with God's creatures, you learn they have souls. And what makes their souls less important than mine?"

He sniffled, then cleared his throat. "So now you know my secret, don't you, my beauty?"

Clapping his gloved hands against each other to warm them, he glanced at the sun and at her, then said, "Well, then. I'm going to gather up some supplies for the two of us and try to suss out a plan for you. I shouldn't be gone for more than a half a day. There are just a few supplies I might be needing. And I ought to check a few traps to see if I can snatch up some dinner for the two of us. Best rest up in the meantime, my kotenok."

Veru listened until she couldn't hear him anymore, and then she finally laid down, putting her head on her paws. As she waited for him to return, she was surprised to realize that not only had she not thought of Stacia or Nik the whole time she'd been with the young man but she hadn't even thought of her wound.

CHAPTER 12

A Single Tree Makes No Forest; One String Makes No Music

Time passed slowly as Veru waited for the young man's return, and she drowsed in the shadows of the pit while at the same time keeping her ears flicking back and forth for any signs of his heavy footsteps. Once she heard the faint sounds of something but realized it was the scurrying of a small creature. Its scent was sharp and almost bitter, and it hit the back of her nose like garlic or onion.

It dug a hole into her pit and stuck its whiskered muzzle in and looked around. Deciding to emerge, it was halfway out of the hole when all at once it seemed to catch sight or smell of her because it froze, its front feet dangling in midair. Veru huffed at the brown-and-white furball, and the brave thing bared some impressively long teeth and squeaked at her threateningly before hastily wriggling backward and tunneling away.

I wonder what those would taste like, she thought. *Probably onions.* She'd eaten wild game with her soldiers before, but she'd never thought of lemmings or other small burrowing creatures with such disinterest. As a tiger, she looked at such a tiny thing and knew instinctively that it wasn't worth spending her energy.

Even if it walked right into her mouth, and she swallowed it whole, the amount of fur and bones versus meat and fat was disproportionate.

Eating it would probably give her tremendous gut pain. All those tiny bones would only serve to get caught in her teeth or jaws. They might even puncture her stomach or throat. The fur could make her gag, and consuming a live animal, though markedly easier, could damage her going down. Only a wounded or desperate cat would try to hunt such an animal. She was built for much larger prey.

Just then, her long, lean stomach rumbled, reminding her that she was indeed wounded and desperate. Perhaps if the lemming returned she'd risk a bellyache to fill the emptiness. In fact, Veru was stretching as far as she could, trying to see into the dark little hole, sniffing for traces of the long-gone lemming, when she heard the heavy footfalls of the young man returning. She collapsed down into a sitting position again and waited for his face to appear at the top of the pit.

"Privet, krasivye tiger. Are you hungry? I've brought food," he said from atop the ledge.

She could hear him busily gathering wood to get a fire going. Veru realized then how cold the weather had become. Though she was fairly protected from the wind being trapped within her deep dirt walls, even so, a gust swept inside on occasion and ruffled even her thick coat of winter fur.

The young man was dressed warmly in a parka and a balaclava, but he'd surely need a fire and possibly a tent if he meant to spend the night outside. After he got his little fire started, and she heard the crackles and smelled the scents of pine, grass, and woodsmoke, he squinted down at her in the shadows.

"Good. Your dish is still upright. Look out now. I'm pouring your water."

He emptied what must have been a full skein of water and then, when she'd licked the dish dry, a second. *It must have been heavy for him to carry that much water*, she thought. In addition, he tossed the bodies of four cleaned rabbits, their fur, heads, and legs removed, as well as two other small mammals she couldn't identify.

"It's not much for one of your size," he admitted as he watched her scoop up one after another, crunching bones and swallowing her meal in large bites. "But it should get you through the night at least."

He disappeared again, and she heard him fussing by the fire. "Hope you don't mind," he said, "but I saved one for myself."

Soon Veru smelled the aroma of animal fat as it hit and sizzled on hot coals. Normally, such a thing would make her salivate. Instead, she laid down, her meal finished, and licked the remains from her paws and around her mouth as best she could. *It's a waste what he's doing,* she thought. *All that delicious fat is seasoning the wood and the air instead of lining his belly. And the marrow in the bones is dripping out and away from the meat. He'll need to eat again far too soon. If he ate like a tiger instead, he'd be far healthier.*

Veru, sated and sleepy, rolled to her side and wondered if she was going to think like a tiger from now on. How odd would it be if she turned human again and began serving raw meat at dinner parties? Still, there was some truth to idea that the lifeblood of the animal was wasted when cooking. Perhaps there was a happy medium where meat could be cooked partway.

She listened to the young man eat, and when he was finished, he tossed his bones into the pit in her general direction. Veru sniffed at them but didn't eat them, except for one cooked leg he didn't finish. Then he shuffled around a bit, digging in his bag. Setting it aside, he sat on the lip of the pit with his long legs dangling over the edge, placing a strange round instrument on his lap, a kind Veru had never seen before.

"Would you like some music to soothe you to sleep, little tiger? Perhaps it will take your mind off that steel trap around your ankle, eh? I promise I'll figure out a way to get that off for you tomorrow." Rubbing the back of his neck, he added, "I'll admit—I'm not quite certain at this point exactly how I'm going to do it. Perhaps if I pray for an answer, something will come to me, eh? My papa usually sends me an inspirational dream when I ask for one. He is my guardian angel, after all. Speaking of which . . ."

He held up the instrument. "This here belonged to my father. He invented it. And always told me he was inspired by his guardian angel, his papa, my dedushka. Both of my parents were musicians, you see. Making and playing instruments was a skill passed down in our family.

"Many generations ago, my shepherd ancestors created the first musical instrument in our country. It was a pipe called a rozhok. At first they used it to herd and call sheep, but then they learned that different shapes and trees made new sounds. Music became the main source of our income. My family played at festivals, weddings, holidays, and all other celebrations.

"My dedushka was particularly skilled at playing the garmoshka. I can do a passable job with that one, but it's not my favorite. All he ever wanted to do before he passed on was to obtain a commission to play at the capital for the royal family, but then the tsar was killed, and so was his dream.

"After we buried my dedushka, my parents pressed on, teaching me how to play all the traditional songs even though I was young, and I even began writing some of my own. Papa had to invent ways the three of us could play more than one instrument at a time since I was their only child.

"From a very young age, I became skilled enough to play most any wind or string instrument, the only difficulty for me was carrying them." He took a few moments to tune the instrument, then he strummed a few notes. "Ironically, I have the same problem now. Even though I'm strong enough to carry and play anything, I can't exactly cart them around with me." Placing his hands across the strings to still the notes, he added, "This domra, a balalaika, and a zhaleika are all I have left now of my parents." He went back to picking the strings quietly. The notes drifted up and away from him, out into the darkening evening.

"They died about ten years ago of malignant cholera. I nearly died as well. If it hadn't been for the ministrations of my aunt, I'd be buried next to them in the old churchyard. Now I live with my aunt and uncle and their twelve children."

The young man began to softly strum his instrument, picking at the various strings mindlessly as he spoke.

"When my uncle was injured working in the forests, they became desperate for money. Though they didn't want to do it, I insisted on helping by allowing them to sell my inheritance—my parents' musical instrument collection. Those items helped to sustain the family over the years.

"After I became old enough, I joined their family business, trapping and selling furs. When that's not going well, I play or sing for money, when I can find the work, but a lone musician doesn't earn as much. We travel far distances as trappers, so I bring these with me sometimes to practice and to help me pass the hours." He lifted the instrument. "I only have three left now. Anyway, if you'll indulge me."

Setting the polished instrument on his lap, he began plucking the strings in earnest, beginning slowly at first and then moving faster and faster. The skill with which he played was breathtaking. His fingers danced across the strings so quickly, playing a melody so bright and happy it made Veru completely forget she was stuck in a pit in the middle of nowhere.

She closed her eyes and imagined twirling, raising her hands in the air while snow fell around her in soft, fluffy flakes landing on her cheeks, hair, and cloak as her skirts billowed out. Then as Veru kept dancing, she was no longer alone. Warm hands, toughened by wind and work, grasped her own tightly and held on to her so she could spin even more wildly. Rich male laughter tickled her ears, and she laughed in unison.

All at once, the song finished. She felt desperately disappointed and breathless and thrilled all at the same time. As the last notes drifted away into the starry evening and disappeared, Veru opened her eyes, wishing she could catch them and bring them back. She was surprised that the laughter was still there, as were the snowflakes.

Fat, white puffs floated down lazily from the dark sky, landing on her furry ears, her nose, and her paws and then slowly melted. The young man was leaning over, looking down at her and chuckling, his blue eyes gleaming as he lifted his winter cap and pushed back his dark blond hair.

"You liked that one, didn't you?" he asked, propping his instrument on his knee. "I've heard stories of music taming savage beasts, but I don't think you're too savage at all, are you? How could you be when you purr like a house cat?"

Purr? Veru was horrified to realize at that moment that a telltale rumble was indeed coming from her chest. How humiliating! Worse than that, she couldn't seem to stop it. The seesawing vibration was something that appeared to be connected to her . . . her heart. She felt happy. Veru didn't know when she'd last felt joyful.

Truthfully, she knew she shouldn't be feeling that particular emotion now. She was stuck in a pit with a steel trap around her leg; she had no idea where Nik or Stacia could be; she'd been cursed to the form of a tiger, been run out of the palace, the empire was in a shambles, there was a strange sorcerer with an army either attempting to take over the capital, or on the road searching for her and her sister; and her beloved mother had just passed away.

But for some reason, being around the young fur trapper made Veru forget things of which she should be cognizant. He was entirely too distracting and far too . . . effervescent for her liking. Besides, he was a particularly good-looking young man, and she didn't trust men like that. Chiding herself, Veru shook her head, raining slush all around her. *I'll certainly be muddy tomorrow*, she thought. This was followed by the notion of, *My hair must look like a bird's nest.*

Then she remembered it no longer mattered what her hair looked like. She had no one to impress. The good-looking young man wasn't helping her or speaking kindly to her because he was *in love* with her. He was simply a good person. And as far as his effervescence went . . . he wasn't doing it to influence her or gain her favor. She was a tiger. He played her a song because he loved music. That was all.

Still, somehow Veru managed to get her purring to stop and laid her head down to try to sleep. Just then the good-natured young fellow leaned over to say, "Spokoynoy nochi," and grinned again before disappearing. Soon she heard a soft snoring sound from overhead and the hoo-hooing of an owl.

Huffing out a steaming breath from her nostrils, Veru laid down on her side, shifting to make her leg more comfortable, shut her eyes, and thought, *Good night, indeed.* Rest well, young man.

—

Veru woke in darkness, used to doing such a thing in the winter season as a human with the limited daylight hours, but her tiger body told her she should roll over and keep sleeping. It wasn't even sunrise yet, but the early hours brought both the musical young man and Veru a surprise neither of them would soon forget.

She had awoken abruptly, not to the sound of the young man descending quietly into the pit like she should have under normal circumstances, nor to his near presence when he approached her with his heavy footfalls. Instead, she'd been jolted awake when she felt the screeching pain of her leg being torn open once again as the steel trap was disengaged from her back ankle.

Instinctively, she whipped around to protect herself, tucking her injured leg beneath her and roared, only to realize her muzzle was now tied with a rope, and she felt dizzy to the point of stumbling. Veru was confused. It was still very dark. She couldn't smell anything or anyone except the young man. *Why has he come down now, in the middle of the night? Hadn't he said he'd be coming down in the morning? Why is he awake so early? Is he leaving me?*

As for him, the young man in question was surprised the tiger had woken up at all. He thought he'd found enough of the valeriana root to keep the large animal asleep for many hours if not a full day. In fact, he'd worried it had been too much. That he might have killed her outright. It had just been his good luck to come across a patch of the spent flowers near one of his traps, and then it had taken some time to pack each carcass full of the stuff. He was lucky she'd been so hungry that she didn't notice how he'd carefully sewn each one shut with the herbs inside.

Danik rationalized that even if it had been too much, he didn't want the poor creature to suffer. He highly doubted she'd survive with the type of injury she had anyway and debated putting her out of her misery himself depending on how bad her wound looked. What he certainly didn't expect was her fast recovery.

He'd waited several hours to make sure she was completely asleep. Only after he was certain, checking by tossing some large rocks into the pit and seeing she didn't even flick a furry ear in that direction, did he risk throwing down his woven ladder. The first thing he did was tie a slip rope around her mouth, just in case. It wouldn't stop the claws, but at least she wouldn't bite him.

Once that was in place, he bent down with his torch to try to get a good look at her leg. Truthfully, it didn't look too bad. It wasn't bleeding and didn't even look sore. In fact, if it weren't for the steel trap biting into her ankle, he'd say she wasn't injured at all.

Gently, carefully, he lifted her heavy leg, maneuvering it away from the other so he could stand on the springs. He'd have to in order to apply the necessary force to open the jaws. When he did, he could hear the meaty squelch as the trap wrenched itself free from her flesh, tearing a fresh wound in her mostly healed foot.

Danik gasped as hot, new blood wet the ground. He was trying to make sense of it when the foot disappeared, and he was suddenly faced with a very angry, extremely large tiger.

He held up his hands and spoke softly, unwilling to step off the trap while she was still so close. "Now, now, my krasivaya kotenok. I know it hurts," he soothed. "I was only trying to help. If you'll just back away a bit, I'll make sure this trap doesn't get you again."

Veru's body trembled, and she managed a plaintive sort of whine, then she collapsed sleepily against the side of the pit and watched him with half-hooded eyes as he took a tool from his pack, quickly disassembled the trap, and placed it into his bag. Tying it closed, he stooped to refill her water bowl, then took hold of the thin rope keeping her mouth shut.

Without a word, he climbed the bouncing rope ladder, and when he reached the top, pulled it up and gave the thin rope around her mouth a yank. It came free with just a sharp tug, and he rolled it around his hand and then placed it, too, in his bag. "Try to sleep now," he said softly. "I'll find you more food in the morning."

Not only did Veru sleep; she slept soundly. It was midday, in fact, when she woke next. She was surprised to find the young man had not only kept his word but had also provided a means for her escape. There were more rabbits for her in the pit, but there were also a handful of small mammal carcasses left atop the long tree trunk he had rolled into the pit as incentive for her to climb out.

After eating and licking her water bowl clean, she stood and tested her weight on her ankle. It was fully healed—a miracle she was grateful for yet still didn't understand. Only slipping once, she bound up the tree trunk, scooping up the bits of food as she went, and finally exited the awful pit, grateful for the young man and eager to greet him personally, only to find he'd vacated the area. Veru sniffed around his fire and determined he'd left many hours before. The coals were cold, and there was no warmth in it at all. Nor were there any signs of his footprints remaining in the snow.

For once, Veru had no idea what she should do or where she should go. She let out a loud roar, listening for an echoing response from her sister or a sign of Nik, but she heard nothing in reply. Though she was a large animal, she'd still need to climb a hill to get a general idea of direction. For now, she supposed she should continue in an easterly course, following the rising of the sun and keep the setting of it on her tail.

She'd also need to find water and more food. It wouldn't be as easy to hunt without her sister, but she was sure she could manage on her own. Veru set out, and it didn't take her long to come across the young man's scent. Realizing he was headed east as well, she decided to track him for a while and rationalized it was good hunting practice, and it wasn't at all because she missed his company.

Finding the stream he'd stopped at for water, she drank her fill for the first time in several days and washed the crusty blood from her fur. After catching a small fish for a snack, she then pressed forward, picking up his trail on the other side. Soon she realized, just as evening was coming on, that she wasn't the only animal stalking the young tracker.

It just took a moment for her to figure out why. His scent was not just that of a man, which was enticing aplenty if an animal was big enough and hungry enough, but this particular human also carried with him the scents of many other animals, dead and bloody ones. That might scare off some, but it wouldn't scare off a pack. Certainly not a pack so large.

She picked up her pace, hoping she wasn't too late. As she moved, her breaths came out in white puffs that dampened her already wet coat. Not that she could feel it. The outer layer of her coat was so thick and heavy it kept the rain, the snow, mud, and cold from penetrating, for the most part. Then she had a nice warm inner coat as well as a thick layer of fat and muscle.

Even when she wore several layers of petticoats or heavy woolens beneath her armor, she'd never felt so warm. Fur had always been highly prized to line cloaks, boots, gloves, and coats, and Veru couldn't deny fur felt luxurious and warm. There was nothing else like it. Not in the wide world of textiles. But never again could she wear such a thing next to her human skin and not remember it had once belonged to a creature such as what she was now.

How could she employ hunters like the young man she tracked? True, most hunters did not prey on animals like her. They revered tigers. Feared them, even. But so many other living things died. Their legs caught in the same awful traps. It wasn't something any creature should suffer. Still, she ate them, didn't she? Wasn't it better not to waste? To remember the gift of life?

Veru didn't know all the answers. But she did know that even the brief time she had been caught in a trap, had experienced pain and fear and suffering, had changed her. She would continue to think on it. Perhaps there was a better way. It was interesting to her that she found she'd like to discuss options and possible solutions with the young hunter. Though he killed for work, Veru judged him to be a kindhearted man. One who was gentle of soul.

Catching the fresh scent of the pack and the frenzy of their hunt, she picked up speed. If she was going to save the gentle hunter, Veru would need to hurry. Snow had stuck to the ground in some places, and as her long body stretched out into a run, her claws retracted and the large paws worked like snowshoes, keeping her atop the drifts.

Veru had wondered why the fur had grown so long between the

pads on her paws. It looked different than a cat's or a dog's feet. Now she understood—the long, thick fur not only kept her feet warm in the cold but it served to silence her footfalls. Even with her excellent hearing, she could barely hear the sound of her own running.

All was silent in the copse of trees when she slowed. Soundlessly, she stalked from dark shadow to dark shadow, blending into the white snowdrifts and the golden leaves, watching, waiting, sensing prey all around her. The trees thinned, opening to a little glen where a solitary figure stood near a campfire.

In the darkness all around him, hungry yellow eyes gleamed with ill intent. The man didn't even notice as he pulled a musical instrument from his knapsack and began to play. For just a moment, Veru was lost in the haunting, plangent song. She imagined that he might be playing it for her. Perhaps he missed her already, or maybe he thought she was dying.

Almost unable to help it, she closed her eyes. That's when she heard the first howl.

Chapter 13

If You're Scared of Wolves, Don't Enter the Woods

As the music danced in her mind, it was like Veru was lost in a stage play she'd seen performed long ago by a traveling troupe visiting the palace. Gray wolves, the villains of the theater, leapt from the trees, howling and circling their intended prey, uncertain when or exactly how to attack. They danced around their human victim, lured in by scent and his music. The man carried no visible weapon, only his instrument. The hungry wolves yipped and darted around their prey, salivating as they waited for the signal from their leader.

The music crescendoed, then suddenly ceased. Had the player been killed? Veru's vision went red. Predatory instinct and, above all, the desperate need to protect took over. Something inside her snapped. She moved without thinking. There was a snarl and a yelp that was quickly silenced.

A new player entered the stage.

The wolves hesitated, uncertain. Finally, the leader gave the signal, and, almost as a unit, they barreled toward their victim. Then two things happened at once.

Another creature, much larger, shot out of the trees, taking down two wolves in a fierce, fast attack, ripping open the throat of one and the belly of the other. Steam rose from the fresh wound as the young wolf shuddered, whimpered softly, and died, his guts spilling out onto the fresh packed snow. The large golden tiger lifted its head, blood dripping from its fangs, and puffed a hot breath before turning to target another wolf.

To the wolves, such an act made no sense. The great predator had killed; why wasn't it eating? Meanwhile, their own target had hefted a pack full of the delicious scents of sable, fox, polecat, and mink, donned wooden skis covered with deerskin hide, and was now pushing through the snow with large carved walking sticks, picking up speed quickly.

Three wolves chased after him, running fast in pursuit, hunger making them ignore their fallen pack members. Two remained with the dead, whining and licking the faces of the fallen. Three more died quickly, torn to pieces by the jaws and claws of the great enraged beast. No, four. A fifth still fought the predator. How could it be so hungry? Did it mean to eat them all? Perhaps she was crazed, they thought, or taking the territory for her own.

Wounded, their alpha signaled to regroup. They'd find prey elsewhere. The important thing now was to hide from the large wolf killer. He'd cede the territory, and the pack, such as remained, would move on. Silently, they slipped into the shadows and disappeared, leaving their dead behind.

Veru shook her head and sniffed the air, instinctively understanding the fight was finished. Had she just fought off a pack of wolves? The scent of the ferocious animals quickly vanished. She sniffed the cooling body of the wolf at her feet, wondering if she should pause to eat so as to replenish her energy, but then studied the ski tracks of her hunter. Unfortunately, the three wolves who followed him did not appear to veer off to heed the call of their alpha but had kept up their pursuit.

It was a good idea to escape on skis. The young man had been able to cover a lot of ground very quickly, especially since the terrain led downhill. She caught sight of him every so often, but she was growing tired. The fight had drained her. She'd been bitten several times, and there was a nasty gash on her ribs, but she could feel them healing as she ran.

Her stomach rumbled. The meager meals she'd been eating weren't enough to stave off the cold and help heal her body. Veru also knew another fight was likely. She regretted not tearing off a hunk of warm flesh when it was readily available. Still, she pressed on, determined to save the young man's life who had risked his own to save her.

She came across the first dead wolf one hour later. Apparently, her hunter had used one of the traps in his bag and set out a tempting morsel. The poor creature had stuck his head in the trap to pull off the meat, and it shut on his skull, killing him instantly. Veru pitied the animal but was glad it had been quick and that she needn't fight him herself. Quickly she picked up the chunk of meat that had fallen aside in the snow and gulped it down while still running.

By the time she caught up with her young hunter, he'd positioned himself in the hollowed cave of a rock. She could tell by the smell that it had once been used as the home of a bear but had long since been abandoned. He'd quickly built a fire in the opening and had an impressive stockpile of firewood, which meant either he or someone else had used it as a shelter before. He stood behind the fire holding out a long hunting knife as the two wolves, both young females, paced back and forth on the other side, growling menacingly.

He'd made camp before sundown, but night had fully fallen at that point, it being winter and only a few hours of daylight. There was no moonlight at all. Only the cold light of the stars and his fire, but Veru found she could still see very clearly. As such, it was evident to her by looking at his face and form that the young man was not only exhausted but injured. He favored one leg heavily.

There would be no more running for him until he healed. It would be up to her to take out the determined wolves. She was about to head down to attack them, when she hesitated, thinking there might be a different way. Her father had taught her from a young age that the best result in battle was to defeat your enemy without raising a weapon. Sometimes that meant diplomacy, sometimes he used scare tactics, and other times he simply outwitted his opponent.

Just because she was bigger and could defeat them with her teeth or claws didn't mean she had to. It was time to be the commander her father had been. Instead of springing on the wolves like she'd done before, she decided to try facing them in open challenge. That way they'd have an opportunity to run, if they preferred, saving her from a fight she didn't want.

Filling her lungs and puffing herself up as big as possible, something that worked in war as well, Veru leapt down onto the path leading to the rock cave, snuffed, and then roared so deafeningly she was sure she could have brought down an avalanche under the right conditions.

The wolves spun, sat on their haunches, yipped, and whined, but didn't budge. Instead, they stayed stubbornly in place, trembling. So Veru took one step closer, and then another, letting every sharp claw click down separately with a scissor snick, her mouth open as she let her chest rumble with a deep, menacing growl that promised pain, disembowelment, and death.

One wolf stood, her tail tucked. She whimpered, looking at her companion. Then she sat again, her tongue lolling and dripping. The other watched Veru with steady, wild eyes, but her body shook with fear. Finally, after Veru let out another roar and crouched to pounce, they bolted, running so fast one slipped on slick ice and scrambled quickly, falling behind the others who outpaced her in the snow.

She watched them until she could scent them no more and then turned back to the cave opening. Her young man stood there, squinting in the darkness, knife still pointed out. His hand slightly shook. When she entered the circle of firelight, she paused, looking up at him across the fire. It was then that she realized her fur still bristled, and the rumbling sound still emanated from her chest.

Making oneself as puffy and large as possible was definitely something that felt unnatural for Veru, especially around men. So, she reverted to her normal way of doing things, shook her whole body as if she was ruffling her skirts, and then, as demurely as one could when one was a tiger and not a lady, she sat, attempting to bat her eyes, which only served to irritate her, so she stopped and flicked her tail back and forth instead in what she presumed looked like a friendly sort of way.

"I . . . I wondered if that was you," he said. "Part of me hoped it was. Then I also hoped it wasn't. I'll understand if that doesn't make sense. It doesn't make much sense to me."

Veru thought that about summed up how she felt too. He hadn't yet dropped his hand with the knife, so it was obvious to her that he was still frightened. She supposed he should be. Veru was a dangerous animal, after all. She'd probably be scared, too, if she were him. To put him more at ease, she slumped down, placing her back to the fire so she could guard the opening to the cave. That gesture seemed to do the trick.

She could hear him finally move from his position. His normal footfalls were awkward, staggered. He limped over to his pack. "Are you hungry? I don't have much left. But I expect you deserve something for saving my life."

He tossed her a raw hunk of meat. Veru licked it and then swallowed it whole.

"Here's to hoping that was enough for now, little lapa. Speaking of which, it appears to me as if your paw has healed while mine is now injured. How's that for justice?"

Settling himself down on the other side of the fire, he pulled off his thick boots and examined his foot. Veru lifted her head to look at the damage. She could see his ankle was swollen with a purple bruise on the side.

"Looks like a bad sprain," he said. "Best to leave the boot on, else it will continue to swell. I don't believe it's broken though." As he pulled his boot back on, he winced, but smiled at her. "Too bad I don't heal as easily as you, eh?"

Veru snorted and put her head back on her paws, closing her eyes.

"I don't have any water, but there's a nice fast river not too far from here," he said. "I'll head over there in the morning. Might take me a while. I'll have to carve you a new bowl, but if you're patient . . ." He yawned and closed his eyes. "It's the strangest thing. I should be more frightened of you than the wolves, but I'm not . . . I'm very relaxed." His words were becoming more drawn out, like he was having trouble forming them. "It's just that I'm so tired," he said. "I . . ." then Veru heard a soft, musical snore.

She found she rather liked it. Within a minute, she was asleep too.

—

The next morning, she was awake before the sun. Her young man snored loudly in his little cave. She thought his staccato snore was probably what woke her. The coals from the fire were still warm but they wouldn't be for long. Veru managed to use her paw to maneuver some sticks of kindling that had been laid aside on top of the coals.

Once they caught, she opened her jaws wide and wrestled some larger logs onto the fire. The wood sunk heavily into the old coals and smoked for a while before catching, the flames eating the old mosses first before starting on the bark. After they were merrily crackling, she headed off through the fresh snow to look for the river the hunter had described.

It didn't take her long to find it. Her nose seemed to catch the scent of fresh water on the air. It was a crisp smell, a bit ticklish. She could almost taste it on the back of her tongue. After drinking deeply, she caught herself four fish, which took her the better part of an hour, and made quick work of devouring them, then batted two more to shore.

Unfortunately, one of them wriggled its way back into the river and disappeared, but then she managed to catch a much larger fish, so she didn't mind. Though she tried to be gentle with them, they were still pretty badly mangled by the time she got them back to the cave.

When she dropped them with a thump by the fire, she apparently startled the hunter, who was intently carving a bowl from a large piece of bark. He dropped his knife.

"You scared me, little kotenok," he said, picking up his knife. "I thought you left me." Shifting, he grabbed one of his walking sticks and got awkwardly to his feet. "What's this?" He stopped dead when he saw the two large fish lying there in the snow. "Well, I see you found the river. I'll assume you drank, then."

He sighed. "At least one of us will have breakfast this morning. I'll have to make do with sbiten. I don't think I'll be able to head up there today. Despite wearing my boot, my ankle swelled up pretty bad during the night. I'll pack it in snow for a while and see if that helps."

The hunter shifted, taking a step back inside the cave but heard movement outside and turned just in time to see the golden tiger nudging the fish toward him with her nose. She then walked several steps away and sat down. "Are you"—he gestured to her and to the fish—"did you just . . ." His words trailed off, and then he laughed. "I must be seeing things. Perhaps you're full, then? Very well. Spasibo. How about I cook them up and share them with you, eh?"

Veru snuffed but remained in place, laying down with her head on her paws. The young hunter hobbled over, cleaned the fish, leaving the guts on the snow for her, and placed it whole right on top of the hot coals. It smelled good to Veru as it cooked, but it was interesting that the raw food smelled just as good if not better.

Standing up, she wandered over to the cave, slowly enough so as not to scare him, and then laid down again, scooping up the fish innards. Then she began licking her paws. After which she rolled on her side and napped lazily as he finished cooking his meal. Veru felt happy hearing him make appreciative little noises as he ate and licked the hot juices from his fingers. It was nice to see a man salivate over the food she'd caught for him instead of her body for a change.

When he was sated, with a full cup of tea at his side, he tossed her half a fish, which she quickly polished off, then he sat with his back against the wall of the cave and pulled out the strange pipe he'd been playing the night before, just before the wolves attacked. After blowing a few practice notes, he teased her, asking if she had any requests.

"No? Then I suppose I'll just play you something I've been tinkering with lately." He started, then suddenly stopped, lowering his instrument. "It occurs to me that we haven't been properly introduced. My name's Danik. Ohchen priyatna. But then we've met before, haven't we? It's too bad you can't tell me your name."

Lifting the zhaleika to his lips, he began playing, and Veru didn't realize she'd started purring again until his song ended, and he laughed, pointing it out. In the late afternoon, she drank at the river again and hunted fish, which, as it turned out, were ridiculously easy for her to catch. Again she returned with two large fish for Danik. He seemed to accept the idea that a tiger was hunting for him rather easily, all things considered.

After three days in the cave, he was ready to emerge and continue on his journey, claiming that his ankle was strong enough now to forge ahead. He said an awkward sort of das vedanya and began walking in a northeasterly direction. For a time, Veru just stood there at the cave entrance, not knowing what to do, exactly. Should she continue to follow him?

It was clear now that their paths were beginning to diverge. Yet she knew he was still vulnerable. He moved slowly in the snow, using snowshoes now instead of skis. Before he went too far, disappearing over a hilltop, she'd made her decision. Bounding after him, she followed, not exactly in an obvious way; she didn't walk out in the open as he did but stayed out of sight in the tree line. And she didn't follow too closely either.

Around noon, he figured out she was there. He must have caught a flash of her in the trees. "I see you, little paw," he called out. "You need to be careful in the trees. That's where hunters like me place their traps. I'm going to head in soon to check on one. It would be better if you stayed a bit closer if you're intending to follow."

Veru didn't know what to do. If she growled or roared in response, she might frighten him. Wishing she could speak, she blew a sharp breath of air from her nostrils while nodding her head and emerged from the trees slowly. The sound she made reminded her of her sister's sarcastic snort or derisive laugh. Again, it was very unladylike, but it seemed to put Danik at ease. He drew closer, and after he dipped into the forest for a time, emerging with a fresh fur and meat—some of which he wrapped in oil paper and placed in his pack, the rest of which he tossed to her—he began whistling, and walked beside her.

That evening they camped in the open with just a hill at their backs. He played for her again, this time strumming his domra. Veru laid closer to him than she had before, more adjacent to the fire than opposite. The night was cold, and in the morning, when his snores woke her, she was surprised to find his hand tucked between her head and paw.

Raising her head caused him to shift in his sleep. He grumbled and moved closer to her, pressing his face against her side and both hands between them to keep warm. Veru laid her head back down and tried to keep quiet. He slept longer than he usually did, and when he finally woke, blinking the sleep from his eyes, he didn't quite seem to know what she was at first.

Since he clutched at her coat, yanking on it slightly as if to tug it closer or over him, Veru assumed he must have believed she was a fur blanket of some sort. Turning her head toward him, she snorted a warm breath over his cheeks. Drawing back, he rubbed his face, confused, and then understanding dawned, and he scooted back away from her so fast he knocked his head against a tree trunk.

Veru just laid there still, unmoving, watching him. Then finally, she yawned widely, turning her head away so as not to frighten him with her long fangs, then got up, hind end first, and stretched from her paws to her tail and moved to the other side of the dead fire, waiting to see what he wanted to do.

"Uh . . . right," he said, taking off his balaclava and running a hand through his dark blond hair, mussing the long locks so they fell over his ocean-blue eyes in an appealing sort of way. When scraping the same hand across his face, Veru noticed again the pleasing curve of his high cheekbones, the strong, defined chin, and the generous, easy smile. The raspy sound of the light blond growth of new beard on his jaw was something that also caught her attention.

"So, I appreciate the not . . . killing me in my sleep. Especially as I value my . . . you know, life," he said.

Veru was used to men speaking awkwardly or feeling uncomfortable around her. Usually it was frustrating. She was irritated by it, for the most part. This experience was the first time she ever felt the urge to comfort a man and put him more at ease. Perhaps it was due to her being a tiger. She simply wanted him to know she wasn't going to kill him. She refused to believe it could be anything else.

He rose and began packing, mumbling things like, "Strangest thing," and "Never seen the like," and "Maybe I died out there, or I'm dying right now, and this is all a waking dream."

Veru wasn't sure what came over her at that exact moment, but she walked up to Danik, slowly, her head down and pressed it against his leg. He froze completely still in response. "Okay . . . what are you . . ." When she didn't move but did that strange chuffing sound again and rubbed her head against his knee, almost knocking him over, then did the same to his second knee, he dropped his pack and put his hand on the top of her head to steady himself.

"Now, now, girl. Don't forget—I've got a bad ankle. You'll knock me over."

Instantly, Veru sat and looked up at him.

He stared down into those storm-gray eyes, and at the same time she gazed back into his. "You . . . you understand me, don't you?" he asked in wonder. That strange purring sound started again in the tiger's chest. Swallowing, a thought came into the hunter's head, one he couldn't shake. He knew it was dangerous. And terribly stupid. But he did it anyway.

Danik lifted his hand, slowly, purposely. It trembled, and Veru could see the whorls of his fingerprints, the calluses from his work and his music, and the scars and color on his skin from working outdoors. She knew he wanted to touch her. Veru could have moved away in that moment. But she didn't want to. It surprised her, but she wanted the contact.

Men had tried touching her before, and typically she never ever allowed it. The tsarevna Verusha was highly adept not only in the art of evading the unwanted hands of diplomats and suitors but was skilled enough with a knife to keep it between her person and anyone, soldiers included, who attempted to get a bit too close. She'd also always kept Nik or her sister between herself and everyone else as a sort of human buffer system.

With Danik, it was different. He didn't want to touch the girl, the tsarevna, or even the soldier. He wanted to touch a tiger, a beast, an animal capable of ripping him to pieces. This hunter of wild things was unexpected. He was like a soldier who hated war or a captain who loathed the sea. This man killed animals but also seemed to care for them.

There was something about his gesture that was innocent. That felt raw and vulnerable. He wasn't trying to take from her. Instead, he was offering. *But offering what?* she wondered. Kindness, perhaps? That he was curious was certain.

As he reached for her, stepping closer, she felt something more. It was akin to her relationship with Nik. Similar, but not quite. She felt powerful, not used, or helpless. Veru knew she could destroy him with the swipe of her paw, but she didn't want to. In fact, she . . . she wanted him to touch her.

Looking into his dark blue eyes, as deep and full of mystery as the Bering Sea, Veru felt the pull of him like a riptide. The hum of her purr intensified in her chest. It made him braver. Danik swallowed. His Adam's apple bobbed, and her eyes fell on the warm pulse at his throat, not because she wanted to rip into his jugular but because she wondered how it would feel to press her lips against it and smell him up close.

Then his hand was on her head. He didn't move at first. Just left it there. When he stopped shaking, he slid it to her ear, feeling the shape of it and then to her neck, sinking his hand into the deep fur and stroking it as if he were unable to help himself. Veru turned her head when he began to scratch, and her claws extended of their own accord. Never had she felt something so unbelievably relaxing. It was better than easing into a hot bath full of flower petals.

So good did it feel that she almost didn't hear him when he said in amazement, "You're so beautiful, my golden devochka. My kotenok."

Though she knew he didn't mean it in the same way all those other men did, there was something about hearing those words that made her melancholy. It was the same thing every man she'd ever met said to her, with the exception of "kitten." Though, if she considered it long enough, there had probably been some irritating older gentleman who might have used that name for her once.

Even knowing it wasn't really his fault, she backed away from Danik and sat, saddened that it had been her fault that the magical moment between them ended and wondering if there was something wrong with her. Not for the first time, and certainly not for the last, she cursed her beauty and wished she could be appreciated instead for her mind or her skill with a knife.

How lucky her mother had been to find someone who truly saw who she was and loved her inside and out. She could just have easily been married to some old man who used her up and tossed her aside the moment her first hairs became gray. At least she took some comfort in knowing not all men were so fickle. Her father hadn't been. She just needed to find a man like he had been. A task that proved not as easy as one would think.

Danik's frown and furrowed brow showed her that he didn't understand what he'd done wrong. Conceding, Veru turned back and was standing beside him, with Danik bravely stroking a hand down the length of her spine when both of them jumped with a terrible mix of fear and guilt at hearing a roar of displeasure coming from directly behind them. It caused Danik to stumble and fall, and Veru to mentally curse herself for not being as vigilant as she should.

Then they heard a voice that came from an unseen person. A voice Veru knew all too well. It said, "Keep your peasant hands off my tsarevna and back away from her unless you want to be eaten by her sister."

Chapter 14

The Truth Is Always Simple

Danik scrambled to his feet, looking from his golden tiger to the larger reddish-orange one standing a few feet away, her fur bristled as if ready to pounce. "A . . . a sister?" he asked in confusion. "And you . . . you *talk*? In a man's voice? I'm sorry, but I don't think I understand."

"Of course you don't, you glupec. Just move aside so I can make sure you haven't harmed her."

As Danik watched, a boot appeared, after having been tossed into the snow beside them. It was soon followed by a second, and then a man materialized out of thin air. Danik, who had gasped and quickly made the sign of the cross to ward off evil spirits, took a brave step, putting himself between the stranger and his golden tiger. He held up one hand and pulled a chain with a dangling cross from around his neck, brandishing it at the young man, saying, "Begone with you, sorcerer. Her bones and teeth are not meant for your potions. It's bad enough you've bewitched one of the sacred spirits," he said, indicating the red tiger. "I'll not let you have this one as well."

Nikolai snorted and raised an eyebrow. His forehead dripped with sweat, and his cheeks were red and appeared hot and feverish despite the cool air. His eyes sparked with a crazed intensity. If Veru could have told him to stop, she would have. Nik always listened to her, or at least he used to. Perhaps she'd never really known him at all.

Veru huffed and took a step toward her sister, happy to see her, but when Nik beckoned her over to their side, clearly intent on using his magic against her hunter, she wanted to send a clear message that Danik wasn't to be harmed. She angled her body in front of her hunter as if to protect him. When she did, both her sister and Nikolai snarled.

"Move away from him, Veru. I don't want you to get hurt."

The golden cat narrowed her eyes and sat stubbornly. If anyone was going to get hurt, it wasn't going to be her.

As for Stacia, she didn't understand why her sister was wasting their time. They needed to move on. She didn't know why Veru had fallen behind in the first place. It was just like her to head off on her own, batting her lashes at some boy while she was stuck trying to pick up the slack. If she could just stay focused, they'd be halfway over the mountain by now and could get back to the palace and deal with the fallout of leaving. Didn't she understand what was at stake?

Meanwhile, it was clear that the hunter had no intention of letting the newcomer just leave with his golden cat. He intended to fight off the interloper.

Though Nikolai was certainly not the largest, heaviest, or most muscular of their soldiers, both Stacia and Veru expected the brawl to be over with fairly quickly. To say the tussle resulted in unexpected insights was an understatement. Not only were the twins surprised with Nik's willingness to fight Danik but they were amazed with his ease and confidence. It wasn't his usual predisposition.

More often, when tasked with fighting, Nik was bumbling and awkward. His stance was always wrong, and he relied on Veru's constant coaching. The only reason he hadn't been dismissed was Veru's sponsorship. Most of the men preferred his light touch when it came to Veru. Not only did they believe he wouldn't hurt her but they also didn't think he even could.

Still, the twins knew the only way they could justify keeping Nik in the Royal Guard was to train him in another skill. He hadn't taken to the idea of medical training at first, but when Veru insisted that once he was properly trained she'd have no other surgeon in battle, he clicked his heels together and left immediately to seek out the head physic.

Their military doctor reported his progress to them often, stating that while Nik appeared to be interested, his mind often drifted and that his questions occasionally bordered on the macabre and once on the obscene. Veru laughed that off, certain the doctor must have misunderstood. Nik was blunt, to be sure, but that was why she liked him. He never hid who he was from her. Even if he was a buffoon, he was her buffoon.

But now Veru realized there was much more going on with Nik than she'd ever believed. First, he possessed magic and had never told her about it. Then they'd never really had a chance to talk about how he'd come to be in league with the strange monk who'd try to heal her mother and then impersonate a suitor either. Why he would betray her in such a way, she didn't understand. Also, there was the question of how he knew all the secret ins and outs of the palace.

The only thing that was clear was that she didn't know her friend at all.

Even so, what she did know was battle. And what she saw didn't make sense. Having magic, Nik could easily use it to best his enemy in combat, and he wasn't. He intended to fight, and he wasn't looking for a fast exit or eyeing her for help either. In fact, the ineffectual soldier she'd always encouraged before was nowhere to be found.

All of them had been extensively trained in hand-to-hand combat, Nik included, and Veru herself had sparred with him often, so she was well-versed in his skill set, or so she thought. But the Nik she saw now held out his hands and arms at the ready in a powerful stance as he tried to outmaneuver his opponent and reach his goal—her. In all her fights, in all her training with Nik, she'd never seen him move with such dexterity and power. Frankly, it shocked her. She could also see the sweat coursing down his face, and the thought came to her that he might be ill.

Then there was Danik, her hunter and musician. She knew he

was no soldier. But as she studied his trim and lanky form, she realized it was a bit too early to call the fight. With Danik's tendency to slouch, and the easy way about him, and knowing Nik was trained soldier with a few surprises up his parka, she assumed their little tussle would be over quickly. With Nik being the natural winner. But now she wondered.

They locked arms. Nik flipped Danik onto his back in the snow and then headed toward her, a confident smirk on his face, assured he was immediately victorious. Suddenly, his face changed as his feet were pulled out from beneath him, and he fell to the ground with a hard splat. He was dragged through the snow and tossed like a bag of hay several feet away. If Veru was human, her mouth would have formed an *O*, and her brows would have lifted all the way to her hairline.

Though it was true Danik spent long hours outdoors, she now realized the slouching appeared to be mostly due to his intense focus on his instruments. Veru cocked her head. It was true that heavy parkas tended to hide the shape of a body, so she couldn't see much of Danik's frame. To her, he'd appeared wiry, but perhaps that was more due to her current size and shape. All humans were small compared to her.

The fight continued for a while longer, and Veru noticed that Nik was panting heavily. Something was wrong. It was then that Stacia roared plaintively. Danik turned his attention to her sister, and that was when Nik finally decided to use his magic. He cast some kind of spell on Danik, who would have probably defeated Nik on the next blow.

Danik froze in place, lifting his hands. "What have you done, wizard? Can you not fight me like a man? Using your magic to blind me is dishonorable."

Nik ignored Danik and stumbled over to the golden tiger, fell to his knees beside her, and wrapped his arms around her neck.

"Veru!" he panted. "Are you okay? Have you eaten? Did this man hurt you? I'll kill him if you like, just give me a signal. It took so long to find you! Now that we've . . . now that we've finally found you . . . I'm feeling rather . . . dizzy. I think I'll just sit down for a moment. If you don't mind."

Nik's eyes rolled into the back of his head, and he fell face-first into the snowbank. Veru made a grumbling sort of squeak and leapt toward him, nudging his body, but it didn't move. Then she turned as her sister let out a rattle and also slumped to her side. Stacia's eyes closed, but her breathing was steady.

Quick as a flash, she ran back to Danik, who, still blind, clutched feebly at the fur on her back. The golden tiger began guiding him to her fallen friend.

"I don't understand what's happening here," Danik said. "That man said the other tiger is your sister, which makes sense. But he also called you a tsarevna and used the name Veru. The only Tsarevna Veru I've ever heard of is the royal Tsarevna Verusha Irena Vasilia Stepanov, who, as far as I know, is still at the capital and is *not* a tiger."

Veru growled softly and directed the hunter to Nik's body, then poked her nose in Danik's bag. He reached out a hand and found the bag. "What is it? You're hungry? No. You want food? For them? I see. Well, I don't see. Not really. Hold on. I think my vision is coming back. Yes. It is."

Danik blinked rapidly, his eyes watering. Veru could tell when he got his eyesight back completely. He laughed and looked around at everything. Then pointed at Nik, gritting his teeth. "That man is evil. I don't like him."

Veru nudged Nik's body.

"Maybe you want to help him, but I'm still thinking it over. I don't trust him."

She sat down, and he glanced over at her sister, who was slumped on her side. "Well, her I don't mind helping. She needs food and water. I can do that much at least. I don't have any food left though. We were going to head out to check some more traps today."

Danik took a long look at the golden tiger, and the two visitors collapsed in the snow. "Are you sure I can leave you alone?" Reaching up to Veru's ear, he touched it lightly, gave her a lopsided grin, and stood as best he could and hobbled a few steps. "All right. But if he steals you away while I'm gone, I'm going to set my most vicious trap for him, and it's going to hurt." He warned, "Oh, and if he touches my instruments, I'll come up with something even worse."

Before he left, Danik picked up Nik's leg and dragged him over to the fire, not caring that the inert man's head hit several rocks on the way. Danik only turned the fallen man over when Veru stood next to him, making a sort of whining noise. "Fine," he said when it was done. "I can't move the tiger, but I think she'll be fine. I'll even put some snow in the pot for the grand mag-*ass's* tea and fill the hole I dug next to it again with snow for you tigers to drink from. If he wakes up"—he gestured with his hands—"nudge him toward the teapot with a claw to his backside or something."

As he headed out, Danik stopped to pick up Nikolai's magic boots and then chucked them hard at Nik's feet. They landed, bouncing on the bare ground of the hollowed-out spot where they'd slept the night before, next to the listless man to whom they belonged. Veru laid down next to Nik to keep him warm, watching as Danik disappeared.

Once the fire was going again, it was quite warm. Soon all was silent, and it began to snow. The hole was now full of melting snow, and the teapot was bubbling, leaving Veru with nothing to do but guard her sister and friend, watch for Danik's return, and think.

Within a few hours, her young hunter returned with a medium-sized boar. Veru knew that his kill was not something he'd caught in a trap but something he'd hunted on his own. It didn't take him long to cut his catch into sections and set some meat roasting over the fire. He cut up several pieces for her and then placed more by Stacia.

The scent of fresh meat was enough to rouse her sister, and Stacia began licking the food. At first with her eyes closed, and then she managed to swallow a few bites. Invigorated, she lifted her head and took more, gulping down her meal in large pieces until every bit was gone. After a while, she got up on shaky legs and walked over to the fire to drink deeply of snowmelt.

Nik had also roused at the scent of food but had to wait a bit for it to finish cooking. Danik, with an expression of great aggravation, thrust a tin mug of hot tea into Nik's shaking hands. He sipped the steaming brew at first, then began gulping it in earnest and refilled the cup. When Danik passed him a large plate of meat, he didn't even say, "Thank you," or take the offered utensil. He just lifted large portions to his lips with his fingers and chewed and swallowed as quickly as possible, the grease dripping down his chin and fingers.

Danik watched him across the fire with a look of disgust, picked up a fork, and began picking at his own plate. His eyes kept darting to Veru, and Nik and Veru could see they were loaded with questions, but Danik kept them contained, at least for the moment. Instead, he watched them in silence, preferring to observe instead.

After Nik polished off several helpings of roast boar, he finally sat back with a sigh and placed his hand on Veru's back. "Thank you for the food," he said formally. "I . . . apologize for my actions of before. I did not mean to accuse you of anything. My only excuse is that our trip has been harrowing. I have a duty, you see, and . . . anyway . . ." He trailed off as the golden tiger rose and moved out of his reach.

The young man had begun stroking her head and back, and apparently, she wasn't having it. She still hadn't come around to Danik's side of the fire, but as the hunter lifted the fork to his mouth, he couldn't help the smile that lifted the corners of it. He chewed and mumbled, "A duty. Right."

"Yes," Nik echoed sharply. "A duty. In my worry to find Veru, I forgot the toll traveling so far so fast takes on our bodies." Turning to glare at the golden tiger, Nik scolded, "We've crossed the entire Siberian taiga looking for you. I hope you're happy with yourself."

The golden tiger wrinkled her nose in a snarl. She appeared to be very unhappy with the man. Danik, though still puzzled as to their exact relationship, felt his hackles rise and his temper flare. He set down his own mug of tea, and said sharply, "I'm certain she didn't *mean* to leave you. Especially as seeing you're such a charming fellow and all. Not that I have an obligation to tell you, but for your information, when I found her, she was caught in a trap. She's very lucky she healed from her injury. It was quite an awful experience for her, in fact."

This seemed to have an effect on the young man. He actually winced and began speaking softly to the golden tiger, saying things Danik could not hear but wished he could. Then, more loudly, Nik said, "Yes. Well. I'm just glad we found her. We thank you for your help, sir. Perhaps if you can give us your name and residence, we can see to it that you receive a commendation of some type when our task is completed."

Danik snorted and shook his head in disbelief just as he felt the press of a large animal behind him. "Well, hello there," he said, grinning at the big red tiger. Stacia was nudging his bag, looking for more food. "Here you go," he said, holding out his plate. "You can finish mine. I'm full anyway."

She took a hunk of meat gently from his plate and dropped it into the snow beside him, settling herself down next to him. Then he slid cooked boar ribs in front of her, which she grabbed between her paws. They, too, were gone quickly, and when they were, she rolled to her side sleepily, her tail flicking back and forth.

Carefully, Danik lifted a hand and touched her back. Stacia lifted her head and glanced at him, curious, but then laid back down, eyes shut. Within a moment, she began to purr. "How marvelous!" Danik said. "You purr as well." At the same time there came a sharp, low, rumbling growl from the golden tiger. Her dark gray eyes were fixed on Danik's hand as if she wanted to eat it right off his arm.

"All right," Danik said, raising his hands, with a grin and a wink at the golden tiger. "I get the message."

Nik narrowed his gaze on one tiger and the other and then on the stranger seated across the fire. "So," he began again. "As I said, we'd like to thank you for your help and hospitality. If it's not an imposition, we'd like to stay here overnight and then head out on our journey in the morning. We're quite a distance from where we were headed."

"Oh? Where were you headed?" Danik asked.

"That's none of your concern, peasant," Nik snapped rudely.

The golden tiger growled, baring her teeth at Nik.

Grimacing, Nik said, "That is, what I meant to say was, while we are very grateful for the sacrifices you've made on our behalf, we're on official business, so if you could try to curtail your natural curiosity, we'd appreciate it." The tiger's chest rumbled again. He continued. "And rest assured, I'll be certain to take down your name and information so you can be sent a more than generous compensation for any losses you've incurred." He turned to the tiger. "Will that do?"

The golden tiger turned away from him and began licking her paw.

"I see," Danik replied. He gave Nik a tight smile and a nod. Dusting his hands, he rose and explained, "Well, it's fine with me if you all want to camp here another night. Since I'm just a . . . peasant, I wouldn't expect to have much say in such things anyway. As such, I'm just going to go gather some more firewood for the night. If, of course, that is acceptable to the grand mag-ass?"

Danik gave a tight, crisp bow and a flourish, and when Nik didn't even notice the insult but just nodded and began rummaging in his pack, Danik laughed softly. When he was ten or so paces away, he turned around and added, "Oh, I forgot. Tsarevna Anastasia, would you like to come with me? There are wolves in this area, and the thought occurs to me that I might need a protector. If not, and you're still feeling fatigued, then perhaps the tsarevna Verusha might wish to accompany me instead?"

Both tigers immediately rose from their positions and trotted after him while Danik stood there, feet planted in the snow with a wide, knowing smile on his face. Nik stopped his rummaging, his face turning bright red with anger, but he didn't seem capable of response. With both tigers at his heels, Danik turned, whistling, and headed off into the trees, followed by his companions.

When he returned, still whistling, he set his armful of wood and kindling down near the fire and began adding more sticks to the crackling flames. When he was positioned across the fire once more, staring at the obviously livid man across from him, he took out his favorite hunting knife and began sharpening it. "Perhaps you and I should start again. It appears that unlike you, I was taught good manners.

As such, introductions are in order. My name is Danik Andronovich. I'm a hunter and a musician. I don't expect you to shake my hand in friendship at this point, nor do I seek a reward for doing the right thing."

Pausing, Danik set down his sharpening stone, reached out, and placed his hand on the golden tiger's neck, then pointed the tip of his knife at Nik. "But I will have you understand that I would have saved her regardless of her title—rich or poor, old or young, human or animal.

"Now, as for you, I still haven't figured out who or what you are. For all I know, you are the one who did this to them. What *is* clear to me is that you possess a magic of some sort. Whether that magic is good or evil remains to be seen. I don't consider myself qualified to make such a determination. And I don't I trust you to tell me the truth either."

Danik picked up the stone and began sharpening his knife again. He glanced at both tigers, who were now solidly on his side of the fire. "I'm not certain how they feel on the matter. On the surface, it appears as if they mean you no harm, but for all I know they could be"—he waved his knife in Nik's direction—"ensorcelled to obey you. So, until I am satisfied as to what your intentions are with these two creatures, who appear to answer to the names of our royal tsarevnas, I don't intend to let you or them out of my sight."

Nik was so angry he could barely speak. But he swallowed it down, much in the way he did when he dealt with his father oh so very long ago. If the twins hadn't been watching him at that very moment, he'd kill the hunter. It would be too easy. He'd slip on the boots, grab the man's own hunting knife, and slit his throat. But then he looked at Veru. At the way her eyes never left the lean hunter's face. He knew he couldn't. She'd know. She'd never forgive him. Nik's hands tightened into fists.

"Is that your final decision?" Nik asked smoothly, quietly, managing to let not a hint of the emotion he felt escape.

Leaning forward, Danik smiled. To Veru, the gesture was much different than the ones he'd given her before. This smile was much darker. It showed teeth, reminding her of a tiger's fangs. It was full of determination and power. It was a smile that could kill. She found she rather liked it. That he was even capable of it came as somewhat of a surprise to her. Yes. She liked her lanky hunter. Veru liked him very much.

"It is," he replied. "And just so you know," Danik added, "I am no glupec."

CHAPTER 15

Miracles Frequently Arrive in Storm Clouds of Trouble

To make matters worse, the hunter then took out a musical instrument of some kind and began strumming it, not stopping for hours. Hours! Nik yanked his cap down over his ears, trying to stuff the flaps into his eardrums, but it was no use. The man even hummed and occasionally sang. If he could have gagged him, he would have.

It wasn't that Nik had never heard music before. The barracks were often filled with the sounds of various instruments night after night. There was always clapping and dancing. The problem was that music was always associated with celebration and drinking, and those two activities were something Nik avoided at all costs.

His first memory of music and dancing had been during a Christmastide celebration with his mother. For once his father had been in good spirits. Even his mother was in a rare happy mood. Their family had actually gone to a service, since the townspeople had just finished building the brand-new little church and their father wanted to see what all the fuss was about. Not that he'd contributed anything to it in money or labor. No. Not his father. Nik's good old papka just wanted to make an appearance and see if there was anyone around he might wish to impress.

As such, his mama was full of brightness and hope for a change.

They'd stopped at the market, and somehow either his mama or one of his siblings had asked their father at just the right time if they might have some nuts. Papka, not willing to be embarrassed in front of the other men, acquiesced and bought them, making a big fuss over Mama, claiming it was her Christmastide gift and handing her the package with a gentleman's bow and even a kiss on the cheek.

When the merchant clapped happily at his display, Nik's father grinned widely, and even added a few other items to the purchase, including a large bottle of rum. The whole family seemed cheered by the trip to town. When they arrived home, his mother began cooking. She made a Nesselrode pudding for the first time that day. His father even donated some of his rum to flavor it. Nik recalled it being the best thing he'd ever eaten in his life.

That evening, after feasting like kings, Nik's mother took out a box he'd never seen before. She said it had been a gift from her parents when she married their father. Opening a little drawer in the bottom, she took out a key and inserted it into a keyhole, then wound it until it stopped. With her children gathered round her, their tiny tummies full, and their hearts and faces overflowing with Christmastide happiness, their mother seemed joyful too. For the first time in Nikolai's memory, she seemed happy and peaceful, and to Nik, that day she looked like an angel.

The little box began to play a merry and bright tune. The young children clapped in delight and began twirling about the room. When it stopped, they asked her to make it work again. This time, she had Nik wind the box. "How does it play?" he asked. "There's no man inside to work the instrument."

"Open it and look," his mother answered with a secretive smile meant just for him.

He did, and Nik was fascinated by what he saw.

"It's like the comb I use to pull the tangles from your sister's hair," she explained. "They make a sound when they pass over the little metal bumps on the wheel."

"Da!" Nik replied excitedly. "I see it, Mama!"

"Good, moy syn," she replied with a soft smile, then set down the music box and held out her hands. "Now, how about a dance with your mama?"

"But . . . I don't know how."

"I'll teach you. Just follow my steps."

As his mother waltzed with him around the room chanting, "Raz, dva, tri, raz, dva, tri," over and over and laughing as they took turns spinning each other around, his father watched the two of them from his chair in the corner of the room. The liquid in the bottle of rum he'd bought slowly disappeared as he watched his family celebrate. He didn't join them, but his gaze never left them. Instead of dulling his vision, if anything his eyes grew brighter and more focused as they danced. Sadly, his thoughts were far from being "goodwill toward men."

That night, when the young children were all tucked into their beds and Nik had just finished his outdoor chores in the barn, his father, still warmed by rum and his mother's sleeping body, took hold of his first-born and abused him, sorely, wickedly. Nikolai's papka had hurt him before physically, certainly. But to force the same attentions on his son that he did on his mother was not only cruel and vicious but sick.

When his father stumbled back to his bed, Nik vomited all over himself and laid in it, crying for hours. He'd only just cleaned himself and the floor and climbed into his own bed next to his siblings before falling into a nightmarish, restless sort of sleep, when his father called out to him to get up and come help him with the morning chores.

Never again did Nik celebrate, dance, or sing. And never again did he laugh or smile in his mother's presence. He wasn't absolutely certain his mama knew what his father had done to him, but whether she did or didn't, Nik still blamed her. He hated himself for it, too, because a part of him loved her still. It didn't matter, though, because just thinking about her made him want to vomit.

Just like hearing music did.

Veru had asked him, begged him even, time and again to join her at one party or another, and he always made an excuse. He couldn't dance, he'd say. Then she'd reply that she'd teach him. Or he'd tell her that he hated dressing up. She'd only answer that she did too. Nik would try to distract her, saying she wouldn't even notice if he wasn't there anyway what with all the pretty-boy suitors her parents had lined up for her. They'd all be stupid as boulders, of course.

Inevitably, she'd laugh at that and agree with him, which was always a relief. Truthfully, he panicked thinking about a suitor coming to call on Veru. It had never been likely her parents would choose someone ill-suited for her. The tsarina had been particularly intelligent and observant when it came to the aristocracy. And Veru's mama wasn't stubborn about bloodlines either. If she hadn't found a suitable match for either of her daughters from those of highborn lineage, then she would have looked elsewhere.

Nikolai had no doubt that the matches she orchestrated for both her daughters would have pleased not only herself but the both of them, and it would have benefited the empire as well. Such was the skill set of the tsarina Ludmila Marianka Sashenka Stepanov. Though their mother had accepted the friendship between Veru and Nik, he had seen the tsarina eyeing him on more than one occasion, and he knew what it meant. Even without words, her message was clear.

The tsarevna Verusha is not for you.

Though she was gone, he still felt her knowing gaze on him. He knew he wasn't worthy. He knew he didn't deserve her. What he really deserved . . . Nikolai didn't want to think about. But by heaven, if he couldn't have Veru, then he'd make absolutely sure whoever did was worthy of her. The man who came to court her would not only be sun-god beautiful and the most skillful politician but he'd also treat her as an equal and be able to protect her at least as ably as she could herself.

Frankly, Nik wasn't sure such a man existed. Even so, he certainly wasn't going to have some smug, music-playing, hair-in-his-eyes, crooner-slash-hunter run off with the most eligible, most unique, most magnificent woman . . . er . . . tsarevna-turned-tiger in the realm either. Nik didn't care if she hated him for it. He wasn't going to let it happen. If he had to protect her from herself, he would. That's what friends did for each other.

Finally, the man stopped his infernal strumming, and it was like all the tension in Nik's muscles could finally melt away. He rolled to his side with his back to the fire and had just closed his eyes and started to breathe deeply when a tail hit his face. Sputtering, he cracked open an eye, trying to brush the bits of fur from his mouth and was about to lecture Veru for taking so long to come back to his side, when he realized in the darkness it wasn't Veru but Stacia.

"Who invited you over here?" he said moodily. "Keep your tail out of my face, would you? Next time, I'll bite."

In response, the big red tiger lifted her head from her sleeping position and bared her fangs. He got the message but snorted anyway. "Yeah, yeah. You have bigger teeth. So what? I'm not afraid of you, Stacia."

It was quiet for just a moment, and Nik was just about to drift off when Stacia suddenly lurched at him, snapping her jaws just a few inches from his face. He screamed and then laid there panting while she blasted him with a steamy breath from her nostrils, her chest puffing in a noise that sounded to him suspiciously like tiger laughter.

"Cut it out, I said!" he barked, doing his best to wrestle her away, though she was far too heavy for him to move. She allowed his feeble pushes to work, though, and repositioned herself away from him, laying down and giving her tail a final flick in his direction. After that, the camp fell silent until morning.

—

The next day no one spoke at all. Nik was all glares and seething hostility, while Danik was full of whistles and smiles. The tigers appeared to be in good spirits, lapping up the snowmelt from the campfire and the remains of the roast boar that Nikolai and Danik set out for them. Once their packs were on their backs, Nik having donned his other pair of boots, seeing as how the tigers made it clear they intended to walk with Danik for a time by avoiding him and his touch, Nik finally broke the silence, and said, "Well, hunter, where are we headed?"

"Since you asked, I'm thinking I need to figure out what kind of magic you're practicing, Grand Mag-ass."

"I'll thank you to stop calling me that."

"Maybe you will. If I choose to call you something else. But seeing as how you still have atrocious manners and have never bothered to tell me your actual name, I don't really have any other option now, do I?"

Danik grinned, turned on his heel, and said, "Let's move along, Mag-ass."

Stacia could almost see the steam coming out of Nik's ears. She'd never seen him react that way to anyone before. To the other soldiers, he was always deferential. When they mocked him, he let Veru fight his battles. Never once had she seen him stand up for himself. It was interesting.

Most of the time he was simply mooning over Veru, or serving Veru, or asking her where to find Veru. Never had she seen him take the lead or offer insight or direction. He constantly sat at Veru's heels, waiting on her beck and call. He'd never had a voice before. For the first time in . . . ever, she felt she was seeing the real Nikolai. Not that Veru was noticing her friend or his reactions. She appeared to be mooning herself, over the hunter.

Even now Veru was walking right beside the hunter, completely oblivious to her sister or Nik. Every once in a while, the hunter's hand would drift down to touch Veru's head or stroke her neck. Stacia found it fascinating. Veru didn't typically encourage male attention. She wondered what exactly had happened between the two of them during their time apart.

"If you must address me, call me Nikolai," Nik said from a few paces away.

"Nikolai. And where do you hail from?"

"I said *if* you must address me."

"It's a long walk," Danik reasoned.

Nik grunted angrily and spat, "The capital."

"I didn't ask where you worked. You weren't born in the capital, were you?"

"*No*," Nik replied with pursed lips and a bitter, heated expression. "Why must you pry into my life?"

"Simple. You ask me to trust you with the lives of these tigers. Would you not do the same?"

At that moment, Veru looked over at Nik, and his hard expression cracked. "Yes," he answered. Stacia noted that when Veru eyed her friend, his shoulders dropped, and his angry tone diminished to the point of falling away completely.

"Fine. My name is Nikolai Novikov. The small family farm where I was born and raised once laid alongside the Pinega River. It is now gone. The home and barn burned to the ground many years ago. I am responsible for its destruction, along with the deaths of my parents and siblings. I'm the only survivor. Someday I might share the details, but not today."

Stacia was immediately interested in what happened. How old had he been, she wondered. She'd known since he showed up with the monk that there was much, much more to Nik than she had ever believed, but responsible for the deaths of his own family? Was it accidental, or did he mean murder? Just how far would he go to get what he wanted? Clearly much farther than either of them had ever suspected. That he would admit such a thing was nearly as shocking. What did he expect to gain from it? Redemption? Love? Forgiveness? Understanding? Glancing over at Veru, she was surprised to see her sister still staring straight ahead. Did she already know? Didn't she care about her friend? Or had she already cut him out of her life?

If such a tragedy had happened to one of her soldiers, Stacia would have pulled him out of the ranks and sent him in for evaluation. Long ago she'd learned from her father that those who have ongoing battles in their minds sometimes get confused on the battlefield. They make mistakes, very often dangerous ones that could lead not only to tremendous losses but even catastrophic outcomes in war. He'd taught her that it's better to keep them home or send them to specialty training.

Nikolai must have lied in the interviews. That's the only way he would have been allowed into the Royal Guard training. Unless . . . Veru . . .

Stacia again looked over at her sister, but there was no sign or sound of sadness or empathy. She simply stared straight ahead as she walked.

There was, however, a sign of pity on the face of the hunter. His eyes were now fixed on Nik.

"I . . . see," he said. "I'm sorry for your loss."

Nik scoffed. "Why are you sorry? It's not your loss."

"No. But like you, my parents are gone. I never had any siblings. I envy you that."

"I wouldn't. Too many children are a blight on the world. It's like too many kittens. They must be drowned, else they overpopulate the area."

Stacia let out a steamy puff of air. She realized then that if Nik's mental state hadn't already been troubled, it certainly was now. Perhaps the stress of caring for the two of them was making it worse. Perhaps he already knew he'd lost his place, his hope. That what he'd done had not only risked their lives but might destroy the empire. She briefly wondered if he might be under the influence of the sorcerer even now, but she dismissed it. There had been no sign of him.

It was clear that adding the hunter to the mix wasn't aiding Nik's mental state either, but on the other hand, Stacia could also see the benefits of having an experienced hunter who knew the area helping them. She decided it would be a good thing to keep an eye on Nikolai Novikov.

Danik, oblivious to Stacia's thoughts, glanced over at Nik. "I can see you've given this much thought. Though I disagree with you, we'll speak of this another time, when you're less sensitive about the subject."

"I highly doubt that will happen."

Shifting his pack, Danik said, "Pain fades over time. Old wounds cause stiffness, and there are some that fester and need a great deal of digging out or even amputation before they can heal, but in my experience, a body naturally wants to heal."

The hunter winked at Veru and gave her a nod, which again made Stacia wonder what, exactly, the two of them had been through. His words and tone indicated he might have witnessed Veru's healing abilities firsthand, and he had mentioned finding her in an animal trap of some type and that she'd been injured. Stacia wasn't sure it was wise for the young man to know everything about them, but at the same time they needed allies, and her instincts, both human and animal, told her to trust the man. She tended to rely on instinct, even before she'd turned into a cat.

There was also the fact that Stacia liked what the hunter said and the way his mind worked. He was clearly bright and intelligent. As to his thoughts on pain and healing, she generally agreed with the things he said and found wisdom in his counsel. Like Nik, she was still in pain, though it was of a different sort. She and Veru were still healing from the death of their mother.

Stacia didn't know how Veru felt about the loss of their home, the potential loss of the empire their parents had built, and the deaths of many of their closest guards, but to her there were too many to allow herself to think about. When she did, she felt herself shutting down. Going numb. It made her feel like rolling over in the dirt and sleeping through the days, not eating, or drinking, just sleeping until one day she didn't wake up. How could she move forward when loss clung to her like weights around her feet, holding so tightly she couldn't budge?

Perhaps her sister had found recovery of a sort during her time with the young man. Music had always brought their mother peace. In truth, Veru was much fonder of the musicians than she. Stacia preferred the ringing knell of sword clash to the plucking of strings, and the lilting melodies of pipes tickled her spine until she wanted to dance out of her chair and head out of the room to clear her head.

But she could admit it took a great deal of precision and skill to do what he did. Watching his fingers play on the strings made her whiskers twitch, but it reminded her of stringing a taut bow and aiming it at a knot on a tree. When she hit her mark, she could almost hear the arrow sing in the air. His music was not all that different. It required practice and exactness.

That level of determination was something she admired and rewarded in her soldiers. Stacia was also appreciative of the way he'd handled Nikolai. He was firm, intelligent, and he had a backbone. Yes. The hunter had potential. Perhaps there was more to him as well than just hunting and music.

"Sometimes you don't heal," Nik said. "Sometimes a body dies. Then sometimes it comes back again."

That statement caught Stacia's attention.

Giving Nik a puzzled sort of look, Danik replied, "I'm not sure about the coming-back part, but you're right about healing. Still, I've found that if a body has the right motivation, healing can happen in most cases."

Grunting, Nik refused to speak further on the matter.

Toward afternoon, they stopped to check a trap but found nothing. It only took a moment for Danik to reset it, and they pressed on.

By late afternoon, the winds had pick up and clouds had filled the sky, making the heavens as roiling and dark as an angry sea.

"We'd best find shelter," Danik said. "It looks like a bad storm."

"Do you think it will blow over by tomorrow?" Nik asked, speaking loudly over the wind and holding his hat on his head so it wouldn't blow away.

After a brief search of the sky, Danik replied, "I'm uncertain. Storms like this don't normally hit at this time of year. When they do, they're unpredictable. Some blow themselves out quickly, but others can last days or even weeks before a reprieve."

"Weeks?" Nik puffed out a breath and glanced back at Stacia and then at Veru. "The thing is . . . the longer they're gone, the more likely the empire will fall. In fact, there might not even be an empire *left* for them to run if I can't get them back by the end of winter."

"Right," Danik said. "Well, since you haven't really told me what you're trying to accomplish, *exactly*, I'd say we should first prioritize. Let's not worry about the empire just yet, shall we? How about instead we worry about riding out the storm first? You know, surviving? The first time I went out hunting with my cousin and started complaining about my feet, he said, 'Don't look at the mountain in the distance. Just focus on the hill in front of you.'"

Danik clapped Nik on the back and grinned. "What do you say we give it a try, Nikolai mag-ass?"

Nik narrowed his eyes and threatened, with his finger raised, "One more time and I'm getting out my book of spells."

Danik began walking backward, his grin still wide. He caught his hat in his hands just before it blew away. Dark blond hair blew in his eyes. Though the snow and wind stole the sound of his words, Nik could still hear the echoes of the hunter's laughter and just barely make out the phrase by reading his lips, "Do you promise, Maaaag-assssss?"

"Gah!" Nik screamed into the icy particles of snow and wind and stomped behind the irritating man, trying to catch glimpses of Veru before she disappeared into what would soon become a blizzard.

As he walked in Danik's footprints, his head down and his feet sinking deeper and deeper into the snow with each passing moment, he cursed the man with every word he could think of and then, when he ran out of words, he began inventing new ones. Every step marked a new descriptive term for the man, and it soothed Nik somewhat that he could yell his feelings as loudly as he liked, and the man couldn't hear him.

"Pretentious . . . blathering"—*stomp . . . stomp*—"narcissistic . . . overbearing"—*stomp . . . stomp*—"incorrigible . . ." Nik couldn't think of another word, so he paused for a moment, and then the perfect term came to mind. Raising his arms in the air, he shouted loudly, "Povesa!"

Pausing, he glanced around, expecting to see Stacia at least, but no one was nearby. When he looked down, he found he couldn't even see Danik's footprints any longer. In fact, he couldn't see more than two arm lengths beyond his body now in any direction. Panic grabbed hold. He was lost. Nik was about to start cursing *himself* for being a glupec when someone grabbed his arm from behind.

"There you are!" Danik said. "Good thinking shouting like that. The tigers have exceptionally good hearing, even in the storm."

Nik saw a flash of gold and red next to the man. Both the tigers were heavily covered with snow. Stopping near Nik, they shook themselves hard and snow splattered on both him and Danik.

"Best stick close to each other now," Danik said. "Easy to get lost in a storm like this. What were you shouting anyway?"

"Nothing important," Nik said.

Stacia, who kept herself pressed close to Nik, forcing him to walk next to Danik, looked up at him, and despite the freezing temperatures, his face turned red under her scrutiny.

"So where is your next campsite?" Nik yelled above the wind.

Danik shrugged. "Don't have one in this area. I just usually find whatever works."

"No cave? No supplies? No stream or river? Nothing?" Nik screamed incredulously.

Shaking his head, Danik said, "This one came on quick. We're out in the open here with no trees, mountains, or hills, for at least a day in any direction."

"We're not going to survive out here in this. Where's your next shelter?" Nik asked.

Danik rubbed some snow off the golden stubble on his cheek. "There's a small farming town about three days northeast of here called Polensk. When I trade there, the priest will often let me sleep in the stables behind the church. It's the closest shelter."

Shivering, Nik glanced down at Veru. Her entire body was once again covered with snow. Quickly he whipped off his pack and crouched down. Pulling out his magic boots, and with only a moment's hesitation and a single curse, he thrust them at Danik. "Okay, here's how this is going to work. Since you know where we're going, you put these on, and they help you walk or run very, very fast. You'll also be invisible—that is, we won't be able to see you either. We can move at the same speed you do, at least I think we'll be able to, but the catch is, you have to be touching us. Otherwise, you'll lose us like we lost Veru, and out here, that will be a death sentence."

Danik took the magic offering with a raised eyebrow, then quickly slipped off his snowshoes, handing them over to Nik, who stared at them a minute, knowing he'd never run quickly in them, but put them on anyway. After shoving his foot into the first boot, Danik realized they were too small for him. He was about to yank them off, when, somehow, the fur and leather stretched and reformed itself, covering his foot perfectly. Danik laughed. "This is amazing!"

"Yeah. I know," Nik said grudgingly. To his surprise, Danik didn't disappear. It seemed that part only worked in tandem with his tunic, which was still in his bag. Nik wasn't going to complain about that or offer anything else. "Huh," he said. "Never mind about the invisible thing. I can still see you."

Taking Nik at his word, Danik put on the second boot, held out an arm, and wrapped it around Nik in a half bear hug so tight, Nik wished with all his might he could push the hunter's arm away, but he knew it was the safest thing for the moment. Since Veru was on the hunter's other side, the man bent his lanky form in an uncomfortable position, tugging Nik along with him so he could wrap his other arm around her neck.

Nik wasn't sure how they'd travel that way, but he went ahead and put his arm around Stacia, too, hoping the boots would work with the four of them. "Take a few steps at first," Nik said, "to see if it will work with four. It might be that you have to be touching all of us. In that case, I'm not sure what we'll do."

Together the group walked awkwardly and then tried trotting a few steps, but it quickly became apparent that Stacia could not keep up. Even wearing snowshoes, Nik was moving faster than Stacia as a tiger, that meant the magic only worked with the person being touched by the boot wearer.

"It's not working," Nik said as they ran back to her.

"It was worth a try," Danik replied, bending to remove the boot. He'd gotten one off and was hobbling in the snow, trying to balance to slip his foot back into his old boot, when a powerful wind knocked him down on his back. Veru stuck her face near his, and when she did, her paw touched the forgotten magic snow boot. Instantly, the fur and fabric began knitting itself around her paw, and the laces lifted of their own accord. They stretched out, encasing her other legs, then broke off, creating three new boots.

When her feet were covered with the new magic snow boots, now colored gold and white, the laces continued to move up her body, enclosing her chest and circling her belly. Quickly they molded and hardened, becoming a gold leather saddle encrusted with diamonds and gemstones.

Instead of a bridle and reins, the laces created an elaborate carved handhold made of gilded copper wire. Thin gold-leaf panels fanned out behind the saddle, unrolling along her flanks and down her back to her tail. Each one looked like a peacock feather with a large silvery gemstone, the same color of her eyes, placed at the tip.

Nik stood still, amazed at what he saw, while Danik sat frozen in the snow, his hand gripping the second boot. It was Danik who moved first, quickly pulling off the second boot. "Tsarevna Anastasia? Would you mind coming closer?"

Swallowing, still not moving, Nik said only, "She . . . she prefers Stacia."

"Stacia, then," the hunter said as the red-striped tiger approached, blowing a puff of warm air into his face. "If I may, Tsarevna," he said, and held out the magic boot for her front paw.

She lifted a paw gingerly and barely touched it to the boot when the same amazing enchantment began its work on her. This time the boots and saddle changed to a new color. Instead of the white, silver, and gold like her sister, Stacia's saddle was made of the finest black leather, sable, and mink fur.

The back portion also fanned out but in a different shape—less featherlike and more geometric. It was also a bit more intricate than her sister's, and it gleamed with sparkling opals, pearls, diamonds, obsidian, and onyx. In the center, where the black braided handhold wove itself, the saddle created the largest, most brilliant emerald either of the men had ever imagined.

When Stacia turned toward them, Nik noticed for the first time just how green her eyes were. They were the same color as the emerald. The black suited her, too, he thought. It was dignified. Regal. Also, she was still in mourning for her mother, so it was appropriate. Not for the first time he had the impression that he was looking at the next tsarina and that he should bow. Instead, he just dipped his head in a respectful nod, but he didn't think she noticed.

"Obviously we are meant to ride," Danik said. "Is such a thing proper?"

"I don't know about proper," Nik said. "You're the hunter. Are they strong enough to carry us?"

Danik scoffed. "Even if they were simply average tigers, which I assure you they are not, they would be strong enough."

"Okay," Nik said. "We'll try it. But you must stay together," he warned the tigers. "And if you tire, stop. Agreed?"

Veru made the chuffing sound, and Stacia echoed it. They moved next to each other and waited. Hoisting their packs, both men headed toward Veru. When Nik insisted he take Veru, Danik held up his hands, not wanting to argue. Danik tried throwing a leg over Stacia, but he was violently repelled as if thrown off by magic hands.

Nic tried with Veru, and the same thing happened. They tried again with the same results.

As they laid in the snow, Veru and Stacia switched, each heading to the other man. This time Danik was a bit more reluctant to try, but when Veru nudged his boot, he got up. He stuck a foot in a stirrup and swung his leg over, settling successfully into the golden saddle. Nik frowned and hurriedly did the same with Stacia.

Still moody, Nik dug his heels into Stacia's sides, earning him an irritated growl from the big cat. She headed over to her sister regardless. "Now remember to stay close to us. You'll have to lead since you know the direction of the town."

"That's if I can find it in this mess."

"Let's pray you do. Or even this miracle might not save us."

With that, Veru and Stacia began to run, picking up speed and stretching their legs. The men bent over their bodies, trying to shield their faces from the stinging snow and ice.

Though Nik could tell Danik was communicating directions to Veru by bending close enough to her ear so she could hear his voice, to him it looked like the murmuring of a lover, and it chafed him worse than the leather saddle beneath him.

Hour after grueling hour, they pressed on, and then somehow, through the ice and snow and awful dark of night, Nik spotted a light, then two, and three, and suddenly, before him was a surprisingly welcome and familiar sight. Even though Nik had never been back to a church again since that Christmastide service so very long ago, knowing he had nothing to believe in and could never trust anyone again, there was something about seeing those soaring onion domes, belfries, and chapels that promised warmth and safety that made him desperately wish he was wrong.

CHAPTER 16

In Russia, the Church Domes Are Painted Gold, So God Takes Notice

Danik pressed forward to a stone wall that surrounded the church and reached up to find a hidden lever. Once they were inside the wall and had the gate secured behind them, the tall trees and the high wall blocked out a good deal of the wind. The two-story building was fairly large for such a small town and even appeared to be sporting not one, not three, but five domes.

Nik's little church had only raised one dome. He wasn't certain that more domes meant more faith in the membership or more importance to God or even a larger populace, but more domes certainly meant more cost in construction. Danik led them around the back end of the church to a smaller structure and opened the barn door, letting them inside.

Once the doors were shut, they all shook the snow off their bodies and found a clean, empty stall far away from the other animals. The few horses, milk cows, and nanny goats made a fuss at first when they smelled the large predators who entered their cozy little home, but luckily the church didn't own too many farm animals, and they settled down quick enough when the tigers left them alone.

Danik thought this behavior very odd. Under normal circumstances, any prey animal should have driven themselves crazy, kicking the stall and screaming until the priests rose from their beds to find out the cause of the ruckus. He suspected the storm was the cause of their strange behavior, while Nik argued it was likely the magic.

Even if Veru or Stacia had an opinion on the matter, they either didn't care overmuch, or realized they couldn't communicate their thoughts on the subject regardless. Whichever was the case, the twins were exhausted from their long run and collapsed on the hay Danik and Nikolai spread out for them in the stall. Letting them rest, Danik set out to find a few supplies left in the barn for travelers. He returned with some blankets, a lantern, and a large metal can stuffed with kindling.

When the lantern was lit and the fire had been started, he filled a pot with water from an ice-crusted barrel outside, brewed them both some tea, and began cooking a pot of oats from the feed left for the horses. Then he filled the trough with water for the tigers. "I'll have to hunt or trade furs for meat for the two of you in the morning," he said. "For now you should rest. I know you're hungry from that run. Let's see if we can get those saddles off you."

Veru and Stacia looked at one another. Both were weary to the bone. They stood again, shaking the last of the melting snow off themselves, and Veru took a step toward Danik. Then, before he could touch it, the saddle shifted, moving and shrinking. Stacia's moved of its own accord as well. Soon they'd transformed once again into laces that slipped off their backs and drew in on themselves until they formed just one boot each. The tigers danced, backing up in the small stall, and the snow boots slipped off their paws, forming human-sized footwear once more.

Nik picked them up and placed them in his pack. After a long drink, Veru and Stacia slumped down in the straw on their sides and closed their eyes. "I'm worried about them," Nik said. "Running with the boots takes a lot out of you. Eating is necessary after a long run."

Danik stroked his cheek. "I could try to wake the rector. See if he has any meat. I'm not sure how he'd handle it if I tried to ask for a quantity large enough to feed them. I was hoping to disappear before I had to explain their presence. Or ours, for that matter."

"There's a goat back there. We could give them that."

"I'm not sure the priest would take too kindly to the idea of losing his favorite cheesemaker."

"Like you said, we'd disappear before he knew."

Danik grew cross. "Perhaps you soldiers take what you want, but that's not how it works out here in the hinterlands. The rule we abide by is to leave behind as much as you take or work it off. And if you can't recompense those who give appropriately, then you leave double or even triple the next time around. If all of us took without giving, people would stop making a place for us, and then where would we be? Traveling is difficult enough as it is. All it takes is a few unscrupulous people to ruin it for the rest of us. I, for one, don't want to be stuck out here without a safe haven. That's as good as a death sentence. Isn't it?"

Nik held up his hands. "Fine. We'll do it your way. But I'm warning you—if I think Veru is failing, I'll cut off your arm and feed that to her before I let her die."

"Believe me, I won't let it get that far. I'm a trapper. I'll keep them alive. Besides, you're the city boy. You probably smell more like home cooking than I do. I'm sure she'd rather eat you first."

"Shut up," Nik said, kicking some straw, getting dust in Danik's mouth, and making the fire spark.

"Stop acting like a soplyak," Danik said, banging the cookpot with the metal spoon. "You'll start a fire. An uncontrollable one, I mean." Bending over to stir the meal and grunting in satisfaction, he scooped some oats into a dish and thrust it into Nik's hands. "Here, eat and try to sleep." Picking up his own bag, he took the pot with the remaining hot oats and stood up. "I'm going to set some traps. I'll be back in a bit."

Nik finished most of what was in his bowl quickly. Kneeling by Veru, he held out the bowl with the tiny remaining portion at the bottom. "You should eat something—try to lick it out." She wouldn't even open her eyes. But at least he could see that her chest was moving in a rhythmic pattern. Giving up, he tried with Stacia. "Are you hungry?"

The red tiger had a difficult time opening her eyes as well but managed a soft rumble in her chest. Her tongue darted out toward Nik's bowl. A glob of sticky oats clung to her rough tongue. She swallowed it and went back for a second and third lick, keeping at it until no trace of the oats remained. He dipped the bowl in the water and brought it back to her. She downed three bowlfuls, splattering him in the process with a mixture of trough water and tiger spittle.

"Thanks a lot," he said when she laid her head back down. He stayed long enough to see her exhale a long, weary breath, and then her body began moving like her sister's in a steady sleeping rhythm. Nik placed a hand on her shoulder and said softly, "Seriously, Stacia, spasibo. Thank you for carrying me through the snow. You saved my life. I won't forget it."

Nik tried then to give some water to Veru, but she wasn't interested. All he got from her was a very slight moan or growl. Either that meant she wanted to be left alone, or she was very bad off indeed. Still concerned, he laid down, fluffing the straw as best he could to make a pillow, and nearly the moment he shut his eyes he was fast asleep.

Nik didn't stir at all until very late the next morning when he was awoken by the sound of movement and snuffling in the straw nearby. At first he couldn't recall where he was, exactly. It was very dark in the barn, and he could hear the wind and sleet beating hard in fits and starts against the sides of the structure, sending freezing gusts of air through the cracks in the wood. Panic seized him for just a moment when he sensed the presence of another man nearby, but then he counted slowly, deliberately relaxing his muscles as he listened to the sounds around him, letting his dreams and nightmares fade and reality take over.

Slitting his eyes open at last, he could see that Danik had built up the little fire again and was alert and moving around. Nik wondered how long he'd been asleep or if the hunter had slept at all. The snuffling sound was coming from Veru. The hunter knelt beside her, his hand on her neck. Apparently, he'd just gotten her to drink. Yawning sleepily, attempting to appear at ease, and not at all bothered by the fact that the hunter had been able to coax Veru to drink but not himself, Nik asked, "How's she doing?"

"A bit better," Danik replied. "She's eaten some. It revived her enough, I believe."

Curious, Nik rose to a sitting position. He discovered then that hay stuck to every inch of him, including his hair, but Danik had somehow managed to end up hay-free. He tried swiping it off, only to find the little sticks had penetrated the fabric of his clothing. Grunting in irritation, he started plucking it free and tossing it aside. "What did you feed her?" he asked as he plucked.

"Mostly mice. A few rats."

Nik's mouth fell open.

Danik went on. "Look, I know it's not preferred, but it's what's available. They're nice and fat in the winter, so they've got a little bit of meat on them at least. It's better than nothing. Don't you think?"

Nik smacked his mouth in a distasteful way and gave the hunter a sour look. "Vermin? You fed the tsarevna of the Kievian Empire vermin?"

"Tsarevnas. Plural." Danik turned and stared down his nose at Nikolai. "You seem to have a rather bad habit of forgetting Tsarevna Anastasia. Why is that, I wonder? I would think you'd be grateful to the lady who saved your life."

"I am, of course . . ."

"Would you rather they starved?"

"No . . . but . . ."

They were interrupted by a banging on the barn door, which was then subsequently opened. A friendly voice called out, "Privet, puteshestvenniki. I saw your light and brought some food and blankets. It seems the storm is going to last a bit longer, so . . ." Though Danik had risen to his feet quickly and tried to head off the visitor, he hadn't been quick enough.

The young man stood just outside the stall, looking in, with the open door pressed against his back. His face was as pale as if he'd just been visited by a heavenly messenger. As Danik approached, the frightened priest turned, allowing the door to nearly close on its squeaking hinge. He didn't run, though, or drop the stack of blankets, which was something. Nik had to give him credit for that.

"Zakhar. Wait," Danik said, holding up a hand. "Please let me explain."

The priest swallowed, turned back, and then thrust the blankets into Danik's hands and closed the stall door firmly, making certain he stood on the opposite side of his visitors. He made the sign of the cross and mumbled a prayer, then wet his lips and nodded to Danik. "Yes. Explain, but quickly, my friend."

"Zakhar, this is Nikolai Novikov. Nik, this is Zakhar Balakin, the head student of seminary training here at the Saint Vladimir II Cathedral. He's in his final year of study before entering the priesthood and taking the final vows."

"Priyatna Poznakomit'sya," Nik said politely.

"Yes, yes," the young cleric said stonily with a barely perceptible nod, his eyes fixed on the large animals behind Nik. "It is lovely to meet you as well on such a beautiful day as this. God has blessed us, has He not?" He tried to smile, but it was a half-hearted effort, and it faded rapidly. After that, the priest crossed himself and mumbled a silent prayer again.

"Zakhar, calm down," Nik said. "They're not going to hurt you."

Gripping the stall door, the priest gave Danik a look of panic and replied in a tone that was half irritation and half anger. Nik pressed his fingers over his lips to stop himself from laughing. He figured if Danik could make a priest angry, he shouldn't feel so bad. "What is this you are saying, hunter?" the priest asked. "How can you mean they will not hurt me? Do you think I am as faithful as Daniil, who sat all night with the lions? *No*. I assure you. I am not. God knows I am no prophet. Every day I beat the wickedness from my breast as I prepare myself for my calling, and every day I know I fall short."

The priest demonstrated the act by actually thumping his fist against his chest. When Nik heard the hollow sound coming from the priest, he actually did laugh, but quickly controlled himself when Danik gave him a glance that promised retaliation.

Not even noticing the laugh, Zakhar continued his litany of self-recrimination. Danik opened the stall door, standing with his own back to it to keep it open, while the priest clasped his hands behind his back and began pacing. "Surely, there is not a more ill-prepared student working under the illustrious Bishop Rudimov. I shall fail in my studies, and when I do, I'll return to my hometown in shame."

"No, Zakhar, you won't," Danik said. "You're the smartest man I know. Bishop Rudimov must believe it too. Why else would he make you the top student of your class?"

The priest paused in his pacing. "Personally, I believe it's due to his thinking I need to practice my leadership skills. I fear he finds them lacking."

Danik took hold of the priest's shoulders and shook him. "I need you to stop running down this mental road like you always do and put that big brain of yours to better use."

"Yes, my friend, of course. How can I help?"

"See?" Danik put an arm around the priest's shoulders, turning him toward the stall and guiding him inside while grinning at Nik. "That's why I came here. It wasn't just for shelter. If anyone can figure out how to help the tsarevnas, he can."

Scowling, Nik jerked to his feet. "Hold on. We never agreed to bring more people into this. How do you know you can trust him?"

Danik looked at the priest and jerked his head toward Nik with a can-you-believe-what-he-just-said expression. "Uh, because of this?" Danik said sarcastically, yanking on Zakhar's cassock.

"Hey. Stop that! Show some respect for the calling," Zakhar chastened, pulling his black robes away from Danik's fingers and smoothing out the wrinkles. When he wasn't satisfied with his robe, he started tugging on the belt, attempting to adjust it, when the other two men suddenly stepped in front of him, blocking the view.

"How about we keep that thing knotted up properly?" Danik said. "We wouldn't want to offend anyone of a . . . um . . . delicate nature."

Zakhar frowned. "What are you two going on about? There's no one else here."

When he began removing his belt again, Danik grabbed it and cinched it tight. "Yes . . . there . . . *are*," he insisted. "We told you." He jerked his thumb over his shoulder and whispered, "The *tsarevnas*."

Zakhar looked from Danik to Nik and then over their shoulders at the two cats behind them who sat still in the straw, watching the whole interaction. At that moment, Veru lifted a paw and gave it a long lick. Lifting an eyebrow, Zakhar straightened his shoulders, gave the two men a tight smile, and said, "I see the problem."

"You do?" Nik asked hopefully.

"Yes," he answered with a monkish mien. Slowly, he began backing out of the stall. "We do have some training in counseling for those who have been"—he fluttered his fingers together and wrinkled his nose—"*addled* in their thinking for one reason or another. I'm certain we can set up some sessions that will help you—"

Danik cut him off. "I don't think you understand, Zakhar."

"Oh, but I do, my friend," the priest replied with a condescending sort of head bob. "Let me just find the right person who might understand your particular . . . affliction, and then I'll introduce—"

"Exactly," Nik said, catching the priest by the arm before he could escape. "Allow me to make proper introductions."

"No. That's not necessary," the priest said. The tranquil appearance he'd been momentarily displaying on the surface melted away like fat in a hot skillet. Now the man was crackling and sizzling with emotion as he attempted to wriggle out of Nik's grasp.

Nikolai could sense the man's fear escalating. He was nearly ready to bolt, and they couldn't have that. "Stacia," Nik said, "if you will kindly block the door, he might accept the fact that we're not going to allow him to leave."

The large red tiger rose, and the priest nearly clawed Nik's face in an effort to move away from the big cat. Nik obliged him by stepping around him, placing his own body in front of the priest's, allowing him to cower in the corner of the stall.

"There now," Nik said. "You can see there's no escape until you've heard us out. We mean you no harm, sir. I know it must feel difficult to set aside your fear, and yet you must. Until you do, your mind will not function as it should, and according to Danik, we need the knowledge you possess. At the very least we could do with some supplies and the certainty that you won't cause a panic among the seminary trainees or the townspeople while we are in residence."

After the priest had calmed himself somewhat and nodded mutely, Nik waited a beat and then, taking pity on him, added, "You might close your eyes and breathe in deeply. Hold it and count to five, then breathe out while counting to five again. Do this for a series of five to ten times until you feel yourself centering. Remember that you are alive, and while you are alive, no matter what trials life brings, you still have a chance to overcome them and attain your goals. If you wish to pray during this time, you may. Whatever helps you focus is a good thing."

They waited while the priest did as Nik suggested, breathing in and out, in and out. After a few rounds of deep inhales and exhales, his body relaxed, and he seemed much calmer. "Better?" Nik asked.

"Yes, spasibo," Zakhar admitted. "Where did you learn such techniques?"

Stacia was wondering the same thing at that moment. Nik didn't answer the question though. Instead, he summoned her. "Tsarevna Stacia, will you come and greet young priest Zakhar?"

Uncertain as to how exactly she should "greet" someone formally as a tiger, Stacia walked over next to Nikolai and glanced up at him briefly, hoping for some kind of suggestion. When she didn't get one, she then attempted what she would have done had she been asked to welcome someone of status in the grand ballroom while wearing a formal gown and a tiara. She extended a regal head nod coupled with a slight curtsy, but she suspected it ended up looking more like a tiger stretching its back.

"Veru?" Nik said next, turning to the golden tiger.

The golden tiger rose to her feet and walked over to Nik, then sat down next to him, looking as regal as a tsarina on a golden throne. To drive the point home, Nik placed his hand on top of Veru's head and gave Stacia's shoulder a brief pat, showing he was unafraid.

Clearing his throat, Nik began. "Several weeks ago, a dark sorcerer entered the royal palace with an undead army. His intention was to force one of the tsarevnas into wedlock." Nikolai glanced at the tigers briefly but went on. "As you may have heard, their mother, the tsarina, has recently died, leaving them as the heirs to the empire. When weaving his magic spell, the sorcerer discovered they were in possession of two charms left to them by their mother. I was aware he had long been seeking these charms, but I did not know the sisters were in possession of them."

Stacia and Veru wondered if Nik was purposely leaving out his role in inviting the sorcerer into the palace to make himself look better in the eyes of the others or because he desired or needed their trust or if he simply couldn't admit it to himself.

"As far as I can tell," Nik went on, "the charms have no monetary value but are magical in nature. Somehow the sorcerer became aware they had the charms and dropped the charade of a suitor, choosing to attack instead. This is when the sisters were transformed into the creatures you see before you.

"I was not a direct witness to this change, having taken a severe blow to the head. But their soldiers, such as survived, were. One of their men-at-arms roused me after the attack and bid me take them to his mother's people on the far side of the mountains, where they have stories of such transformations occurring. He hoped they might know how we may be able to change them back.

"We . . . bumped into your hunter friend along the way. He, too, is hearing this story for the first time. As a priest, I do not know your views on magic. I am in possession of some magical gifts of my own, and I have seen such things used for both good and evil.

"As for me, I don't care much about the morality of such things. In my experience, I judge most everything and everyone evil until they prove themselves otherwise. Trusting others is not easy for me. But I will do anything to help them. And if that means leaning on the two of you," he concluded, glancing at the priest and Danik, "then I'll suffer it. For their sakes."

Zakhar said nothing for a beat, and then he stepped forward. To Nik's surprise, he put a hand on his shoulder, offering him an understanding smile. "Someday, my new friend, you are welcome to share the history that led you to become the man you are today. I am more than happy to hear the tale. If you wish to invoke the seal of the confessional, you may. I am always at your disposal."

Taking a step back, he straightened his cassock and bowed deeply. "My royal tsarevnas . . . no . . . *tsarinas.* I am deeply honored to welcome you to our humble cathedral and will endeavor to make your stay here as comfortable as possible. In addition, I will devote every mental faculty at my command to the resolution of your extremely interesting dilemma. Please grant me forgiveness for my awkward and most embarrassing display."

He straightened abruptly. "You must be famished! Danik! You should have said something," he hissed testily, punching his friend in the arm as he quickly exited the stall. "I'll be right back. I just need to raid the larder."

They heard his footsteps running to the barn door and then the sounds of him heaving it open. A moment later he returned. "Er . . . how do they feel about the preparation of the food? Should the meat be well done or partially cooked?"

Danik snorted. "Tigers usually prefer it raw."

"Right, right."

He ran off again, and Danik called out, "I just fed them rats and mice, so don't overthink it. Just bring them something *big*."

"Yes, of course," Zakhar said as he pulled the barn door closed.

"And don't forget to keep this to yourself!" Nik added.

True to his word, Zakhar brought them a huge roast for dinner that evening. It was cooked rare.

—

Unfortunately, or perhaps fortunately, the storm didn't blow over for many days. Though Zakhar kept them fed, he wouldn't be able to hide how much meat had gone missing from the kitchen stores for long. Danik promised he'd hunt some big game as soon as he was able to, after the weather broke.

Zakhar appeared one night, when they'd been there about a week, very eager to share a discovery he'd made.

"So what is it you want us to do, exactly?" Danik asked.

"It's as I said. I have taken vows not to touch the sacred texts or enter our school of study after hours, but you have not."

"But don't you consider yourself breaking vows by having us do it for you?" Nik asked.

Zakhar paused and thought about it for a moment. "Perhaps this is why you are here. God's laws should not be broken, this is true. But not all laws are God's, though there are many who would make the unlearned believe otherwise. It is for this reason I decided to study the doctrines of the church. Don't misunderstand me—I have a deep and abiding faith. But I have seen those in high positions abuse others and take monies, offering forgiveness to those who have no intention to change or display any feelings of penitence. I study because I wish to follow the Lord and His law, not necessarily laws instituted by men, especially those I deem unjust.

"Still, our bishop is a good man. And I honor my word. Yet I know the texts. Christ was able to save the woman taken in adultery while not breaking a law technically. He also paid a tax with a coin from a fish's mouth. In this case, I feel I am not strictly breaking a law I have promised to obey, and yet I am still helping those who need my help. This is a charity and a kindness, is it not? I feel in my heart it is the right thing to do."

"I like the way you think," Nik said. "So what are we looking for?"

"I asked our bishop if he knew of any texts related to tigers. My expectation was that he would say no. However, when he took a day to consider it, he recalled one. It was not contained in a book, but it was an ancient scroll kept in a golden box. Not even he had ever read it, as it has always been handed down and kept secret. He has sworn to protect it and never to open it. The vault it's contained in must be opened with a key he keeps on his person or on his bedside."

"I can do it," Nik said quickly. "With the boots, he won't even see me."

"But how will you know where to find the box?" Zakhar asked.

"Simple," Nik said. "Draw me a map."

Chapter 17

A Story Is Soon Told, but a Difficult Work Is Not So Soon Completed

It didn't take Zakhar long to return with a pot of ink, paper, and a blotter. Working by lantern light, he quickly sketched out a very detailed drawing of the cathedral. Both Nikolai and Danik were amazed at the precision and neatness of his work. When they commented on it, he said, "This is much of what we do for our studies. We copy old texts, translate books from one language to another, and occasionally add our own artistic flourishes. I've been able to commit many passages of scripture to memory through duplicating pages over and over again."

Nik pointed to the outline of the cathedral. "This looks like . . ."

"A cross?" Zakhar suggested. "Yes. It is meant to look that way. This is a double cruciform or two-piered cathedral. It is a symbol of Christ. When you enter the doors, the mind should be drawn to holy things." Zakhar paused for a moment, then straightened. "There is much symbolism found within the church and the ornate rituals therein. I confess I delight in the exploration and study of such things, but unlike most of my brethren, I also find signs of our Lord in the more natural and simple things of the earth, such as the birds that sing in the morning outside my window or the flowers that bloom in the springtime."

"For me, God is in music," Danik said, clapping his hand on his friend's shoulder. "When I want to feel close to God, I just imagine I am singing with His angels. Perhaps that isn't good enough for some, but I've found it is enough for me."

"The day I went to church was the day God destroyed my life," Nik said. "So I'd prefer it if the two of us stayed on opposite sides of the universe. I'm sorry if that offends you."

"My new friend, don't apologize for your feelings. You are not the first I have met, nor do I expect you will be the last to impugn God for worldly sorrows. I do not condemn you for doing so, nor do I imagine does He. What griefs you have experienced in life only He and you know. Someday I hope you will look upon Him as I do. For me, it helps to picture God not as a destroyer or as a negligent, withdrawn figurehead but more as a kindly grandparent or as a wise old monk."

"I . . . I don't have any experience with any of those," Nik replied. "The only men I've ever known older than myself have been evil."

"Well then," Zakhar said, "I will think on this further and pray for you, my friend. Perhaps an answer will come to one of us when God, or you, is ready to share more, da?"

Nik gave Zakhar a nod, and the priest turned back to the drawing.

"Now, where was I? Ah, right. Where you would normally enter is here, at the porch through the main doors. The area just beyond that is called the narthex. Then you hit the main body of the building, called the nave. You'll see the bishop's throne there and two wings; this area is called the transept. You'll be entering the building at that door with my key. The east transept contains a picture gallery. There's a hidden door on that side that opens behind some curtains.

"Once inside, you'll head into the nave, turn right, and then instead of entering the sanctuary—where you'll find the altar, the candelabra, the censer, and so forth—you'll head up to the second floor through a door hidden in the mural of Saint Peter. This will take you to the bishop's living quarters. His key will be on a leather strip hanging about his neck or on the bedside table next to him. I'll bring you some shears to cut the string.

"After you obtain the key, assuming you haven't woken him and caused an alarm, then you head to the west transept. Use the key to open the vault containing the cathedral library. Head down the stairs. Once inside, you'll find shelves and shelves of books and the tables and chairs we use for our study. When Bishop Rudimov showed me the box, he locked it up in a large cabinet on the far back wall. It was approximately here." Zakhar quickly drew a series of bookshelves, desks, and the cabinet and circled it.

"That's fine," Danik said. "But what I don't understand is how one key can open the door, the cabinet, and this box. That doesn't make sense. Did you see him open the box?"

"No," Zakhar said. "The same key opens the vault and the cabinet. It's the master key to everything inside the cathedral. Some of us, like me, have keys to the outer building. As to the box, he didn't open it, so I don't know if his key will work with that."

Nik asked, "Is it built like a music box?"

"A music box? I'm not sure. Why?" Zakhar asked.

"I have a little experience with those," Nik explained. "My mother had one. The key is sometimes stored inside the box itself, in a hidden compartment."

"That would be helpful," Danik said. "So when do we do this?"

Zakhar sucked in a breath. "Tonight."

—

That evening the wind and snow blew only lightly. Danik hoped it was enough to cover their tracks by morning. He'd accompanied Nik to the side door of the east transept, and they'd used Zakhar's key to enter the building. The cathedral was quiet; the seminary students, cooks, and priests were all asleep, as it was well past the midnight hour.

Wind rattled the windowpanes as they slunk through the dark passageway lit by nothing but fleeting reflections of moonlight peeking through clouds reflected off the snow-covered ground. Finally, they entered the nave, and Nik, invisible while wearing his tunic and magic boots, took hold of Danik's arm. "Meet you on the other side," he whispered, and then he was gone, heading up to the bishop's apartment to secure the key.

Danik heard the soft snick of a door and saw a passageway open and close behind the bishop's throne, then he quietly made his way across the room and through the west transept, stopping to wait by the locked door. He estimated it would take Nik approximately the same length of time it would for him to complete a song, so he tapped one out with his fingers on his leg. When he finished the first song, a second, a third, and began a fourth, he started to worry.

Nik headed up to the apartment, proud of the fact that he was quieter than a mouse tucked into his winter bed beneath layers of white snow. There wasn't even a stutter in the bishop's soft snores to indicate his sleep had been disturbed. The problem wasn't Nik. It was the sleeping posture of the bishop.

Zakhar's information was accurate in that the bishop wore the key around his neck. The issue was that the bishop apparently slept on his stomach, and he was a bit on the beefy side. That meant removing the key from around his neck was going to present something of a challenge. It wouldn't be impossible; it just meant waiting until the bishop rolled over.

Nik did exactly that, but the bishop was soundly, deeply, comfortably asleep. After several moments of waiting, Nik decided he needed to take further action. Looking around, he found a quill and tried tickling the man's nose with the feather tip. All that accomplished was eliciting a sneeze and a rather phlegmy snort.

He knew then that more drastic means were necessary. Taking hold of the man's quilt, he gave it a little tug. The man tugged back. Nik pulled again, this time removing the quilt to the other side of the bed. With eyes still tightly shut, the bishop reached out, grasping at nothing until at last he found the blanket and yanked it back over himself, then proceeded to snore as before.

Frustrated, Nik slowly removed the man's pillow in tiny degrees until his head fell, startling him awake. "What? What was that? No, sir. Not in my church," he mumbled, grabbing his pillow from the floor where Nik had dropped it. He stuffed it beneath his head and rolled to his side. Nik mouthed a thank-you to the universe and waited a beat for the man to start snoring again before moving closer.

The gold key hung on a leather cord tied about the man's neck, and Nik examined it from a few different angles, trying to see where he could slip the shears against it without having the cold metal touch the man's skin. Finally, he found a good spot. Taking a deep breath, he stepped forward and made the cut.

Sadly, the key slipped down the man's nightrobe before Nik could catch it. The strip of leather still hung outside his neckline, so, very slowly, he took hold of the tie and pulled it up, up, up until it came free. Just in time, too, because the bishop giggled, rubbed his chest, and rolled to his other side.

Nik got out of the apartment with his prize as quickly as he could and headed down to the rendezvous point only to bump into Danik at the door. He took hold of the other man's arm, guiding him as quietly as he could toward the west transept, and the two made their way over to the vault.

"What took you so long?" Danik hissed as Nik removed his boots.

"He was sleeping on top of it," Nik replied. "You have to know that things aren't always going to go easily and account for it."

"That's easy for you to say when you aren't the one waiting."

Fortunately, the rest of their escapade went according to Zakhar's plan, with the exception being that the vault was incredibly dark. There were no windows at all in the cathedral basement, so they stumbled about a great deal and were constantly on alert thinking someone would hear them and come down to check on the noise. Apparently, the wind was sufficient to block out most of it.

Once they found the cabinet, it only took a moment to discover the box. Locking everything behind them, they returned to the barn, doing their best to cover their tracks, leaving the snowfall to do the rest. If everything went according to plan, they'd get what they'd need and return the box, along with the key, before anyone was the wiser.

By the next morning, they realized it wasn't going to be that easy. They'd believed the key would be needed to open the box, but that wasn't the case at all. Zakhar arrived early, bringing some breakfast and a small haunch of deer meat for the tigers.

"Do you have it?" he asked excitedly.

"We have it," Nik replied with a yawn. "But we haven't figured out how to open it."

"Let me have a look."

Danik handed the golden box to Zakhar and took out his hunting knife, portioning the deer meat for the tigers. Once they had their breakfast, he cleaned his hands with the warmed water from the fire and began preparing their own meal. Nik sat back against a post, sipping hot sbiten with his eyes half closed.

Meanwhile, Zakhar was flipping the box upside down, left, and right, over and under, pressing on jewels and twisting different knobs. When a small piece of the lid clicked, and he pulled it open, he crowed gleefully. "I knew it," he declared. "It's an elaborate puzzle box. I've only heard of these, but I've never seen one."

"A puzzle box?" Nik said, opening his eyes. "What's that?"

"They can be simple, requiring only a few simple moves, or they can be very complex boxes requiring more than one hundred moves. So far, I've only managed a few. My guess is that this one is a complicated box with lots of levels."

He kept at it while they ate, discovering a magnetized gemstone that was embedded in a removable piece of wood. If they held it on the underside of the box, they could hear something moving back and forth inside. Zakhar was certain that was the key that fit into the keyhole he'd just uncovered. They just needed to access it. Unfortunately, he needed to head to seminary classes, so he left the box in the hands of the other two men for the morning, promising to return and bring them an early supper. Zakhar had hoped to retrieve the key and the box before the others woke that morning, but he couldn't take one without the other, so they'd have to wait and risk the bishop discovering one or both was missing.

Nikolai and Danik took turns trying to solve the puzzle, until finally Danik had the idea to push down on a small piece they'd both been overlooking on the corner. It must have opened something inside the box, allowing the key to drop into another compartment. Once it was there, they slid open the outside wall, allowing the key to fall into Nik's palm. He inserted it into the keyhole on the top, and with a click, the box fell open.

Four sets of eyes stared down inside the box—two human and two tiger. Hands shaking, Danik reached inside and carefully took out the rolled piece of parchment. They debated for a moment if they should wait for Zakhar to return, but it was only midday, and they'd have to wait for several hours. Unable to resist, Nik tugged on the leather tie, loosening it, and unrolled the scroll.

Holding the parchment up to the light, Nik squinted at it for several long moments and then passed it off to Danik, saying, "I can't read it. It's in some other language."

"Let me see."

Danik perused it for time as well but was equally frustrated, though he did take some time to admire the beautiful art in the margins. "Uh, Nikolai?" he said. "Take a look at this."

He pointed to some beautiful renderings of tigers, with very familiar coloring.

"Yeah," Nik replied, after a moment of comparison. "I'd say it's them. Unless you've come across any that look like them before."

Danik shook his head. "Stacia maybe, but she's much redder than most tigers. They tend to be more orange. And I've certainly never seen any that look like Veru." He took the parchment back and pointed out a section at the bottom. "Doesn't that look like a cat to you too?"

"Not sure," Nik said. "Might be a panther of some type."

The two spent several hours studying the drawings, trying to figure out what they might mean. When Zakhar arrived with the evening meal, they showed him the scroll, and when he unrolled it, he, too, was fascinated with the art, but told them he couldn't read the text either, even though he was well-versed in several languages. Then he peered at it more closely and gasped, tracing his fingertip lightly over the whorls and ink, focusing intently on one section.

"What is it?" Nik asked.

"Did you see something we didn't?" Danik pressed.

Zakhar stepped back and turned away, clasping his hands behind his back. He paced a bit, mumbling to himself, saying things like, "It can't be," and, "Impossible." Finally, he turned back and smiled at the others. While rolling up the scroll tightly, he told them that that the bishop had instructed all the students to look for the missing key, and it was imperative that the gold box and the key be returned as soon as possible.

He'd brought a waterproof leather bag for them to wrap the scroll in, and as he carefully rolled the beautiful work and stored it, he hoped the suspicion he had didn't show on his face. Like them, he believed the art reflected the tigers, but unlike them, he was skilled enough with letters and scrollwork to recognize the work of certain reputable artists, especially those he'd seen often. And Zakhar could absolutely identify work done by his own hand.

Though Zakhar had no recollection of creating such a piece, and it was much more masterful than anything he'd ever done, he'd found the hidden signature instantly. That he didn't know the language meant nothing. It could simply be a copy of something he didn't know. But how could it be? Had he created it before, during a waking dream? Or perhaps someone had duplicated his style? But why? It didn't make sense.

What was clear to him was that he was involved. He had felt it from the moment they'd explained their situation. As much as Zakhar loved the church, when they moved on, he'd need to go with them. It was as simple as that.

Handing over the bag, he said, "Will you trust me?"

"Yes," Danik said instantly.

"Depends," replied Nik.

"Your magic boots and tunic. Will you let me borrow them?"

"Why?" Nik asked. "What are you going to do?"

"The storm has broken. Already I have risked much to supply you with food. Tomorrow before sunrise is the time to leave. I'll use the boots and tunic to return the box and leave the key on the bishop's staircase, along with a letter saying I have decided to return home. I will accompany you on your trip. If you will have me, that is."

"Of course we will have you," Danik said immediately.

"I'm not certain about this," Nik replied, rubbing his chin.

"It is not you I ask, gentlemen," Zakhar said quietly, his eyes trained on the tigers. Getting down on one knee in his cassock was awkward, but he managed to do it and bowed to the two tigers. "My tsarinas, I have come to the realization that there is a part I need to play in this. If will you accept me, a humble priest, as your servant on this journey, I offer my services. I cannot provide protection in the way of swordsmanship, but I sense you can take care of yourselves in that regard. I am, however, well-spoken; and I'm well-versed in many languages; and I'm good with maps, quill, and ink."

Raising a finger, Danik said, "I, uh, am also good with maps."

Zakhar waved his hand, trying to shush Danik, while keeping his eyes trained on the tigers.

"Will you have me?" Zakhar asked earnestly. Never in his life, even since he joined the priesthood, had Zakhar wanted something more. The mystery of the work done by his own future hand intrigued him. He needed to understand the how, the why, and the when. Every part of him knew he must accompany them at all costs.

Stacia glanced at her sister, who rumbled in her chest in reply. Then both cats approached the brown-eyed priest and sat down before him, inclining their heads in a gesture that the men took to mean approval.

"Thank you," he replied with a smile and reached out to pat Veru awkwardly on the head before rising and tripping on his robes.

After Zakhar exited the barn with the magic boots, the bishop's key, and the empty gold puzzle box tucked into his pack, leaving them with instructions to meet him outside the cathedral wall an hour before dawn, Nik said, "I sure hope we can trust him."

Danik clapped a hand on Nik's back. "I still don't trust *you*, if that's any consolation."

With a snort, Nik built up his straw bed, put some more wood on the fire, and tried to get some sleep. It was going to be a long, cold night, or several nights, before they found shelter again.

The moon was bright on the snow in the predawn hours as they made their way outside the cathedral walls the next morning. They had the tigers walk first so they could obscure their tracks in the snow and then hid in a copse of trees as they waited for Zakhar to appear. Finally, they saw him emerge from the gate in the stone wall. Quickly he found their trail and followed it into the trees.

"Do you have the boots?" Nik asked.

"Yes. Here. Take them," Zakhar said, pressing them into Nik's hands.

While Nik turned and placed the boots down on the ground near the tigers, Zakhar took off his heavy pack and opened it, showing Danik what he'd brought.

"Redistribute some of this to your bags," he said. "The cooks aren't going to be happy with me after seeing how much food I've taken, but we have to feed the tsarevnas."

"Thank you," Danik replied, moving some of the food to his bag. "I'll hunt when we have time to stop."

"When we have time? I'm afraid I don't understand."

"You will soon," Nik mumbled from his crouched position.

There was a *whoosh* as the magic boots transformed around the paws of each tiger, but this time instead of fancy saddles, the laces created long leather reins and straps that tied each tiger next to one another. Then they lifted in the air and wove together an ornate double-benched white sleigh, trimmed in gleaming black.

When the magic was finished, Stacia danced in place, a jeweled collar of onyx around her neck with a large emerald resting in the center on her chest. It was attached to a set of black diamond–studded reins and a harness. The laces on Veru seemed to have a difficult time deciding what to create. At first it settled on a shaft bow, but then the design switched to the same jeweled collar and harness as Stacia's, but hers was made of gold and silver, with a huge white diamond at the base.

Zakhar's eyes rested on that priceless gemstone, and his fingers twitched. "Look at that," he said with something akin to awe and reverence. "Think how many of our suffering children such a prize would feed and house."

Glancing up at him in that moment, Veru wondered for the first time in her life just how many children there were under her authority that went without food or shelter. She knew her mother had programs set up, but honestly, she hadn't paid much attention to them. She'd been much more concerned with the Guard, border patrol, and diplomacy efforts. There was so much she didn't know. She looked at the gemstone adorning her sister. Such things were beautiful, indeed, but they meant little to her and her sister. Neither twin cared much for the jewels or crowns or furs that came with their station.

There were times when they dined well at the palace, and there were certainly foodstuffs they enjoyed. She, in particular, enjoyed trying new dishes with spices and flavors offered when guests or diplomats from other lands visited. It was one of the reasons she wanted to command the military. That way she could explore the far reaches of the empire. Veru had an intense desire to see, taste, and experience everything the world had to offer. She wanted to meet the people, learn their customs, taste different foods, and study new languages.

Of course, she'd serve her own country and people at the same time. She'd always told herself that she'd be the best daughter of the empire she could be and would lead the military capably. But what if her dream was selfish? How could she head off to explore the things she wanted when her own people were suffering without the basic necessities of life? She was always willing to suffer alongside her men when it came to long marches, scanty food, or fighting the elements. Veru had learned to put her men first, and in return they trusted her to lead.

And yes, they'd encountered hungry faces along the way and had parted with blankets and rations when they could spare them. She'd always informed her mother of such things upon her return to the palace. But who would take care of those people now? Stacia? Her sister and the troops who followed her practiced the same policies Veru did. They'd never spoken about the many, many programs their mother had run on her own. Who would take those over? Perhaps it no longer mattered. If they remained tigers, there would be no more empire. No one to watch over the people. For the first time in her life, Veru felt anger over what had been taken from her, from them. They needed to fix their tiger problem and then return and defeat the sorcerer who had done this.

The laces danced in the air next to Stacia, as if waiting for something or someone else before finally settling down. The red-and-black-striped tiger, oblivious to the thoughts of her sister, narrowed her eyes, sensing the magic was trying to tell her something important. It was portentous. As if trouble loomed, or something was coming for them. She could almost grasp it, but she was unable to define it.

"I . . . I had no idea the magic could do this," Zakhar said.

"We didn't exactly either," Danik replied with a grin. "Glad you brought food though. They'll really need to eat after this. I also hope you brought a map."

"I did," Zakhar said, running a hand along the beautiful sleigh. "Why?"

"Because we need to get to a military outpost on the far side of the mountains. Climb aboard. Priests carrying food get to sit first."

Zakhar took the back seat with all the packs and traps, leaving the front open for Danik and Nikolai. Picking up the reins, though hesitant to use them, Nik said, "Are you ready, ladies?"

Stacia cocked her head back to look at him, and Nik could have sworn she was smirking. Leaping forward, she began to run. The sleigh slid to one side and then the other, threatening to capsize at first, but then Veru started running, too, and they soon found a rhythm. Pulling together, they moved faster and faster, and before long the countryside around them blurred, and everything became white.

CHAPTER 18

Death Is Not Found behind Mountains, but Right behind Our Shoulders

It took them two days to reach the Ural Mountains and another two to climb the mountains and find the road that led to a military outpost overlooking the West Siberian Plain. Since they agreed it wouldn't be smart to introduce the tigers to the soldiers at the outpost, Nik and Zakhar went to gather information from the soldiers, while Danik and the tigers hunted.

Veru managed to catch a ground squirrel and a marten, but Stacia only found a nasty badger who refused to come out of his hole no matter how deeply she dug. He used his long claws and sharp teeth to cause her enough trouble to make her give up on him and take the squirrel Veru dropped at her feet instead. Since they were only out hunting for a short time, Danik returned with just three fat grouse, which would be enough for dinner for the men. They returned to their meeting place to find Nik and Zakhar waiting.

"What did you discover?" Danik asked them.

Nik answered, "Not much. It seems this area is populated by Samoyed peoples, not Evenki."

"Will they hunt the tigers?"

"I don't know," Nik answered. "Some live in the forest, others along the rivers. They live in clans and claim territory based on family lines using signs or symbols of their clan to designate borders."

"Did they say where to find the Evenki?"

"The man I spoke with believes they are located much further east. Almost all the way to the sea."

Danik removed his hat and slapped it against his thigh. "That far? Is it even safe for us to travel across the lands of the Nomadic Alliance? I know the tsarina was passing laws to protect those who wanted to immigrate to the empire, but I don't know how easy or safe it will be for us to travel through. Tell me again exactly what instructions the soldier gave you before departing the capital."

Pacing, Nik thought and said, "The man told me head to an outpost and ask for directions. Then he mentioned something about hunting and bringing a gift of meat or pelts to the people in exchange for information. He warned me to tell no one about the tigers until we found his people, the Evenki, saying they would believe us and help us and that we should ask for a shaman. He never mentioned any other tribes or clans."

"Right. So he had to have known that his mother's people were located on the far side of the Nomadic Alliance. If he did, then why have us stop at an outpost? Why not tell us to travel all the way to the Great Sea?"

"He said his father had been stationed at one, and that's how he met his mother, who was Evenki."

"That doesn't make sense," Danik said. "If the Evenki are located that far out, why would they come to the borderlands? How would his parents even have met?"

"I don't know. Trade, maybe?"

"Council meetings," Zakhar suggested. "The Nomadic Alliance council leaders would have met with diplomatic leaders from the empire from time to time. It would make sense for them to travel to more neutral territory when discussing accords. A traveling diplomat would have taken a contingent of soldiers stationed at the outpost, especially those who knew the traditions and languages of various clans."

"Then we need to seek council leaders. Perhaps they will know how to find the Evenki or the shaman we seek," added Danik. "I say we head out, walking at a normal pace. Let me set some traps so we have some furs and meat to trade with. Then we'll see what we find. I figure the least we'll get is information."

Agreeing with Danik, the men headed down the mountain and out onto the Great Siberian Plain. They made camp along the Ob River, and Zakhar and Nikolai learned how to bait and set traps from Danik. Within a week, they had a growing pile of squirrel, arctic fox, ermine, otter, lynx, rabbit, and even some highly prized sable.

He taught them how to skin, flesh, and stretch the pelts, reserving the meat for themselves or the tigers. Once Nik had been taught how, he took to the skinning of the animals quite easily, which Danik appreciated. Skinning the animals had always been the part of his job that he'd hated the most. Zakhar was also happy to let Nik do the job, though he didn't mind the stacking or the stretching. Counting and numbers had always been something of a fascination for him.

When he asked Danik the price each pelt would fetch at market, he kept a running total on parchment and began calculating the numbers against how many meals each pelt could provide for the hungry. Soon Zakhar was the first to rise in the morning, very excited to see what catches could be found in the traps, and he was very quick to remove the animal and bait the trap afresh. Though he still prayed over the fallen creatures of the Lord, he counted it a blessing that their flesh could be used to feed and clothe the hungry and naked.

Zakhar would even hum or sing songs of thanksgiving as he wrung the mud from the bodies of the poor dead creatures. Danik, though he loved music and singing, and despite the fact that hunting was his work, had never developed a fondness for it. He didn't deny the beauty of the furs, or their warmth, and he even agreed with Zakhar about the money and the feeding of children, but to him the memories of taking the feathers or the fur from the animals would never leave his mind.

He'd come across bands of hunters who were so thorough in their work that they left no trace of animals behind to repopulate the area. These men didn't hunt for meat or to create a warm coat or blanket but to line one of many cloaks of wealthy men or to fill a wardrobe with beautiful colored fur coats and hats that were rarely used.

It saddened him in a way that made his heart ache. On nights when he played his music, he'd seen creatures of the forest draw close, even when he had a roaring fire between them. He'd fed forest squirrels before and watched them play and their antics as they stuffed their cheeks full to the brim with nuts and then scurried to hide them from one another, screeching when a fellow dared to dig up his brother's hidden stash, making him laugh.

To him, each animal had a soul, just like the tsarevnas. Even when he didn't know Veru for who she was, he knew she was special. He couldn't have killed her even then, no matter how beautiful her coat. The thought that some man might end her life simply to use her as a floor decoration or to hang her on a wall sickened him.

Though it was his job, Danik felt that someday there would be a reckoning for what he'd done. Following the tsarevnas and serving them was a small way he could pay a penance. He felt he owed it to them and to every creature he'd hunted to keep the tigers alive. If there was a way to make a livelihood from his music, he'd prefer to do that, but without his parents, he wasn't sure how.

Still he played at night, even while noticing that Nik cringed every time he did. He thought to inquire about it, but Nik simply rolled over and tried to sleep. It was obvious he still didn't want to share anything about his past. Even so, the music was the only thing that soothed Danik after a long day of hunting. It was how he apologized to the creatures that remained. Most of the time his songs were melancholy, but occasionally, he remembered the squirrels or the birds and played happy, lilting songs for them.

When Danik announced they had plenty to trade, they set off downriver, seeking signs of a settlement. The first group they came across were less than friendly. In fact, they shoved the three men to the ground, grabbed their bags, rifled through them, and took everything they had.

Then they used their fishing spears to point them in an opposite direction so they'd clearly get the idea to vacate the clan's family lands.

"Well, that didn't exactly go as planned," Danik said, circling back to the camp.

"Not at all," Zakhar agreed. "It was a good idea, though, to leave behind the tigers and most of our gear and pelts. I'll calculate our losses when we return. Thank you for that, Nikolai."

"Yes, thank you," Danik echoed.

"Right. Well. I've learned from a few tough lessons over the years. There are some things I'd rather not risk."

"Makes sense. I, for one, am delighted that my domra wasn't taken. Spasibo, again."

"Pozhaluysta."

"But are *you* glad, Nikolai, my new friend? You don't seem to enjoy Danik's music, even though he is quite good at it. Do you not find his skills excellent? Perhaps you are used to musicians of exceeding talent, having been one of the trusted palace Guardsmen."

Nik clasped his hands behind his back, an easy thing to do now that his bag was emptied. He spoke hesitantly. "It's not that I don't appreciate Danik's ability. As far as musicians go, I'm sure he's quite good. I simply dislike music in general."

"Certainly not all music," Zakhar exclaimed. "What about songs celebrating our Lord?"

Shrugging, Nik replied, "I'm not too familiar with most of those."

"Music of Christmastide?" Danik asked.

"Those tunes I especially loathe."

"But . . . why?" Zakhar said.

They waited, staring at Nik until he grew uncomfortable. Finally, he said, "My mother had a music box. She loved it, and I did, too, for a while. Then she died, and it was horrible. Anytime I hear music, it reminds me of her death. And that's all I want to say about it."

Zakhar replied in his soothing priest's voice. "I'm so sorry, my son. If you ever wish to talk more of this, you may speak to me of it by requesting a confessionary meeting in private."

Nik snorted. "Sure. When I want absolution, I'll ask you."

"I did not mean to suggest you needed absolution. I merely wanted you to know that I am available as a priest, should you wish to use me as such."

"I'll keep that in mind," Nik said.

"I've never met anyone who hates music," Danik interjected. "How can you blame music for a tragedy like that. It just doesn't make sense."

It didn't seem like Danik wanted anyone to answer. He appeared to be simply talking to himself. Zakhar patted him on the arm as if attempting to soothe his feelings as well. Nik's mouth twisted up in a wry sort of smirk. He wondered if by just saying what he did he'd been able to spare himself music in the evenings. If so, it would be worth it. Nik doubted it would work for long though. Trying to keep Danik from his songs would be like trying to keep Zakhar from his studies.

The priest had brought a fat tome of scripture; it had been one he'd personally been copying from various scrolls, and it was filled with his own flourishes on each title page. Nik didn't tell him, but he thought the artwork quite beautiful. When Zakhar wasn't reading scripture, he was studying maps or creating new ones with various colors of bottled ink and parchment. As they camped that evening, Zakhar worked on his rendering of the tigers pulling their sleigh with the three of them riding along. Nik was holding the reins, and there was a painted smile on his face.

Had he been smiling? He couldn't remember. Actually, Nik hadn't recalled smiling in a long while. The last time he could remember being truly happy was when he'd danced with his mother. Since then he'd been enthusiastic, such as when he thought he might win the affection of a tsarevna, but he hadn't felt happy, at least not in a carefree sense. Glancing over at Danik that evening as they camped, he could almost see the distress on Danik's face. Even without an instrument in his hands, the man was drumming his fingers against his leg.

He sighed, acknowledging that even to him it was too quiet in the camp. "It's fine with me if you want to play something," he said to Danik. "I'll suffer through it."

"No. No. I don't want you to remember your mother like that."

"It's not like you've played that one song of hers anyway."

"Can . . . can I ask what song was it? The one in her music box?"

"I don't know what it was called," Nik said quietly.

"If you hum it, I might be able to tell you the name."

The fire crackled and popped, and when Nik put his hand on Veru's back, she looked up at him with her dark gray eyes. He saw the human girl beneath the face of the tiger at that moment, and something inside him broke. Music filled his mind as he closed his eyes, and the image of his beautiful mama on that long ago night when she'd asked him to dance came clearly to his mind. She'd placed his hand on her small waist and took his other hand in hers, and together they'd twirled on their warped wooden kitchen floor.

Soon real music filled his ears as notes were plucked that matched the tune he'd been humming without realizing it. Quickly he dashed the tears from his cheeks as Danik lowered his balalaika. "It's called 'The Turning of the Troika,'" Danik said. "I'm sorry about your mama."

"Don't be," Nik replied, getting up and heading to the other side of the fire. He laid down, stuffing his empty bag under his head. "She's better off dead."

The next morning they repeated the process, heading in a different direction. When they came across signs of a clan, they took only a bit of meat and a few pelts, leaving the tigers and the rest of their supplies behind, and walked on until they found a group of people fishing at the river. After showing them the items and making a gift of a beautiful fox pelt and a brace of birds, they were taken to meet with the head of the clan.

Fortunately for them, a translator was located who knew enough of their dialect that they could present their case. When Nikolai and Danik weren't certain how to proceed, Zakhar easily took over. They seemed to understand that he was a holy man and thus were very willing to help him on his quest, especially when he said he had a writing he needed to show to a shaman.

They said they had such a man in their clan, and he was brought in and introduced to them. There was then a sharing of certain foods and drink followed by a cleansing ritual. Zakhar was fascinated by the entire process and longed to document every part of it. Then the shaman asked politely if he could see the document they had mentioned. Unfortunately, they had left everything back at the camp with the tigers, but Zakhar, unwilling to say nothing, described the document in detail as best he could, promising to return with it in the morning.

The moment he mentioned the three tigers on the parchment, everyone in the little yurt froze in place. Then they glanced at one another with wild eyes. The shaman hissed a command, saying everyone should leave except the translator. When all had departed, he asked very pointedly, "Have any of you three seen or killed a tiger?"

Zakhar looked at his companions, who nodded. "All three of us have seen tigers, yes. We have not killed any."

"How many did you see?"

"We have seen two."

"And the colors?"

"One is gold and white and the other is red and black."

The shaman sat back and took a deep breath. Then he looked at the translator and said a string of words in their language. Immediately the translator rose and disappeared, ducking out of the yurt opening. He returned with another man who was dressed for travel. The shaman gave the man instructions. When he was finished, the man nodded soberly, then stood by, waiting.

"What's happening?" Danik asked.

The translator presented Danik's query to the shaman, who answered,

"This is our best guide. He will take you to the site of our Great Gathering Grounds. You must hurry. You have only two days to travel many, many leagues before the end of the final winter clan meetings. If you move quickly enough, you may catch up with the one you seek before she travels too far toward home.

"We will give you as many rations as we can spare so you don't need to stop to hunt. When you find her, our guide will make introductions. Should the great leader of the Evenki agree to meet with you, tell her all you have told me, and she will listen.

"If she decides to help you, she will tell you where to find the third tiger, the gray-and-black shadow who stalks the taiga, roaring with his pain, invisible and unseeing. Only then will you be ready to ascend the Dreaming Mountain to find the Storyweaver of the Sky, the One Who Hears All—Above and Below, the White Shaman of the Tundra."

Before they knew it, the three men were hurried from the yurt, the guide following behind them. Runners quickly approached packing their bags full of raw fish, reindeer meat, and extra clothing. The pelt they'd given as a gift was returned to them, and they were shown many more pelts they'd be gifted in exchange, along with a lightweight and sturdy yurt their guide strapped to his own back. Danik attempted to refuse them, but the good people insisted. The three men humbly bowed and promised to return someday bearing many gifts of their own.

Quickly they headed back to the trees where they'd left their things, their silent guide following behind them. When the tigers emerged, he was shocked, but within a few moments, he dropped his pack in the snow and bowed himself to the ground, mumbling words no one understood. Gently, Zakhar took hold of the man's arm and bid him rise.

Nik took the magic boots from the pack left with the tigers while Danik fed them some of the reindeer meat given to them by the clansmen. Once the sleigh was created, they ushered the wide-eyed guide onto the sleigh, offering him the reins, and then the rest of the men climbed aboard. As the tigers began to run, each of the men lowered their heads in fur-lined cloaks to keep the bits of stinging sleet and snow from their eyes and sunk even deeper into their thoughts.

Now they knew they weren't only seeking a shaman. They were looking for a man they'd only heard of in children's tales.

The Storyweaver of the Sky.

The One Who Hears All—Above and Below.

The White Shaman of the Tundra.

As if that weren't enough.

They were also supposed to find a third tiger.

One who was gray and black, perhaps blind, in pain, and, to make matters even more difficult, invisible.

Chapter 19

A Sinking Man Will Cling to Foam

The landscape blurred around them as the tigers ran, and they arrived at the site of the Great Gathering Grounds before they broke up their final meeting. Their little group waited in the trees while the guide disappeared, heading into the melee to find the one they sought. When he returned, he gestured that they should follow him, but held up a hand to indicate the tigers should stay, bowing several times and pressing his palms together in apologetic supplication as he did.

Trailing him, the men wove between bands of people who were breaking camp and setting out in all directions, heading home now that their council meetings had been completed. Their guide led them to a large reindeer-skin tent, one of the only tents left standing in a sea of bare log tentpoles and smoldered campfires. After calling out and hearing a brusque reply, he opened the flap and bid them enter. They did and were escorted to seats by a crackling fire, where they found a woman still adorned in her council attire.

She was a handsome woman with bright, shrewd eyes and a straight posture. Her dark hair was braided with colorful strips of dyed reindeer leather and was tied at the ends with tufts of white fox fur and polished animal bone, which also trimmed her magnificent beaded coat. Danik envied the skillfully made reindeer moccasins and might have asked about trading for a pair if he thought such a thing wouldn't be inappropriate.

Before they could even begin to form a word, she spoke in perfect Russian. "So, you have come to hunt our great striped treasure, have you? You mean to take him from us?"

"Not at all, my lady," Zakhar interjected quickly. "We do not come to hunt. We are only here to—"

She held up her hand. "I do not speak to men of the cloth any longer," she said. "You mean to convert my people to your ways. To convince us to be like you. Too many of our young men and women have left us. Seduced by your world. By your promises of a better way of life. Who is to say which way of living is best?" She gave Zakhar a long look. "No. I would venture you have not yet discovered your own path in life. Such a one cannot think to guide others. You are as yet untested."

Next, she appraised Danik. After examining him, taking in his clothing, glancing at his hands, she asked, "What are you?"

"What do you mean?" he asked in reply. "Do you ask about my family, my town, or my profession?"

"Yes. Exactly."

Danik opened his mouth, but he was uncertain where to begin.

"I see. You, like your priest, are lost. And you?" she asked, turning to Nik. "It is easy to discern you have the stance and training of a soldier, and yet there is much more to you beneath the surface as well. And I fear if I pierced the skin I would uncover a putrefaction so vile no surgeon or shaman could cut it away quick enough for it to heal." Leaning forward, she picked up a stick and jabbed it into the flames, then held the hot poker up, gesturing to the young man. Looking into Nik's eyes, she said, "There are some sicknesses you must burn out. Only sweat, tears, and searing pain will bring an end to the suffering. Even then, there's a chance it will reemerge. A watchful eye is key."

She sighed and tossed the stick back into the flames. "Very well. If we are meant to leave things of great import in the hands of the untrained and inexperienced, then so be it. Take me to your tigers. Perhaps they will not prove to be as disappointing as you three."

The men rose uncertainly, feeling as if they'd just been scolded by a schoolmarm, and headed out the tent flap. None of them questioned taking the Evenki leader to the tigers; they just obeyed. Within a few moments, they were standing back, watching her as she assessed the tigers as boldly as she'd just done with them.

Absolutely unafraid, she walked around them—first Stacia, clucking her tongue as she did, and then Veru. When she was finished, she said, "I don't know how it is that your people managed to harness this magic. Even if the tiger tokens were traded or gifted to your parents, it shouldn't have worked. It's meant to belong to our people. You can't keep it. You must give it back. Even if you were one of our people, it is a sacred trust. One must be deemed worthy to carry a tiger token and wield its power. Grave evils come upon the one who attempts to harness the magic unworthily."

"That's just it," Nik said. "We want to lift this curse so the tsarevnas can go back to their land and fight the demon who is trying to take over the empire. The soldier who sent us here said your people could help. His mother was Evenki."

"How old was this soldier?" the leader asked.

"Perhaps the same age as yourself," Nik replied.

She laughed in response. "I am much older than I appear." Clasping her hands behind her back, she turned and looked up at the sky. After a moment of silence, she said, "That young soldier could be any of our sons. So many of them leave us searching for a better life in a land not watched over by our ancestors. We have lost far too many of our youth in such a way. They abandon us for the bright futures they believe come from living in ever-expanding metropolises. What they often find is a poor existence. One without purpose, family, and home, and one where they slip into the neglected and castoffs of society." Spinning, she asked, "Why did he not accompany you himself?"

"He stayed to fight and protect the empire," Nik said simply. "He is . . . was very brave. We don't really know if he's still alive."

"Hmm," she said. "He's alive. We would have heard otherwise."

"I . . . I think he must have recognized the magic wielded by the sorcerer. That man was looking for some simple charms worn by the tsarevnas. I believe he has more of these tiger tokens. He was extremely powerful. In the forest, he read my mind, and he commands an army of the dead."

The leader of the Evenki began pacing, her eyes narrowed. "I see. We have heard whispers of this man—this sorcerer of whom you speak. He has left the palace, I think, and has gone on the hunt. Many tigers have been killed. I suspect this is his doing. He is searching for these two. This must be why power and magic are draining from our lands. If this man has begun collecting the Tokens of the Tiger Emblem, then he can bring about the end of all things. Already hunters are returning empty-handed. River water is polluted and sluggish. The fish refuse to spawn in them. The snows are coming later each year, and the winters are harsher, the summers hotter. The reindeer are dropping calves too early. Now I understand why all this is happening. The above and beneath are out of balance."

"So you'll help us break this curse and free the tsarevnas?"

"You do not understand," she said. "The tigers do not come as a curse. They come as a gift. They are a blessing to our people. If they show themselves in your tsarevnas, then they have deemed them worthy hosts, even if I do not see it myself."

Mumbling a few words in her language, she shook her head. "I must find out why." Then softer, with a pained expression, she added, "Perhaps it is something I have done. Regardless, the error must be repaired for the good of all." Approaching Stacia and Veru, she asked politely, "Will you change so we can talk?"

The tigers blinked and looked at one another.

"Why will you not change?" she asked, a wrinkle appearing between her brows.

"What do you mean by 'change'?" asked Danik.

"I mean transform to their human selves."

"Transform?" Nik said incredulously. "They've never done that since they changed the first time."

"Not once?" she asked with surprise.

"No. Never," Nik replied.

"Interesting," she said. "And when did their first transformation . . . I mean, when did they alter their forms into tigers for the first time?"

"When the sorcerer attacked them at the palace. That would have been . . ." He began calculating on his fingers. "The night after was a half-moon. We've passed another half-moon since and are nearing a third."

She was quiet for a moment, and then she turned quickly, saying, "Come. We must hurry."

"You'll help us, then?" Zakhar asked.

"Yes. But I believe it is you who have been sent to help me."

"I don't understand," Nik said.

"I know you do not. Be patient and I will try to explain as best I can."

When they arrived back at her tent, she issued orders, and the entire structure was broken down in a matter of minutes. The only piece that remained was the large pole at the center. The clansmen who had traveled with her began heading east on their own, packing her large tent with them. They'd seemed hesitant to leave her behind, but no one argued with their leader. She dismissed their guide, sending him back on his own to reunite with his clan. He smiled at the three young men, clapping them on their backs and giving them a respectful nod before leaving.

Then, with her own bag on her back, the leader of the Evenki walked back with them to the tigers and watched with fascination as Nik readied them for the trail. When she saw the laces flutter in the air next to Stacia as if trying to create a third harness before settling into two, she sucked in a breath. "It means to create the Transcendent Troika. I've heard stories of such a thing told to me by my grandmother as told to her by her grandmother and hers before, but not a one of them were a witness to it."

She climbed into the sleigh. "We must find Iriko."

"Who's that?" Danik asked.

"He is my son—the gray tiger that you seek. But he will be hard to find. You see, he is the one who has truly been cursed."

"Where do we go?" Nik asked, offering the reins to the Evenki leader. "Would you like to take them . . . um? We don't even know what to call you."

"You may call me Matriova, and no, I do not wish to guide the tigers. In fact, you should let them take us where they will. When we draw near to Iriko, they will sense him. His presence will call out to them. If they instinctively desire to form the Transcendent Troika, the magic will pull them where they need to be."

"Is your son truly invisible and blind as the other clan suggested?"

For a moment, the Evenki leader, Matriova, was quiet, then she said, "Iriko was not always. But yes, he is blind now. He can, however, be seen if he wishes it, but even so, he is invisible to his people, for he has been banished."

"Banished!" the three men said at once.

"But may I ask why?" added Zakhar.

Matriova sighed deeply, then snuggled into her fur-lined cloak. The tigers began to run, and the sleigh rocked side to side before the world blurred around them. "It is a long story," she said. "And it is one that we do not usually share, especially with outsiders, but perhaps the time has come for a change to our way of doing things."

Before she began her story, Zakhar took out a fresh sheet of parchment and a pot of ink, raising his quill to tap her on the shoulder, asking with his eager expression if he could document her tale. Giving him a long, thoughtful look, she nodded. He handed his pot of ink to Danik, who tried to keep it warm enough in his hands so Zakhar could keep writing, which was difficult on the bumpy terrain. But Danik knew his friend well enough now to know that Zakhar was only jotting down notes so he'd remember, and then he'd fill in the details later when they had time to spare and plenty of fire or lantern light.

"Iriko was my last child," Matriova began. "I have had many children and several mates over the years. And I've outlived all of them. Such is the way of our clan leader. You see, the one who wears the tiger token is granted an exceptionally long life."

"Then you mean that you—"

She held up a hand. "I know you are young and impulsive, but try to listen without interruption as best you can."

When she saw the men nod in agreement, she continued. "When

one of us senses it is time to leave this world and make the long journey to join the sky people, we examine our offspring carefully and select the one we think will be the best suited to carry on as a leader and protector of the people. A few years ago, I announced it was *my* time to journey to the sky people and step aside. I would imagine there are several husbands waiting for me there, each one singing his best song so I will choose to enter his tent in the sky and live with him. Truthfully, not a one of them had a good enough singing voice to catch my attention.

"After gathering my children together, I selected Baikali, my beautiful, strong daughter, to take my place. Before I can pass the leadership of the clan to her, she must first take on the responsibility of the tiger and wear the tiger token for one year. Then, if she and the tiger agree with one another and the bond is sure, she will also take on my leadership role."

"When exactly did you take on this role for yourself?" Danik asked.

Matriova was quiet for a moment. "I don't count years like most people do. But I have seen many of my children marry, grow old, and join the sky people. I've seen thousands of nights, season upon season. I lingered only because I was waiting for a daughter who was special. One who I felt was ready to carry the burden. It is not an easy thing to wear a tiger token—one of those special charms, as you called them."

"Is that why Iriko is banished? The tiger needed to be passed to a female?"

"No. That is not the reason. And no, the charms have been worn by men in the past, but in my tribe, it has always been passed traditionally to females. As I was saying . . . it is not an easy thing to wear a token. They are special.

"In fact, they are pieces of a very powerful emblem or seal. When combined, they give the person who holds it power to change the world. A long, long time ago, the pieces were contained within our borders, or so the legend goes. Over time, they disappeared, one by one. Lost to the ages. It is one of the reasons our peoples venerate the tiger. To destroy one results in one of the worst of all punishments."

Zakhar interrupted, "Let me understand: When you wore a tiger token, or a piece of this tiger emblem, you could change back and forth into a tiger at will?"

"Yes. But to do so required me to pass a test."

"What sort of test?" Nik asked.

"The test is different for each person. For some it is a test of bravery. For others a test of knowledge. The tiger must deem you worthy."

"What happens to you if you fail the test? Do you not become a tiger? Or can you not change back?"

"It is not that simple. Your tigers, your tsarevnas, haven't even begun their trials yet. With the Evenki, we choose our candidates very, very carefully. Never, to my knowledge, has an aspirant failed a test, though it has taken some longer to access their full abilities than others."

Nik spoke up. "You said you selected your daughter to replace you, yet here you are. And your son is the tiger, not your daughter, so what happened? Did she fail the test?"

"No. Baikali did not fail. She was halfway finished with her first year wearing the tiger token when the terrible accident happened. The reindeer were just coming into their winter coats, and the leaves were kissed with fire but hadn't yet fallen, and my son Iriko wanted to fish. He was a boastful, proud, fractious boy and prone to thinking his mother's advice and counsel were about control and not about keeping him safe.

"He loved ice fishing, and that year the ice came early. I warned him that it wasn't safe, and he needed to wait for it to harden before he tried it. He told me he would obey, but one morning I woke to find his favorite pole missing. I sent Baikali out to find him since she could scent his path and bring him home. She discovered her brother easily enough, but when she went out on the ice to confront him, she was still in tiger form. Baikali was much too heavy for the ice, and it cracked. Both of them went under.

"With the tiger token, she would have survived, but she was determined to save Iriko. She switched to her human form and held on to him, swimming for an opening. He was only a boy of twelve back then. He clung to her desperately, clawing at her neck and clothing, not realizing that in his desperation, he tore the token from her body.

"Baikali managed to thrust him up through an opening, but she was swept away beneath the ice. Iriko returned to us many hours later, clutching the token in his hand. We found my daughter's poor broken form two days later when the ice melted. She'd drowned, her body bruised, turgid, and pale. We buried my beautiful daughter with her feet pointed east so she could watch the sun rise every morning. It was a tragic death, and though I knew the boy was young, I blamed him for killing our hope. For destroying my vision for the future with his thoughtlessness.

"Ashamed by having caused the death of his sister, especially knowing how important she had been to the Evenki, which I had made abundantly clear to him, Iriko sunk into despair. He tried to beg forgiveness from me and the people, but there was no way for him to make restitution for what he'd done. There are some things that, once broken, are gone forever.

"Iriko tried to return the tiger token to me, but no longer would the tiger recognize me as its companion. Instead, it bonded to Iriko, but Iriko, in his shame and misery, defied the tiger spirit. His soul grew bitter and dark, and he refused any attempts the tiger token gave as a test. Since he was determined to defy the tiger, turning a blind eye to its call, his own eyes grew dim. Soon his demeanor proved too volatile for the people, and he was banished.

"I regretted my harsh treatment of him then, but I didn't see any other way to remedy the situation. The people wanted him gone. They considered him bad luck. A wanderer who brought only wickedness and vengeance. I had no choice but to do as they asked, as much as it broke my heart. So you see, not only did I lose my daughter but I lost my son as well. And the people lost the gift of magic they'd relied upon for centuries.

"It was a tragedy unlike anything I'd ever experienced. Until now, the magic Iriko possessed was the last hope for our people. I'd feared it was gone from our lands forever. But perhaps all is not as I thought. Perhaps the magic has found its own way to return. Maybe I was too hasty, too quick to judge. Maybe there is still something left for me to learn before I join the sky people."

Zakhar had been scratching furiously with his quill, only stopping long enough to dip it in the inkpot held by Danik, but now he paused. "I think there is never an end to one's learning," he said. "Perhaps even after we join the sky people there is more to be learned. Don't you agree?"

Matriova snorted. "I thought you men of the church believed only in heaven and hell. Are you trying to say you now believe you may have a place among our sky people instead?"

Tilting his head, Zakhar blinked rapidly. Whether that was due to deep reflection or bits of sleet disturbing his vision, Danik couldn't be certain. Zakhar finally answered, "To my way of thinking, though the stories of our origins on this world differ, there are basic fundamentals in common enough to ascertain certain things that ring true across cultures.

"Those who treat their fellow man with goodness and kindness, who value life and live in such a way that they leave behind more than they take, people who edify and teach the young, passing on their wisdom and values, will, when they depart this world, return to the bosom of their creator, living in a condition that is typically defined as a place of peace and joy.

"In that sense, yes, when my time here is finished, I would hope I have contributed enough and sacrificed enough for others to have earned a position with my creator. I am content in the knowledge that a being powerful enough to bring life and such diverse beauty and wonder to this world is perfectly capable of revealing to us our role or further wisdom should we have need of it. I see no point in foisting my personal theories on others since that's all they are at present—theories. Though I do admit, I am committed to the study of God and His law."

"You are a strange priest, indeed, young man. But I . . . hear wisdom in your words. I will ponder them further myself and perhaps . . . I will amend my policy of speaking to men of the cloth in your case."

Zakhar lowered his head. "I am honored and look forward to such a day, for it is obvious I have much to learn from one such as yourself."

There was a sudden jerking of the sleigh as the two tigers unexpectedly veered to the north.

Matriova grabbed on to the sleigh's side to right herself and said, "They must have sensed him!"

Their speed increased, and Zakhar was forced to set aside his paper and stopper his bottle of ink. It was all they could do to hold on. They sped past a large river and then a lake and a second even larger body of water before climbing a series of hills. Then they came to an abrupt stop. The tigers panted hard, and when the passengers stepped out of the sleigh, the laces immediately unwound, and the two tigers collapsed in the snow.

Nikolai and Danik hurried to their sides, offering them meat, and began searching for firewood so they could melt snow to water. As the three men worked, Matriova walked slowly, her eyes searching the area and studying the ground, looking for tracks.

"He's here," she said. "I can sense him."

"I don't see anything," Zakhar said, joining her, lending his hunter's eye.

"Nevertheless. My son is here. He's studying us somehow. I believe he senses our presence as we do his."

When everyone was settled, Zakhar and Danik headed out into the trees to hunt. This time with only simple traps and nothing large enough to catch a tiger. Danik didn't want to trap Iriko by mistake, remembering Veru's poor leg as it tried to heal over and over again against the steel teeth. When night fell, they returned with a few birds and roasted some of the meat left in their packs. Stacia and Veru were exhausted and slept deeply. Soon the men laid down to doze as well. Only Zakhar and Matriova remained awake, as he was showing her the pages he'd drawn.

He'd just unrolled the scroll he'd recovered and discovered to his delight that she knew the language, when she shushed him at hearing the crack of a branch. The circle of firelight didn't light much area past their small camp, so they peered into the darkness, looking for traces of life.

"Hello?" Matriova called out. "Is that you, son? Please come out."

They heard a snarl and a deep growl in response. Immediately, Stacia and Veru rose from their sleeping positions and darted quickly toward the trees. They disappeared into the darkness beyond the campfire. Danik and Nikolai rose as well, blinking sleep from their eyes.

"What's happening?" Danik asked.

They heard a roar and a tussle in the snow. Then all went quiet.

"Should we go after them?" asked Nik.

"Wait," Matriova said, holding up a hand.

Straining, they heard a noise, very soft, like a rhythmic pulse that grew louder. They realized it was the sound of paws on snow. Soon they saw the dark shadows of the tigers followed by a third shadow. When they stepped into the light, Veru growled softly, and Stacia whined. Behind them, treading in the snow barefoot, as lightly as the two tigers had, was a young man, tall and handsome.

His long, dark hair hung loose down his back. The reindeer tunic and leggings he wore no longer fit and were torn in places. Where the tunic should have been closed, he'd cut it open down the center to account for his expanding, muscular chest, and he'd ripped off the arms and widened the holes so his arms could fit through. The leggings hung on his narrow hips and were now far too short to provide any warmth from the snow. Around his neck hung an all too familiar charm.

A keening sound came from Matriova as she took in the sight. Zakhar could see crystal tears coursing down her cheeks. His heart broke for the older woman, but then he looked at the young man, and he saw nothing but flint in his expression.

"Oh, my boy," Matriova said. "My Iriko." She rose and removed her own fur-lined cloak to wrap around his shoulders.

But as she was securing it, he grabbed her hands, stopping her, then stepped back, wrenched the beautiful wrap from his body, and tossed it mercilessly to the snow, saying, "I am no boy, woman. And I have no mother. You should know better than to try to warm a glacier. Don't you remember that ice feels nothing?"

Chapter 20

The Eye May See It, but the Proof Is in the Tooth

For a moment all was silent except for the crackle of the logs as they sunk deeper into the fire. Zakhar and Danik instinctively wanted to protect the older woman from the snarling young man. As for Nik, he felt frozen in place. It was as if he were watching a play in which another boy was speaking words he longed to say to his own mother.

He could almost see how the words cut her, and yet he could also see how the young man needed his mother to see him, to love him, despite the things he'd done. It was there, but it was buried so deep, he doubted anyone else but him would see it.

Veru and Stacia sat on opposite sides of the new arrival, their eyes trained on him. He was what they'd been looking for, and they hadn't known it. They could feel the tiger clawing at his insides. It raged and paced, longing to emerge and greet them, but the young man had built up a very effective cage. His tiger spirit was trapped. Because of this, he was going mad. The tiger inside him foamed in fury, fuming and bellowing, leaking angry poisons that festered and boiled.

"You are not made of ice, Iriko. You are my son," Matriova said. "I claimed you as mine the day you fluttered in my womb, and every day since my thoughts have been with you. Though we've been apart, I have not forgotten you."

"You abandoned me!" Iriko shouted.

"No! The people rejected you. I had a duty—"

"You had a duty to me!"

Iriko's breaths came quickly, and his hands tightened into fists.

Matriova stepped closer and touched his broad shoulder. "You're right, my son. You're right. I should have left with you. Perhaps someday you can find a way to forgive a very old woman."

She shifted closer to him, lifting her cloak once again and speaking to him comforting words in her native language. This time he allowed her to tie the cloak around his shoulders, but when she was done, he stiffened his body again and said, "Why have you come? Why now? Tell me quickly so I can refuse your request and return to my solitude."

"Very well," Matriova said and held up a hand to stop Zakhar when he was about to protest and suggest some manner of diplomacy or breaking camp first. "I am helping these people on their quest. They need to be guided to the Dreaming Mountain so they can meet with the White Shaman of the Tundra. At long last two of our tiger tokens have returned to us, but they need help. These men have vowed to assist them."

"Help?" he spat. "*You* never needed help."

"This is different. They are not . . . of our people," she said, glancing down at the tigers at her feet. "They were not prepared as we are for this responsibility. They wish to . . . to separate themselves from the tiger spirit."

Iriko stepped forward and stretched out a hand until he took hold of his mother's shoulders. "Is this possible? You never mentioned such a thing was an option."

Saddened, Matriova said softly, "I didn't know you hated it that much. To abandon the tiger spirit once it chooses you is not an easy thing."

"Nor is it easy trying to live up to everyone else's expectations and constantly failing," Iriko said.

"I . . . I understand," she said.

"Do you? How can you possibly? You always lived up to everyone's expectations. You've never seen the people's faces"—he paused—"or at least heard their voices fall in disappointment over your actions."

"Perhaps not in the way you're thinking. But yes, I've seen disappointment before, son."

Iriko grunted. "Perhaps. But you were not responsible for the death of your sister. The one everyone depended on, were you?"

Matriova sighed. "No. But I have made my own mistakes over the years. Each one of us must learn from our own errors and walk our own path to knowledge, mustn't we?" Biting her lip, Matriova turned and walked back to the campfire, thinking. At last she spoke. "Very well. If you also wish to disconnect yourself from the tiger spirit, then you will need to ascend the Dreaming Mountain as well. These two need your help," she said, indicating the two tigers. "They don't know our lands. And I am too old and feeble now to manage the climb. If you agree to take them and manage to either make peace with your tiger or break connection with it, returning the token so our people can select a new carrier, then I will send word you are to be reinstated as a member of the clan."

"I'm not sure I want to be a member of the clan any longer."

"Surely it's better than living out here alone."

He shrugged. "I've been doing fine on my own."

Veru made a sound like a chuffing noise and rubbed her body along his leg. Stacia growled and stretched up, knocking her head against his hand. "Settle down now," Iriko said with a rueful laugh. "Is it that you are worried about me, ladies, or do you like me that much already?" He paused. "I know what you're saying, but you don't understand what I'm capable of." He cocked his head as he stroked Stacia's head. "Are you doubting my hunting skills or the fact that I don't have any footwear?"

"Wait a minute," Nikolai said. "Can you . . . can you hear them?"

"Yes," Iriko answered matter-of-factly as he ran a hand down Veru's back. "It seems I can understand them, but they cannot hear one another except through me. Can't any of you?"

"No," Danik said.

"This is fascinating," Zakhar said. "I need to document this immediately. Perhaps we can return to the fire? I have so many questions."

"Of course," Matriova agreed. "But first, Iriko. Will you take them?"

"I'll . . . consider it."

Veru yowled and pushed against him, which made him laugh. They all noticed the stern young man appeared very much different when he laughed. They could see the boy lurking behind the face of the angry man.

"I know. I heard them, Verusha," Iriko said. "Fine, *Veru*. What kind of a name is that anyway?"

He put his hand on Veru's back, and she guided him to camp, where he found a seat by the fire. The tigers sat down next to him on either side. When Danik brought them some raw fish, Veru nudged it over to Iriko, who snatched it up and took a large bite, not even caring that it was uncooked. "A tsarevna, you say? Wait, both of you?"

Nik raised a hand and then quickly lowered it. "Technically, they're the tsarinas."

"Is that right?" Iriko replied with a smirk, glancing in Nik's direction. Veru looked at Nik at the same time, twisting her head and neck in the same way the young man did, as if looking Nik up and down and obviously finding him lacking. "And what are you to them, exactly? A footman?"

"No. I . . . I polish Veru's armor and do other various . . . jobs."

"Armor?"

"Er . . . yes. Can you please ask her—"

Iriko held up a hand, ignoring Nik's query. He cocked his head, clearly listening to something Veru was telling him, and then burst out laughing. Nikolai didn't know if she was talking about him, but his face colored anyway.

Zakhar raised a hand, then realized what he was doing and added, "If I may, I have many questions I'd like to ask now that I have an interpreter of sorts."

Matriova put her hand on his arm and said, "Hold off on that for now. The three of them are cementing their bond. There will be time for that later. If they are to truly form a Transcendent Troika as the legends say, they'll need to work together in perfect harmony."

"Troika. If I recall, I saw images of something like that on the scroll." Zakhar became distracted, rummaging through his papers.

Nikolai stood and said, "Yeah, well, if we can't talk, there isn't much point in waiting around right now, is there?" He picked up a stick and thrust it into the fire and told Danik he was going to head out to look for more firewood.

When Danik pulled out his domra and asked if anyone had a musical request, this time being especially pleased that he could ask Veru or Stacia themselves, they answered that they would prefer to speak to Iriko just then. Danik said he understood and tucked his domra away, but he was disappointed at their answer. He'd always thought the tigers enjoyed his music. He climbed into his blankets and rolled away, trying to ignore the soft murmuring and laughter coming from the other side of the fire.

As for Matriova, she often glanced at her son but was more than thrilled at seeing him interacting with the other tigers. It warmed her heart to see flashes of the boy she'd once known appearing in the face of the sullen man he was now. She hoped that at least Iriko would not, in fact, choose to abandon the spirit that had chosen him. Of all people, she knew the power and responsibility that came with a tiger's life, but she also knew the loneliness and abandonment of living without it.

She didn't understand why it had stayed with her son instead of returning to her, but she had thought about it constantly over the years. Matriova had waited many decades to pass on the token. Her daughter had been the perfect host, a more excellent candidate she couldn't have hoped to find among all her people. Everyone knew it and looked forward to Baikali ruling in her place. She'd been so perfect, in fact, that Baikali hadn't hesitated when she saw the need to save someone else—her younger brother.

Matriova didn't think she'd been nearly as prepared when she'd accepted the tiger token. In fact, she'd been more like Iriko—impulsive, quick-tempered, and selfish—but over the years and through the trials and experiences the tiger gave her, she'd been able to mature, become more than what she'd been. Perhaps the tiger was drawn to Iriko. It knew, somehow, that her son needed its guidance.

If she were being honest with herself, she'd confess that she missed the tiger. It had been a part of her for so long that the tiger had become a piece of her identity. It was her friend when she was alone. It protected her from the elements. It strengthened her in times of weakness. Were there things she gave up? Certainly. But in her view, there was so much more she'd gained by wearing the tiger token than she'd lost.

The real test for her now was about seeing the tigers of their people bond with outsiders. Did these two girls who'd been born with wealth, all the opportunities that power and an empire could give them, really need more? How could she learn to accept that the gift that meant so much to her people could fall into hands so soft and pampered? What did they know of loss? Of sacrifice? Of struggle? Of doing without? Did they even understand what the tiger tokens meant to the people who lived in this land? Could they possibly understand?

And worse. If she saw that great gift withdraw from her people, what would they have left? Could she ever reconcile the feeling that she had known the tokens were within her grasp and she had done nothing to reclaim them? Could she trust that the White Shaman of the Tundra would know what to do and that it would be the best thing for her people? Then again, what if she made a mistake and did something that protected her own people but caused the destruction of another? Could she live with that?

But what of the Transcendent Troika? Had the time finally come? Was it to be these three who formed the envisaged masterpiece? They were so unprepared, so unskilled, so . . . unwilling. But . . . if there was one thing the ancestors had taught her over the long, harsh winters, it was that the direction of a great stampeding herd could be impacted by something as simple as a blowing leaf. Perhaps there was more to them than what she could see on the surface. Matriova rubbed her temples, feeling an ache in her head as she thought of these weighty issues.

Of course, the young didn't think of such things. They only considered where their next meal was coming from, how long they could sleep before their mama kicked their foot to make them rise to work in the morning, or who might be winking at them from across the fire. Not for the first time, she longed to join her people who had gone on before—the wise ones who sat at the open doors of their yurts watching them as they smoked pipes and laughed at the silly worries of the still living, their laughter and smoke twirling overhead to make the lovely colors of green, blue, pink, and purple in the winter sky.

Zakhar didn't feel a bit sleepy. First, he documented all he could about meeting Iriko and how the newcomer had interacted with Veru and Stacia. When he felt their conversation had dwindled to more mundane topics, he decided to move on to more important things. He wanted to take advantage of the time he had with Matriova and pulled out the scroll so she could help him translate it.

After painstakingly copying her translation for the better part of an hour, Zakhar knew he'd need to share it with the others. It was quite obvious that the document had been meant for their eyes, but there were details included that were still a mystery to him, including how and when he recorded the document originally. He asked Matriova again and again what her thoughts were regarding certain passages of text, but she said she had no context or knowledge of such, even though she'd carried a piece of the tiger charm herself for a bit longer than four hundred years and had heard stories passed down for generations before herself.

Her best advice was to ask the White Shaman. Not even in her lifetime had she met him, though in her younger days she had attempted to ascend the mountain. She told Zakhar that though tigers were allowed to climb the mountain, they never encountered the White Shaman, at least as far as she was aware. Instead, they were sent a dream, one that helped them in their life journey. When they woke, they would find themselves back at the mountain's base.

Those who persisted would find they became confused and turned around until they lost their way. Soon they were no longer allowed to climb, and some even lost the memory of the mountain completely. When Zakhar asked her if she'd ever had a dream on the mountain, she replied she had, but she refused to share with the priest what it was and told him when she'd awoken, she was at the mountain's base. After that she'd journeyed home, never to make another attempt.

Now that they'd translated the scroll, both of them became quite excited by what they'd read. Zakhar couldn't wait to copy it again in his own language and make an attempt to imitate the beautiful artwork surrounding it, but he knew, though his hand had made the scroll, at that point in his life he wasn't nearly a skilled enough artist to replicate it. The realization was stunning and awesome. He wanted to tell someone, but who and when? Would they think him crazed or that he'd imagined it?

As he discussed the scroll with Matriova, both of them felt there were symbols and meanings in the art to discover that went far beyond the simple words of the text itself. Some of it felt distinctively Russian to Zakhar, though he wouldn't dare suggest as much to Matriova. He didn't think she'd take such a thing well.

Together they read it, each mumbling the words to themselves, trying to make sense of the passages of text.

In dire times, at world's end,
Some must face a daunting task.
Choose to embark,
And leave their mark,
Troika three the mount ascend.
There the truth they must unmask.
Seven spirits bless the land
Pass their tests and wisely rule.
But if instead,
You cling to dread,
Raging beasts will gnaw your hand,
As you become death's vile tool.
Learn from those who came before,
Should you ever start to drift,
Beware desire,
Trust, but inquire,
Lean upon your tiger's roar,
Capture every gilded gift.
Then as champions, you'll arise.
Brimming with a brilliant power.
Distinct, each one,
Shining, each sun.
Rising to boreal skies,
And prolong your terrene hours.

Zakhar quizzed Matriova, taking notes and making his own as long as possible. Finally, when his eyes and the dwindling fire allowed him to work no more, he carefully stoppered his inks and cleaned his quill tips, then rolled up the scroll, vigilantly storing his work, before falling into a deep sleep.

By the time he woke the next morning, everyone else was breaking camp. "What's going on?" Zakhar asked sleepily as he rubbed his eyes, shivering now that the fire was completely out.

Matriova answered, "I hope you don't mind. I shared the basic information of the prophecy from your scroll. At least what I could remember. It appears to correspond with what we were already planning to do anyway, which was to try to get the three tigers to the Dreaming Mountain. After that, who knows? Iriko has agreed to accompany you that far at least."

When the group was ready, Matriova placed a pack on her back, including snowshoes and the sturdy little yurt gifted to Danik, as well as a nice supply of dried fish. Iriko returned his mother's lovely cloak, securing it on her shoulders himself.

"Are you certain you don't wish to come with us?" he asked.

"No, son. It is enough that I was able to reunite with you. If I die on the journey, I am ready now."

"But I won't know where you are buried."

"That won't matter. It's only a body I'll leave behind—an empty shell. You'll know where to find me. Just look up. I'll be there. Watching over you always, my son. I hope someday you'll find a way to forgive your old mother. And remember: no matter what you choose, I love you. I've always been proud to have you for a son."

Iriko nodded. He took a step closer to her, reaching out and groping the empty air with his hand, feeling for her shoulder. She took it and squeezed it, guiding his palm to her face. "You're shorter than I remember," he said.

"No, I'm not. You're just taller."

He hugged his mother and said, "Thank you. I . . . I'll talk with you from time to time."

"And I'll answer."

They touched their heads together, then when he had his hand on Stacia's back again, using her eyes to see, she turned to Zakhar and said, "If you ever have time to seek me out, assuming I survive my journey, I wouldn't mind talking with you again, young priest."

"I, too, would enjoy further discussion," Zakhar said in reply. "Perhaps we can talk about God and the ancestors on our next visit," he suggested.

"I think I might look forward to that conversation."

"Then farewell for now. May the snow be solid beneath your feet."

Matriova grinned. "I like that expression. I'm going to use that one."

"Feel free," Zakhar answered, and then climbed into the sleigh next to Danik.

"And, son?" the older woman said, turning back one last time.

"Yes?" Iriko replied.

"Don't forget to forgive yourself as well."

With that, she was gone, disappearing around a hill. Iriko could still hear her for a while and tracked her footsteps, but then he was distracted by Stacia's voice. He'd been fascinated by the story of the magic boots and how they'd turned into a sleigh and reins. The tsarevna's irritation came through loud and clear to him as he fingered the gemstones along her collar.

Why are you standing there instead of letting your tiger out? Stacia demanded. *Can't you see the magic means to make a third place so you can help us pull?*

It's not very kind of you to sit back there and make us do all the work, Veru added sulkily.

Iriko laughed, almost seeing the pout in the tone of her voice. "Back home the women do most of the work while we have meetings. We smoke and sit around a fire and make all the decisions while the women have the babies, make dinner, collect the firewood, and—"

Soplyak. You're full of rubbish, Stacia said. *We know your mother is the leader. What are you trying to pull?*

"I'm not pulling anything," Iriko said, stretching his big arms over his head.

Veru said, *That's the point. You're trying to get out of pulling.*

"Is that the way for a proper tsarina to talk? I wouldn't think fine young ladies such as yourselves should be using words like that," Iriko said with a chuckle. He paused for a moment to hear their reply and then roared with laughter.

Annoyed, Nik leaned forward and asked, "Can we get going? Please?"

As if reading the minds of the tsarevnas, Zakhar asked, "Can you change to a tiger? Have you ever? I'd like to record that in my notes."

Stomping over to the sleigh, by holding on to the harnesses, Iriko's expression turned back into the angry young man with muscles entirely too large. "No, I can't, for your information. Sorry, ladies. You're on your own. I'll tell you where to go though. You be my eyes, and I'll be your voice." Turning to the men, he added, "I'll also let you know when they start to wear themselves out. Reins, please," he said to Nik.

Reluctantly, Nik handed them over. "So you can see through their eyes, can't you."

"I can. The three of us are bonded. I can feel their hunger too. Not that any of *you* care about that."

"What do you mean?" Danik said, standing up to address the stranger. "Of course we care about . . ." He turned to Veru and Stacia. "Veru, you can't possibly think . . . of course we care . . ."

Iriko smiled, his teeth as white as the snow and all as straight as pillars except for one little gap between his front incisors and his two canines, which were slightly snaggletooth. This gave him an even more feral appearance when he grinned. "It's just too easy," he mumbled to himself.

Without saying another word out loud, he picked up the reins and turned his head in one direction and the other. The tigers mimicked his movements precisely. Zakhar was fascinated by this and wanted to capture the strange light in Iriko's glacier-blue eyes and how they dilated suddenly when he linked with the others.

Then the tigers broke out into a run. Danik, who was still trying to communicate with Veru, collapsed backward. If it hadn't been for Zakhar, he would have gone over the back of the sleigh and fallen off, and the way Iriko was laughing at the sound of the poor man's struggles, none of the others were certain the sleigh would have been turned around to collect their fallen warrior.

Shrinking back down in his seat, Danik gripped the side of the sleigh and held on. Not for the first time, he regretted seeking out their new companion. Nikolai was thinking the exact same thing. Zakhar was thinking only of the scroll and his journals and when he could begin working again, while the three tigers were now focused on only one thing: the mountain that seemed to be calling to them even though none of them had ever seen it or stepped foot on it before.

CHAPTER 21
A Beard Doesn't a Philosopher Make

Meanwhile, the Storyweaver of the Sky, the White Shaman of the Tundra, the One Who Hears All—Above and Below, also known to the mother who gave birth to him as Vesako Alingida, a name that meant Old Man with a Spear Who Lives on a Mountain, a prophetic name if ever there was one, heard nothing but the soft echoes of his own snores within the hollow of the mountain cave he called home. Though it was blistering cold outside on the icy slopes, the cave was full of natural coal, so it was easy enough for him to keep a fire going at all times.

As for food and water, there was enough snowmelt to provide him with water for drinking and bathing. He foraged a bit in the summer and grew a few herbs and mushrooms that he used for food, tea, and visions, and then there were a few loyal acolytes he allowed to bring him supplies once or twice a year. But that early morning it wasn't the sound of one of his followers on the mountain path or an animal, and it wasn't the impending arrival of the three tigers he was waiting for that woke him.

All had been proceeding as it should have been, and he had been resting up for the trials that would soon be requiring his utmost attention, when an unusual disturbance alerted him to a change in the cosmos. Rising from his sleeping mat, he headed to the opening of his cave and looked up at the night sky.

Sure enough, he spied an upheaval of balance large enough to cause a crack, an opening in the passage between worlds just to the right of the polar star. Through it shot a ball of fire so bright he had to shield his eyes. Down, down it fell until it crashed nearby, causing the entire area to shake with its power and the tremors even resulted in the fall of a few of his favorite trees, much to his dismay. Vesako stood there for many hours, his hands clasped behind his back, watching the area until the rising and the sinking of the sun, the short burst of rays encompassing the puffy dust cloud created by the object for the briefest of moments.

Still thoughtful, he turned and went about the motions of creating a second fire, passing between them himself, trying to discover the meaning of the crack in sky and the fallen object and how it might impact the upcoming trials of the three tigers headed his way. Perhaps there was some portent to the timing, he mused. Vesako didn't believe in coincidence. Not since he was a very young man, anyway. He sipped cup after cup of hot tea and meditated, but the answer eluded him. Finally, after two days, he laid down on his sleeping mat again, exhausted, but slept fitfully.

Long before the fleeting rays of winter daybreak, his eyes flew open. He sensed another presence in his cave. "Hello?" he said. "Make yourself known to me. I mean you no harm, be you animal, human, or spirit. Reveal yourself."

Sitting up, he searched the cave by the waning light of the fire and saw nothing, so he closed his eyes, feeling for the intruder. "There you are," he said with his eyes still closed. Opening them just a crack, he stepped into the darkness, where a transparent form huddled. "Do not be afraid," Vesako said. "I mean no harm to you. Come, come. Warm yourself by my fire, and we shall take a look at what you are."

The ghost drifted closer. Vesako knew instantly there was a connection between himself, the wandering spirit, and the opening between universes. Something was amiss, and it was now his job to repair the damage. But first he needed to make contact. Hesitantly, the spirit hovered near the fire for a moment, but then it moved toward the cave opening as if it wanted to escape.

"Now, now, hold on for just a moment," the White Shaman said. "I can help you if you'll allow it. You've traveled a great distance, and you're probably frightened. If I could just . . ." He stretched out a hand as if to touch the entity, and at the exact same time the specter reached out a hand as well. Their fingertips brushed against each other, and the White Shaman felt something he never thought he'd experience.

I would call it déjà vu, the ghost spoke in his mind.

"This word is something I've never heard before, and yet I understand it," the White Shaman said in response. "Why is that, I wonder? And why can I hear your thoughts? Are you a tiger in your world?"

A tiger. Perhaps I have discovered a kindred soul. I am not. Though I have worn the amulet. I don't see one on your person. Did you wear an amulet at one time?

"Amulet. Another word I am unfamiliar with. We call them tokens or perhaps an emblem. Are you a shaman on your world?"

A shaman? How interesting. No. I am a . . . the ghost chuckled. *I'm more of a mentor or a father figure to the tigers on my world these days. At one time I trained them for battle, but that was a long, long time ago. You speak a different language, one I've never heard before, yet I understand you as well. How is that possible, I wonder?*

"I believe you understand, because I understand," Vesako answered cryptically. He then walked around the ghost, trying to see deeper using his shaman eyes, but it was like looking at water. He saw only his own reflection. *Could it really be? Impossible! Incredible!* He asked, "How did you come to be in the state you are now? Why are you here? Was it the war?"

I suppose you could say I came here as a result of battle, but it's not a war such as you believe.

"Is it not, my friend? Aren't we all fighting the same war?" The White Shaman clasped his hands behind his back and paced, thinking. Perhaps the cosmos thrust this one upon him because he needed help. Or maybe the upcoming trials would be more challenging than he perceived, and he would need the aid of this one.

Help! Yes. I am in need of help. It appears I am lost and cannot find my way home.

"Perhaps we can be of aid to one another, my friend."

I am willing, of course, though there isn't much I can do in my current state.

Straightening his shoulders, the White Shaman said, "What is clear is that we have been brought together for a purpose. You have been sent here to help me, and I will also be a means of helping you. But first we must do something about your soul."

My soul?

"Yes. A soul isn't complete without its corporeal frame. Eventually, your spirit will wander and become lost. Completely purposeless. It's quite possible you will even go mad. There is a reason you were drawn to me, you realize."

There is?

"Absolutely. I am your kindred soul on this world. I am certain of it. I felt it when our fingers touched. When I study you with my seeing eye, it is like looking at myself in a still pool. When one meets a kindred soul, also called a mirror, or a reflection, it can be a good meeting, or it can be a terrible thing."

But we don't look alike.

"Don't we? I cannot see your mortal frame, so I have no reference. The physical makes no difference. When you fell, a passage was opened between worlds. Our souls can be very alike or very different, depending on the fit. Some worlds are so different that there is no place for a kindred soul. Some are never born on one world. But the cosmos makes up for it by putting two kindred souls on the next world in the form of twins."

How fascinating.

"This déjà vu you spoke of is a sign of it. When you experience such a thing, it is because your kindred soul has or is experiencing something similar on their world, such as when we touched fingertips. We nearly joined then."

Joined? I'm not sure I understand.

"If you aren't a shaman on your world, you wouldn't. As a shaman, we spend time separated from our corporeal frames. We explore the realms of the spirit to learn, and then we must seek our bodies and merge once more, becoming a soul again in truth. Some go too long apart, and it weakens their bodies to the point of decay. When that happens, they can never return. They become wandering shades who haunt the living. It's a terrible thing."

But you're implying, then, that my mortal frame, as you put it, is not on this world.

"That's right."

Then where is it, do you think?

"I couldn't possibly know. But I can help you seek it. I just hope we can find it before we're too late."

And if it's on another world?

"We still might be able to find it."

Are you saying we have the ability to travel between worlds?

"Not everyone can, obviously. But yes. I can teach you how." The White Shaman clapped his hands together and rubbed them, a gleam of excitement entering his eyes. "I have to say, I haven't been this animated in decades. This is going to be fun, isn't it?"

I don't believe I ever considered myself to be an annoying sort of person. Now I can see why Miss Kelsey might find me tiresome on occasion.

"Tiresome? Who finds us tiresome? Most people who are granted an audience consider themselves fortunate to be allowed in our presence."

On second thought, I do think there is much we have to learn from one another. A drop of humility might go a long way with you, my friend. Your humble living circumstances notwithstanding. I only hope we can accomplish this feat before my corporeal form expires.

"You might get lucky. It could be simply floating frozen in the cosmos." The White Shaman looked around his cave. "You don't care for my home? Where do you live?"

Let's just say I'm very glad I can't feel the frigid air. I'm more used to a hot climate, as I spend most of my days on the continent of India.

"Indeeah? I've never heard of such a place."

Truly? How curious. You can travel between worlds, and yet you don't discover the continents of your own planet, preferring instead to remain on a glacier at the top of the world. The ghost glanced out the cave opening at the swirling lights. *Well, at least you have a lovely view. But let us make haste. I would like to keep the use of my extremities. Though I am simply a spirit at present, I daresay I can feel the cold seeping into my fingers and toes. How do we proceed?*

"Come, then. I will prepare a special tea. After I've consumed it, I'll begin walking from the back of the cave toward the fires, passing between them. You'll then come from the opposite side and head toward me. We'll meet in the center, and by the time I get to the cave opening, you should be with me, sharing my body. That will hold you together until we find yours."

Is sharing your body safe? It won't cast out your spirit?

"It should be safe enough. That is unless we never find your form, then it might become a problem. And no, you cannot cast out my soul. At least I don't believe you're strong enough, should you be so inclined. Normally, a visiting soul cannot do such a thing, assuming the host doesn't go willingly. Which I won't. We'll be able to share information easily, and you can then see all I do, though I'll still be in charge of my body."

I can't take it over?

"Not unless I allow it."

Can I leave anytime I want to?

"Yes."

Very well. Make your tea. I promise you I won't linger. If we don't find my body, I'll . . . Well, I don't know what I'll do, but I don't want to end up wandering.

"You won't have to. At that point I can help you find your way to the sky people if that is your desire."

Sky people?

"You don't have sky people on your world?"

Ah. You are speaking of an afterlife.

"Yes. That would be an accurate translation."

Then yes. You can help me journey to the sky people at the appropriate time.

"Very good." Vesako could sense the spirit watching him closely as he prepared his tea. "You do this also, don't you?"

I do, though I do not use psilocybin mushrooms.

"That's an interesting word. Psilocybin. What does it mean?"

It means that the mushrooms you use to create visions or dreams contain a drug or a chemical that affects your mortal frame. It alters your perceptions of time and space and, or, auditory, sensory, visual, coordination, etc. It can also cause panic and anxiety.

The White Shaman stopped chopping. "I sense you are older than myself."

Perhaps. I don't know when *you are. For that matter, I don't even know* where *you are, other than the Arctic, based on my assessment of the sky outside.*

"Where are you?"

Earth.

The shaman laughed. "Earth. Good. I, too, am on Earth. This is the Dreaming Mountain in the lands of the Native Alliance. It is two moons past the winter solstice in the Year of the Broken Reindeer Antler."

I . . . I am from . . . the spirit stopped. *I hesitate to share too much information. I don't want to impact your history.*

"Ah. I understand. This is a wise course. Though you and I *must* share information with one another, no? Perhaps if we make a vow not to disclose such details we discover with others, and only use our findings to aid our tigers in their purpose on our own worlds?"

Yes. I believe such a promise would be adequate for our purposes. Very well. I promise you I will not share information about your world with my own tigers or any other until or unless such time as is appropriate, and it does not impact mine or your own world or any other in any way.

"Wonderful. And I agree to the same. Shall we begin, then?"

We shall.

The White Shaman stared down into his hot cup of tea. The chunks of floating mushrooms spinning like little pieces of flotsam on a quiet pond. Setting down his cup, he picked up another and filled it with hot water, saying, "I believe I shall try a cup without the . . . what did you call it? Psilocybin? If it doesn't work, I can always go back to it." He grinned. "Never let it be said I cannot be taught something new."

After he downed his mug of tea, the two versions of the same man—one a shaman and the other a spirit from another place and time—stood on opposite sides of two fires.

"Are you ready?" the White Shaman asked.

I am, the ghost replied.

"I am Vesako Alingida, the Old Man with a Spear Who Lives on a Mountain, the Storyweaver of the Sky, the White Shaman of the Tundra, the One Who Hears All—Above and Below, and I have found my kindred soul. At this time, I offer to share my mortal frame to house his wandering spirit." He shook a gourd filled with rattling beads that danced musically. "Now you pronounce your name and intentions and begin your walk."

Very well. I am Anik Kadam, mentor, teacher, soldier. I intend to share the form of my kindred soul on this world. I also intend to find another who is lost.

"Fascinating. Now walk toward me. We will find your companion as well. I promise you. She isn't gone forever, my friend from a different world."

How did you know it was a woman? the ghost asked as they walked closer.

"I don't know, come to think of it. I—"

Their fingertips touched, and then a powerful energy, like the magic felt when the lights were particularly bright in the dark sky, pulled them together. The cave spun, and then they were both standing in the same place, looking out of the same pair of eyes.

"Did it work?" Anik asked, using Vesako's voice.

This was followed by a deep chuckle. "Can't you tell?" the White Shaman asked. "Doesn't it feel a bit tight and uncomfortable? Like you're wearing someone else's shoes?"

"Yes, now that you mention it. In fact, this reminds me a bit of the Divine Scarf. We can use it to change our appearance, though we are still ourselves on the inside. It's as if we are wearing someone else's skin. It was one of the gifts we recovered."

"A gift, you say?"

"Yes. Have your tigers made the attempt to break their curse?"

"Curse . . . we do not consider the tiger form a curse." The shaman began pacing but suddenly stopped, and instead of clasping his hands behind his back, he touched together his two pointer fingers and tapped them on his chin.

"There is much we need to discuss before your tigers arrive."

"I agree, Anik Kadam. We should also meditate. This is how we will find your companion . . . ah, Nilima. She is your . . ."

"She's my granddaughter, of a sort."

"Granddaughter?" Vesako grinned. "I always wondered what it would be like to have a family. You must tell me about your wife. Is she beautiful?"

"She was. She's with the sky people now. But she was lovely."

Vesako sighed as the image of a pretty woman with long dark hair came to mind; he realized it was their wedding day. She had some type of delicate tattooing on her slim fingers, and her beaded dress, so radiant and brilliant, wasn't nearly as bright as her smile or how proud he'd felt when she slipped her hand through his arm. He sat down, crossed his legs, picked up his mug, and sipped. Never in the White Shaman's very long life had he ever smiled more than once in a day, and not to his recollection had it ever been so wide.

CHAPTER 22

Don't Divide the Pelt of a Bear That Isn't Dead

It took the little group three days traveling at top speed to get to the Dreaming Mountain. When they reached the base, they stopped. By that time Danik and Nikolai were both furious with the newcomer, Iriko, who had assumed full responsibility for the tigers and the journey. Though he was younger than the other men, he was much larger, bolder, and brasher. It wasn't that they were particularly frightened of him; it just seemed like less trouble to let him have his way.

Iriko also had the ability to communicate with the tigers, and that was worth something, even if the others resented it somewhat. Danik and Nikolai did, however, take great pleasure in blaming him for running out of their carefully preserved stash of meat. Iriko, though in human form, retained a tiger-sized appetite, and by the time they stopped, they were out of food entirely.

Apparently, Iriko, being unable to see the provisions, ate freely, assuming there were more. With nothing left to feed the exhausted tsarinas, and the men, with the exception of the priest, spoiling for a fight, the three others decided to head out in different directions, trying to hunt some game for the tired cats, each man feeling incredibly guilty for their own reasons.

If any of them had ideas about trying to hold Iriko back from wandering off on his own due to his disability, he quickly proved he needed no such pampering. With the heightened senses of a tiger, he lifted his nose to the air and padded off without so much as a fare-thee-well to his newfound companions.

Meanwhile, Zakhar took advantage of the quiet to build up a little fire and spend time making more copies of the prophecy, trying his best to figure out the meanings of various passages on his own. He thought to share it with the others from time to time on their journey, but with tempers raised, a good moment never came. The others were always arguing about something or another. He did take the opportunity to read his work to the napping tigers though. They lifted their heads and blinked, acknowledging that they were listening, though they couldn't respond without Iriko nearby.

He was deep in his work, catching up on his chronicles of the journey thus far, when Nikolai returned. He'd apparently set a few of Danik's traps and had been planning to make their camp a bit more comfortable for the evening.

"What are you working on?" he asked Zakhar as he prepared the sleeping furs.

"I'm trying to draw a likeness of Iriko and his mother, but I fear I'm not doing either of them justice."

"May I take a look?"

"Certainly."

After a long moment of perusal, Nikolai handed the page back to the priest. "It's good," he said. "But you've forgotten the most important piece."

"Did I?" Zakhar said, quickly scanning the page. "I have the cloak here and the fact that he's wearing no footwear. I'm still working on his musculature, if that's what you mean. I don't often see specimens with his, shall we say, bulk."

Nik snorted. "I'm not talking about his physique. I mean the tiger token."

Clucking and shaking his head, Zakhar said, "How foolish of me. I was caught up in the emotion of the reunion between mother and son and forgot the purpose for which we were seeking him out. Forgive my disregard. I will attempt to correct my mistake immediately."

Shrugging, Nik returned to his work. "Isn't that your true purpose? To repair family bonds and help people find renewed joy in life, whether with one another or with God?"

Zakhar lifted his head and considered Nik's statement. "It is."

"Then why feel sorry for doing your job?"

"I . . . I wish to contribute to the group as best I can."

"Believe me—if you can help us keep the peace, you are contributing."

"I'll try, but . . . I fear I am failing in that regard as well. I've left you to your squabbles and instead have become absorbed in my studies." Zakhar went back to half-heartedly scratching on the page but then stopped. "Nik?" he asked. "Is there something you'd like to talk about or perhaps some guidance I can offer regarding the infighting between you three?"

Nik sighed. "No. It took time with Danik. It will probably take more time with this one. The weird thing is . . . if he was a cat, I'd probably get along with him better."

"It's interesting, isn't it?"

"What's interesting?" Nik asked, dragging a felled log closer to their fire.

"How the new addition has, in some way, bonded you and Danik."

"I suppose," he agreed, sharpening Danik's axe before splitting the log. "At least the hunter hasn't played any music lately. Seems melancholy because of it too."

"I agree." Zakhar bent his head over his paper again, careful to shield it from the light snowfall. After a moment, he called out, "Nikolai?"

"Yeah?"

"I'm afraid I cannot recall what the tiger token looks like. Perhaps you might be able to describe it for me?"

"Why not just look at it when Iriko returns?"

"I suppose I could. But the others . . ."

"You mean the tokens worn by Stacia and Veru?" Nik shook his head. "I never got a good look at those. I can describe them the way they were explained to me though. It might be better to get the description from the horse's or tiger's mouth, as it were, while we have Iriko to serve as a translator."

"What about the others—the tokens worn by the Death Draughtsman, the man you brought from the forest? Did he show you those?"

"No. But after what Matriova said, I believe he has at least one of them, maybe more. She said they'd been lost to her people. If two of them fell into the hands of the tsar and tsarina, who knows where the others ended up. But from what the Death Draughtsman told me, I got the sense he'd been collecting them."

Danik returned soon after that with a few birds. He'd placed the rest of his traps, hoping to catch some animals. They had roasted one of the birds and fed the tigers the other three before Iriko returned dragging the heavy carcass of a large deer behind him. Though Nikolai and Danik were happy they'd be able to fill their own bellies as well as the tigers', they wore unhappy expressions, especially knowing Iriko had left without a trap or a weapon of any kind.

It was a puzzle to Danik in particular, how a blind man with no obvious weapon could not only track and take down a deer but then manage to find their camp again. Lifting his shoulders, he gestured silently to Nik, pointing at the deer. In response, Nik simply shrugged and shook his head, equally clueless, mouthing "I don't know."

Iriko paused where he was crouched over the beast and said, "You realize that even if I wasn't able to use the eyes of the two tigers sitting near you, I'd still know you were talking about me. I can hear you moving your mouths."

Flicking his long hair back from his face, he added, "Can you toss me a knife, Priest?"

Zakhar said, "Certainly," but then seemed hesitant to throw it, assuming the tiger who couldn't see wouldn't be able to catch it, resulting in an injury.

Iriko sighed and reached over to grab it from his hand, cutting himself in the process. A few drops of his blood fell into the snow, but Iriko took no note of it and began hacking limbs off the deer. "If you want to talk about me, I'd prefer you do it to my face," he said to the others. "If you can't bring yourselves to do that, I'll just assume you're too cowardly."

"If that's the way you want it," Danik replied.

"No holding back, then," Nik added.

"How did you track it?" Danik asked.

"With my ears and my nose," Iriko replied.

"But wouldn't it run when it saw you?" Nik asked.

"Yeah. But I climb a tree or a hill or hide and wait for it to come to me."

"What happens if it gores you?"

He held up his hand where he'd grabbed the knife. It had already healed. "No problem."

"Okay, so how do you kill it, then?" Danik asked.

Iriko shrugged. He pulled out a makeshift ivory knife from inside his vest. It was polished and sharp, and Danik realized he was looking at bone. "Sometimes I use this. Sometimes I just grab them around the neck and hold on until they stop breathing."

"Hey," Zakhar said. "If you have that, why'd you want my knife?"

Iriko smiled then and winked, but at no one since his eyes were focused on an empty space. "I can always use a backup."

Satisfied, but still shaking their heads, Nik and Zakhar helped him carve up the beast and feed the tigers, saving a portion to place on the fire. Danik then openly scolded Iriko about leaving a trail of blood behind him that would attract every predator for miles. Iriko laughed and called Danik a trus and an old grandmother worrier before consuming most of the half-cooked deer roast and climbing halfway into a bed of furs, leaving his burly chest exposed to the freezing air. It only took a moment or two before he began snoring loudly.

Sated, the tigers rested deeply, too, and one by one the other men also drifted to sleep, lulled by a gentle but cold breeze and the twinkling stars overhead. With the hot fire warming their backs and the steady, deep snoring sounds of three large predators nearby, the three average human men felt as safe as anyone could be when sleeping in the frozen Siberian wilderness in the deep of winter.

Unfortunately, they were awoken by the snuffling of something large, with fetid, hot breath, that pawed at the remains of Iriko's kill, and it wasn't a tiger. It nudged Zakhar, still deeply asleep in his furs, pressing him deeper into the snow. His eyes flew open as the breath was knocked out of him, and he gasped as he stared down a dark open maw surrounded by dangerous white teeth. Just as he was wondering if it was to be the end of him, the large creature's attention was caught by something else, and its heavy paw lifted off his chest.

"A great white bear!" Danik cried, throwing off his furs and reaching for his hunting knives, quickly tossing Nik the axe. "Nik, see about Zakhar. I'll try to distract it."

As Danik pulled a torch from the dying embers, the tigers sprung to action. They roared and leapt, one on either side, challenging the bear by swiping the air just next to him, barely missing Zakhar, who was being awkwardly pulled away from the bear's stamping feet by Danik. Then, with a great bounce, the bear was upright, standing on hind legs and bellowing.

The breath came back to Zakhar at once, and it was as if he couldn't stop himself. He screamed. Panic seemed to invigorate his limbs, and he scrambled away from the bear and the tigers faster than a lightning strike. Within a moment, he was thirty, forty paces away. Then suddenly, he stopped, remembering his precious papers. He was about to head back toward the waning fire, praying that his careful work wouldn't get trampled, but slipped on an ice patch.

Sliding down a hill, Zakhar tumbled end over end and came to a stop on top of a strangely shaped pile of snow. That's when he heard the soft cry coming from a dark opening behind a bunch of brambles and branches. He got awkwardly to his feet, his bruised ankle causing him to limp, and headed toward the opening to investigate the source of the cry.

With the men out the way, the tigers felt free to attack. Bloody gashes now appeared along the bear's hindquarters and back. They heard a scream as the bear managed a savage bite on the golden tiger.

"Veru!" Danik cried. One of her shoulders was torn and bloody.

Then Iriko finally joined the fray. He leapt boldly upon the bear's back, wrapping his arms around its neck as if to strangle it with his bare hands. It bucked wildly, trying to throw him off, but it couldn't rid itself of its passenger. Nik wondered where Iriko had been. It was as if he had come out of nowhere. Nik glanced over at Iriko's sleeping furs, and they were covered with snow. He hadn't been sleeping in them recently, at least not recently enough to see the bear.

Waiting for his opportunity, Nik, who had slipped on his magic boots and tunic, came very close to the tumult and, finally, thrust his knife up and into the bear's side. This injury, in addition to all the other attackers, proved too much for the poor, hungry bear, and with a final frustrated bellow, it turned on his heel and ran off into the dark dawn.

Nik ripped off his tunic quickly so they could see him. "I stuck him with my knife," he said. "I don't think he'll be coming back." His voice trembled as he stared at the knife with blood dripping freely from the blade. He'd helped Danik kill and skin animals before, but they were small and it hadn't been dark. They hadn't felt like . . . like that night . . .

"It's a she-bear," Iriko said. "Show me the knife."

"What good will that do?" Nik asked, irritated at being doubted and the fact that he still wasn't in control of himself.

"Just hand it over," Iriko said. "There's no time to argue. She'll probably double back."

Nik blew out a shaky breath and thrust his knife into Iriko's open hand, nicking him in the process. The larger man carefully measured the blade from hilt to tip using his thumb and fingers. Nikolai stared at the blood as it drip, drip, dripped onto the white snow. If it had been daylight, all of them would have seen Nik's face go white at the sight of it. He swallowed. *There was so much. It was his fault. All his fault.*

"The blade's not long enough," Iriko said, flicking the knife so it stuck in the snow at Nik's feet. "A bear that big, you need a knife deep enough to penetrate the layer of fat. You might have stuck her, but you only made her mad." His mouth twisted up into a mocking smirk. "This is why you people need to stay on your side of the mountains. Not only do you know nothing about how to survive in the true wilderness but you couldn't even tell that was a female bear."

"That's enough," Danik said. "You are the reason she was even here. I told you—you left a trail. Any blood that was spilled tonight is something you'll have to answer for."

Iriko folded his arms across his mostly naked chest. "I can protect myself," he said haughtily.

"I'm sure you can," Danik replied. "But that doesn't discount the fact that Veru was injured."

Iriko's smug expression fell away. As if he could sense exactly where the tigers were, he approached Veru and knelt by her torn shoulder. Veru was licking a paw and paused, looking up at him. Stacia was licking her sister's injury and whining, but she backed away at Iriko's approach. Nik could see when Iriko used Stacia's eyes to assess Veru's injuries. Iriko had the decency to wince, but then his face hardened, and he waved a hand in dismissal. "They'll heal," he said as he stood.

"Perhaps," Danik said. "But healing requires energy. That means more hunting, more resources. And what about the bear? Is it fair to her? She was just hungry."

"I, um, hate to interrupt this very important lesson, especially since Iriko really needs to be taught a few things," Nik said, still feeling jittery, "but I just noticed that Zakhar is missing."

Danik looked around. "Did anyone see him leave?"

"Good riddance," Iriko said. "One less mouth to feed."

When Danik gave him a look, Iriko threw his hands up in the air and said, "Fine! I'll track him. Just keep in mind, you were the one talking about conserving our resources."

"I'll go with him. Will you stay with the tigers and watch camp in case the bear returns?" Danik asked Nik.

Nodding, grateful to be left behind, Nik sent the two men on their way and took his time folding his tunic as he tried to get his thoughts under control. He then selected a much longer knife from Danik's pack. To his shame, his hands still shook as he sat quietly in the snow, his free hand on the nape of Veru's neck, as they kept watch. Petting her soft fur as she healed from her wound soothed his soul, and eventually his mental anguish eased.

Not seeing or hearing any sign of the bear's return, Nik's eyes fell on Veru's wound as it knit itself back together. When she was healed, he used a bit of snow to clean the blood from her fur. Stacia sat on his other side, and soon he let the long knife fall. He put his hand on her back too.

As the three of them sat together waiting for the others to return, they each thought of how very far they had drifted away from their dreams and their home and wondered if there was a way to return, and if they did, would they even find a home there, or was it gone forever. What home meant to each of them was different in that moment, but they found comfort in being together, knowing that they all had suffered loss and hardship. It united them in a way and kept driving them toward the same goal.

Stacia and Veru blinked rapidly as puffs of snow drifted lazily around them. Maybe it would be easier to just give up, to consign themselves to live as what they were now. Their eyes stung and burned, but they couldn't cry, at least not like humans did. Their sorrow just made them feel heavy, like they wanted to lay down and not move.

As for Iriko and Danik, it was fairly easy to track Zakhar. Unfortunately, the great white bear was headed in the same direction. They heard the bellow and began to run. When they found Zakhar, he was at the mouth of an ice cave playing with a small bear cub and cuddling a second.

From the top of the hill where Zakhar had obviously fallen or slid down, Danik sighed and asked, "What are you doing, you glupec?"

"They were crying," Zakhar replied. "I couldn't help it. Aren't they cute?"

"Well, now their mama is returning, and she's already mad and hungry. It's time for you to come back. Put down her babies and say a prayer for yourself that she doesn't come after you."

"Ah, that's it. They're hungry. Danik, can we give them some food?"

"No," Iriko answered. "We need our food. The mother bear can hunt on her own."

"Can she though?" Danik asked. "She's injured now. I think you can do without a meal or two so she and her babies can live."

Iriko blinked once and then twice, his blue eyes unfocused. "You aren't like the other hunters I've seen. They take and take with no thought of saving. Most hunters would have looked at that bear and seen only the wealth in her fur. But this one"—he jerked his thumb in Zakhar's direction but missed him completely—"wants to be a kormilica, and you want to feed the mother, who would eat you if you gave her a chance."

"Yeah? Well, we'll be feeding that bear an injured priest in a minute if we don't get him out of there."

"Um, there's a slight problem," Zakhar said somewhat sheepishly as he tried and failed to nudge the polar bear cubs back into their cave. "I seem to have twisted my ankle. I'm not sure I can get up the hill."

"Fantastic," Danik said under his breath. Then, shifting his pack off his back, called out, "Hold on. I'm coming down."

Iriko threw out an arm to stop him. "I will do this for you. Wait here."

"No, Iriko. Wait!" But Danik's words had no effect.

With a mighty leap, Iriko was down and standing next to Zakhar. Before the priest could protest, he wrenched the man to his feet, flung him across his back, and with a series of running steps, he was up and at the top of the hill. "There," he said, yanking Zakhar from his back and dumping him in the snow as if he were nothing more than a sack of potatoes.

"Ow!" Zakhar said in protest, clutching his ankle.

"Er, thanks," Danik said, helping his friend to his feet. He put Zakhar's arm around his shoulders, and the two began to hobble back to camp. They'd only gone a few steps when they heard the mewing cry of the two bear cubs, who were making a desperate attempt to follow them.

"Poor things," Danik said. "You're right. They're hungry." Pulling Zakhar's arm away and steadying him, he said, "Iriko, hold on to Zakhar for a moment. I've still got some meat in my bag."

Grunting, Iriko rolled his unseeing eyes, but obeyed. He was about to pick Zakhar up again and toss him over his shoulders when the priest protested and said, "Just let me lean on your arm for a moment, would you?"

Danik tossed a bit of roasted deer meat down to the two cubs, who ran after it, playing with it for a moment before ripping it apart and devouring it. "Come on," he said, taking Zakhar's arm again. "Let's get some distance between us and them, before Mom comes back."

After they returned to camp and Zakhar was settled, getting all his papers in order, Danik asked Nik to borrow the boots. He sped from trap to trap, collecting all of them and any animals he'd caught. Quickly he decided on which they wanted to skin and keep for themselves and which they could spare, and he left a pile of them at the lip of the bear's cave so they'd have food for several days, then he sped back and removed the boots.

The group took stock of their supplies and divided up the remaining meat, giving the tigers enough for the journey ahead and saving some for later, then they packed up everything and were about to place the boots on the feet of the tigers when Iriko held up a hand.

"The mountain isn't far from here. This is a magic place. A place for tigers. We don't know if the three of you will even be welcome to set foot upon it. I think it's best if you stay here and camp. Or, even better, head back to the nearest settlement and wait for our return."

"Absolutely not," Nik began.

"You need me," Danik protested.

"I think we should listen," Zakhar said, putting his hands on the other men's shoulders. "He could be right. What if the mountain rejects us? We're only human, after all."

"But my job is to protect the tsarevnas," Nik said. "It's my duty. What if they perish there, and I was down here roasting a fish? How could I live with myself?"

Iriko snorted. "Like you could catch a fish."

Nik's face went purple. "You arrogant . . ." He couldn't help himself; he began chanting a spell, a dark one, one he'd promised himself he'd never ever use, and Iriko's breath cut off.

"Stop that immediately," Zakhar commanded, shaking Nik. "You don't really want to do that, and you know it."

Nik ceased his spell, and Iriko started breathing normally. Veru glanced up at Iriko and then at Nik and growled softly. Wincing, Nik looked straight into Veru's eyes and said, "I'm sorry. I didn't mean it."

Her growl cut off, but it was Iriko who answered. "No harm done. I suppose I deserved it. Didn't know you were a budding shaman."

"I'm not. I'm a . . ." Nik didn't know how to finish that sentence. "Well, I'm not a shaman," he said lamely.

"I have an idea," Danik said. "Since our shaman here has those magic boots, and we're heading to a magic place, why don't we let the magic decide?"

"What do you mean?" Iriko said, folding his arms across his beefy chest.

"I mean let's put the boots out for the tigers, and if they create something for all of us to head up the mountain, then we all go; but if not, then we'll agree that those of us of a human nature will . . . stay behind. Is that acceptable?"

Nik shook his head nearly imperceptibly at Danik, not wanting to take the risk, but Zakhar voiced loudly that he agreed, making the decision for them.

"I suppose I can agree to that," Iriko said.

Danik handed Iriko the boots, and he walked over to Stacia's head, placing a palm on her shoulder and tracing it down her leg. Then he said, "Okay, boots, you decide: Do you want all of us to go or just us tigers?" Placing one on her foot, he turned and put the other on Veru's, then stood back and waited to find out what would happen.

This time, instead of a large sleigh, the magic boots created two things long and low to the ground, one was harnessed to each tiger.

"What are these?" asked Zakhar as he clutched his waterproofed bag of precious papers. "What does it mean?"

"I've seen these before," Danik said.

"So have I," said Iriko, using Veru's eyes to examine the rigging attached to her sister. "But only with dogs, never with tigers."

"Of course not with tigers," Nik replied in a mocking tone. "Like you could put a tiger in a harness."

"They're meant for two and two. I supposed that means we can go," Danik said cheerfully. "Can you drive one?" Danik asked Iriko.

"I suspect the tigers will be doing most of the driving," Nik suggested. "And don't get any ideas about me riding with him," he said, jerking his thumb at Iriko.

"Fine." Danik said. "I'd be thrilled to ride with you, Mag-ass." Nikolai glared at him, especially when he heard Iriko roaring with laughter, but Danik just grinned back and turned to Zakhar. "Will you go with Iriko? You'll sit here on the sled, and Iriko will stand in the back to steer."

The priest nodded. "I can do that. But don't you think we need to ask the sisters what they think? Tsarevnas," he said, nodding to the tigers deferentially, "do you agree to allow us to accompany you up the mountain? The choice is ultimately yours, I should think."

Stacia and Veru looked at one another, and Veru could see her sister's slight head dip. She didn't want to break up the group. Veru felt the same way. They'd come this far together. It felt right to continue that way. To Stacia, the group reminded her of young soldiers sent off on a training mission together. When they endured hardships and learned to rely on one another, it cemented friendships, and they bonded. Perhaps that was the purpose of this journey.

As for Veru, each person was a vital piece. Each added a unique talent or gift. If they learned to work together, there was no telling what they could accomplish.

"Stacia wants you to come," Iriko said. "She believes the magic of the boots is an indication that the mountain wants us to stay together. And she also said having you along might be of use should they start to fall asleep and begin dreaming.

"Veru says without your help they never would have made it this far. She thanks each of you for your sacrifice and asks if you are willing to go just a bit further. She promises she will not forget your efforts on her behalf."

The men nodded and smiled, saying, "Yes, Tsarevna," and, "Happy to serve, Tsarevna."

"I'll steer this one," Danik said. Elbowing Nik, he teased, "Climb aboard, Mag-ass. You'll be responsible for our supplies."

Once they were all settled and their bags strapped on, Danik nodded to Iriko, and the young man spoke to the two tigers in his mind. *Are you ready to climb the Dreaming Mountain?*

I can't help but notice we have to carry your dead weight, Stacia said to him in reply.

Iriko laughed. *I promise as soon as we find the shaman, and we can rid ourselves of these tigers, I'll carry anything you ask. Besides, after that, the only thing of weight the two of you will have to carry are your heavy skirts and royal head-bashing scepters, right?*

That shows what you know about running an empire, Stacia replied. *I'd like to see you try it.*

What happens if we do start to dream? Veru asked nervously. *Your mother said—*

Don't worry about that. If it happens, we'll deal with it then, said Iriko.

Veru said, *But you didn't tell the others that you—*

Iriko interrupted. *They worry too much. Besides, it only affects tigers. At least I think it does. Anyway, your many suitors are going to get jealous again if I'm talking to you for too long. So let's get going, then, shall we?*

Stacia gave a very unladylike snort that caused Danik to run to the front to check on the harnesses.

"They aren't too tight on her, are they?" he asked Iriko.

"No," he replied, trying ineffectually to cover a snort of his own. Then, turning to the other two men, Iriko said with a wide grin, "They're ready."

"It's about time," Nik said with a grumpy expression.

Still grinning, Iriko flicked the reins. *Told you so*, he said to Veru and Stacia as they began to run up Dreaming Mountain. *Jealous!*

Shut up, you Irik-*tating thorn in my paw.*

Just save your breath for the mountain, Your Royalness Queen Anastasia. And while you're at it. Mush! Iriko quipped, slapping his hand against his thigh.

Chapter 23

When Many Take Hold, the Load Isn't Heavy

I'll mush him, Stacia thought, before grunting and beginning the hard pull up the mountainside, taking the lead.

They climbed for several hours. The ascent was easy at first. Snow was packed along a trail that led up a winding, gradual climb. As long as they stayed single file, they were safe enough, so there wasn't any danger of a fall or a snowslide.

When Iriko said the tigers needed a break around midday, they ate and boiled enough snow to refill their waterskins. The tigers drank heavily of the snowmelt they poured out for them and ate enough deer meat to energize them without weighing them down.

The daylight disappeared quickly, but they continued with the light of the stars and the moon to guide them, and they arrived at a stopping point that had obviously been used by others before. The trail ended abruptly in the clearing, and the moment they stopped, the magic boots began to retract from the sleds and harnesses they'd created and changed into boots once more.

Danik and Iriko explored the area, while Nik and Zakhar began assembling a fire in a circle of blackened rocks that had seen a great amount of soot in days gone by. By the time Danik and Iriko returned, the others had a crackling blaze going.

"What did you find?" Zakhar asked.

"Nothing good," Iriko replied.

"There's no place we can see with a path to the top," Danik explained. "At least not one that can accommodate tigers."

"That's not exactly true," Iriko said, contradicting Danik's report.

Glancing at him in confusion, Danik asked, "What do you mean?"

Iriko rubbed his jaw and turned to the sheer rock wall behind them. "I think this is the turning point."

"Turning point?" Zakhar said, dusting his hands on his robes and standing up. "What do you mean?"

"A turning point. A choice. Most tigers can change back and forth between human and cat. But not us. Something's wrong with the three of us. We don't know what. Maybe it's our upcoming trials, or that we weren't meant to be tigers in the first place. But true cats can go back and forth. They can retain the power of the tiger even when taking their human form. A cat can't scale a sheer rock mountainside like that one behind us, but a man with the strength of a tiger could, at least in theory."

"Hold on. I thought getting up the mountain was the trial," Danik said.

"Oh no," Iriko explained. "That's only the beginning. Some ascend the mountain, some don't. All trials begin and end with a dream. Let's just say, you'll know your trial when it happens."

"But didn't your sister go through them?" Nikolai asked.

"No. Like me, she had the power of the tiger, only she could transform at will. But she hadn't come to the Dreaming Mountain for her trials yet. Our goal is to remove the tiger, not go through the trials. That's why we don't want to fall asleep. Get it?"

"Wait, Iriko," Zakhar said. "Let me understand. So even without the trials, you have the tiger's gifts?"

"That's right."

Zakhar pressed, "So you're implying you could scale that rock there, even blind, and get up to the next ledge, however high it may be, just by climbing? And that your people could do this without the aid of ropes or tools or other such helpful implements? Second, you are indicating that this particular ledge may be some sort of choice?"

"I believe so. It might have been a test, not a trial but a . . . well, like I said, a turning point. Those who lay down and go to sleep end up back at the bottom. They have a dream. One that will guide them in their duty, help them navigate their lives, but they never reach the shaman. Those few who are determined, who conquer the mountain, may in fact attain their goal. It hasn't happened often that any are successful, but there is a record of it happening."

"Ascend the Dreaming Mountain . . ." Zakhar mumbled to himself. "Wait just a moment." He pulled out a paper from his bag and scanned it, then read, "It says, 'Learn from those who came before, should you ever start to drift . . .' Perhaps that means drifting asleep. We should take a lesson from those of your people who have been here before. I agree with Iriko's summation. I think we should climb."

"Wait just a minute. Let's assume you two are correct, and those of us who aren't filled with the strength of a tiger somehow manage to climb this rock face and survive it. How are we going to get Stacia and Veru up there?" Nik asked. "There's no way a tiger could climb that."

Iriko walked over to the rock and put his fingers into a crevice, feeling carefully for a handhold. Then he placed one foot and a second. He scaled the cliff wall three or four feet, testing each hand and foothold carefully, then he turned and let go, falling gracefully into the snow twenty feet below.

"Easy," he said, dusting his hands in such a way that caused his arm and chest muscles to ripple, which made Nik roll his eyes in disgust. "I'll harness them to me and carry them up."

Absolutely not.

No, Veru said to him in protest.

"Now, ladies," Iriko said out loud, holding up his hands. "Just listen to my idea."

"See? They don't like it. Let's stop and consider our options," Danik said. "He does have a good thought, just not a well-executed one."

"What's that supposed to mean?" Iriko said, crossing his arms over his chest.

"Obviously *you* have the ability to scale the cliff. But you can't see where it ends or how high it is. That's both good and bad. You have no fear of it, and that's good. For you. And yes, we'll need you to climb it—in fact, probably more than once. But there's no need to risk everyone's life in the process. First, are we certain this is the only way up?"

Iriko cocked his head, listening to the tigers and consulted with them silently before addressing the group. "Stacia and Veru are in agreement. This feels right," he announced. "But they are also in agreement with Danik that we should examine every option."

"Fine." Danik then turned to Nik. "Nikolai, do you think your magic can be guided at all? Can you try to direct the action in some way? Say to make harnesses to carry the tigers such as Iriko suggests?"

"Possibly. But why? I thought you said it was dangerous."

"Oh, it still is, but my thought is to have him go up and then use those muscles of his to support us by using harnesses and ropes he ties off up top as we climb. That will help us in the ascent since we aren't tigers. Once we have two or three of us up there along with our supplies, then one can remain here, harness a tiger, and the rest can pull her up."

"Yes!" Zakhar said. "That should work much better than carrying one while climbing and risking two lives at once."

"Fine," Iriko said. "I suppose I 'see' the logic. Of course, all that depends on our budding shaman. We're assuming he can make it work."

Nik said, "You all are assuming a lot. As far as I can tell, the boots work how they want. Did you forget I said it was possible, not probable?"

"Sounds like a trus's way of avoiding risk, if you ask me."

"You talk as if you know me. You don't. You have no idea what I'd be willing to risk, so don't assume anything!" Nik got in Iriko's face and poked him hard in the chest just to make certain he got the message. "I'm not afraid of you. In fact, I've faced far, far worse than a spoiled soplyak like yourself and lived to talk about it, so bring it on."

Iriko's white grin was wide. "You want to fight? It's been some time since I tossed a man down a mountain, but I'd be happy to see the tail end of you." He laughed. "That is, I'd relish 'seeing' the tail end of you flipping over your head again and again and again as you tumble and bawl like a detka through the eyes of your podruga." Iriko started throwing a fake temper tantrum, then stopped himself by sucking his thumb loudly.

Nikolai's face tightened with anger, then, to everyone's surprise, instead of attacking the man, he grabbed the boots, ran to the cliffside, and, after yanking them on his feet, leapt onto the rocks and began climbing.

Everyone's mouths dropped open in shock, including Iriko's. His thumb fell out, the mocking forgotten as he turned toward the sounds of a still-livid Nik climbing the rock face. Somehow, though he was an amateur climber at best, Nik managed to ascend thirty feet in just a few seconds. When he started to slow down, and the adrenaline wore off, his body trembled, his foot slipped, and he dangled by just his hands for a dangerous moment before finding another foothold.

Both Stacia and Veru panicked and screamed in Iriko's mind to hurry and help their friend, but the young man was already moving before he heard them. Thanks to the tsarevnas' trained gazes on their friend, Iriko was halfway to Nik when the magic shoes decided to lend aid of their own accord.

The laces grew into strong cords that pounded into the cliff, making powerful rings, while others wrapped around his torso and legs, creating a belt and harness. Then others stretched high above his head, disappearing into the mist, and he could feel when they tightened on something far above him and began to pull him upward.

Soon Iriko was next to him, climbing slowly alongside. The ropes didn't stretch out to help him like they did with Nik, but Iriko didn't seem to care about that. His only thought was to ensure Nik's survival. As they continued to climb, he carefully coached Nik on how to locate the best places or what he should look for when he needed to rest for a moment. With his enhanced strength, he could support Nik when his arms or legs trembled or pass him a length of cord that was too far out of reach.

There was one point, near the top, where even Iriko needed to pause. It would require a literal leap of faith. Only a tiger could do it, and even Iriko couldn't sense what waited for him. Would he land safely atop the cliff on an outcropping or hit another ledge and plummet to his death? There was no way to be certain.

Nik felt that they were surely at the top. The cords created by the boots ended in the fog bank just above them. Iriko wasn't so sure, and he was too far above the tigers to use their eyes. The two men clung nearly upside down on a section that widened and spread over their heads in a ledge, but there were no other options for them. He knew he must somehow leap over it, or they had to turn back and go down.

Nik wasn't able to pull his body up and over a ledge curved in such a way using only his arm strength. With his legs dangling beneath him, he wouldn't have the upper-body muscle, even as a trained soldier. Iriko wasn't even certain he could do it with the strength of a tiger to aid him. Especially when he wouldn't be able to see what waited for him over the ledge. Was it another section of sheer rock cliff, or was it a resting spot? Had they finally come to the end of their journey, or would this be the end for them?

Legs shaking, Iriko shut his eyes and thought about his sister. She'd been so brave. Baikali hadn't hesitated when it came to saving his life. He'd never thought of himself as being in the same league as her, but maybe if he at least tried, she might someday be able to forgive him for what he'd done. Maybe his ancestors would perhaps give him the opportunity to be a servant to her in the afterlife. He thought he might like that. Gathering his courage, he leapt.

Nik watched in awe as Iriko's large body moved in the air. His legs dangled in space, and then somehow, by the sheer force of his will, he drew himself up and over the incline, twisting and managing to get a leg over the edge. Then he was up and enveloped in the fog above them. Waiting for the sound of Iriko's landing up top or, even worse, the sound of a crash, and his body falling and hopefully not brushing against his own since such a thing would absolutely cause Nik to lose the fragile grip he had on the cliff himself, Nik held his breath. But there wasn't a sound.

A moment later, the cords shifted, moving violently. Nik cried out, his hands and feet slipping from their holds as he grasped the rope for dear life. If it wasn't for the belt around his legs and waist, he would have surely fallen. Then he was being yanked up, and quickly.

Within just a few moments, he was unceremoniously dragged over the lip of the rock and into the fog, where he was embraced by a very large, very sweaty bag of muscles that smelled slightly like raw fish and moss.

"Get off me," Nik mumbled against Iriko's fur vest. "I'm glad to be alive too. Try not to squish me in the process of celebrating."

Iriko grabbed Nik's shoulders and shook him, too hard. "Who knew your temper would get the both of us up here?"

"Yeah. Well . . . now that we're here. What do we do next?"

Cupping his hands, Iriko shouted down. "We made it! Send the priest!"

Irritated again, Nik asked, "How do you expect Zakhar to climb up here in robes?"

Iriko shrugged. "I'll help him. Take off the shoes and we'll see."

Bending to remove the boots, Nik grumbled, "I don't like the casual way you play with people's lives."

"Maybe I do it because I don't care that much about mine," Iriko answered as he caught the magic boots Nik tossed in his direction. The laces had retracted when Nik removed them. He hoped for Zakhar's sake that they would work to help Zakhar just as they'd saved Nik.

"Don't care? Why would you say that?" Nik asked.

"Because it's true." Iriko walked over to the edge and glanced down as if judging the distance. Nik didn't know if he could actually see using Stacia's or Veru's eyes from where he stood.

"If I could die, I would," Iriko said softly. "I've tried to. Repeatedly. Turns out it's not as easy to kill a tiger as one might believe. It isn't right that my sister is gone, and I got to live. The people needed her, and I was foolish. She shouldn't have saved me. End of story. If there was a way to trade places with her, I would."

"Is that why you left? To try to end your life?"

"You sure ask a lot of questions, don't you?" Iriko said. Then he grinned and took a step off the edge of cliff, with the magic boots in hand. As Nik ran to the edge to peer down, he realized he couldn't see a thing through the fog, but he did hear Iriko's whooping scream of delight on his journey down.

—

Good. It seems like they're cooperating after all. They're going to make it to the top. All they need to do now is figure out which trail is the right path to the top, and we'll be seeing them in just a few short hours. Then we can start them off on their real journey—the trials that await each of them.

But surely, it would be kinder to offer them guidance now, Vesako, and not expect them to face such hardships on their own.

Bah. You cannot teach a baby to walk by moving his legs for him, can you?

No. But . . . you can still encourage. Offer open arms and hope and catch them when they fall.

Sometimes the pain of falling is necessary for growth.

Not always.

The two mentors floated out of body in the fog, watching the progress of the young people. The one from another world, Anik Kadam, appeared to be very concerned over the possibility of their demise. He cared about them already. Anik's emotional connection to them was interesting to the White Shaman, Vesako Alingida. The two men had spent the equivalent of a lifetime together, drifting through the cosmos in thought, though in the physical world it had only been a few days. Vesako had not only come to admire and respect Anik but trusted him completely.

Do you not believe there is growth to be found in the trials we have prepared? Vesako asked.

Of course, Anik answered. *I only ask that you consider our involvement. Instead of watching from a distance and allowing the universe or the cosmos, if you prefer, to deal out cards at random, isn't it nobler to give just a tiny push from time to time, a gentle nudge, so that instead of unwanted consequences they each become their best selves? In so doing, they might all have an opportunity to forge a life of happiness and joy.*

Does that not take away their freedom of choice?

Not as I see it, Anik replied. *They are who they are. We do not manipulate them, only drop in clues or aid from time to time so they might have their best chance to grow.*

You are playing at being God, Vesako said.

No. I am being a father. But perhaps you are right, in a way. Many religions think of God as a father.

I thought your religion believed in many gods and goddesses.

Let's just say that over the decades I have become vastly open to the idea that I might not know everything.

It seems to me you know a great deal.

Ah. You yourself have taught me there is so much more. So very much more.

And you have taught me the same. Very well. With this group of young people, I agree to take on a more . . . parental role than I have in the past. Perhaps you will join me on this adventure. I sense you aren't yet prepared for your journey home.

No. I still haven't found Nilima.

At least we've recovered your physical form as we journeyed through the great expanse together. Though you aren't ready to travel home with your corporeal form as yet, we will continue to practice until you are. It won't take you long, my friend.

The astral version of Anik smiled at his friend. *I still have much to learn from you. Thankfully, walking through the cosmos as we do doesn't affect the timeline. I don't know how to repay you for your kindness.*

You will repay me when we save my world from this villain, and my young people are safely journeying on the path they need to be walking after having passed the trials we've developed for them. Then you'll be ready to help your own tigers.

Yes. I will help you, and you'll train me at the same time. Thank you, Vesako.

Spasibo, Anik.

Good, Vesako said. *The men are on top, and they're bringing up the tigers now.*

The first tiger had reached the top, but the ascent was far from complete. When the second was harnessed, there was a frightening moment when the rigging began to slip. Stacia teetered, her heavy front half falling out. Though Iriko tried desperately to right her, and she clawed his arm and chest deeply, opening his skin all the way to the bone, it was very apparent she was going to fall and from a very high place.

The rope tried to reweave itself, but she was so heavy the cords snapped repeatedly, and in her desperation, she severed many of them. Stacia scratched at the cliff and shouted in her mind, *Help me!* to Iriko, who screamed various instructions and concerns back to her. At that moment, she felt like she was going to die. Stacia wasn't ready. She was supposed to die in battle, in some moment of glory, not dangling from bootstraps on the side of a snowcapped mountainside in Siberia as a tiger.

At least she'd see her beloved mother and father again. There was some comfort in that. Her heavy body dropped several feet, and a piteous roar escaped from her throat. She dangled now by only a cord wrapped painfully around her back paw. It hurt. She moved her tail back and forth, instinctively trying to right herself. Iriko moved down slowly, trying to line up his body with hers. She could smell the blood dripping off him.

Hold on. I'm coming, he said to her mind. But it didn't matter. It was over. She'd already given up.

Then there was a different voice in her head. It was comforting and familiar somehow. She felt a warm presence near her too. It was as if someone was touching the ruff at the back of her neck, calming her.

The voice said, *Clear your mind. Focus. Tell the laces how to lift your body. You know where your equilibrium is found, where your tiger form is heaviest. That's right. Instruct the cords. Fashion a harness that suits you. Do not forget—you are in control, not the magic. Around the chest. Very nice. Now have them gather you up, slowly, turning your body in just the right way. Good. When you reach the top, tell the others there is a final challenge that awaits you before you get to the top. You must decide together which path is the right one. Remember: when you work together and listen to the experiences of all, in most cases, you will find the right way.*

Vesako returned to Anik, and they watched until everyone reached the top and then the two men returned to Vesako's body. They still shared one form for the time being, as Anik hadn't yet learned how to jump forms, but Vesako kept Anik's body in order until the other man was strong enough to return to it.

You did very well with her, Anik said.

It felt right. I'm happy you were here to advise me. Perhaps my universe was calling out to you, and that's why you're here. I fear I haven't been a good mentor these past decades. I've sent the dreams, yes, but been largely uninvolved with the lives of the young people. I certainly never thought of taking a direct role, such as yourself.

I disagree with your self-assessment. I think we are both here to learn from one another. Without you, I don't believe I will be able to serve my tigers well either. I must confess—I'm eager to see the next phase of your tigers' journey.

It will be difficult for them.

As the experiences my tigers have faced have been. But I would hope that in the end it's worth the effort.

Yes. Learning is the point of life, is it not?

Indeed, my wise friend, indeed.

Chapter 24

Go to the Verge of Destruction and Bring Back…

"Tell me what the voice said exactly," Danik requested as the little group came together at the top of the high cliff.

It was dark and all of them were exhausted, but none of them dared sleep. They were far too frightened of entering a dream and then ending up back where they'd started at the base of the mountain and being forbidden to try again.

Patiently, they waited as Stacia communicated to Iriko what she'd heard and felt as she dangled on the side of the cliff, fearing for her life.

"After the voice told her how to save herself, it said there was a final test waiting for us," Iriko explained.

Zakhar had pulled paper and ink from the supplies and was quickly scribbling details as they were discussed. "Would you say the voice was male or female?" he queried.

"Does it matter?" asked Iriko.

"I only ask because I suspect it might have been the shaman. He is described as the One Who Hears All—Above and Below. Perhaps this means he can know what's happening on the mountain and can lend aid or not, depending on his whim."

"Maybe," Nik mused. "But I don't recall any mention that the White

Shaman was a man. Besides, there's no way for Stacia to really know, is there?"

"Perhaps not," Zakhar agreed, waving the hand holding the quill. "Please, go on."

Iriko translated, "The voice, which to her sounded like a man, not that it matters, told her there is a final trial and that we'd all need to consult together to find the right path."

"Work together," Danik said, rubbing a hand over his new beard growth. "That sounds fun." He sighed and considered their surroundings, then brushed the snow from his pants and stood. "Shall we do some reconnaissance, then, and figure out where these paths are?"

"Might I venture," Zakhar asked, holding up an ink-stained fingertip, "that we stay together? Perhaps wandering apart from one another may lead to unfortunate consequences."

"Okay. We'll wait until we're all ready," Danik said.

As they spoke quietly together, recovering from the ordeal of scaling the mountain, Nikolai and Danik took a moment to look out over the cliff at the surrounding countryside. To the south, the land stretched out as far as their eyes could see, only blocked by puffs of fog and cloud. In the distant west, they could see the Ural Mountain range, with bits of blue and green and white. And the little bit of north in their view that wasn't blocked by trees was white with blueish blobs of taller white, which they surmised were likely glaciers.

The sky was clear and crisp and black, with the brightest, coldest stars, and it was lit with waves of color—purple, green, yellow, and blue. To Stacia, Nik, and Veru, it was the most beautiful thing they'd ever seen. Zakhar was too wrapped up in his work to notice. As for Danik, he had seen such visions before, though never at such a height. To him, the dancing lights were creating a song he was desperate to pick out on an instrument. There was no time for it now, and it pained him somewhat. Music always helped him organize and calm his thoughts.

As for Iriko, his reflections were not on his surroundings but with his mother. He sensed she was not long for the world. The tiger inside him was mourning. Matriova was cold, growing quiet and still. Within the next day, she would be gone. Another member of his family would soon join their ancestors and become one of the sky people. What would she think of him then, when she could see him all the time—see all his mistakes and shortcomings. Would she love him as she said she did, or would she reject him, once and for all? Perhaps if he succeeded in passing the tiger on to someone worthy, she could somehow forgive him at last.

Nik distracted him from his thoughts by placing the boots on the tigers. They grew into the sleds as before, and silently the men took their places. This time the tigers didn't seem to know the right direction. Veru started one way, while Stacia tried another. Almost reluctantly, they followed Iriko's suggestion and went in the same direction, though none of them were certain of its validity.

They headed off toward the south only to find the path led nowhere. Another path up the back of the mountain seemed to have great promise, but again came to a dead end. They returned to their starting place and discussed what to do.

"Perhaps it's time to use our strengths and work together instead of relying on magic," Danik said.

"Or the instinct of a man cub," Nik joked half-heartedly. The fact that Iriko paid neither him nor his comment any mind was a certain indication the man was distracted. But instead of asking him what was wrong, he turned his back to the others and bent down next to Veru. "What do you suggest?" Nik asked as he removed the boots from the tigers.

Addressing Zakhar, Danik said, "You have an artist's eye. Take a good look at our surroundings. What do you see?"

After studying the view carefully, he took out a fresh sheet of paper and dropped down to quickly sketch out some trees and the large mountaintop behind them. "I see five possible paths," he said, drawing them between the trees.

"Are you certain?" Nik asked with interest, crouching down beside him. "I only saw the two."

"Oh yes. There are indeed five. Three are hidden by branches or trees, but they do lead out of this clearing."

"So which one do we take?" Iriko asked. "You're the hunter," he said, lifting his chin to Danik.

"Yes, but I'm not sure those skills apply. Besides, you hunt as well."

Iriko simply shrugged and turned his head away as if he no longer cared about the journey.

"We've already been down two of them, and they led nowhere," Nik said.

"The voice also said it's a test," Iriko reminded them after Stacia insisted he speak for her.

Show us, Veru said.

What do you mean? Iriko asked silently.

Let's see each path and then get a feel for each one. Then we can return here, discuss it together, and decide, Stacia suggested.

"The tigers want to see all the paths, then we can talk about it further," Iriko translated.

"Fine. It's a good idea." He leaned down to pick up his pack and handed one to Nik. "I think we should walk at this point. Are you ready, Zakhar?"

"Yes."

"Then show us where to go."

They set off as a group with Zakhar leading the way, his map open in front of him as he plodded awkwardly through the snow.

"Aren't your legs freezing?" Nik asked, after seeing the priest's damp robe hemline trailing along behind him.

In answer, Zakhar lifted the edge of his robe and showed off a pair of breeches tucked into his boots. "They belong to Danik," he said. "He loaned me an extra pair some time ago."

"Then why continue wearing the robe? Why not dress as warm as the rest of us?"

"I'm warm enough," he answered in response to Nik's question. "Besides, when I put my robes on, I made a promise to God. Breaking it feels wrong. Bending it a bit, I think He'd understand. It's the heart that makes one worthy in His esteem more than what one wears, don't you think?"

Nik blinked and wiped a bit of snow from his face. “I don’t believe I’ve ever given consideration to the thoughts or intentions of God. I guess I always figured if He was aware of me, or of anyone, assuming we were worth His notice, then He’d have stopped all the evil in the world. Seems to me He just doesn’t care all that much.”

“Perhaps He cares more than you think. Did you ever consider the possibility that evil has a purpose?”

“No. Evil is just evil. It’s wrong. It shouldn’t be here.”

“Ah,” Zakhar said. “Here is the third path. Do you see it leading up past the tree line?”

As the others walked around the path, looking for some type of clue, Zakhar put a hand on Nik’s shoulder. “Consider a tiger, for example. To the deer who is chased down and eaten by one, it might be seen as a monster, a villain, or evil. Is such a thing evil to you?”

“No. It’s just survival. The tiger wouldn’t kill unless it was hungry or afraid.”

“What about an animal plagued by sickness? It strikes out and kills for no reason other than the madness in its mind. Is this evil?”

Nik thought for a moment, then answered. “No. All animals are innocent. They can’t control what happens to them. If they are sick due to having eaten something wrong or have become rabid, then it’s not their choice. They aren’t thinking rationally.”

“But would you not agree there are some people born who, not of their own choice, might be sick in their mind? Who might do things they cannot control and would not do if their mind or environment were healthy? There are many scriptural examples of Christ cleansing lepers or ridding people of demons, which allowed them to reintegrate with society. He did not see them as evil or as bringing this condition upon themselves.”

“Maybe not,” Nik answered. “But surely some people become evil due to their nature or their choices.”

“I would agree with that. Keep in mind that I’m not trying to bend your thinking to one way or another. Just to allow the idea that some things we might think of as evil may simply be that we don’t understand what has happened to that person to cause them to behave in such a manner. Shall we proceed to the next path?"

Nik nodded, and they walked on, continuing to speak of one thing or another, but not of the thing Nikolai really wanted to talk about. Deep inside, he'd always had a suspicion that because of what his father had done, it meant there was something wrong with him too. What kind of a boy could kill his own family and feel nothing?

Wasn't he, by definition, evil?

Certainly, he was broken, at least.

Though his mother and siblings were gone and had been for a long time, he felt haunted by his past. Perhaps it was all the talk of sky people from Iriko and Matriova, but it was almost as if ghostly specters hung above them in the air, watching them, and the idea filled him with nervous energy. He was also exhausted, just like the rest of them. But they still had a long way to go before they could rest.

After checking the next two trails, they reconvened and discussed their options. Danik, the hunter, felt like the fourth trail was the one to take. He recognized some broken tree limbs and other signs that indicated someone had passed that way before.

Iriko had no preference, but generally agreed with Danik. Veru and Stacia were deathly afraid of the fifth path. It closely skirted the side of the mountain and appeared to be very treacherous. They didn't care which of the other paths the group attempted as long as they avoided the fifth path.

Nik and Zakhar liked the third path—it seemed to have the most upward trajectory. This made sense to both of them, as they assumed the White Shaman would be at the top of the mountain.

"Why do you think the White Shaman lives at the top?" Danik asked.

Zakhar shrugged. "I just assumed we were heading to the top."

Chiming in, Nik added, "No. He's right. Not necessarily. Iriko, are there any particular things a shaman uses or would like to have around?"

"He'd need food," Zakhar said.

"And wood," Danik added. "There's plenty of that on the north side of the mountain."

"Also water," Iriko said, growing animated for the first time. "He'd need mushrooms, herbs, sunlight, and . . . and a fire!"

They all froze. Both tigers lifted their noses, Iriko imitating them as well.

It's that way, Stacia said.

The path we don't want, Veru added.

"I think you're right," Iriko replied out loud. "They believe it's the fifth path. The most dangerous one. There's a tinge of smoke on the air, and it's not coming from the top. It's possible the White Shaman doesn't live on the mountain but inside it. There might be a cave opening around this way."

"It feels right to me too," said Nik.

"And me," Danik and Zakhar responded together.

"If we're all in agreement, I suppose we should go. We'll have to go single file," Iriko said.

"This time we should go first," Danik said, indicating the other regular human men. "We'll do our best to clear the path of snow and watch out for dangerous ice patches. You follow with one tiger in front and one behind. Use their eyes to help your footing. Hopefully, the path will widen soon."

The group set out, and though the trail was steep and slick, they made it successfully up to a series of caves with only a minor slip, which happened when Veru stepped awkwardly on a rock that gave way. Luckily, Iriko caught her in time and pressed her body against the side of the cliff until she could find her traction once more.

It was fairly obvious which cave was the one they were seeking, as it had a series of stone steps cut out, leading to the opening. They wove back and forth up the side of the mountain, arriving at the cave entrance just as the sun broke over the horizon.

Inside, the cave was pitch-black, but they heard a scuffling that could have been from an animal of some type. Danik took a step back, searching for his hunting knife, but Iriko held out a hand to stop him and shook his head slightly. "It's not an animal," he whispered with near reverence.

"S priyezdom," they heard a voice say. "You made it—how wonderful." Then the shuffling grew closer, and the person added, more quietly, "I know. I know. You said they would. I suppose you win that one." This was followed by a soft chuckle.

Then whoever was inside the cave made several noises. This was followed by a tiny blaze of light and a crackling sound. Soon not one but two fires blazed to life. When Danik's eyes adjusted, he looked up, wondering where the smoke would leave the cave, and to his surprise, he found not one but a few of what seemed to be natural evacuation points in the ceiling. Though the walls were blackened, the White Shaman's home was fairly warm, considering the temperature outside and the fact that it was open to the elements.

"Come. Come in," the shaman said. "You must be tired. I've prepared some small repast, but I'm afraid I don't have much. If you'd like to hand over that last, large piece of deer meat, I'd be more than happy to roast that for you as you sleep. You'll all need the energy where you're going."

"Going?" Nik asked, removing his bag. "But we just arrived."

"Yes. You did, young soldier. And quite a trip you've had too. Met some interesting characters along the way, did you? One even tried to eat you. Good! That experience will serve you well."

"How do you know so much about us? Have you been watching us?" Zakhar asked.

"Not in the way you're thinking. I'm not omniscient. It's my purpose, you see. I oversee all things related to the tigers. Have been doing so for quite some time now."

The White Shaman stopped and tilted his head as if he were listening to something. "No. It's fine that they know that. Everyone here knows that." There was a pause, then he continued. "Yes. I agree. It may be different on your world. You might have to . . . what was the phrase you used . . . 'keep your cards close to your chest'? Well, I've never gone with them before, so how would I know exactly what to say? I usually keep my distance. Allow the air of mystery to impress them, as it were."

Danik cleared his throat. "I'm sorry to interrupt, but were you addressing us?"

"He was not," Zakhar said. "He is conferring with someone we cannot see. At least not with our senses."

"So he's . . . a bit off?" Nikolai asked, whispering quietly to the priest.

"I wouldn't think so," Zakhar replied. "He doesn't seem to be lacking in any way otherwise. Incidentally, just because someone is communing with the unseen does not indicate a lack of mental function. There are many religions, not just my own, that believe in beings that exist beyond the span of our own mortal view."

The White Shaman chuckled. "You're right. This *is* going to be fun." Then he spread his hands and smiled. "Forgive me," he said. "I haven't addressed a group this size in . . . well . . . ever. Please sit and make yourselves warm by the fire."

When Iriko and the tigers came in, the White Shaman took an extra moment to peer into the eyes of Iriko. He had to look up, since the shaman was on the shorter side, and Iriko was rather tall. The younger man bore the scrutiny and proximity of the other man with uncharacteristic patience. When he was finished with Iriko, the shaman turned his attention to both of the tigers.

After this, he held out his hands to Danik, who blinked in stupefaction for only a moment before figuring out what the man wanted. Opening his bag, he took out the last wrapped piece of deer meat and handed it over.

"Very nice," the shaman said almost gleefully, before placing it on a spit over the fire. "I needed to put some meat on these old bones." He then giggled at his own words and began going about the business of brewing some tea.

Zakhar, meanwhile, intended to work more on the prophecy or at least ask some questions and take notes while he had the opportunity, but as he sat there in the warm little cave, allowing his body to relax at last, he could feel the exhaustion taking over. "Would you mind terribly if I rested my eyes for just a bit?" he asked the White Shaman. "I mean, will it make a difference if we sleep now? Or will sleeping mean we end up back at the base of the mountain? Because I don't think I can do that again."

The White Shaman gathered some mugs and began filling them with his hot brew. "Why don't you all drink some hot tea first? It will warm your bellies before the food is ready. Then you can sleep. I promise you won't end up back at the base of the mountain. I have a pile of extra furs near my cot if you'd like to borrow them."

Zakhar stood and distributed some of the furs while the rest made themselves comfortable using their own belongings. Only Iriko and the tigers sat stiffly at attention. The White Shaman passed around steaming mugs, and all the men began to sip. Then he brought two large dinner bowls over and set them before the tigers.

"You two need warm bellies as well," he said, pouring a large pot of tea into each one.

Stacia and Veru stared at their bowls, with little bits of floating herbs and dark blobs of mushroom. They sniffed, and the herby smell wasn't unappealing. They tentatively lapped up and swallowed a bit, surprised to find it was sweet. By the time they'd finished, they looked up to find Zakhar, Danik, and Nik were already sound asleep, and Iriko was even beginning to look drowsy, his lids half closed.

Stacia slumped down. Her body felt so heavy. She looked at her sister, heard steady breathing, and saw the golden tiger's eyes had fluttered shut. Only at that moment did she begin to suspect there was some sort of sleeping potion in the tea and was relieved that whatever it was had not killed her sister.

He's done something to us, Iriko. Iriko?

The tiger stuck in the form of a man was fast asleep now as well.

"They cannot hear you any longer, young tsarina," the White Shaman said. "But don't despair. You'll be joining them soon."

Are you killing us? she asked, only slightly concerned that the idea of her demise didn't cause her as much despair as she thought it should.

"Absolutely not!" the shaman replied with an offended tone. "I'm simply aiding you in the acceleration of the quest you so recently began. In this manner, time will be of no consequence, and I will be able to guide and watch over you in your trials. I should think you might be comforted to know that when you rise, you will be that much wiser, that much more prepared for the mortal journey that awaits."

But we don't want the trials. We only want—

"I am well aware of your aims, young lady." The White Shaman sighed. "Do not misunderstand. I do not take away your choices. You still have them. But life is meant to be a series of experiences. Trials and errors and opportunities to stretch and strengthen yourselves. This is simply . . ."

The red tiger began snoring.

The White Shaman cleaned out his pot and began brewing a new batch of tea, this time only adding a tiny portion of mushrooms while trying to ignore the quirked eyebrow he sensed from his friend.

It's only a bit, he said, justifying his own potion. *Besides, we'll need to watch over them for some time before returning to check our own physical form.* He wrinkled his nose. *And these young men will need a bath. I daresay the tigers smell better. And that's not something I say often.*

As his companion laughed, Vesako turned the meat, his mouth watering at the smell of the delicious roast. *Why do you think the young always want what's easy?* the White Shaman asked.

That's an easy one. It's human nature, Anik replied. *Everyone prefers the easy path. No one relishes the climb.*

But climbing is how your body gains strength, Vesako said.

Yes. But there are different kinds of strength, aren't there?

They'll need all of them, I fear, if they are to face what lies ahead, Vesako mused.

Anik asked, *Tell me again: What have you designed? How are these trials different than the challenges my tigers have and will face?*

The White Shaman pulled off a tiny section of roasted venison and popped it into his mouth. Chewing with relish, he answered, *It is similar in many ways. They must endure obstacles, opponents, work together, and are granted certain gifts or powerful items along the way. Unlike in your world, instead of obtaining items for a goddess, they must conquer their own fears and learn to work with the tiger in order to best be a guardian or servant of their people. If they choose to abandon their task or remain stuck in place, not moving forward but forever remaining in a state of . . .*

Limbo?

Limbo . . . that's an interesting word. I like it. Then the tiger eats away at them, until they become something that haunts the living. Much like the one they must face in the end.

My tigers, too, must face a demon. It really doesn't seem much different.

And yet it is, isn't it? On the surface, at least.

I suppose all things are. The two of us eat different foods, don't look alike, speak different languages—

And yet we are the same at the core, are we not?

Yes.

The two men who shared one body were quiet, each keeping to their own thoughts as they listened to the breathing of the young people. When his tea was ready, Vesako bustled about the cave, arranging each young man and woman and tiger in a comfortable position; then he took his time dining on a nice piece of deer meat, preserving the remaining portion for when he next woke to tend to the bodies; then he returned to his sleeping cot, covered his own body carefully with his fur blankets, and said out loud, "Are you ready, Anik, my friend?"

I am.

"Then let's get started."

Raising his cup of tea to salute his sleeping companions, the White Shaman of the Tundra, the One Who Hears All—Above and Below, the Storyweaver of the Sky, downed the contents of his mug in three large gulps, feeling it warm him all the way to his belly. Then he closed his eyes and began to drift. With his new companion, Anik, at his side, he began to weave a story, the greatest tale he'd ever fashioned. Into it he placed not only himself and the one from another world but he also added a hunter, a priest, a soldier, an outcast, and two tsarevnas, one with hair as golden and soft as morning sunshine, while the other's braided crown was as red as Russian poppies.

Yes, he thought as Vesako hummed softly, allowing himself to enter the story at last. *This one will indeed be the finest tiger tale I've ever woven.*

At that final thought, the White Shaman of the Tundra began to snore.

Outside the Dreaming Mountain, the sun had already disappeared, and the Arctic lights commenced telling a story of their own, but tonight they sparked with a new kind of magic, one that wove brilliant shapes and colors not seen in a millennia, an indication that something new, something special, had just begun.

EPILOGUE

The More You Know, the Less You Sleep

"Hold on. You aren't stopping there. Surely," Kishan said, wide awake, though it was now very, very late.

"I'm weary, and you, my boy, are still sick. You need your rest."

Anik Kadam stood, drained his now cold mug of tea, and stretched his neck and back. As he went to the little sink to rinse out the mug, he added, "We should really think of adding some more comfortable chairs to this hut. Especially if you insist on staying out here in the middle of nowhere."

Kishan slumped back on his pillow. The story had distracted him from both his illness and his depression for a while, but now both hit him again with a deep, drowning fatigue. "What difference does comfort make?" he groused.

"Who said I was talking about your comfort? Here." The older man passed Kishan a cold glass of water. "Hydrate yourself and try to get some sleep. I'll stay with you, if you like."

"Will you tell me what happened next to the young people?"

Kadam felt the younger man's forehead. The fever would break in the morning if Kishan could just bring himself to rest.

"I'll make you a bargain. If you sleep for at least six hours, which will allow me to give my old bones a break, I'll tell you the next part of the story. Deal?"

"Agreed."

Kishan shut his eyes, and his breathing steadied and slowed until it quieted into a gentle rhythm, indicating he was at last asleep.

Putting up his feet, Kadam was about to shut his own eyes, when he heard a voice in his head.

I thought you didn't like using mushrooms.

Kadam smiled and replied, *Hello, old friend. It's not a hallucinogenic type. The kind I gave him simply helps with stress and sleep.*

Do you really think telling him what happened will strengthen him?

I don't know. I just don't want my boy to suffer. I know what it's like. Being alone and knowing . . . too much.

Do you regret it?

My time with you? Or knowing what I know?

Any of it. All of it. I know I regret it.

You regret meeting me? Kadam replied with surprise.

Not at all. I regret the path you chose for yourself.

Ah, you mean my impending death.

It doesn't have to happen.

We all make choices. You know that. You taught that principle to your tigers.

I did.

And I saw firsthand what losing one of your own did to you.

The White Shaman sighed. *Well, if you think it will help him. Feel free to share everything. Leave no detail out.*

I'm sure I won't. Not with you buzzing in my ear.

Anik, I . . . I'll stay with you, if you like. When it happens, I mean.

I'd like that, Vesako. But we're not quite yet at the end of my tale.

No?

No. There's still a bit more left to tell.